TEARS
OF
FROST

By Bree Barton

Heart of Thorns
Tears of Frost

TEARS OF *Frost*

BREE BARTON

 KATHERINE TEGEN BOOKS

An Imprint of HarperCollins Publishers

Katherine Tegen Books is an imprint of HarperCollins Publishers.

Tears of Frost

ISBN 978-0-06-244771-5

Typography by Joel Tippie
19 20 21 22 23   PC/LSCH   10 9 8 7 6 5 4 3 2 1
❖

First Edition

For the girls. All of us.

KINGDOMS

The Opalen Sea

River

Northern Peaks

Haer Killian

ian Village

Ilwysion

Foraois Swyn

Refuj

Caves

Fojo Karaçaō
THE FIRE KINGDOM

Glas Ddir
THE RIVER KINGDOM

The Red Salt Mines

Dead Man's Strait

Ice Caves

The White Lagoon

The Salted Sea

Ice Pits

AUTHOR'S NOTE

In the world of this trilogy, magic is born of a power imbalance. Magicians carry inside them a long history of subjugation, including rape, bodily harm, and abuse. Because this book delves more deeply into their magic, it delves more deeply into these subjects, too. In many ways this story is my meditation on sexual assault and depression, two threads that for me have always been intertwined.

Everyone's experience of assault and/or depression is unique. I've done my best to represent them with fairness and sensitivity.

I believe stories work in two ways: they transport us to a place we have never visited, and at the same time, they resonate with the truest parts of who we are. In this way, books can be powerful agents of healing. But when a book transports you to a place you no longer feel safe, that resonance can be painful and retraumatizing. I do not ever want to do my readers harm.

If you need to put this book down at any point—even right now—please do so. Take care of yourself. That is the most important thing.

And if you are suffering, please never be afraid to reach out for help. On that note, I've included a list of resources in the back of this book. I know from personal experience there are always people ready to offer support, even when it feels hopeless. In my own life, the best gift I have ever given myself is learning how to ask.

Bree Barton

Long before blood poured from flesh,
and breath clung to bone,
before the ancient runes were ground to glass
to shift shapes in the aether,
back when mothers whispered truths
cloaked as once-upon-a-times,
Know this, little ones, they said.
When day breaks, frost becomes a flame.
When dusk falls, beasts become the prey.
And when the moon is weeping,
the witches do their reaping.

—Addi proverb

28 DAYS TILL THE WEEPING MOON

My dearest sister,

Let me tell you a story.

Once upon a time, there was a reinsdyr. She had soft gray fur with white patches like spilled milk. The reinsdyr lived alone, apart from the herd, in a snow-sugared forest. When she grew hungry during the long winters, she wandered closer to the mountains to find food.

From their den, the ice leopards watched the reinsdyr graze the fields below. They saw her munching on roots and frostflowers, nibbling pink apples and mushrooms with tiny caps. They rejoiced when she found a nest of robin's eggs or an arctic char flopping beside the lake, knowing she would grow fat and flavorful. "A reinsdyr is only as good as its meat," they said, "and we need meat to survive. You cannot change your nature."

While the ice leopardesses nursed their young, the largest, fiercest leopards left a trail of frostflower petals, luring the reinsdyr up into the mountains.

They waited. They did not have to wait long.

When she came, the leopards proposed a trade. "We will give you food," they said, "if you give us something first."

So the reinsdyr gave them what they wanted. They were not gentle, and they were not kind.

Perhaps you have heard this story before, dear sister. It is an ancient legend of the snow kingdom, a story the Luumi tell their children before tucking them in at night.

They tell me you have awoken, that you are traveling to the land of ice leopards and reinsdyr just in time for the Jyöltide celebration. But your place is here with me, not in Luumia. You belong by my side.

Zaga has sharpened my men into a keen, deadly blade. They are hunting you, joined by an army a thousand Dujia strong.

I trust you will come willingly when they arrive.

All my love,
Angelyne

Chapter 1

FUGITIVES

THERE WERE FIVE OF them. Thick chested. White faces filthy with dirt and scruff. After stomping through the forest each day, they sat around the fire at night, roasting fatty goose legs and swigging tin cups of stonemalt. Coarse men, eating and drinking and farting like the brutes they were. From the shadows outside their camp, she listened to them swap stories about the brawls they'd won and the girls they'd lost.

She had no plans to kill them.

Not at first.

She knew Angelyne had sent the men to track her down and haul her back to Kaer Killian. So far they'd done a piss-poor job. If anything, they were keeping her fed: she circled back every morning and sifted through the charred remains of their camp-fire. Slurped greasy meat off leftover bird bones. Drained the dregs from a forgotten flask. She even shat in a man's hat the morning he was fool enough to leave it behind. He came back for the ugly rag and had it halfway to his head before he started screeching. She'd laughed so hard from her hiding spot she nearly gave herself away.

If they thought they were tailing her, they were mistaken. The advantage was hers and she intended to keep it. She would die before letting them drag her back to the castle.

But Pilar d'Aqila was a decent sort of person.

She'd give them a fair shot at dying first.

As Pilar lurked on the outskirts of their camp, her thoughts grew darker, more violent. The men spoke of the servant girls—girls she'd met at the castle—ranking them by the firmness of their breasts or the plumpness of their asses.

"I like 'em pretty and pint-sized." The first man slapped his thigh. "Spunky, too."

The fifth man, who seemed to be the leader, groaned. "Too spunky is no good. They make trouble when you grab them for a kiss."

The story he told next, to a chorus of claps and guffaws, made Pilar's blood burn.

She didn't know the men's names, but she didn't need to. *First. Second. Third. Fourth. Fifth.* The order in which she would destroy them. Like notes on a scale, one leading to the next.

She knew she should keep quiet and concealed. Five brutes, one girl: the odds were stacked against her. But the fouler the men got, the fouler her temper.

By the time the river rats shoved a fresh-caught prisoner into the circle—hands bound, potato sack over his head—her fists were itching for a fight.

"Look what I found," said the third man. "Our thief."

Pilar's pride flared—*she* was the one thieving, not this clod in a potato sack. The fourth man kicked the back of the prisoner's legs and his knees buckled. He dropped dangerously close to the crackling fire.

The fifth man stepped forward and whipped off the sack. Kneeling on the forest floor was the prince of the river kingdom.

Former prince, anyway. Last surviving son of Clan Killian and all that.

Quin looked rough. His eyes were wild, his blond curls matted with dirt and leaves.

"Please, wait. I can explain." He fumbled for the leather pouch looped onto his belt, hands clumsy from the ropes around his wrists.

"What's this? Gold?" The fifth man snatched the pouch, tested its weight, and laughed. "You think we want your coins? The young queen has put a fine price on your head. She sits on *all* the Killian gold."

He stooped to look his prisoner in the eye. "Have you been stealing our food, Your Highness? Sucking down our scraps?"

"N-no," Quin stammered. "I swear to all four gods, I haven't."

Pilar balled her fists so tight, her nails cut into her palms. The prince wasn't her responsibility—but he didn't deserve to be punished for her crimes.

The fifth man had a hungry gleam in his eye. She knew that gleam.

"Take a man's meat and he might forgive you." He scraped a dagger from its sheath. "Take a man's malt and he'll slit your throat."

To hells with it. Pilar attacked.

She launched herself from behind a tree and into the circle. Skidded through the fire with the side of her boot, kicking a spray of smoldering coals into the first man's face. Sparks scorched his eyes as he leapt back cursing.

The second man lunged, grabbing a fistful of her glossy black hair. She clenched his fleshy palm tightly to her skull. Slammed her free hand into his elbow, popping the bone backward. He screamed.

She wasn't done.

With her feet firmly planted, she hinged at the waist, spinning him in a half moon until he lost his balance and plowed into the ground. The bigger they were, the harder they fell. She crushed his nose with her boot—the sole of which was still mildly on fire from the coal trick—stamping out the embers on his face. Two birds, one boot.

The third man let out a war cry and grabbed her from behind. He hooked his brawny arm around her neck and tried to drag her down. Not a chance. She arched her spine and thrust her hips back, driving both elbows hard into his ribs, over and over, until she heard the bones crack. Her hand swung between his legs, palm up, striking his groin. He gasped and stumbled backward.

The fourth man was hardly worth mentioning. One solid punch to the throat and he crashed to the earth, strangling on a broken windpipe. The gurgle like a song.

There was a rhythm to fighting, a tempo. The men lumbered. She danced.

A fist collided with her face.

She took the punch gracefully. Not that knuckles to the nose ever brought much opportunity for grace. She staggered back as red streaks clouded her vision.

"Demon witch," growled the fifth man.

She spat blood-saliva. "Why don't you grab me for a kiss?"

He took the bait. Grabbed her wrist and pulled her closer. His other hand was occupied—with the dagger, she noticed. Not ideal. He swiped at her and she dodged the blade, barreling into him instead of away. The boldness of the move surprised him. She balled up her trapped fist and clasped her free hand over it, using her shoulder strength to wrest her arm out of the spot where his grip was weakest. One of her favorite tricks.

He looked impressed.

"Aren't you going to enthrall me, little spitfire? I'd welcome your sweet touch."

Rage flooded every muscle of her body. In her mind she saw the cottage by the lake. Wooden rafters. Dirt floor. Broken horse-hair bow.

When the man raised the dagger, she smashed her arm bone into his, knocking the blade off course. Then she flattened her free hand and rammed all five fingers into his milky blue eyes. *Don't only block—counterattack.* That was her training: *Defend yourself, but do not hesitate to hurt him.*

Her fingertips had eye juice on them. She didn't care. All her training was worth it, even the ugliest parts.

Pilar seized his wrist and wrenched it, loosening his grip. The dagger dropped—directly into her sticky hand, which was ready and waiting.

"For the girls," she said. "All of us."

She plunged the blade straight into his heart.

He burbled air and blood, then sank—*not* gracefully—to the ground. The quiet was pleasant. Or it would have been, if not for the groans and whimpers of the surviving men.

"Pil?"

She whirled around, ready to take on a sixth, before remembering there was no sixth. Just Prince Quin, kneeling on the forest floor. Staring at her in shock and disbelief. Which was kind of insulting, when she thought about it.

"Pilar Zorastín d'Aqila." She spat a long red dribble into the fire. "Only my friends call me Pil."

Never mind she didn't have any.

Pilar wiped her mouth on the back of her hand, leaving a brown smudge on her tawny gold skin. Shook her short black hair out of her eyes. Crouched and yanked the blade from the fifth man's chest.

In a few strokes she sliced through the ropes binding Quin's hands.

"Thank you," he murmured, rubbing his wrists. She wondered how he'd managed to escape Angelyne's magic when he couldn't even escape five men. The prince wasn't exactly built for a life on the run.

He met her eyes. "I owe you one."

The words jarred. This was the boy she'd shot by arrow—an arrow meant for Mia Rose. The boy she'd plied with rai rouj their one drunken night on Refúj. The boy whose sister was dead because of her.

If anything, *she* owed *him*.

Pilar made an instinctual decision. Her favorite kind.

"If you're headed to the snow kingdom," she said, "come with me."

"How did you know I was going to Luumia?"

"You're running too, aren't you?" She slid the blood-slicked dagger into her boot. "Two fugitives are better than one."

Chapter 2

LIKE A BLADE

THE SILVER COIN CLANKED against the flask in Pilar's pocket as she and Quin moved swiftly through the woods. The pale trees were tall and twisty with blue needles at the top. Swyn, the river rats called them. To her they looked like music, a forest of white treble clefs.

Pilar felt for the coin and ran her thumbnail over the grooves. Once she crossed Dead Man's Strait and sailed into Luumia, the name engraved on the coin would prove useful. In twenty-seven days the Weeping Moon would rise. That night, on the steps of the Snow Queen's palace, she would come face-to-face with the person she'd risked everything to find.

Till then, all she had to do was survive.

Her knuckles were bruised, lip swollen. She could imagine her skin purpling beneath her sharp, dark eyes. But she felt no pain. Pilar was viciously alive.

Quin cleared his throat once, then twice.

"If you have something to say," she said, "say it."

He cleared his throat again. "Your nose is bleeding."

"I took a fist to the face. Your nose would be bleeding, too."

"Then why don't you heal yourself?"

"Because I don't want to."

"Is that why your face looks like that?"

She stopped walking. "Explain yourself."

"The cut you got from the guards." Quin motioned toward her cheek. "You still have the scar."

Months after the guard's glove sliced her cheek open, it still hurt. The blow had fractured her cheekbone. Whenever she moved her jaw, a jag of pain shot all the way to her forehead. At night her eyes blurred, black fleas dotting her vision.

"I don't practice magic," she said. "Not anymore."

"Even to heal yourself?"

"I like the scar. Adds character."

The longer answer was more complicated: the scar made her look battle worn, yes, but it also served as a reminder. *Never trust anyone. Not even your own mother.*

She cocked her head. "You of anyone should know the cost of magic."

"I do." Quin bit into the words. "Though if I may be so bold: you seem equally content to murder people with arrows and blades."

9

"Like the man I killed moments before he slit your throat."

"He wouldn't have hurt me."

"How naive can you be?" She shook her head. "You didn't deserve to die. Not when I was the one stealing their food. Though I did return it. In a manner of speaking."

She waited for Quin's expression to fade from confusion to horror. Then she grinned.

"You'll need to keep up, Killian. Those won't be the last guards my mother sends for me."

His laugh was hollow. "Those guards were looking for me, not you. You've been gone for weeks. Haven't you wondered why no one was looking for you?"

Pilar frowned. Come to think of it, until the five men, she hadn't encountered any guards since leaving the castle. But she'd chalked it up to good luck.

"Zaga doesn't need you," Quin said. "She has a new daughter in Angelyne Rose. A *stronger* daughter."

"I know you're just trying to hurt me," she spat. "Stop dancing around what you really mean. You want to talk about Karri? Then talk."

She hated that she could still see Princess Karri, Quin's older sister, bleeding red onto the snow. Stomach pierced with an arrow. *Pilar's* arrow. She could see herself, too, shrinking back into the woods like a coward, terrified by what she'd done. All because her mother told her to.

"I don't care how many innocents you shoot with your bow, Pilar Zorastín d'Aqila." Quin's eyes blazed green. "Unless you can enkindle the whole kingdom—unless you, too, can crawl inside people's hearts to make them want what you want—Angelyne is stronger."

"Even if I *was* still using magic," she growled, "I would never enkindle my Dujia sisters. That's not how magic is meant to be used."

"We are in violent agreement about that."

Pilar turned and stomped through the forest. She refused to think of Karri, Angelyne, Mia Rose—anyone from that awful night. Instead she plunged her hand into her pocket and busied her fingers with the coin, tracing the name carved in the silver.

You'll see how strong I am. Stronger than she ever knew.

Zaga was a liar. For years she had deceived the Dujia sisterhood, peddled magic as a way to "topple the old power structures." Pilar had drunk it down like a frosty pint of ale.

Magic, as it turned out, was just another way to hurt people. The most dangerous way of all.

Now Pilar thirsted for revenge. First she would kill her mother. Then she would kill Angelyne Rose, queen of the river kingdom—and Zaga's new pet.

But if Pilar was going to kill them without magic, she needed help.

She dragged her thumb over the first letter etched into the coin, a snaking silver S.

Snow Wolf.

If she wanted to join forces with the greatest Dujia killer in all four kingdoms, she had to find him first.

In the beginning, Pilar didn't hate magic. What little girl wouldn't fall in love with making her own flesh sing?

By five she knew how to coat her skin in pleasing shivers. At eight she could grow the bones back together after breaking her leg.

Pilar watched the other children on Refúj. When they were sick or hurting, their mothers mended their broken limbs and drew the fluid from their lungs. Zaga did none of those things. She was a whisper on the walls of the cave, a harsh invisible voice. Pilar knew if she wanted even a sliver of her mother's attention, she'd have to be a good Dujia. Not just good: the best.

So she practiced. Night and day. She bent herself into the shape she thought her mother wanted. If Zaga lived outside her body, Pilar was physical. She had no interest in subtle magic tricks. She loved ramming her thumb into a person's wrist, stopping the blood in their veins.

Pilar had another reason to like unblooding. This was the dark magic that had left her mother's left arm dead at her side. Zaga never talked about who hurt her, but of all the magic Pilar could use to win her mother's attention, surely unblooding would do the trick.

It didn't.

Still, she practiced every day. Zaga had taught them all that magic was a way for women to reclaim their power. Pilar believed it.

After what happened in the cottage, she stopped believing in anything.

"I have to piss," she said.

"Lovely," Quin muttered. "By all means, don't let me stop you."

"I get the feeling you're not used to frank conversation."

"Frank is one word for it. I was going to say you're egregiously blunt."

"My finest feature. That and my jawline."

Pilar loved her body—it was compact and supple, flexible and strong—but she resented the constant need for maintenance. That was the magical perk she missed the most: With magic she could compress the fluids of her body, go days without needing food or water. She could tweak her moon cycle, confining the flow of blood when she didn't want to be bothered. She could even restrict her bowels.

Pilar had yet to meet another Dujia who could magically condense a shit.

She ducked behind a tree and unbuckled her trousers. Quin whistled a tune—to cover the sound of her piss hitting the blue needles, she guessed.

"Do all bodies make you nervous?" she said. "Or just mine?"

"I wouldn't say *nervous* . . ."

"You should sing yourself a lullaby next time I take a squat."

She could practically hear him grimace. "You're a little rough around the edges, aren't you?"

"I didn't grow up with servants emptying my chamber pot every night."

Quin coughed. "I emptied my own chamber pot by the time I was eight."

"Commendations for your bravery."

"You're impossible."

Pilar yawned. "I must act different from the girls you grew up with."

"Different*ly*."

"And look different, too."

With her chin-length black hair, angular brown eyes, and amber skin, no one would mistake Pilar for a river rat. All the Glasddirans she'd met were fair skinned and liver hearted. Light eyes, dark hearts.

"Naturally," Quin said. "You're from the fire kingdom."

She smiled, proud of her Fojuen heritage. But her pride soured. As her mother always reminded her, she was only *half* Fojuen.

Her mother could rot in four hells.

"To be honest," said Quin, "other than my mother and sister, I didn't grow up with many women."

"Aren't you forgetting Mia Rose?"

Silence.

Still crouching, Pilar peeked out from behind the tree. Quin's brow was creased. If she'd meant to get under his skin, she'd succeeded.

Pity flashed in her chest, followed by resentment. Why was everyone so smitten with Mia Rose? She was cocky, entitled, self-righteous. A classic river rat. Only a girl that pigheaded could think she knew everything when she knew nothing. Not even how to save her own neck.

Of course no one else remembered it that way. By stopping her heart, Mia had become a hero. Mia Rose, the martyr. Mia Rose, the warrior. And so on.

Pilar hated how even the most awful people turned into saints the moment they died.

"Are you finished?" Quin called out, gruffer than before. "We should get going."

She stood and buckled her trousers. Checked to make sure the silver coin was safe in her pocket. Rounded the tree until they stood face-to-face.

"What's the hurry, Killian? Got somewhere to be?"

"Yes." His eyes bored into hers. "As far away from that castle as I can get."

The heat of his words surprised her. Before she could respond, he turned on his heel and walked swiftly through the forest.

"*Now* who's egregiously blunt," she muttered.

Quin didn't hear her. He was already blazing past the tall twisted trees, confident she would fall in step behind.

Pilar was curious about Quin. Growing up on an island of magical women, she hadn't met many boys. No princes.

During her months disguised as a scullery maid in Kaer Killian, she'd watched him from a distance. In the beginning he struck her as a typical spoiled royal. At least with those full lips and high cheekbones, he was less of an eyesore than the shriveled grandfathers of Refúj.

Then, on the night before his wedding to Mia Rose, she'd heard him play piano.

For a long time she lingered in the shadows outside the library, struck by the sad, sweet melody. Watching Quin at the piano—the fierce way he touched the keys—made her fingers ache for her violin.

When his would-be bride barreled into the library, the music stopped abruptly, and Pilar hurried back to the scullery with hardened resolve. She'd come to the Kaer to complete a mission: kill Mia Rose. She pushed Quin's song away as she sharpened her arrow in the dark.

Of course then she'd failed to hit her mark—not her finest moment—and one week later, a still-very-alive Mia and Quin appeared on Refúj. When the prince danced drunk and shirtless, batting his eyelashes at Domeniq du Zol, Pilar realized he'd been bottled up for years. All it took was one generous dose of spirits to crack the bottle.

She wished she had a dose of spirits now.

As they walked through the white and blue trees, Quin broke the silence.

"Why don't you go back to Refúj?"

"My mother broke the most sacred rule of the sisterhood," Pilar said. "She killed another Dujia. They'd put my head on a spike."

"The women I met don't seem like the heads-on-spike type."

"Everything is different now."

She had other reasons, too. Even before Zaga's betrayal, Pilar wasn't exactly beloved on the island.

"Why don't *you* go back to Glas Ddir? Those are your people."

She frowned. "Now that your father is dead, aren't you actually king?"

"Right. I'll just waltz back in and tell them I'm the rightful heir. I'm sure Angelyne will happily abdicate the throne, as long as I ask politely."

"Who said anything about politely?"

"Says the girl with a death wish." He jerked a thumb toward the forest at their backs. "You don't take on five men otherwise."

"Wanting to fight and wanting to die are two different things."

"Who taught you to fight like that? Your mother?"

Pilar laughed. "That's like asking if a snake taught me to walk."

"Whoever she was, she should be commended. I wouldn't last five seconds in hand-to-hand combat with you."

Quin was wrong. He wouldn't last three.

He was also wrong about her teacher being a she.

"What's in Luumia?" Quin asked.

"Ice leopards, the White Lagoon, bottles and bottles of warm buttery *vaalkä* . . ."

"You know what I meant."

Pilar shrugged. "I'm looking for someone."

"Me as well."

"Want to tell me who?"

"I do not."

Pilar arched a brow. "How are you planning to find this mysterious someone? You're a river rat who's hardly ever left the Kaer. The snow kingdom is massive. With lots of snow, I hear."

"I could ask you the same question."

"Mine won't be hard. He's a Luumi warrior. When the Weeping Moon rises on the last night of Jyöl, he stands on the steps of the Snow Queen's palace, cloaked and masked. They say he can go up against the most powerful Dujia—and win."

Quin frowned. "You're a Gwyrach. Why are you looking for a man who kills Gwyrach?"

"*Dujia*. Not Gwyrach. I don't answer to that word."

"I don't care much for 'river rat,' either."

"Fine," Pilar growled. "No demons, no rats."

Quin nodded, satisfied. He plunked himself down against a tree and pulled a hunk of stale bread from his satchel.

"Aren't you going to offer me some?" she said.

"No."

"Royal ass."

Quin chewed and swallowed, then folded his hands over the leather pouch on his belt. He tipped his head back and closed his eyes.

For a moment he looked exactly like his sister—the first time she'd seen the resemblance. Something about the hardness of his jaw, the way he lifted his chin. It startled her.

Pilar plopped down beside a twisted tree and closed her eyes. It was useless. No matter what she did, Karri was always there.

All those months Pilar had watched the prince in Kaer Killian, she'd also watched the princess. Karri had no shortage of talents—she bagged a boar on every hunt, trounced her weapons master in every fight.

She was also kind. More than once Pilar saw her filch a stallion from the castle stables and ride into Killian Village. Karri talked to people in smithies and alehouses, pubs and brothels. Even children hungry in the streets. She didn't just talk: she listened. The Glasddirans loved her for it.

Her father did not.

Pilar knew how it felt to have a parent hate you for who you were.

Karri would have made an excellent queen. And now she was dead. Pilar could never forgive her mother for telling her to shoot that arrow. But she could never forgive herself for doing it.

Pilar shook her head to clear it. Regret was passive. It eroded you from inside out, like a poison.

Revenge was active. Like a blade.

She had the dream again. Alone in a dark cave. Staring into a black sheet of ice. Sometimes she took the form of a demon, sometimes a witch, sometimes just a girl. Behind her own face, she always saw the same thing in the reflection: Princess Karri bleeding out onto the snow.

Pilar drove her fist into the ice, again and again, until it shattered like glass.

But this time, there was someone else.

Mia Rose stepped out of the shadows. She stooped. Wrapped her fingers around a broken shard. Looked up at Pilar.

It's over, Mia said.

She raised her arm, the shard glinting silver.

Pilar awoke to Quin's screams.

Chapter 3

DIRT AND BLOOD

"Wake up. Wake *up!*"

Pilar shook Quin by the shoulders. She whispered his name. Yelled it. Even grabbed her leatherskin and doused him with water. A powerful sleeping terror had taken hold, his screams loud enough to rouse an army.

If more guards arrived, she could take them. But if her mother sent Dujia instead of men? Even if Pilar *did* use magic, she couldn't fight off theirs. Not alone.

Only twenty-six days till the Weeping Moon. Pilar's best shot at finding the Snow Wolf was to be at the queen's palace on the last night of Jyöl. She couldn't afford to be captured.

She punched Quin in the face.

Not hard. She didn't want to hurt him, just wake him up.

She succeeded.

"Where am I?" Quin sputtered as he jolted upright. He rubbed his nose. "Did you just *punch* me?"

"Yes." Pilar was many things, but she was not a liar. "You were about to get us both killed."

"Nice to know you have my back." Quin let out his breath, his shoulders slumping. "She was right beside me. I saw her. *Touched* her."

He'd been dreaming about Mia Rose.

In the castle, when Zaga paraded Mia's lifeless body through the Grand Gallery, Pilar had felt a tangle of emotions. Mia was naive, yes—and disgustingly superior—but did she deserve to die?

Then again, did she deserve *not* to? Mia had been so intent on saving her sweet baby sister, she'd dragged them all back to the Kaer and straight into a trap. Mia was the reason Karri was dead. She was the reason Pilar and Quin and everyone else got enkindled. She'd played right into Zaga and Angelyne's hands, and been too stubborn to see it.

"Since we're both awake," said Quin, yanking her back to the forest, "we might as well keep moving."

She watched him pluck the blue needles off his jacket, face raw with pain. When he saw her looking, he stood. Wiped his eyes with the back of his hand.

Pilar didn't understand what Quin saw in Mia Rose. But she didn't have to. Despite all the death and misery she had dumped into his life, one thing was certain: the prince was still in love with Mia Rose.

Mia Rose was dead.

Pilar and Quin made decent fugitive companions. She was better at tying strong knots. He was better at cooking dead things. But the banter they'd struck up the first day had ground to a halt after he dreamed of Mia.

Typical. Mia Rose wrecked everything, even from the grave.

"Ask me a question," Pilar said as they trekked south. "Anything."

"All right. How did you escape?"

"Not to brag," she said, clearly bragging, "but I knew where the scullery maids kept the spirits they smuggled in. Most Dujia are less powerful when drunk, or at least sloppier. So I stole some rai rouj and slipped it into my mother's cup. Angelyne's, too."

She cocked her head. "How did *you* escape?"

Quin hesitated.

"Have you seen my father's Hall of Hands under our new queen?"

Pilar shook her head.

"In the slivers of a moment when Angelyne's enthrall weakened," he said, "when I came back to my senses, I would go to the Hall. There are no longer hands swinging from the rafters. There are bodies stacked on the floor."

"*Bodies?*"

"Your mother sends guards to every village to demand allegiance. All those who refuse to kneel to Queen Angelyne get carted back to the Kaer, where they're subjected to all sorts of magical atrocities. A tower of bodies rotting in the Hall."

Pilar frowned. That was dark, even for her mother.

"What about the smell? Don't people get sick?"

"Angelyne can heal those she wants to. But yes. Agreed about the stench." He ran a hand through his blond curls. "Most of the men carried protective stones. Rings and amulets made of uzoolion and other rocks. I assume they grabbed hold of anything rumored to fight magic. I saw runes, charms, talismans looped around their necks or tucked into their pockets, and I—"

"You looted the bodies."

He let out a long breath. "I needed some way to withstand the enthrallment. I would never have been strong enough."

When Quin's eyes fell to the leather pouch on his belt, her eyes followed.

"That pouch isn't full of gold," she said, realizing. "Those are the stones you stole."

He stiffened, like he was afraid she would scold him. Honestly, she was impressed. Never in her wildest dreams would she have imagined gallant Prince Quin pickpocketing the dead.

Pilar felt a stab of excitement. "Killian. You know what this means? If we have enough of the right stones, we can weaken Angelyne's magic. She's beatable."

He shook his head. "The moonstone grows more powerful by the day. It seems the more people Angelyne hurts, the more people she *can* hurt."

Quin's expression blackened. "She practices with other stones, too. Strange gems I've never seen. I think she may be storing her magic in new places, bewitching objects we'd never even recognize."

Pilar frowned. "I've only known three stones to affect magic. Fojuen to strengthen, uzoolion to weaken, and lloira to store a Dujia's healing gifts. Sounds like Angelyne has found a way to warp that, too."

"I know it was wrong," Quin said quietly, "stealing those men's stones. I'm not proud of it."

"Why? You survived."

Pilar knew better than anyone that survival did not come in a silken bonnet. Survival meant dirt and blood under your fingernails.

It meant killing someone before they killed you first.

Chapter 4

FOR THE BOTH OF US

Two days passed, then three. On the fourth day, Pilar felt the air grow colder. In the distance she saw big white mounds in the earth. Ice caves.

"We're nearing the border," she said to Quin.

"I imagine so."

Once they crossed Dead Man's Strait and entered the snow kingdom, they would go their separate ways. The idea flooded her with panic.

"Here's a question," Quin said, as they trekked through the snow. "Do you know what happened to Domeniq du Zol?"

He said it almost casually, like an afterthought. But she heard it. The catch in his breath.

Pilar missed Domeniq, too. He'd been her one true friend on Refúj, even if the friendship was brief. She remembered his kind, crooked smile, the way it lit up his face.

She also remembered the way he and Quin danced together at the Blue Phoenix. Sweaty. Close.

"I never saw Dom in the castle," she answered honestly.

"I did," said Quin, and she realized he'd been baiting her, that he'd known the answer all along. "Your mother uses him for magic practice. Sometimes she sends him out with the guards to round up more bodies for the Hall. She and Angelyne enkindle him, make him do and say all kinds of atrocious things he would never do."

"How do you know what Dom would do? You'd only just met."

"I know he's good," he growled. "And wise. And generous in spirit. More than I can say for you."

She held up a hand. "I wasn't arguing with you, Killian. Just asking."

Quin's eyes met hers for a moment, fierce. Then he looked away.

"We both know Dom was playing both sides. Training to be a Dujia Hunter, while secretly protecting his Dujia family. But the rest of the river kingdom doesn't know the truth. To them he makes a powerful example. He's the last surviving Hunter, now serving the new queen."

"What about Griffin Rose? Fearless leader of the Circle of the Hunt? He's still alive, too." Pilar snorted. "Though last I heard, his mind is so far gone he slurps soup out of a shoe in the castle dungeons. Looks like all those years spent murdering innocent Dujia finally caught up to him."

"And yet you're seeking his Luumi counterpart," Quin muttered. "You're a tangle of contradictions."

She wheeled around. "*I'm* a tangle of contradictions? Griffin Rose married a woman who was enthralling him! A woman who never loved him, but loved my mother, of all people. Griffin Rose, assassin of Dujia—and father to two Dujia daughters, one now dead."

Quin stopped walking. "You might show some respect when you speak of Mia Rose."

She glared at him. Mia and Karri were the two frozen lakes they tiptoed around. Pilar didn't tiptoe. She was sick of not speaking her mind.

They were about to have their first real conversation, like it or not.

"I know there are things you want to say to me," she said. "You just don't have the courage to say them."

"You're not a very gentle person, are you?"

"There's no place for gentleness in this world."

"I think there's nothing this world needs more."

He began to hum.

Pilar recognized the melody. She was back in Kaer Killian, lurking in the corridors the night before the royal wedding.

It felt like a lifetime ago. She'd been so righteous in her mission. Kill Mia Rose, enemy of the Dujia. Save her sisters. Return to Refúj a hero, and finally clear her name.

Sometimes the things you wanted most were the very things that destroyed you.

Quin's hum was tender. She couldn't bear it.

"Stop," she said.

He stopped. Took a breath.

"You want me to talk about Mia?" he said. "I miss her. I think about her all the time. Sometimes I lie awake at night, just to see if I can conjure up a memory of her freckles."

"Why?" Pilar swallowed the softness in her voice. "Are you drawing a portrait?"

"Are you always this heartless?"

For eighteen years Pilar had been told to trust her heart. *Feel instead of think,* said her mother. *Trust your heart, not your mind.*

Her heart had failed her.

"I think," she said, "that you're doing a piss-poor job of moving on."

"I'm not trying to move on. I'm trying to grieve."

"Mia's the one who stopped your sister's heart! You should hate her."

"I don't hate people."

"Liar. Everyone hates someone."

Quin's green eyes flashed with more pity than anger, which was worse. She wanted to wound him. Better to hurt him before he hurt her.

"You're a coward," she said. You shouldn't even be here. If you were brave, you'd find a way to beat Angelyne. If you had even one speck of courage, you would go back to Glas Ddir and save your people."

There it was. The spark of rage in Quin's eyes.

"Don't tell me what I should or shouldn't do. After a lifetime with my father, I've seen what hate can do."

"How could you grow up in that castle, with those people, and not hate them? Don't you hate your father for everything he did?"

"The minute I give in to those feelings," he said, his jaw working around the words, "I'm no better than he is. You think hurting people makes you strong? I think it makes *you* a coward. You hide behind your fists so you don't have to feel anything. Can't you see I'm grieving?"

He tugged a hand through his curls. "It isn't just Mia. I lost my sister. My whole family."

"My mother was my whole family. She betrayed me."

"I know."

"She used me to kill innocent people. I only shot Karri because she told me to."

"I know." He looked her straight in the eye. "You do not have a monopoly on grief, Pilar. Even if you won't admit it, I know you're grieving, too."

Why was he being so kind? She was giving him fire, and he was shoveling snow onto it.

"You don't get to tell me how to grieve," she snapped.

"Of course I don't. But I believe grief has power. It flows through us whether we want it to or not. If we ignore it, the grief builds up inside us and leaks out in all kinds of ways. If

29

we remember what we lost, the grief gets stronger—but we get stronger, too."

"Your sister is dead because of me. Mia is dead because of me. I nearly killed *you* with my arrow! Why don't you hate me?"

"I'm angry. I'm terribly sad. But I don't hate you."

"Fine." She clenched her jaw. "Then I'll hate myself enough for the both of us."

When he placed a hand on her arm, she flinched. She was no longer there with Quin. She was in the cottage by the lake. Lying on a hard dirt floor, staring up at the wooden rafters, long beams casting shadows like a cell.

A punch she could take. Gentle touches scared her.

On instinct, she shoved Quin away, pushing him off balance. When he stumbled to the ground, her chest ached.

She didn't want to hurt him. Not really, not at all.

Quin was right. In the fight between her fists and her feelings, her fists would always win.

When she spoke, her voice was steady again.

"I want to give you something, Killian."

"What could you possibly give me?"

She extended a hand and pulled him to his feet.

"I'm going to teach you to fight."

Chapter 5

SERENADE

WHEN IT CAME TO sparring, Pilar was the best fighter she knew. That wasn't pride speaking. Or it *was* pride speaking, but pride rooted in fact.

Quin, on the other hand, was terrible.

"You're not very good, Killian."

"I've never done it before!" he huffed. "This is all new to me."

"You want me to bake you a chocolate strudel?"

"I want you to be more patient."

"Patience was never my strong suit."

Quin had taken to the idea of sparring immediately, which was a relief. Pilar couldn't return what he'd lost, but at least she could teach him to protect himself. Finally she had something to offer. Something a girl like Mia Rose could never give.

Beads of sweat clung to Quin's brow. The yellow sun was gone, crushed by the bloated white blob of the moon. Pilar wasn't tired in the slightest. When she fought she felt like someone had poured rai rouj into her veins, spiking her blood with heat.

"I told you, keep most of your weight in your lower half. You're skinny so it's even more important to have a strong base. Stop standing on the earth like a sprite."

"Do sprites exist?"

"Everything exists. Now fix your form and come at me again."

Quin charged forward, swinging his arms wildly. She swiped her foot behind his ankle and sent him crashing to the ground. Somehow he fell forward instead of back.

"Ow," he moaned into the dirt.

"Sorry. You're already dead."

"I'm trying!"

"Try better. And bend your knees next time. If you don't bend your knees you might as well be standing on two sticks. What happens to sticks? They break."

She couldn't believe how much she sounded like Orry. He was in her head.

Three years earlier, when Pilar was fifteen, a young married couple had arrived on the island. Morígna, the Dujia, was a musician. She gave Pilar her violin. Her husband, Orry, was a fight teacher. Orry was jovial and charming, passionate about showing his students how to protect themselves. Pilar trained with him daily. Who cared if the other girls didn't like her? The lonelier she felt, the harder she fought. For the first time, her ever-ready fists were a gift, not a curse.

"Don't rotate your shoulder forward," she told Quin. "You want to stay grounded and strong. Hug your elbow tight to your body—it'll give you more control. Then twist your body and pivot your front foot. The thrust of the leg accelerates the punch."

"Where do I punch my opponent?"

"Cheeks, nose, or under the ear where the jaw attaches. Three weakest spots on the human face. Of course at the moment it doesn't matter where you hit—you're throwing punches like confetti. Start with palm strikes. That'll keep your fingers protected." She demonstrated driving her palm into Quin's nose. "It's a good trick. With enough force you can shove the nasal bone into his skull."

"Sounds messy."

"Fighting is messy. It's one part choreography, two parts improvisation. For you right now, it's three parts staying upright."

"You're good at this, you know."

Pilar felt a surge of pride. The adrenaline rush she always got from sparring was so much better than anything she'd ever felt from magic. In the early days, Orry told her she was special. She would stagger home each night, bruised and bloody and blazingly alive.

"Water," Quin gasped.

Pilar scooped snow into her leatherskin and handed it to Quin, who gulped down the icy slush. The prince looked good with a little color in his cheeks.

He wiped his mouth on his sleeve. "Thank you."

"Drink up. We're not finished."

"But I'm exhausted."

"Sometimes exhaustion can be helpful. You can't trick your

body—it'll show you where your weaknesses are."

"What's in your pocket, Pilar?"

Her jaw clenched. "Nothing."

"I see you touching it when you think I'm not looking."

"It's just a coin."

She tossed it to Quin to shut him up. He laid the coin flat on his palm and squinted at the symbol side.

"This is the seal of Luumia. Ice leopard with a frostflower underfoot."

"Ten points for Clan Killian."

He flipped the coin over and read the hand-carved inscription. *Snow Wolf*. That must be your famed Luumi assassin." He cocked a brow. "You mean to tell me we've been looking for a dog?"

"Are you mocking me?"

"Not at all. I miss my dogs every day." Quin chucked the coin at her. She caught it handily.

"Nice reflexes," he said.

"My third finest feature. Bluntness, jawline, reflexes."

"I thought it was self-hatred?"

With a roar, she tackled him from the side.

The coin went flying as Quin fell backward. She climbed on top of him, straddling his chest.

"Never, ever let them get you on the ground. Most men are a lot bigger than you and me. The second he's on top of you, he's already won. Now try to get away."

Quin squirmed beneath her. An image of a broken horsehair bow flashed through her mind. She locked her knees tighter, forcing herself to focus on Quin's face. His hair was mussed, his eyes piercing green. Pilar had never seen him from this angle before. She liked it.

She drew the dagger from her boot.

"Sorry," she said. "You're already dead."

Quin drove his palm into her nose.

The impact knocked her head backward. Hard enough that she saw a spray of white stars. Her knees loosened, and in a flash Quin shifted his hips beneath her. She keeled onto her side as he wriggled free.

"Success!" he crowed. He snatched the dagger from where she'd dropped it. "Sorry. You're already dead."

He was being smug, but it was the first time she'd seen Quin really smile. And she had to hand it to him: he'd nailed the strike. Her ears were still ringing.

Pilar brushed off the coin and dropped it into her pocket.

"Nicely done."

"Four gods." Quin's jaw dropped. "Was that a compliment from Pilar Zorastín d'Aqila? We must commemorate this moment."

He pulled a flask out of his satchel. Murky reddish-brown liquid swirled inside, and at the bottom: a dead sqorpion.

Rai rouj.

"Where in the Duj's name did you get that?" she said. The prince was full of surprises.

He shrugged. "You never know what you'll find in a heap of dead men."

35

They built a fire and sat on the hard ground, passing the flask of rai rouj between them. With every nip, Quin loosened. Here was the drunken, dancing boy Pilar recognized from Refúj, back before everyone betrayed everyone else.

Truth be told, she was feeling a little loose herself. She loved the scalding comfort of rai rouj, even if it made her fractured cheekbone throb and the black fleas blur her vision. She felt better than she had in months.

"You know," Quin said, "I actually quite enjoyed sparring. I haven't worked that hard in . . . ever?" He rubbed his shoulders and groaned.

"It's good to have someone knead your muscles after fighting." Pilar's cheeks flamed. "Not that you'd want me to."

"On the contrary! I'd be delighted to have you pummel me with your tiny fists."

"They're not tiny." They were absolutely tiny. "You've seen what I can do with them. I have very strong hands."

"Show me." Quin peeled his shirt off in one smooth motion, until it got stuck around his head. "Help!" he said, his voice muffled. "My brain is too large, it can't get free."

She leaned forward and gave the shirt a good tug.

"Typical," she said. "Your head was inflating again."

Quin's body was smooth and golden. She'd only seen one man naked before, and he was hairy in all the wrong places.

Pilar knelt behind the prince. When she dug her thumbs into the muscles at the base of his neck, he cried out. She froze. Were her hands only good for causing pain?

"Don't stop," Quin said. "For the love of four gods, do not stop."

Only then did she realize the cry was the *good* kind.

She began to knead his knotted muscles with her knucklebones. As she moved slowly across his back, she grazed the white scar beneath his shoulder blade: the place her arrow had gone through.

She could apologize. *Should* apologize. But she'd never been good at saying sorry.

Apologies reeked of regret.

"Who is the Snow Wolf, Pilar?" Quin murmured. "I know there's something you're not telling me."

Her hands stopped. If she told him who the Snow Wolf was—who he *really* was—he would look at her with pity. She could imagine nothing worse.

"Since you're suddenly so interested in honesty," she snapped, "who are *you* looking for in Luumia?"

Quin reached for his shirt. "You'll judge me for it."

"Probably." She crossed her arms, defiant. "But I'm not going any farther until you tell me."

He yanked the shirt down over his neck.

"All right," he said. "I want to save Domeniq."

The answer caught her by surprise.

Pilar pointed behind them. "Domeniq is *that* way."

"Yes, thank you. I do have a basic grasp of geography."

Quin picked up a twig and stabbed at the ground. "You say I've abandoned my kingdom and my people. But I never wanted to be king. My sister was born to sit on the river throne—and unlike me, she actually wanted it. Karri was bold and brilliant and bighearted."

For a moment his eyes shone brighter. Then his face went dark.

"But we'll never get to see her reign. Today, watching the things Angelyne does to innocent people . . . let's just say I've come to understand how much we've lost."

All the regret Pilar had fought against so hard was creeping back. Not only had she robbed Quin of his sister—she'd robbed an entire kingdom of their rightful queen. Karri would have protected the people of Glas Ddir. Angelyne wanted them to suffer.

Pilar swiped at the heat behind her eyes. "You didn't answer my question. What does any of this have to do with Dom du Zol?"

He snapped the twig in two. "Dom doesn't deserve what they're doing to him. I want to break him out, take him somewhere they can't reach him."

The blood was rushing to Quin's face. He exhaled.

"But I can't do it alone. They say a just ruler will never stand by while innocent people suffer. I think, if I can make my case to the Snow Queen, she might help me."

"You're joking." Pilar blinked. "*That's* your grand plan?"

"See? This is exactly why I didn't want to tell you. I knew you'd—"

"You're going to Luumia so you can pop in to the palace for a cup of tea?" She let out a low whistle. "That's all you royals know how to do, isn't it? Throw yourselves at the feet of other royals.

What makes you think the Snow Queen will be able to help you save Dom?"

"Forgive me," Quin spat, "for trying to save the one person I still care about. The only person I have left."

The words stung.

"Look," she said, hardening her voice. "It's fine you like Dom. You can dream about saving him all you want. But until you come up with a better plan, that's all it is. A dream."

From the look on Quin's face, she knew she should say something else. Something nicer. But suddenly he was rising to his feet.

"Do you hear that?"

He tipped his head to one side. Listened.

Pilar stood. She heard it, too.

Music.

She shut her eyes, drinking in the sound. Each note bent the air around it. Only one instrument could do that.

"Do you think it's a trap?" Quin whispered.

Her eyes flew open. Anything was possible, but it seemed unlikely the guards would follow them all this way to serenade them at the Luumi border.

"Shh," she said. "Don't ruin it."

She'd never heard a song so beautiful, or so sad.

"I have to see who's playing," she said.

Pilar didn't wait for him to answer. She turned and followed the violin.

Chapter 6

BRUISED ASS

THE VIOLINIST WAS A boy.

He was young, no more than twelve or thirteen, with tawny amber skin, dark freckles, and rounded eyes. He wore a fur cloak over a rough white tunic with purple diamonds in the wool. Pilar wasn't sure, but she thought this was a costume for Jyöltide, the annual solstice festival.

The boy hunched on a wooden stool, violin tucked under his chin. His slick black hair poked out in every direction like a happy, sloppy crown.

Excitement whirred in Pilar's chest. The boy was Addi, the indigenous people of the snow kingdom. That meant they were closer to the border than she'd thought.

She noticed something else about the boy's face: it was wet and puffy. He'd been crying.

"He's incredible," Quin whispered as they peeked through the twisted trees. The boy's fingers glided over the catgut strings as he stopped them against an ivory fingerboard. If Pilar had learned on a violin like that, instead of the old, banged-up corpse Morigna dragged from the river kingdom, she might have been incredible, too.

"You play, don't you?" Quin said, his voice low in her ear.

What had given her away? The smile that always crept into her eyes when she heard music? The way her fingers twitched, aching to hold the violin?

Her longing burned down to a deep and coiling shame.

"No," she said. "Not anymore."

A loud crack and whistle made them both look up. The boy looked up, too.

The southern sky was breaking.

The stars were falling. Pilar didn't know how else to describe it. They hurtled down as arrows of light, so bright she shielded her eyes. But they were falling up, too, each star curving in on itself. Spinning, whirling. Unzipping the seams of the sky.

The shimmers formed shapes in white silvery purple, flowers and beasts. Some stars drew letters, spelling words in a language Pilar didn't know.

"The Illuminations," Quin murmured, staring up at the sky in awe. "I didn't think the Luumi had them anymore."

"What are they?" she shouted. No need to be quiet now: the stars were shrieking so loudly they drowned out every other sound. "Are they magic?"

"I think they're made of fyre ice."

She shook her head. "I come from a land of volqanoes. I've seen fire, and that isn't it."

"Not fire. Fyre ice. It's a gemstone—with trace amounts of magic, if I'm not mistaken. My . . ." He hesitated. "My old music teacher was Luumi. He'd never seen them himself, but he told me how, when his parents were young, the royal family put on a spectacular display at the end of Jyöl. The Illuminations lit the sky above the palace on the darkest night of the year, when the—"

"Weeping Moon rises," Pilar finished. "But that won't happen for weeks."

"Not to mention they haven't had the Illuminations in almost twenty years. If the lights *have* returned, this must be some kind of precursor to the real display."

He frowned. "But my teacher told me they mined all the fyre ice decades ago. It was the primary source of heat and light in the snow kingdom, and without it, thousands of Luumi died."

"I thought Luumia was a land of progress?"

"Socially, yes. The Luumi embrace their magicians. They embrace everyone—there's none of my father's hate. But after two decades of scarcity, life in the snow kingdom is a bit bleak."

Just as quickly as the sky had lit up, it went dark. The only remnants of the Illuminations were curls of gray smoke.

"Look." Pilar pointed to the clearing.

42

The boy was gone, the stool tipped onto its side. On the snow lay the violin.

She rushed forward. How could he be so careless? You didn't let something that beautiful go crashing to the ground.

Pilar picked up the violin and dusted off the snow. The moment her hands touched the wood she felt a dizzy rush of feeling. The curves of the ribs were magnificent, the neck long and slender. She tapped her fingers lightly on the hollow belly. All she wanted was to play it.

"I'll bet the boy ran home," Quin said. "He probably lives nearby."

His words cracked the fantasy. Pilar's shoulders went slack. How quickly she forgot.

"We should return it," she said.

"Wait," Quin said. "Play me something first."

Her fingers tightened around the neck. "It's been too long."

"Doesn't matter. Play anything." He righted the boy's wooden stool and sat down. "I miss music terribly."

She missed it, too. Pilar eyed the horsehair bow bedded on the snow. She had sworn to never touch a bow again.

And yet. Her left fingers twitched against her thigh. The ache was visceral.

Maybe a few notes. Only a bar or two. Just to see.

She nested the violin in the crook of her chin. Then unnested it.

"Turn around," she said to Quin. "I don't want you watching."

He sighed. "If you insist."

43

He spun around on the stool. Pilar took a breath, stooped, and picked up the bow. It felt like lightning in her fingers. She brought it to the strings.

There was only one kind of magic Pilar still believed in. One kind of magic that a Dujia like her mother could never warp into something evil, no matter how hard she tried.

The magic of a violin when it sang.

Pilar hadn't touched a bow since the night in the cottage. Her fingers remembered the notes, but the cold made them clumsy. Luckily she had a knack for bending a wrong note into a right one. She wished she could fix all her previous mistakes so easily.

In every song, if she were lucky, she'd find one divine moment where she didn't play the notes: the notes played her.

Now was not one of those moments.

She got stuck on a section that had always been a pain in her ass. Her calluses were no longer up, thanks to months of Angelyne's enkindlement and Zaga's watchful eye. One more reason to kill them both. Not that she needed another reason.

After three tries, she lowered her bow.

"I know that lullaby." Quin was still facing the opposite direction. "It's Glasddiran. My mother used to sing it to me."

He hadn't commented on her playing. The only thing worse than failing was when someone saw you fail.

"You can turn around," she said. "I'm done embarrassing myself."

He swiveled on the stool. There was something in his eyes she didn't recognize. A spark.

"Would you like to know what I think?" he asked.

"Are you going to be an ass about it?"

"You're playing a fourth octave. I hope this doesn't offend you, but you shouldn't be able to do that with your level of training."

He'd managed to be an ass while paying her a compliment. Typical.

"You're good," Quin said. "But with practice and rigor, you could be great." He folded his arms over his chest. "I could help you. If you want."

"I thought piano was your instrument."

"I flirted with violin before I settled down." He stood and stepped toward her. "You have good calluses. I felt them while you were kneading my back."

So that was how he knew she played.

"Not as good as they used to be. And I'm cursed with short fingers."

"If you love your instrument, it doesn't matter. And you clearly do." He scratched his cheek. "It's kind of amazing, really. After seeing you fight, seeing you play is like watching an entirely different person."

Pilar frowned. Why couldn't she be both?

"You peeked," she said.

"What if I did? You might as well know you're beautiful when you play."

Pilar didn't know what to say. No one had ever called her beautiful.

"You need to stop clenching your bow so tightly in your right hand," Quin said. "You're not trying to kill it. You want to make love to it." He gestured toward the violin. "May I?"

Reluctantly she handed it over. He tucked it under his chin, mirroring her posture.

"Your shoulders are bunched up in your ears like this, see? You want to make a square with your right arm and bow. And bring your left elbow to where you can see it. You'll reach the lower strings more easily that way."

Quin demonstrated with the bow. With his long, regal fingers, he made it look easy.

"You said fighting is one part choreography and two parts improvisation," he said. "With the violin it's the opposite: two parts choreography, one part improvisation. For you right now, it's three parts not murdering your bow."

Quin clearly enjoyed slinging her own words back at her.

"I think that will help your intonation," he said.

"My intonation is fine," she shot back.

"Look, I play wrong notes, too. It's inevitable. But the violin is different from piano. With violin, you can fix the bad notes before most people can hear them."

She thought that was exactly what she'd done. "*You* seem to have heard them."

"Yes. I can hear them." Quin's smile was sad. "My teacher used to say I was cursed with that particular gift."

When he looked at her, the firelight turned his green eyes gold.

"To be honest," he said, "I'm a bit envious of you. The violin creates a special kind of magic. Every minuscule shift of the fingertips produces a slightly different sound. There are infinite possibilities. Each note can be anything it wants to be."

"I know that already," she said. That was exactly why she loved it. Morígna was fond of saying the violoncello most mimicked the sound of the human voice. Pilar disagreed. Both instruments had their unique voices, but the violoncello picked a fight. The violin asked a question.

Quin lowered the bow. "Do you smell smoke?"

She inhaled. "Yes."

Pilar swung herself up into the limbs of a swyn. Beyond the smooth stretch of white she saw black smoke rising, and in the distance: an ice kabma.

Pilar's heart beat faster. She'd only ever seen sketches of kabmas, the dwellings the Addi carved out of ice, then packed with peat moss and reinsdyr pelts to trap in the heat.

"I think I just found where our violinist friend lives," she called down to Quin.

"But we're not in Luumia yet. We haven't crossed Dead Man's Strait."

"It must be a northernmost settlement—one of the Addi villages flanking the border."

"Maybe they can help us get to the snow kingdom," Quin said.

Pilar dropped from the tree, landing square on her feet. "Then you can have the royals draw you a nice hot bath."

The muscles tensed in his jaw. "Right after I go back to the Kaer to save people, you mean. While you go back to kill them."

"Two sides of the same coin, Killian." She shrugged. "Maybe

you and I should be working together. Makes it a lot easier to save Dom if Zaga and Angelyne are already dead."

He studied her. "Strange, isn't it? The Snow Queen welcomes all Dujia—and yet *you* say she harbors the Snow Wolf, your trusty Dujia killer, within her borders."

"I don't make the rules. Maybe it's how she protects her people. Keep your friends close . . ."

"Thanks, I know the rest."

She sized him up. "All I know is that everyone is welcome in the snow kingdom. Even a warrior like the Snow Wolf—as long as he doesn't hurt the Dujia of Luumia. All other Dujia are fair game."

She yanked the violin out of Quin's hands.

"You really are impossible," he said.

Pilar turned away so he couldn't see her face. When she thought of parting ways with Quin, fear seized her chest. She couldn't explain it. They had nothing in common. Except maybe music. And evil parents. And a deep distrust of magic. And—

"Let's find the boy," he said, nodding toward the black smoke. "If we return the violin, maybe his family will give us a few coins to secure passage on a boat."

"Good idea. That'll at least get us to White Lagoon, the closest port town."

Relieved to be out of her own thoughts, Pilar sprinted past Quin and down the hill, her boots spitting up chunks of snow. The ground leveled off, and suddenly she was slipping on different terrain. She looked down and saw tiny silver bubbles trapped under her feet.

"It's frozen!" she shouted. Pilar had only ever seen the lake on Refúj, clear and blue and never frozen.

So this was what skating felt like. A bird gliding over water.

She stumbled and fell backward. So this was what skating *badly* felt like. A bruised ass.

Quin called after her. "It might not be frozen all the way through . . ."

"Could you try being brave?" she shouted back. "Just this once?"

Pilar felt drunk with hope. She was almost in Luumia. Only three more weeks till the Weeping Moon. With the Snow Wolf by her side, she'd return to Kaer Killian and kill two Dujia to save all the rest. She'd finally be free. Free of her mother. Free of her shame.

She was thinking about freedom when she tripped over the boy's body in the snow.

Chapter 7

FROSTFLOWER

"Put him here," Quin ordered Pilar. "We'll start a fire and get him warm."

Together they had dragged the violinist's body off the lake and into the ice kabma, where they expected to find his family. Instead they found a cold and empty hearth. The black smoke was rising from somewhere else.

"I don't understand," Quin crouched beside the boy. "He was fine just minutes ago!"

Pilar stared at the violinist's face, his dark eyes open. Like he'd witnessed something unthinkable.

She didn't have to check his wrist for a pulse. She knew.

"You have to use magic," Quin said, frantic. "You're the only one who can—"

"It's too late, Killian. He's gone."

If Pilar closed her eyes, she could still see the boy, face bright as his fingers sailed over the strings. If they'd come a few minutes earlier . . . if she hadn't stopped to play the violin . . .

She kicked a tin bucket by the fireplace. Ash spewed everywhere.

"Where's his mother?" she growled. "Where's his father? When I find them, I swear to the Duj, I will rip the tongues from their mouths."

"Has it occurred to you more violence might *not* be the answer?"

"What kind of father abandons his own child? He wasn't there when I needed him the most."

"When *you* needed him?"

She tried to swallow her fury, but it came up like bile.

"I'm talking about the boy," she said.

She felt him studying her. "But you're not, are you?"

Pilar ripped the coin from her pocket and hurled it across the kabma.

"The Snow Wolf." Quin stood, his eyes bright with understanding. "You think he had something to do with—"

"He's my father."

The word felt like ice in her mouth. *Father.*

Zaga had no interest in men, but she had coupled with a man, obviously: that was how babies were made.

As a child, Pilar badgered her with questions. "Tell me something about him. Anything."

"When I told him I was pregnant," her mother said, "he took

the first ship back to Luumia. He said every warrior must lead a solitary life."

"So my father was a warrior!"

Back then Pilar only saw the good. She had a knack for plucking the peppermint candy from a box of shit. As she grew up, the shit began to outsmell the peppermint.

Your father did not want you.

When I told him you were his, he left.

"I want to find him, Mother," she'd declared at fifteen.

"He would kill you in an instant."

"If he kills Dujia, why didn't he kill you?"

There was a small hope Pilar didn't want to give voice to: that her mother was lying. Zaga lied about everything else. Why not this? Maybe the Snow Wolf hadn't known she was pregnant.

Maybe, if he'd known, he wouldn't have left.

And then, during her months disguised as a scullery maid in Kaer Killian, Pilar finally had a chance to do some digging of her own.

One of the Hunters had taken a shine to her. A clumsy, slobbering Luumi boy with a blond beard more like blond fuzz. Every night while he angled for a kiss, she barraged him with questions about the renowned Dujia killer.

Few people had ever seen the Snow Wolf—accounts of his appearance varied wildly—but it had to be him. The boy described his fighting technique as "a blade forged from water, mercurial and deadly." Some skills were trainable, but Orry said you either had good instincts or you didn't. Instincts were something a warrior girl might inherit from her warrior father—even one she'd never met.

"Since you're so keen to find him," her slobbering Luumi suitor had said, "go to the Snow Queen's palace the last night of Jyöl. The Wolf won't let anyone see his face, but he stands on the steps of the palace, cloaked and masked, beneath the Weeping Moon."

The boy had carved "Snow Wolf" on the back of a silver coin and dropped it down the front of Pilar's scullery dress, hoping to curry favor.

He'd curried nothing but a fat lip.

During the darkest days in the Kaer, when the enkindlement cut into Pilar's mind like glass, the coin kept her sane. She would channel all her energy into her fingers, fight Angelyne's magic long enough to reach into her pocket and trace her father's name.

Pilar knew he was a Dujia killer. But then, so was she.

Maybe, if she found him, he would listen.

Maybe he would believe.

"I understand now."

Quin's voice jolted Pilar back to the present. His face was soft. "I wish you'd told me."

Her stomach twisted. How much had she revealed just now, lost in her own memories? She scraped the emotion off her face.

"Why would I tell you? It doesn't change anything."

"It changes everything. You're not looking for a killer. You're looking for your father."

"I'm looking for a killer," she snapped, "who happens to be my father. I need his help if I want to kill my mother. No more than that."

"And after you kill your mother? What will you do once you've claimed your vengeance?"

Whenever Pilar tried to see beyond the moment Zaga's heart stopped, her vision clouded.

"Be honest, Pilar," Quin said. "You want to find your father so you're not alone."

She hated the way he was looking at her, like she was something to be pitied.

"You don't know anything about me."

"I know you're not being honest about what you want. Not with me, not with yourself."

"I am not a liar," she spat. "And I'm not a coward. At least I'm running *toward* something. Your kingdom is in shambles, piles of dead bodies stacked in your castle, and you're running away. Poor little prince, scared of magic. Scared of frozen lakes. Scared of everything."

She could tell she'd hurt him. It made her feel like a clawed beast, unable to do anything but gouge and skewer.

"No one wants to be alone," he said.

She bit the inside of her cheek, eyes blurring with salt. She wasn't searching for the Snow Wolf for a rosy family portrait or a warm hug. How could she make Quin understand?

"I've always been alone," she said. "Always will be."

Pilar shook the tears out of her eyes. "I can't save my family, Killian. There's none to save. And I can't save yours, either. Not your sister, not Mia Rose. I sure as four hells can't save you."

"Maybe I'm not the one who needs saving."

She didn't have time for a retort. Outside the kabma, four wheels smashed into the snow.

"One carriage, three riders on horseback."

Quin had peeled back a flap of reinsdyr hide to peek out the kabma's window. Pilar stood at his side. The crest on the carriage matched the one on her coin: a silver ice leopard standing proudly on a white flower. When the flag rippled in the breeze, the leopard looked like he was slinking forward, ready to pounce.

"We were supposed to go unnoticed." Pilar scanned the kabma. No bulky furniture to conceal them—just straw beds and a round wood table. Four bright red cloaks with high metal collars hung from hooks on the wall.

Only then did she notice the drawings. Dozens of them. They were tacked to the wall—some charcoal, some stained with pigment.

She stepped closer, and her foot knocked into something hard. She'd kicked open a dented violin case. When she leaned down to close it, she saw a white trinket nested inside.

Pilar lifted the trinket from the pink satin.

A frostflower carved from bleached bone.

On instinct, she dropped it down the front of her shirt. She wasn't sure why.

The carriage wheels creaked to a halt outside. Pilar heard the thud of a rider dismount. A woman's deep, coarse voice pierced the kabma's ice walls.

"Foe or friend?"

"Friend," Pilar called. "*Two* friends."

Together she and Quin stepped out of the kabma.

Three women stood in the snow in a perfect triangle, axes slung over their backs. They wore thick furs and snow-fox cloaks. The tallest had bright silver eyes, black hair shaved close to the scalp, and the same cool amber skin as the little boy, only without the freckles. The other two were light-skinned, with crystal blue eyes and long white-blond hair tied up in braids and knots.

The women were older than Pilar—twenty-five, maybe thirty. She wasn't good at guessing that sort of thing. There was something compelling about the way they stood with their feet wide on the earth, their shoulders squared. They were big women, and they seemed proud of their size, comfortable with their strength. Pilar instantly admired them.

"Your voice is mighty," said the woman with the shaved head, thin silver eyes flashing with amusement, "yet you are small."

"You are big," Pilar countered, "yet your ax is tiny."

The woman laughed. "I think I'm going to like you." She fixed her gaze on the prince. "What brings you to the Luumi border?"

Quin shifted his weight. "Unfinished business."

"I wasn't aware the river prince had any business in the land of snow."

So she knew who he was. Pilar couldn't tell if the shaved-head woman, who seemed to be the leader of the guards, was about to clap Quin on the back or hack his head off his shoulders.

A small crowd had begun to gather. Many wore the same bright red cloak that hung inside the kabma, twisted pewter at the neck and a thick white belt at the waist. Others wore reinsdyr pelts and boots made of tanned hide.

In the gray fog, Pilar saw a row of ice kabmas and what looked like a village square. So her instincts were right. This was an Addi village.

The Addi watched the guardswomen, curious, maybe a little afraid.

"Check inside," said the shaved-head guard, waving toward the kabma at Pilar and Quin's backs. The two other guardswomen hurried forward and threw the door open.

Pilar's stomach dropped. She knew what they would find inside.

"It isn't what you think," she began, but it was too late.

"Another one, Freyja," called one of the guards. "This time a boy."

The smile vanished from Freyja's face. She pushed roughly past them, crouched beside the boy's small body. Pilar saw her take his hand gently. She was checking for a pulse.

"We found him by the lake," Quin said nervously. "We tried to revive him . . ."

Freyja stood. "Bind them."

The bigger of the two blond guards seized Quin with one hand. The smaller guard pinned Pilar's arms behind her back. Pilar bent her knees and shifted her weight forward, ready to fight—just as her captor slammed her boot down, crushing her foot.

Pilar swallowed a cry of pain. A broken toe. Maybe two. Her head swam as the guardswoman twisted her arm harder, then reached down and drew Pilar's dagger from her boot.

"So that's it, then?" She fought to keep her voice even. "We're your prisoners now? In Luumia, land of warm welcomes?"

"You're certainly not our friends."

Freyja extracted a piece of black chalk from her pouch and drew a large circle on the door of the ice kabma. She slashed through it with three long lines, making a wheel with six spokes. On the end of each spoke she drew three short dashes.

A murmur rippled through the crowd. This symbol meant something to the people in the village.

Freyja tucked the black chalk into her trouser pocket.

"Lord Dove?"

For the first time Pilar noticed a thin older man sat stooped on the carriage, swathed in such heavy cloaks she could only see his rosy cheeks and the pink tip of his nose.

"What would you recommend?" said Freyja.

"Yes, well, I suppose . . ." Lord Dove rubbed his hands together. He seemed out of place, a gentleman stuck between three rough-and-tumble women. "We really have no choice, do we? She'll want to see them."

"Who will?" Quin asked.

Freyja turned and looked at them evenly.

"The queen."

21 DAYS TILL THE WEEPING MOON

Beloved sister,

My last letter was a lie.

Aren't all good stories like that? As children we are taught that fairy tales are lies dressed up as truths. I think it's the opposite. The best stories are true tales masquerading as fictions. Beautifully crafted, honest lies.

There once was an Addi witch. She had soft skin and long hair that flowed down her back like spun silver. The witch lived alone in an ice kabma at the foot of a mountain. When she grew hungry during the long winters, she wandered closer to the villages to find food.

But the people in the village did not trust her. "A witch will always have a taste for human flesh," they said. "You cannot change your nature." In truth the witch preferred a nice lamb stew to human children, but the rumors clung to her like burs to cloth.

Some of the men took a liking to her dark brown eyes and silken hair. While their wives chipped ice from the frozen lakes or kneaded bread dough in the kitchen, the men stole through the forest to find the witch and propose a trade. "We will give you food," they said, "if you give us something first."

So the witch gave them what they wanted. She ate the warm food. She bore six children. They were half human, half witch. Sometimes she wondered which half were the monsters.

But she loved them fiercely, because this is what mothers do: they love their children, even the most monstrous parts.

The witch grew old. The long years bowed her spine and drew her flesh gently toward the earth. One cold winter, on the night the Weeping Moon rose like a teardrop in the sky, she came to find food for her children, only to have the villagers spit in her face. Even the littlest boys yanked the thinning gray hair from her scalp and called her an old hag. When she fought back, they strung her up in the village square where only mice and crows were there to hear her last breath.

No one knows what happened to her children, if they died from cold or starvation, or if the villagers came for them, committed atrocities too horrible to name. They vanished from the world, preserved only in memories, in ink. But they cast long shadows on those who survived them.

Today the witch is known as the First Soul. She and her six children are the Seven Souls of Jyöl. They live on in the legends of Luumia, a land that has emerged from these macabre beginnings to become a glittering beacon of progress and equality for all.

I have always wanted to see the festival. I do so love a good holiday! The Illuminations of old were a wondrous thing, until Luumia was plunged into darkness twenty years ago, a consequence of greed and an abiding lust for power. But there are murmurings of strange things afoot. They say the Illuminations have returned under the new Snow Queen; that the lights will once again ignite the night sky. My interest in these lights—and their mysterious origins—runs deep.

But alas, I must stay here, righting the wrongs

of this broken land while you draw nearer to the land of promise.

My men tell me you will arrive just as the moon begins to weep. Buy me a festive purple scarf and bring it home, would you? I like to keep Mother's moonstone warm around my throat.

I will see you very, very soon.

With affection,
Angelyne

Chapter 8

DEAD

Mia was drunk.

She slumped in a cozy booth at the alehouse, counting her fingers. Her hands had sprouted more than she remembered.

She was five nips of vaalkä in, maybe six. Honestly? After four they all blurred together. The thing about vaalkä was that it tasted of nutmeg and warm apple pie, served with a salty slab of butter at the bottom of the glass. Quite comforting until it landed in your belly with enough heat to set your spleen on fire.

Or so they told her. She couldn't taste the nutmeg—couldn't feel the heat, even if her body clearly showed the aftereffects.

"What you have to remember," droned her companion, a tall boy with white-blond hair and watery blue eyes, "is that sorcery used to be a man's game. In the Luumia of old, only men were sorcerers. Things were better then, before we were at the mercy of the witch women."

Charming. Mia had made it all the way to White Lagoon, the first town on Luumia's northern coast, where she stood (slumped, rather) in a land shimmering with parity—and she'd managed to find a boy just as parochial as the ones she'd left behind.

"Sorcery is the *u-u-use* of magic," she said, her vowels slurring more than she would have liked. "Not magic itself. Perhaps ye olde sorcerers tapped into a magic that didn't belong to them."

"Ah. So you're one of those." He swilled his barley ale and chewed it noisily. "The girls who blame us men for ruining everything."

"From where I sit, history usually favors the ones with the cocks."

"And here I thought you were a lady." He stroked his mustache, which looked like a wormy white eyebrow pasted over his mouth. If Mia gave it a good hard tug, would it peel off?

"You're in support of the petition, then," he said. "The bid to change our official name from the *kingdom* of Luumia to the *queen*dom."

The word rolled around Mia's head. *Queendom.* She liked the sound of it.

"You do have a queen."

"And what happens to centuries of tradition? To our rich heritage? I'm not going to let some self-righteous witches strip me of my rights."

Mia yawned. The grin slid off his face.

"Am I boring you?"

"Intolbery." She tried again. "Intolerably."

"If you don't want to talk, we could do other things. There are rooms for rent upstairs."

"Also there are rats. But I won't be consorting with them, either."

She was brilliant when drunk, if she did say so herself. For most people, liquor pulped the words to mush in their mouths. For Mia it was the opposite. A nip of spirits removed all inhibitions. Vaalkä gifted her with a tongue of fire.

Albeit sloppy fire.

"Playing hard to get, are you?" He slid a tick closer on the bench. "I like that."

She felt a heavy thud on her kneecap. For a moment she thought she'd dropped her nip of vaalkä—a veritable calamity, seeing as how she was almost out of coins.

But it wasn't her spirits. Mia looked down to see the boy's hand on her knee. He'd somehow found the gap between the bottom of her cropped trousers and the top of her socks, peeled back the fabric and splayed his fingers like a sweaty starfish on her skin.

She couldn't feel the sweat, the heat, the groping.

She couldn't feel much of anything at all.

Mia had woken in a box.

It still gave her nightmares, that first moment. Awakening from the dark into the dark. She hadn't known where she was until she reached up to brush the hair out of her face and her knuckles cracked against hard wood.

Mia couldn't breathe. She was choking, stale air clogging her throat. She cracked her knuckles again, and again, and again, punching at the invisible roof until eventually she found the seam with her fingernails and pried the box open. Only after she'd tumbled out of her coffin, the cartilage in her knees stiff as cold caramel, had she seen the blood smeared across her knuckles, the splintered wood clinging to broken flesh.

She knew then that something was wrong. A thread between mind and body had been severed; a loss of language from her senses to her brain, and from her brain to her senses.

Mia's body had become a shell. She couldn't taste flavors or smell scents. Couldn't feel heat or cold, pain or discomfort—and not pleasure, either. Though she was vaguely aware of her feet on the floor or her hand lifting a glass of spirits, they were more like dull thuds, echoes of sensation. She'd gone numb.

It wasn't only physical. When she forced herself to drink, laugh, and be merry, she felt even more a fraud. It exhausted her, pretending to be normal.

That was the one thing she *did* still feel. Bone-deep weariness. A cloak no one else could see.

It would appear that dying came at a cost.

Her memories of the days leading up to the wooden box oozed through her like wet fog. She knew Zaga and Angelyne had betrayed her. She knew she'd killed Princess Karri while trying to save her. Most of all, she knew she'd left Prince Quin behind. She

had the same nightmare over and over: a terrified Quin screaming her name.

Regret wove itself into the same heavy cloak. She felt numb
from the relentless guilt, and guilty for the numbness. The one
thing she remembered with perfect clarity was the moment she
realized her mother was alive, waiting in the snow kingdom. Seconds later, Mia had pressed two magical stones to her chest in a
last-gasp attempt to stop her own heart.

Evidently, she had succeeded.

Mia didn't know who or what had woken her. She only knew
that she'd sat hunched on the forest floor for what seemed like
hours, blinking in the harsh sunlight as she massaged her adduc-
tors and tibiae, desperate to feel the blood humming in her legs.
She'd expected to find both stones in the coffin: the ruby wren
snarled up in the chain of the moonstone that belonged to her
mother. *Fojuen to stop your heart, and lloira to restore it.*

But there were no stones. Of course there weren't. Zaga and
Angelyne would need the moonstone to continue their reign of
horrors. All Mia found tucked into the corner was a white flower.
Hewn from bleached bone, the bloom had six petals and a small
red bird etched into its heart.

A raven.

My little red raven.

The flower was a clue, the first breadcrumb leading Mia to
her mother.

But if Wynna were hiding in the snow kingdom, who had
stowed the carved flower in the box? Was it the same person who

had carried Mia's coffin out of the castle and deep into the forest, only a few days' walk to the Luumia border? On that note, why in four hells hadn't they stuck around long enough to open the box?

How long had Mia been sleeping?

But she hadn't been sleeping. She'd been dead.

"Are you drunk yet?" her companion asked.

"Not nearly enough."

Mia shifted her hips until his hand slid off her knee.

"What are those?" she asked innocently, gesturing toward the white blossoms hooked onto his belt.

"These trinkets? They're nothing."

She hoped that wasn't true, since it would mean she'd squandered the last hour of her life with an insufferable boy for no reason. In an alehouse full of people, she'd seen his belt of frostflowers and felt a flicker of hope. Mia saw the blooms everywhere—floating magically in the streets, fluttering on Luumi flags—but this was the first time she'd seen one like hers, whittled from bleached bone.

It pained her to have to speak to him. She could tell what kind of boy he was by the way he leaned over the bar, accosting the barmaid. Mia had sauntered up to him acting a little drunker than she was. He offered to buy her a nip, just like she knew he would. The paragon of chivalry.

Regrettably she'd gone a little too far with the nips, her drunkenness moving from performance into reality.

Now she leaned toward him, bending her mouth into a smile

she hoped was coquettish.

"Your trinkets are pretty. Where did you get so many?"

"I collect them." He patted his belt. "The witch mothers hand them out to their daughters like taffy. Supposed to bring them home safely, protect them from us big scary men. Maybe it's we men who need protection! Ever think of that?"

Mia's fingers twitched on the table—and not just because her companion was asinine. *Bring them home safely.* This one nugget of information was more than she'd acquired in weeks of searching.

Everywhere she went in White Lagoon, she asked innkeepers, barmaids, blacksmiths, ship captains, madams, street urchins—anyone she met—the same question. *Have you seen a big woman with hazel eyes and wavy red hair?*

No one had.

The first few weeks, Mia was relentless. Bit by bit, her hope dwindled. She still asked the question, but she'd learned to bolster it with a nip of spirits to stave off the inevitable sting.

With each new disappointment, she cursed herself for her wishful thinking. Spoiled little Mia Rose, a girl who had never lacked for money. Had she really thought she'd arrive penniless in the snow kingdom and "magic" her way into finding her mother? Information cost money. Most things did. If not money, they cost something else.

"But where did *you* get the frostflowers?" Mia pressed. The question came out sounding more desperate than she'd intended, so she poured on the sweet cream. "You certainly don't need some good luck talisman, strapping man like you."

"True. But it makes me look trustworthy, don't you think? Girls love a sensitive man, wearing their pretty baubles. I'm quite the catch."

Mia's stomach soured. Or it would have, if she could still feel it. This boy was another dead end.

She sank an inch into the booth, defeated. Every day she failed to find Wynna meant one more day Quin remained captive in Kaer Killian, enthralled by Angelyne. Mia had promised to come back for him. If she didn't save him, who would? Quin was alone in the world, his whole family murdered, their blood on Mia's hands.

But she would make things right. Find her mother, return to Glas Ddir, destroy the moonstone—and set Quin free.

"My baubles certainly worked on you, didn't they?" Her preening companion slid closer until they were hip to hip.

"Mmm." Mia took a breath. "Have you seen a woman with wavy red hair and hazel eyes?"

Over the last few months she'd asked this question so many times, to so many people, in so many ways. Mia had heard all sorts of answers, but they were never the one she wanted.

"Not many redheads around these parts," said the boy. "Why? Do you miss your mummy?"

He trailed a finger over her clavicle and down her arm, stopping at her wrist.

"Your skin is so soft," he murmured. He pressed his nail into her flesh, so hard it gouged a white crescent moon. Though she felt only light pressure, she could imagine the pain spiking up her arm. She saw the way the boy's face lit up because of it.

A line from her mother's journal came back to her. *Bring your rage into the light and love will heal it.*

Mia didn't want light. She sure as hells didn't want love.

She stared at the boy's hand around her wrist, then into his watery, hungry eyes.

"You're wrong," she said. "It isn't soft at all."

The boy howled in pain. He leapt off the bench and staggered back, his face twisting in shock.

"Witch!" he shouted. "River witch!"

Mia didn't need her sense of smell to know his skin was boiling. The flames hissed and curdled flesh, blackening his shirt-sleeve into shreds. His whole arm was on fire.

Unfortunately, so was hers.

Chapter 9

THE DARKEST NIGHT

Mia stared at the flames licking her arm, spellbound. Her skin puckered as it burned, the way a strip of fruit might dry in the sun. Fascinating.

"I'm on fire!" her companion yelled, knocking down chairs as he tore through the alehouse. "She lit me on fire!"

The other patrons seemed unperturbed. This clearly wasn't the first time a woman had used magic to rebuff a man in this fine establishment.

The proprietress, however, came barreling out from behind the bar.

"Out you go," she barked. "Before you set fire to all my spirits!"

Mia stumbled toward the door. Her legs were wobblier than she expected; she had the distinct impression she was balanced on two slabs of meat gelatin posing as feet. No matter. The gelatins carried her over the threshold just fine.

She teetered out into the night, hobbling across the street and down a narrow alley steeped in muck and garbage, then another, lest the boy feel inclined to come nipping at her heels. Once she was a safe distance away, she sidestepped a pile of what appeared to be human excrement and crouched on the cobblestones, burying her arm in a snowdrift.

A memory burbled to the surface: a virescent hot spring with steam wisping off the water. Piercing green eyes.

The colors melted as quickly as the snow against her skin.

Mia peeled off chunks of charred cloth and flesh, tossing them aside. Her tunic sleeve was ruined. For that matter, so was her arm. She ran her hand over the blistered skin.

Nothing happened.

Mia longed for the sudden shifts in temperature that had confounded her when she first bloomed. The sticky, roiling heat of desire; the bone-shivering ice of fear; the bitter scald of hatred. She even felt nostalgic for the headaches that had threatened to split her skull in two.

Funny how the things you'd hated were the things you missed the most.

Strictly speaking, she still had magic. But she could no longer control it.

Mia stared at her arm, forcing herself to focus. In spite of her faulty body, her brain still functioned passably well. This wasn't the first time she had inadvertently ignited.

She closed her eyes and focused on images of frost, icicles, snowflakes, snowdrifts slushing into rivers, sweet spring flowers blooming on the banks.

When she opened her eyes, her flesh was knitting itself back together around her radius and ulna, then phalanges. Her arm was whole again, freckles uncharred, skin unmarred.

Mia breathed a sigh of relief. She could no longer feel or smell or taste; she couldn't hear when someone was lying or sense their emotions. But at least she could still heal herself.

She wondered how long before she lost that, too.

Mia was exhausted. She supposed she should go home, "home" being the cramped sliver of a cot she'd been sleeping on, owned by a gray-haired innkeeper who sold magical salves. In exchange for a place to sleep and a few coins in her pocket, Mia hawked the woman's wares on the streets of White Lagoon: creams that dulled pain and numbed unpleasant sensations.

The irony was not lost on her.

To hells with going home. She was always tired, yet she hated sleeping—a persistent paradox. As a girl she'd loved the sensation of falling asleep, her feet toasty from the warmer her mother slipped beneath the blankets. But now, whenever she closed her eyes, all she saw was the wooden box.

Mia stood, then stumbled forward, stubbing her toe on a loose cobblestone. She longed for ferocious pain to shoot up her leg. She was broken. Damaged beyond repair. The girl who'd once had all the answers was now a combustible failure.

She would toast her failure with a drink.

As Mia snaked her way through White Lagoon, the streets teemed with both vagrants and landowners, emaciated beggars and glutted red-cheeked youths. The port town was perched precariously between destitution and prosperity. Mia was no historian, but she knew the last two decades had not been good ones in Luumia; a disastrous cocktail of trade embargoes and depleted fyre ice mines had swiftly brought the thriving realm to ruin.

But over the last year, the queen's Grand Fyremaster had discovered new fyre ice pits, and the snow kingdom had sprung back to life. For the first time in twenty years, trade was flourishing, and the eponymous lagoon of White Lagoon—a brief carriage ride from the town itself—had reopened its doors. Heated by the fresh crop of fyre ice, the mineral water was said to have curative properties. Dozens of visitors piled in from Fojo Karação, Pembuk, and other parts of Luumia, lured by the promise of a healing soak.

To Mia, the town of White Lagoon seemed like a street urchin who'd recently become queen. Giddy with unbridled energy and promise, but still dirty behind the ears.

Two women staggered past, laughing. For a moment Mia's heart stopped, the way it always did when a woman passed by. That fleeting clutch of hope she might have found her mother.

But it was only two drunk girls.

As usual, the disappointment smoldered down to anger, followed by an insatiable need to drink the anger down. Mia heard the Luumi word for "spirits," so she followed the girls. They ducked into a wide, low-roofed alehouse she'd never noticed.

Mia donned her best countenance of sobriety and stepped inside.

The alehouse was homey. Fat hickory beams, rosy orange torches, and an impressive collection of reinsdyr antlers on the walls. Not too many patrons—other than the two girls, there was a wiry older gentleman at the bar, and a few others playing a lazy game of kurkits, moving whittled bone pieces from one square to the next.

Beyond the kurkits table she saw the most important thing: casks, and plenty of them.

The barmaid approached with a skeptical expression, her thick white-blond braid swinging like a pendulum at her back. She was dressed in the traditional Luumi costume: bright red frieze, metal-embroidered collar with pewter charms, and a quilted white belt. Mia liked these costumes, though she hadn't seen many since arriving in White Lagoon.

"Good Jyöl," the barmaid said.

The whole town was abuzz over the solstice festival, especially now that so many foreign visitors were pouring in, eager to hear dark and twisty tales. During Jyöltide the Luumi paid homage to mythical Græÿa, the vengeful witch with a taste for human flesh.

"One nip of vaalkä." Mia slid onto a tall stool. "No, wait."

All the alehouses in Luumi offered special seasonal drinks for Jyöl. She would order the strongest spirits.

"A dram of silver death, please."

The barmaid cast her a disapproving look. "Don't you think you've had enough?"

Mia raised a hand in solemn oath. "I swear to you, I have had no silver death this evening."

Technically true.

The barmaid eyed Mia's burnt shirtsleeve hanging off her wrist in scorched tatters. She pursed her lips and did *not* reach for the cask. Mia's irritation flared. This girl was barely in the swell of womanhood—certainly not old enough to condescend.

"Pour her a dram, Sirpa! She looks like the kind of woman who can take care of herself."

Mia turned to see who was speaking. The elder white-haired patron at the end of the bar gave a little wave. His slender frame was bundled in several layers, his white beard full but neatly kept. Underneath his fur-fringed hood, his pale beige cheeks were rosy.

"Thank you," Mia said. "That is *exactly* the kind of woman I am."

Whoever this gentleman was—and he was most certainly a gentleman; his intonation revealed his noble birth—he appeared to have spoken the magic words. The ornery barmaid dipped her head, properly chastened.

"As you like, My Lord."

The barmaid reached for the cask and tossed it smoothly from one hand to the other. She picked up an empty glass.

"Hoarfrost?" she asked.

Mia shrugged. "Why not?"

The barmaid turned the glass upside down and dunked the rim in a bowl of water. When she dragged it through a plate of grayish-white crystals, the rim emerged crusted with rime.

The girl poured three thumbs of the silvery spirits as opposed to the usual two. Magnificent.

"On the house," she said, sliding the dram of silver death across the bar.

Mia lifted the glass and tilted it toward the gentleman.

"A toast to you, My Lord."

He waved her off. "Kristoffin. I insist! I'm far too old and senile to be anyone's lord, least of all yours." He hefted his dram in the air. "Welcome to the queendom of Luumia."

She liked the way he said queendom. Matter-of-factly, as if it had always been that way.

"To the queendom," she said.

Together they tipped back their silver death. Mia had heard a dram of death was both sweet and bitter, pungent with a hint of licorice on the swallow. For her it was tasteless, heatless, and hopefully effective.

"Good Græÿa." Kristoffin set down the empty glass and dabbed his mouth on his coat sleeve. "I'm also too old to be drinking death at this hour, I'm afraid. As the old proverb goes, *A boy drinks to remember. A man drinks to forget.*"

He winked. "To that I'll add: a very old man forgets to remember not to drink."

There was something bewitchingly impish about him. Mia had never met her parents' parents, but she imagined this was how a jolly grandsire would be.

Mia was starved for good cheer. She commandeered the stool beside him.

"Why is a *non* lord drinking at this hour, may I ask?"

She knew it was the right question from the way his blue eyes sparkled.

"Carting precious cargo to our lady queen."

"What kind of precious cargo?"

"I'm sworn to secrecy."

She took the bait. "Yes or no questions, then. Is it jewels?"

"Hardly! Or very dull ones, I suppose."

"Weapons?"

"Not very potent."

"Wild animals?"

"Ha!" Kristoffin chuckled. "Might as well be."

"I give up. You'll have to tell me."

He leaned in conspiratorially. "Foreign goods. Smuggled in from the river kingdom last night, only slightly worse for wear."

Mia fought to keep a smile on her face, even as the invisible cloak wrapped itself around her. She, too, was smuggled in from the river kingdom, and definitely worse for wear: insensate body, memories warped like ink on a wet piece of parchment. Angelyne betrayed her. Zaga betrayed her. Her mother betrayed her the moment she'd resurrected herself in the snow kingdom. For three years, Mia and Angelyne had been forced to relive her death over and over, until it broke them in different ways.

Mia would not—could not—forgive her mother. Still, she needed Wynna's help. There had to be a way to destroy the lloira, to sever the enthrallment and free Quin for good. Before her sister used the moonstone for evil, their mother had used it for good. If anyone knew how to quell the twisted magic inside the pearly orb, it was Wynna.

"Forgive me." Kristoffin slid his empty dram across the bar, dipping his head at Mia. "I can see you are deep in contemplation. I'll leave you to your thoughts."

Mia's attempts to be cheerful had once again failed.

"Wait," she said, as Kristoffin eased himself off the stool. "Have you . . ." She stopped short, loathing how pathetic she sounded, how small.

"Have I . . . ?" he prompted.

She hated having to ask the question. Hated her mother for leaving no clear path, for bequeathing a mysterious bone trinket only to abandon her daughter once again.

Mia lifted the dram of silver death and shook the dregs onto her tongue. She had to ask the question. This could be the one time it yielded the right answer.

"Have you happened to come across a red-haired woman? Big boned? Hazel eyes? You'd remember if you saw her. She's very striking."

Mia heard the wildness in her voice. The mounting desperation.

Kristoffin's blue eyes were kind, but with a glaze of pity.

"I'm sorry," he said. "I'm afraid I can't help. My niece might be able to, she knows everyone. But unfortunately she's in Valavïk."

He took a step toward her, as if he were about to put a

reassuring hand on her arm. At the last second he seemed to think better of it.

"I can't offer you anything concrete, I'm afraid. But I can share a piece of wisdom from an old Luumi poet, a line that has given me much hope over the years. *Sometimes the darkest night sparks the brightest dawn.*"

How Mia wished that were true.

She painted on her most convincing smile. "Thank you. And Good Jyöl."

"Good Jyöl to you, my young friend."

Kristoffin tipped his head in farewell. She watched as he slowly ascended the creaky alehouse stairs.

The barmaid swept both empty drams off the bar, the glasses clinking. "You know who that was, don't you?"

"A very self-effacing lord?"

The girl blinked at her in dismay. "You were talking to Lord Kristoffin Dove."

"Sorry to disappoint, but I don't know who that is."

"You haven't heard of the Grand Fyremaster? The Snow Queen's uncle? The most renowned of all her advisors?"

The barmaid grunted, back to her insolent self. "It was the Grand Fyremaster who discovered new pits in the heartlands. After years of death and darkness, Lord Dove has brought warmth and light back to Luumia."

Mia had heard nothing but *fyre ice this* and *fyre ice that* since arriving in White Lagoon. She tried to imagine doddering Kristoffin Dove as a renowned scientist and explorer who'd saved the whole queendom. It seemed unlikely.

Then again, Mia wasn't the best judge of character. Her sweet little sister had turned out to be homicidal.

From the swamp of spirits, Mia dredged up something Kristoffin had said. *My niece knows everyone.*

His niece the queen.

The barmaid flourished a hand toward the door. "Surely you've seen the frostflowers outside."

Mia's vision blurred until the girl had a double. Brilliant. *Two* obnoxious barmaids.

"How could I miss the floating flowers? They're every two feet."

In addition to all the pine trees dyed Jyöltide colors—pale silver and royal purple—the streets of White Lagoon were peppered with holiday decorations unlike any Mia had seen. The white blossoms hung suspended in the air, inner petals stained a deep violet, as if someone had spilled a thimbleful of purple dye. Most striking were the cold lavender flames flickering at their hearts.

Old Mia would have concocted theories, conducted experiments to test how the mysterious candle-blooms levitated with no ropes, how they burned with no fire.

New Mia was tired. She didn't have the energy to be a scientist. Most days she hardly had the energy to stay upright.

"The frostflowers are meant to light the days leading up to the Weeping Moon," the barmaid said proudly. "Lord Dove has given the Illuminations back to us. On the last night of Jyöl, the story of our people will be writ large across the sky. A testament to all we have survived—and all that lies before us."

Mia belched. The dram of silver death was coming back up her throat.

"If you'll excuse me," she said. "I'm going to spew bile."

Chapter 10

ANGEL OF ASHES

She made it outside, at least.

Mia knelt on all fours, vomiting into the snow. She wiped her sticky mouth on her unburnt sleeve and cursed her carelessness. Without the sensation of nausea, it was hard to keep track of how much she'd drunk.

What was she even doing there? What was she doing anywhere?

As she clutched the snow, retching, a memory rose to the surface—and not one she expected. She saw Pilar d'Aqila, Zaga's ornery daughter. Sharp eyes glassy as she sat enkindled in the Grand Gallery. The girl whose first misdirected arrow launched Quin and Mia on their flight . . . and whose second arrow landed deep in Princess Karri's stomach.

Who had truly killed Quin's sister? Pilar held the bow, but it was Mia who pressed her hands into the wound, snuffing out Karri's life when she'd meant to save it. They had both been lied to and manipulated by Zaga, two pawns nudged exactly where she wanted them.

And yet, when Mia thought of Pilar, she felt no kinship. Pilar had never apologized. Not for trying to kill Mia—and not for nearly killing Quin instead. On the contrary, she'd clearly relished every opportunity to put Mia in her place. During their brief stay in Refúj, Pilar had done nothing but shame and belittle her for being ignorant about magic. As if it were Mia's fault she'd had a heap of lies crammed down her throat for seventeen years.

Even if Mia *should* have questioned the narrative she'd been taught, Pilar was no better. She had grown up privy to her mother's dark magic and twisted ways. Why had she trusted Zaga so implicitly? Why hadn't she seen through the guise?

Mia knew exactly why. Pilar was selfish and stubborn, reckless and obstinate. The girl was too prideful to acknowledge her own mistakes. If she'd seen her mother for the traitor she was, Pilar might have saved them all.

"Are you thirsty?"

A boy stood framed in the alehouse's doorway, red clay tankard clasped in his broad hands. He looked to be nineteen or twenty, with wide-set, rounded eyes a dark shade of brown. His hair was bone straight and shoulder length, glossy blue-black in the moonlight, slicked back and tied neatly at the nape of his neck.

"Good Jyöl," he said. As he held out the red tankard, his biceps swelled beneath his shirt. His skin was the color of pale copper warmed by candlelight. Mia was drawn to the warmth.

"Zai," he said.

She hadn't heard this Luumi greeting. "Zai to you as well."

He gave her a curious look. "You misunderstand me. Zai is my name."

"Oh."

"You're the redhead who leaves a trail of charred flesh, aren't you? They call you the Angel of Ashes."

"My reputation precedes me!" Mia tried to stand but was too woozy. She sank back down. "I only char the flesh of boys who touch me when I don't want to be touched."

"Fair enough. Though I hear you've also charred your own flesh on more than one occasion."

"You hear an awful lot of things, don't you?"

"People like to talk at alehouses. As the spirits flow, so do the rumors."

He crouched and offered her the tankard.

"I think I've probably had enough," she said.

"It's water."

She took a cautious sip.

"Do you want to come home with me?" she blurted.

She'd brought home a handful of night companions over the last few weeks. They weren't hard to find: Luumi boys were infatuated with her auburn curls and freckles. Even after the innkeeper voiced her disapproval, Mia brought the boys back to her cot. As they lay entwined, she would tell them where to touch her, desperately hoping the feeling of their skin against hers would spark heat or sensation.

It did not.

Once she'd even brought home a raven-haired girl, thinking perhaps the soft hands of a girl would arouse her.

They did not.

Mia's desire to feel something was excruciating as every new companion would fumble about, trying to please her and failing miserably. To their credit, they all made a noble effort, with varying degrees of self-confidence. One boy had inched himself slowly down the cot to pleasure her, grinning widely as he crowed, "Prepare yourself!"

If he'd meant "Prepare yourself for nothing," he was correct.

Maybe Zai was different. Maybe, with those strong hands, he'd be able to achieve what others had not.

Maybe, if he came home with her, she wouldn't feel so alone.

"Thank you for the offer." Zai smiled. A genuine smile, albeit sad around the edges. "But I have to stay at the alehouse until we close."

"You work there?"

"I own it."

She blinked and his blurry face snapped back into focus. "Aren't you a little young to own an alehouse?"

"Is this yours?" He was holding her white flower, tracing the bird at its heart. It must have fallen out of her pocket while she retched onto the snow. "I've never seen one with a raven."

"Raven is my name."

The lie came instinctually. These days she trusted instinct more than reason.

"Good. I'd rather not call you Angel of Ashes." He was still studying the flower. "Where did you get this?"

"It was a gift."

"I see." Zai handed it back to her, then stood and brushed the snow off his trousers. "Come down to the dock tomorrow, Raven. There's someone I'd like you to meet."

She struggled to her feet. "Is it about the flower?"

"That's not a flower," he said. "It's a compass."

Chapter 11

DELICIOUS

As Mɪᴀ ᴡᴀʟᴋᴇᴅ ʙʀɪsᴋʟʏ down the cobblestones the next morning, the sun still hadn't risen, the moon staining the sky a cold, quiet blue. Three hours of daylight left Luumia cloaked in darkness well into the afternoon. The Luumi even had a word for how to survive the long winters: *hiio*. Sipping a toasty cup of Jyöltide cinnamon cocoa? *Hiio*. Cuddling up to a crackling fire in a seaside cabin? *Hiio*. Spending precious time with family? *Hiio*.

Wandering White Lagoon utterly alone, devoid of any sensation, and unable to find the one person she'd come to find?

Hiio could go fuck itself.

Mia worried the bone carving in her trouser pocket. She didn't want to get her hopes up—prophylactic pessimism, as she'd come to think of it—but a compass from her mother could change everything.

Of course, she had to learn to read it first.

The town bustled with activity, reinsdyr pulling carriages down the narrow streets. On the wharf, men and women carted barrels from a freshly docked ship. Mia recognized the vessel—she had bartered for passage on this very ship to cross Dead Man's Strait.

"Bartered" was perhaps not the right word. When Mia arrived penniless on Glas Ddir's forbidden southern shore, she had to work extra hard to convince the salty, hirsute captain to take her on board. This was when she'd first discovered her magic was an unruly mistress—she'd meant to set fire to a small Luumi flag on deck, not the mast itself.

At the end of the day, the flaming sail turned out to be more effective.

When the ship deposited her on the shore of Luumia, she had lingered to thank the captain. He'd spat on the ground at her feet.

"One thing you'd do well to remember, girl, is that in this kingdom, magic is a gift, not a blade."

Then why, she'd been tempted to ask, does it make such a handy blade?

Zai hadn't told her where to meet him. Or maybe he had and she'd forgotten.

"Raven?"

It took her a moment to recognize the name as her own. She turned.

"You came," Zai said.

He was more handsome than she remembered, not that she remembered much. Long black hair tied back at the neck; a wooden carton tucked under one muscled light-brown arm, and a cord of rope looped over the other. Mia's face flushed. She'd asked him to come home with her, hadn't she? Not the most tempting proposition from a girl vomiting into the snow.

"Listen, about last night . . ."

"You don't need to explain yourself. I own an alehouse, remember?" Zai adjusted the carton under his arm. "Follow me."

She trailed him down the quay. She couldn't help but admire the breadth of his shoulders, how deftly he shifted the carton from one arm to the other.

A memory of Quin appeared unbidden, so vivid she sucked in her breath. He stood in the river, moonlit gold curls and scintillating green eyes, a smear of freckles over fair, wet skin.

"Are you all right?" Zai asked. With his question, the memory disintegrated.

"I'm fine," she said.

Zai looked nothing like Quin. He didn't move like him, either; he was more surefooted, solid on the earth.

"Are you taking me to stow away aboard a ship?" she teased. "Shall we pretend to be pirates?"

"No."

Zai seemed immune to her sparkling wit. It was disconcerting.

To their right, the ship lowered its gangplank, expelling a host of excited passengers in festive Jyöltide hats and striped purple-and-silver scarves. Mia craned her neck, scanning the crowd for a head of red hair. At this point it was instinctual. Her first few weeks in White Lagoon she'd spent hours lingering at the docks, immune to the cold as she scrutinized every passenger embarking or debarking, absolutely certain she'd see her mother's face.

"Three times as many ships as usual," Zai called over his shoulder. "I've never seen this many visitors for Jyöl."

Mia liked the foreigners. She felt a kinship with people from other kingdoms. Even better: they loved buying magical salves. If she told them the creams were a Jyöltide novelty, her sales would double. "Græÿa's tears," she called them. Or, when she was feeling mischievous, "Witch milk."

"Have you been to the lagoon?" Zai asked, cutting across one wooden ramp and leading her down another.

"No." Admission cost fifty silver coins, and at best she earned five a day selling creams. She had her daily diet of spirits to consider.

"I grew up hearing my parents talk about it," he said. "I just never thought I'd see it myself. Now that the lagoon has reopened, it's changed everything. The crowds can be a bit much, but it's one of those rare attractions that deserves all the praise it gets."

"I'm sure it's lovely. There's nothing like it in the river kingdom."

"We don't see many of you Glasddirans. Not since your king closed the ports."

"I don't think many of us make it this far."

"How did you?"

"Luck, I guess." And magic. And mystery. Oh, and dying helped.

"They say your new queen has reopened the borders."

"There's no telling what the new queen will do," Mia said darkly, and meant it.

Zai's boat was broad and sturdy, much like Zai himself. It bobbed just off the pier, a cheerful yellow canvas stretched taut overhead. Between the boat and pier, a rudimentary rope bridge swayed above the water.

Zai held out a hand.

"I'll manage," Mia said, stepping onto the bridge—and nearly tipping over the side. There was more give to the ropes than she'd expected.

She recovered quickly and clambered onto the boat, Zai a step behind her.

"Welcome to my home," he said.

"You *live* here?"

He nodded. "I don't take her out much anymore. That's what running an alehouse will get you. But she's as good a place as any to bunk at night. I like the sounds of the port. Can't sleep when it's too quiet."

That surprised her. Zai didn't seem like the type to seek out noise.

"This is the galley," he said. "Doubling as my quarters."

The space was cozy, the furnishings simple: a low bench at

a small round table, big enough for a single diner or maybe two squeezed close. In the center of the room a stone slab boasted an assortment of jugs, bottles, bowls, and cutlery. She wondered briefly if Zai was as good a cook as Quin. She doubted it.

In the far corner an unadorned cot was tucked into a nook. An impressive set of reinsdyr antlers embellished one wall, much like the ones gracing the alehouse.

"You like reinsdyr."

"They're beautiful beasts. My family has herded them for centuries."

"The antlers are stunning."

He slipped the rope coil off his arm and hung it from one of the horns. "And functional. We use every part of the animal so nothing goes to waste. We eat and sell the meat, make the skins into mittens, cloaks, and shoes. We even pulverize the antlers into healing salves."

"Yes, I think I've sold some of those."

He set his cargo on a low stool. As he bent to unlatch the carton, his shirt stretched above his bicep. Pale, shimmering blue peeked out: an icy current of ink flowing over his mellow copper skin.

Mia was intrigued. She'd taken the moving ink herself when she first arrived in Luumia, but her mark was a deep purple indigo: a small six-petaled frostflower on the inside of her wrist. Fyre ink, the indigenous Luumi called it. Ink painters pulverized fyre ice into a pigment, which meant they were quite literally injecting magic beneath your skin. To Mia the ink resembled more river than flame; when she held her wrist up to the light, the flower pulsed and churned like water.

People said taking the ink was excruciating—which was exactly why she'd done it. Another desperate attempt to feel something. But the mark cost her nothing: no pain, and no coins, either. One of her night companions was an ink painter, and he'd marveled at her stoicism as the needle pricked her skin.

In her drunken haze, Mia had nursed a wild hope that wearing the six-petaled bloom would bring her closer to her mother.

Another ill-begotten night inked by ill-begotten dreams.

"Don't you get seasick?" she asked Zai. The boat was in the harbor, not the open sea, but still it dipped and listed.

"I have a strong stomach."

Her eyes trailed to see that, yes, it looked quite strong.

"And how are *you* feeling this morning?" Zai asked.

"I've always hated that question. It's judgment dressed up as sympathy. I don't feel sick, if that's what you're asking." Mia cleared her throat. "You said my carving was a compass?"

"Yes. Or part of one. I'll be honest with you: I can't answer all your questions about the frostflower. But my friend Ville is an ingineer. He's very good at explaining the mechanics of how things work. He'll be here soon. You can ask him anything you like."

Zai rubbed his hands together. "Would you like some tea while we wait? It's very rich, brewed with licorice milk. Delicious."

For a moment, Mia wished she could tell Zai the truth. What a relief it would be to confess all the things she'd lost: the sweet scent of blackthorn blossoms; the sharp bite of burnt sugar on lemon custard; the soft, buttery rush of a warm kiss that sent pleasant chills cascading down your spine. She'd only experienced one kiss like that: the night with Quin in the river.

But Mia couldn't tell Zai these things. He was a stranger. More than that, he so clearly lived in his body. How could she ever explain her brokenness to a boy like that?

"No thank you," she said. "I don't drink much tea."

Zai's gaze was steady. Almost as if he were staring *into* her, not at her. The words circled through her skull. *Wavy red hair. Hazel eyes.* Zai owned an alehouse; he knew his way around the town and harbor. He might have valuable information. Why couldn't she ask the question?

But she knew why. She felt small and pathetic, hopelessly vulnerable. For some reason, she cared what this stranger thought. She didn't want Zai to see her as a sniveling little girl looking for her mummy.

So for the first time since arriving in White Lagoon, she bit back the words.

"Can I show you something?" Zai said, his eyes shining.

"That all depends," she said.

But when he held out his hand, she took it.

Chapter 12

DEVIL

ZAI LED MIA ONTO the deck, running his broad hands over the railing. She could tell how much he loved this boat.

They descended three steps, where he stood proudly beside a metal hatch. He opened it to reveal a burnished silver box. Arranged in neat rows were a dozen shimmering stones cut like teardrops and glowing a stunning shade of mauve.

"Fyre ice," he explained, beaming. "A clean source of fuel, freshly installed last week. My boat is one of the first to have it."

"I see you're just as smitten with fyre ice as everyone else."

He was silent a moment, appraising her. "Do you know the history of the snow kingdom, Raven? The *true* history?"

"To be honest, history was never my best subject."

"We use fyre ice for everything. Ever since the first pits were discovered by the Addi, the stones have provided heat and light."

"The Addi?"

Zai frowned. "The Addi are indigenous to the snow kingdom. We've lived here for ten thousand years, before the ice bridges melted. Surely you know this much from your time in White Lagoon?"

She flushed. "Right, of course. I've seen the costumes." She shouldn't have said costumes, it sounded like she thought they were playacting. "The garments, I mean. The red ones with the high metal collars? They're beautiful. And the soft quilted belts! Not to mention the buttons . . ."

Mia was babbling. She took a breath.

"I'm sorry. I just . . . I didn't know they—*you*—had a different name."

"The Addi aren't one people. We don't all herd reinsdyr—there are ocean Addi, forest Addi, snow Addi. Today many of us come to towns and cities to find work, like me. But for the majority of the last ten thousand years, the Addi have lived off the land. That only changed when the Glasddirans came down from the river kingdom three hundred years ago."

"The early settlers!" Mia said. She remembered that much from her father's history lessons, the way he moved walnut shells south from Glas Ddir to represent the ships sailing across Dead Man's Strait into Luumia. "They brought food, livestock, and timber, right?"

"Yes." Zai studied her. "They also brought weapons and disease."

Mia didn't need to feel heat to know her cheeks were burning. Her father had taught her and Angelyne a different version of events. He'd told them how, three hundred years ago, the Glasddirans settled Luumia in peace, warmly welcomed by the indigenous peoples.

Which was absurd, now that she thought about it.

"There are ten different languages among the Addi," Zai said, "but three of them share a word for snow. *Luum*. The colonizers picked and chose what they liked from our culture. They stitched together pieces of our language and beliefs into a quilt that suited them—and discarded the rest. But they liked the word *luum*. So Luumia was born on all official maps."

"What do *you* call it?" Mia asked. "The true name, I mean."

Zai's distinctive smile crept back, sad around the edges. "Luum'Addi. *We are given snow.*"

Mia could still hear Pilar's voice in her head. *There's so much you don't know. And you're trying so hard to know everything.*

Zai turned toward the boat's nautical window, pointing to the vast expanse of snowy tundra to the southwest.

"My family lives in Kom'Addi, a reinsdyr herding community in the heartlands. It's three days' journey by boat, another three by foot. It's a self-sufficient community, but isolated. Fyre ice allowed my ancestors to cook and preserve food, to build kabmas and heal our sick. It was how we survived the long winters. But we were always careful not to use more than we needed."

Zai's eyes narrowed. "When the colonizers came, they wanted our land. Sometimes they traded for it. Sometimes they took it and gave nothing in return. They turned the pits into quarries so they could mine fyre ice in large quantities. They used it to build port towns and cities, to provide heat and light. The royal family in Valavïk demanded an infinite supply of fyre ice to fuel their excesses."

Zai shook his head.

"Fyre ice was not infinite. I was just a baby when the Luumi gutted the last of the mines. People suffered all over the snow kingdom—in the cities, towns, and villages. But people in places like Kom'Addi suffered most.

"By then the Addi were no longer self-sufficient. The Luumi had established trade routes where they exchanged many of our goods: pelts, reinsdyr skins, tools for building kabmas—and fyre ice, of course. We relied on the traders. Our debts ran deep. We had become dependent on other kingdoms to survive."

"Kingdoms like mine," Mia said.

"Exactly. Glas Ddir was our closest neighbor."

He locked eyes on her. "When King Ronan seized the throne and closed the borders of the river kingdom twenty years ago, he dealt the final blow."

"Don't worry," she muttered. "Ronan was no particular friend of mine."

"He caused the perfect storm. With the fyre ice pits newly emptied and trade routes destroyed, thousands of people died from cold, sickness, and starvation. Addi and Luumi alike. Some in my own family."

Something in his expression told Mia he didn't want or need her sympathy.

"Ronan caused so much pain," she said, her voice quiet.

Zai folded his arms over his chest. "You came to Luum'Addi at an interesting time, Raven. The queen's uncle has discovered a new variant of fyre ice, one with a thousand times more power. The new pits are close to where my family lives in Kom'Addi. The Grand Fyremaster has returned to us what was taken: a way to harness our natural source of power."

"I was taught that magic comes from an imbalance of power," she said. "Doesn't that mean something terrible had to happen for the gemstones to be imbued with magic?"

"There are different kinds of imbalances. Long before humans vied for power, the natural world did. Volqanoes spewed lava over the earth. The ocean smashed rocks into sand. Fire lay whole forests to waste, aided by the wind. And don't forget animals. Beasts have never shown mercy to other beasts, at least not when their survival is at stake."

Zai gestured toward the heartlands. "People often misunderstand our way of life. They assume that, since many of us herd reinsdyr and live off the land, we believe in the perfect peace and harmony of nature. But the physical world is violent. It always was and always will be."

Mia thought of the violence in her sister. Three years of turbulent waters brewing beneath a calm facade. Now poor Quin was drowning, helpless against the deluge.

"I suppose it's only natural that Dujia can be violent, too," she said.

"Dujia?" Zai's face was blank. "Is that a Glasddiran term?"

"Oh, of course—you call women with magic witches."

"No. Not witches. That's just how Græÿa has been recast." He let out his breath. "We call them women. It's not as if their magic makes them other than human."

Mia almost laughed. Not at him, but at how different life would be if everyone believed this. If King Ronan had shared this belief, thousands of innocent lives might have been spared. One side saw the Dujia as demons, the other as angels. Why couldn't they just be women?

"In Luum'Addi," Zai said, "having magic is like having a nice boat or a healthy herd of reinsdyr. Something to be admired."

He closed the hatch, sealing in the luminous violet stones. Absently Mia brushed her hands on her trousers—and hit the carved frostflower in her pocket. Zai's voice was so pleasant she'd almost forgotten why she came. How long had they been waiting for Zai's ingineer friend?

Her nerves jangled. The better question was: How long would she let Quin suffer at the hands of Angelyne? She'd sworn to save him, yet there she was, whiling away the morning on a strange boy's boat.

Zai seemed to sense her mind wandering.

"I didn't mean to bore you. I should note that things are better than they've been in years. Today many Addi and Luumi work together, marry, have children. The late Snow Queen was Luumi, but she fell in love with a boy from Kom'Addi, and the fact that they were able to marry and raise a daughter shows you how far we've come."

"Their daughter is the Snow Queen?"

He nodded. "For the first time in three hundred years, some-one like me sits on the snow throne."

Zai cracked his neck and a lock of black hair came loose from the leather band. It suited him.

"The Grand Fyremaster has gone to great lengths to make amends to the Addi. The queen's uncle has found ways to cure the very illnesses the Luumi once brought to our shores."

Mia heard a subtle shift in his tone, a tightening. There was more he wasn't saying.

"If Lord Dove is the late queen's brother," she said, "doesn't that mean he descended from the colonizers?"

Zai looked uncomfortable. "Dove works hard to rewrite his ancestors' legacy. Though you're right. Some things aren't so easily undone."

Before she could ask which things, he pressed on.

"Today many Addi call themselves Luumi. It's no surprise you haven't heard our true history. But some of us try to hold on to our culture, which can be hard to do."

"Like the barmaid at your alehouse," Mia said. "The one wear-ing the traditional dress."

He nodded. "It's called a gohki. And yes. I try to hire Addi where I can."

"This is probably an ignorant question"—Mia took a breath—"but isn't your barmaid blond?"

"Some of us are fair-skinned. Some of us aren't. My grandfather was full Addi with blond hair and green eyes, whereas I'm dark like my mother. It isn't about the way you look. When you're

Addi, there's a knowing in your bones." He tapped his chest. "In your heart."

"Zai!"

A girl's voice was calling from the dock. "You coming, or aren't you?"

"Don't keep our asses waiting on the ale!" came another, deeper voice.

Zai's smile bloomed. A full smile this time. "There they are, right on schedule. My merry friends."

Mia's pulse ratcheted up. "The ingineer?"

"That's Ville, yes. But I should tell you—today is Ville's one day off. He'll be far more talkative if you ply him with some ale first. Once he gets going? Believe me, you'll wish he would shut up."

"I'll buy him an ale," she said, fervently hoping her two silver coins would be enough. "Whatever he needs."

"You'll come with us, then?"

Mia blinked, confused. "Come with you . . ."

"To the lagoon."

Her heart sank. She hadn't understood that part of the arrangement. She had only two silver coins: forty-eight short of what she'd need to enter the White Lagoon.

"The owner is a family friend," Zai said, reading her hesitance correctly. "He lets us in for free."

"Zai, you scoundrel! Who's your lady?"

A boy about Mia's age with a round face and even rounder

belly stood on the pier, a striped purple-and-silver Jyöl scarf tied loosely around his neck. He had the lightest skin of any Luumi she had met. But despite his fair complexion and silvery-blond hair, his hooded eyes were a dark shade of brown—and utterly alive with merriment.

Mia caught herself staring at the exact moment he did. The boy grinned.

"I know, I know." He slicked back his spiky silver hair. "You're smitten by my good looks. I am the fine product of a love affair between two great tribes, both devastatingly attractive. Much like our lady queen." He winked. "No relation."

The tall, shapely girl at his side snorted. "As if there would be any relation between you and the queen, Ville!"

If Ville had the palest skin Mia had seen in White Lagoon, this girl had the darkest: a deep ebony brown with cool, sapphire undertones. She wore skin greases on her cheeks and eyes, dusky blues and plums glimmering like twilight. Her thin black braids were long enough to graze her curvy hips, and her lacy peach bodice hugged a figure so womanly Mia felt childish by comparison.

"Hello and welcome, greetings! Good Jyöl, Zai's new friend." The girl's voice was low and rich, but she spoke at a rapid clip, with just the slightest hint of a Pembuka accent. "I'm Nelladi-nellakin. That's an impossible name, believe me, I know. You can call me Nelladine, or just plain Nell."

Mia stepped onto the quay as Zai locked the door behind them.

"Raven, friends. Friends, Raven. She's coming with us to the lagoon."

"Pretty name!" Nell smiled warmly. "You're pretty, too, so it suits you."

"My name is really pretty too, you know," said Ville. "No one ever says it right, so let me give you a primer. Vee. Lay. *Vee* as in the letter. *Lay* as in . . ." He lobbed another wink at Mia. "You can figure out the rest."

Nell groaned. "Ville, you are atrocious. I refuse to acknowledge your existence. Consider this my official notice that I am no longer your friend."

Ville seemed unflustered by the pronouncement. He grinned at Mia, then at Zai.

"So, you devil. Where's the ale?"

Chapter 13

EXPOSED

THE ACTUAL LAGOON OF White Lagoon was an hour west of the port. A booming carriage business had sprung up, in which visitors doled out exorbitant sums to be ferried to and fro. Enterprising Luumi guides decorated their carriages to reflect popular Jyöltide themes: "Græÿa's Ghost" was a crowd favorite—a bony skeleton swung from the canopy—and "The Grand Fyremaster's Laboratory" boasted bubbling glass beakers tilting dangerously on the roof.

Mia caught Zai eyeing them with grim disdain. But he did stop to admire a plain, boxy carriage that seemed to run of its own accord, ejecting puffs of purple smoke from a pipe at the rear. A small crowd of onlookers had gathered to gape and murmur.

Something about the carriage unnerved Mia.

"What a beauty," Ville said, walking toward it in a kind of daze.

"Fyre ice strikes again," Nell muttered. "He's obsessed." She waved her hands overhead. "Hello! We're headed to the lagoon, remember?"

The boys shuffled back, properly chastised.

Mia was grateful. She realized why she didn't like the boxy carriage: it reminded her of the wooden box.

In the end, Zai procured a simple wagon with two white reinsdyr. When he took the reins, Nelladine swung herself up beside him, leaving Mia and Ville wedged together in the back.

As they jostled over the cobblestones, Mia tried her best not to bombard Ville with questions about the compass. Wait for the ale, she told herself. You've only just met.

After months of searching in vain for her mother, what difference did one hour make?

Meanwhile, Nell gushed excitedly to Zai about a new kind of clay. From what Mia could gather, Nelladine was a potter who sold bowls and tankards to the various alehouses in White Lagoon.

"They call it firesand; isn't that pretty? It's stoneware clay so the specks bleed through the glaze and leave a shiny black patina on the piece, just gorgeous! You'll love it, Zai."

"I run an alehouse, not an art gallery. Are the mugs sturdy?"

"What do you take me for? Of course they're sturdy. Firesand cracks and warps so much less, only one out of five pieces blows apart in the kiln!"

"Will you cut me a deal if I buy in bulk?"

"Zai K'aliloa!" Nell shoved him playfully. "You're a brazen thief. Always taking advantage of my generosity."

Nell was an artisan with her own thriving pottery trade; Zai owned a houseboat and an alehouse. What did Mia have to show for herself? Two coins, a compass, and a missing mother?

The easy intimacy between Zai and Nelladine planted a question in her mind. Surely these two shared more than just an interest in clay bowls.

And then there was Ville, who had zero interest in bowls, clay or otherwise.

"Is your hair naturally that color?" he said, leaning into Mia.

"I don't tint it."

"Good Græÿa." He whistled low. "In Luumia everyone's hair is either black or white. I feel like I've been colorblind my entire life . . . until you walked into it."

Mia had yet to meet a boy who laid it on quite so thick. If they'd been in an alehouse, she might have lit him on fire. But she needed his help.

"Ville's a bit of a rogue, in case you couldn't tell," Nell said over her shoulder. "You can probably tell! So, Raven. Where do you come from? I mean, Glas Ddir, obviously. I meant more specifically where do you come from in Glas Ddir?"

"Is everyone there as beautiful as you?" Ville chimed in. "If so, how do I get a one-way ticket?"

Nelladine rolled her eyes. "Will you at least *try* to be a decent human being?"

"I have an appreciation for beauty, Nelladinellakin. Is that indecent?"

"I hate when you call me that."

"You mean when I call you by your gods-given name? Since you are officially no longer my friend, your judgment simply doesn't affect me. Pity."

Nell let out an exasperated sigh.

"It never stops with these two," Zai said, but Mia caught him smiling.

For her part, she hoped they would keep ribbing one another the rest of the ride. Maybe their joy would be infectious. Maybe her darkness would begin to lift.

The sun still hadn't risen as they approached the White Lagoon, though the morning would soon tip into afternoon. Hordes of well-dressed visitors poured out of the carriages. Giant, speckled volqanic rocks framed a winding passageway that shunted guests to the lagoon's front gate.

And on the far side of the structure, where a cluster of reinsdyr ate and shat—in an area cleverly concealed by the gigantic rocks—Mia saw quite a different tableau.

A row of women hunched on the ground, dirt creased into their hands and faces. Many wore the traditional Addi dress. But whereas the wool of the barmaid's gohki was crisp and carmine, these women's gohki were faded, the red frieze pilled and threadbare.

Three tall men lingered nearby. Though they wore no uniform, their purpose was clear. Every time one of the women tried to wander toward the long queue of foreign guests, the men would guide her back to the others.

"You three go in," Zai said. "I'll tie the reinsdyr."

When he reached for his satchel, Mia saw a loaf of bread peeking out of the leather.

Their eyes met briefly. His face was inscrutable.

"Nell," he said. "Can you take Raven to the disrobing chamber?"

"*I* can!" Ville offered cheerfully.

"No, you absolutely cannot." Nell scoffed. "Men and women have separate chambers for disrobing, thank the moon above."

Nelladine took Mia by the hand, ushering her away before Ville could protest.

"I swear he isn't usually like this," said Nelladine. "I mean, don't get me wrong, he's always bad, just not *this* bad."

On one hand the attention was flattering. But there was something unnerving about it, too. Ville's words roiled in Mia's belly. Did this mean the numbness was fading? If she felt physical discomfort, perhaps other, better sensations would soon follow.

"How long have you three known each other?" she asked Nell.

"I've known Zai for years. As for Ville, only a few months . . . which honestly feels like a lifetime. Sometimes I think that boy would be better off gelded—it would keep him out of trouble, that's for sure. Not that I'd ever wish harm on his poor, godsforsaken balls."

Nell gave a quick wave, and a woman with yellow braids pinned in the Luumi style ushered them to the front of the line.

"It's lucky Zai is friends with the owner," Mia said, impressed.

"Zai is friends with everyone."

Inside, another blond woman handed them each a thick canvas

bathing cloth. Nelladine sauntered down the hallway, pushing open the doors to the disrobing chamber.

The women inside were, in a word, disrobed.

Mia froze. She had never seen a roomful of naked women.

Her eyes drank in all sorts of physiques: women with rolls of flesh on their thighs and bellies; tight, hard bodies with flat chests and narrow hips; dark-skinned women with large nipples like brown blooms, and fair-skinned girls with perky pink nipples no wider than a coin. Bodies shaped like pears, plums, and every fruit in between.

Some were beautiful; others weren't. She saw a thin girl with a baby in her belly and slashes of white marks on her thighs. She saw a big matronly woman with glorious curves and wavy black hair who reminded her so much of her mother. She saw tiny, wrinkled ladies with bowed backs and breasts sagging to their navels, froths of dark, untrimmed hair between their legs.

Mia felt a flash of repulsion. But the reaction was so sudden— and frankly so *mean*—she forced herself to examine it more closely.

The answer came quickly. Shame.

In Glas Ddir such a thing was blasphemous. So many unbridled bodies, so much potential for touching, all that filthy magic stewing skin to skin. Her whole life she had been taught that the female body was dirty, evil, *wrong*.

Mia hated that wherever she went, she took the river kingdom with her.

She wondered if she'd ever truly break free.

"I don't have any bathing clothes," Mia said.

"You don't need any! They provide everything for you, it's very luxurious. They even give you lotions for your skin and hair, see?"

Nelladine flourished a hand toward the candlelit marble slab, where a row of brown clay bowls were filled to the brim with creams and salves. A dozen frostflowers hovered in the air, their violet flames guttering as Nell sat on a wooden bench.

"Put your hands in the ice tub, Raven!" She beckoned toward a large black basin. "The cold closes your pores, makes your skin nice and tight. No more than half a minute or you'll freeze."

Tentatively, Mia sat on the bench, sliding her hands gingerly into the basin. Beside her, Nell dipped a swatch of linen into a bowl of water and swabbed her brow.

"I know what you're thinking. Why wear pigment the day you're going to the lagoon, Nell? Isn't that a lot of fuss if you just have to take it off again?"

She wiped the cloth over her eyelid and lashes. It came back inky blue.

"But I like feeling beautiful. Pretty and womanly, what's the harm in that?"

Nell flipped the blue-smudged cloth around and continued to rub in smooth, firm swipes. Mia felt a twinge of guilt. When Ange-lyne had prattled on about gowns and skin greases, she'd assumed her sister was vacuous. She would not make that mistake again.

"I'm hopeless about that sort of thing," she said. "Maybe some-time you could apply my pigment? Show me how it's done?"

Nell brightened. "I'd love to! Applying pigment always gives me the same feeling I get glazing my clay: you're turning something plain into something beautiful." Her large brown eyes widened. "I didn't mean you're plain! What a thing to say! You don't need a speck of pigment, Raven, truly, you're beautiful without it. I didn't mean to imply—"

"It's all right," Mia said. "I know what you meant."

"Sometimes I talk too much, it gets me into trouble. Don't argue! I know I do."

Nelladine dropped the linen square into the water bowl, pressing it down to soak. She sighed. "I wish the lagoon would buy my bowls, these brown ones are hideous."

She stood, then gasped. "Raven! Your hands!"

Mia had completely forgotten about the ice tub. She pulled her hands out abruptly. Her fingers were sickly white, frost crystals clinging to her skin.

"I said half a minute," Nell cried. "The ice is freezing! How could you not feel it?"

Mia couldn't think of a believable lie. She tried to wiggle her fingers, but they'd gone completely stiff.

"I'm sorry," she stammered. "I was lost in my own thoughts."

"You have been a bit distracted, haven't you?"

Nell cupped her hands around Mia's, rubbing vigorously.

"I guess it's easy for your mind to wander when I go on and on! Thinking about someone you loved, maybe? Someone you lost?"

Mia frowned, realizing Quin hadn't crossed her mind once since arriving at the lagoon.

"It's all right," Nell reassured her. "You don't have to talk about it. We all have our secrets." She gave Mia's hands a gentle squeeze.

"Secrets are what make us real."

A shadow passed over her face, vanishing so quickly Mia didn't trust her eyes.

When Nell removed her hands, the frost had melted. Mia bent and straightened her fingers. They were rosy again.

"Thank you," she said quietly. Had Nelladine healed her with magic, or just good old-fashioned heat? Despite the general Luumi openness on the subject, Mia still felt nervous asking. Another legacy King Ronan had so generously bestowed.

"Now that you're not at risk of frostbite," Nell said, "we can get dressed." She stood and stepped out of her peach bodice, which dropped softly around her ankles.

Nell strolled nude to the hamper, hips in gentle sway, and began to sort leisurely through the bathing clothes.

Mia blushed. She was hopelessly shy about this sort of thing.

And yet. Even if Mia was shy—Raven didn't have to be.

She wriggled out of her shirt and jacket, slid off her trousers, and let the whole twisted clump drop to the floor. Then she unclasped her undergarments and discarded them. It felt simultaneously liberating and terrifying.

"Here, these should be about your size." Nell handed her bathing clothes in festive Jyöltide colors. "Waifish sprite that you are."

Mia had never thought of herself as waifish. In fact she'd always taken pride in her womanly hips, which she'd inherited from her mother. But her hips were no longer as fleshy as they once were. Another side effect of dying.

She slipped on the purple bathing clothes, mortified by how

much more comfortable she felt with garments on.

Nelladine gave a nod of approval. "Gorgeous. Ready? I'm sure Zai and Ville are already in the steam room, waiting for us to grace them with our presence."

Mia swallowed. "You and Zai . . ."

"You want to know if we've ever been together? We kissed once when we'd both had a few too many. It was a mistake."

Jealousy stirred in Mia's chest, followed sharply by self-reproach. Why did she care if they had kissed? This was all a distraction, anyway: she hadn't come to White Lagoon to pine after a beautiful boy. She had a job to do.

But she couldn't help herself.

"A mistake because you didn't like him?"

"Let's just say, if there was a moment that confirmed my lifelong lack of interest in boys, that was the moment." Nell laughed her warm, husky laugh. "But *you're* interested in boys, aren't you? Or at the very least you're interested in him."

"I hardly know him."

"I hardly know a slab of clay when I put it on the wheel, but I still want to touch it." She nudged Mia playfully. "Maybe you should touch yours, too."

The long corridor from the disrobing chamber emptied into the steam room, where people reclined on long pinewood benches. Mia could barely see anything through the white fog.

"Zai?" Nell called. "Where are you? Are you here?"

"What about me?" came Ville's jolly voice. "Don't you want to find me?"

Nell snorted. "I'm sure you'll make yourself apparent soon enough."

The boys materialized. They were sitting cross-legged on the farthest bench, Zai in a white linen tunic, Ville with his pale belly hanging proudly over his canvas trouser tops.

"The lagoon is that way, under the arch." Zai nodded to a speckled stone ramp descending into cloudy water. "You should swim out alone first, Raven. It's really something."

Mia glanced at Ville. She'd been forced to leave the frostflower in the disrobing chamber; there was no space for it amidst all her exposed flesh.

"If you brave the waters of the White Lagoon," Ville said, "I'll reward you with an ale on the other side."

Hope flickered in her chest. "Challenge accepted."

"Don't let Græÿa eat you!" he said with a wink.

Mia edged down the ramp as it sloped into the lagoon. When the water reached her midriff, she took a deep breath and dunked her head under.

She emerged into another world.

Chapter 14

A BLAZE OF SCARLET

THE LAGOON WAS A dreamscape drenched in grays and blues. Steam curled off the water, clouds of fog hovering just above the surface. The hazy dawn light transmuted the visitors into beasts and elves and gargoyles, shadowy black shapes against a pink-limned sky. A land of witches and sorcerers, Mia thought, and the people haunted by them.

The water itself was perfectly white, like bathing in milk. She scooped up a cupful and let it stream through her fingers. Overhead, the moon was plump and shiny as a hardboiled egg.

Mia inhaled. Despite the sulfyr in the water, the lagoon had no sour tang.

Of course it didn't. Nothing had a smell anymore.

She had a sudden flash of sense memory, the echo of a scent inside her nostrils: the sulfyric pinch of the hot spring she and Quin had stumbled across in the Twisted Forest. Suddenly Mia could see his green eyes reflecting the iridescent water, the image so vivid she almost gasped. She'd had more memories resurface in the last day than in the whole last month.

I said I'd come back for him.

Did she, though? She'd never actually said the words. She had simply stared into Quin's eyes in the castle crypt, making a silent promise without a shred of common sense to support it. Considering she'd stopped her own heart seconds later, she wasn't the most reliable purveyor of promises.

Still, Mia was determined. She would find her mother and destroy the moonstone. She would save Quin.

But as she waded into the White Lagoon, Mia found she didn't want to think about the boy she'd left behind. Every memory of Quin only made her feel more broken, more empty.

She swam out farther. The visitors thinned out as the lagoon flowed into rills and runnels. Though she could have easily stood in the shallow water, she kept herself covered up to her chin, mesmerized by the way her whole body vanished into the soft milky white. There were lakes in Ilwysion, of course, the alpine forest she'd grown up in, where her mother taught Mia and Angelyne to swim. But the mountain lakes were crystal clear, nothing like this.

She scooped white water into her hand, letting it sieve through her fingers. What would she say if she found her mother? No matter how many times Mia envisioned their reunion, she'd never been able to script the conversation. When she imagined seeing her mother's face, a swell of feelings took over, joy and love bound up in hurt and blame. She wanted to thank Wynna for everything she'd done—and punish her for everything she hadn't.

Overhead, the dark sky faded into pale blue, a salmon-pink strip smudging the horizon. Soon the sun would rise.

"Remarkable, isn't it?" Nelladine swam up behind her, long black braids twirled atop her head to keep them dry. "Such a strange combination, your bottom half piping hot while the top of you is freezing. Gives me the shivers, in the best of ways."

Mia wished more than anything to feel the shivers. Absently she traced the indigo frostflower on her wrist.

Nell gasped. "I love your ink, Raven! How gorgeous! When did you get it? Your mark reminds me of Zai's."

"Zai's what?" he called out, rapidly closing the gap between them. He swam with strong, powerful strokes, his black hair slicked back and tapered at the neck, his linen tunic clinging to his chest like sealskin.

Ville paddled along beside him, reminding Mia of an actual seal.

"What are you ladies talking about?"

Nell held up Mia's wrist. "Look, isn't that pretty?"

Zai's expression changed. He stood, shaking the lagoon water out of his hair, and examined the indigo mark on her skin.

"This is fyre ink."

She nodded. "The ink painter said now that they've dug new

mines, he's had a surge in business. So many foreign visitors come in asking for—"

"Were you honoring our culture?" Zai said gruffly. "Or mocking it?"

Something had shifted. "I—I'm not sure what you mean."

"He means," Ville said, "that the Addi marks have deep meaning. Just not to you."

Mia blanched. She knew fyre ink was indigenous, but she hadn't put two and two together. Her conversation with Zai about the Addi came rushing back.

"I'm sorry," she said. "I really didn't mean any offense."

Ville's face cracked into a smile. "I'm only joking! It's your skin. Do whatever you like with it. Though, if you write messages on your body"—he raised an eyebrow—"you should know boys are going to read them."

Mia frowned. She turned to Zai to see if he'd been joking, too. But his face was a closed door.

"Show her your ink, Zai," said Nelladine.

The linen was coarse yet supple beneath his broad fingers as he uncapped the button of one sleeve, rolling the fabric into a taut cuff over his bicep's swell.

"Come on, Zai, don't be modest. Show her the whole thing!"

He stared at Nell a moment, then peeled the tunic over his head in one swift stroke.

What Mia noticed first was not the ink at all, but his torso carved into eight neat rectangles. She swallowed. He must have lifted quite a few ale casks to achieve that physique.

Reaching across his collarbone—and over his back and arms—was the ice-blue ink.

Frostflowers unfurled across his shoulders, long tangled roots spilling down the muscles of his back, snaking into dozens of symbols she didn't recognize. On the front of his chest, the ink coiled into a giant six-petaled blossom over his heart.

Mia liked how her own indigo mark looked against her ivory skin and freckles, but she found Zai's icy blue ink even more striking. It transformed his chest into a landscape, glimmering and alive, the gently moving ink like a stream burbling after the first thaw. She had a fierce urge to run her fingertips over the current.

While Mia's mark was still fresh, his were so pale they looked almost like scars.

"My ink is very old," he said, answering her unasked question. "From the last reserves before the pits were emptied. Yours is the new kind." He pointed at the purple mark on her skin. "They say the wrist is the most painful place to take the ink."

"I didn't feel it."

Zai met her eyes. "That, Raven, is the first thing you've said that has truly impressed me."

She was flattered, before realizing there was an insult wrapped in the compliment.

"This conversation is fascinating." Ville yawned. "Fyre ink and frostflowers and aren't we all lovely, impressive people. Now can we please get back to more serious topics? Like what we're going to eat for lunch."

At the lagoon pub, Ville and Nelladine ordered plates piled high with lobster and grilled fish. They ate with their fingers, the tender white meat flaking easily from the bone. Zai's meal was simple: smoked lamb shaved thin and laid atop crusty bread smeared with lemon-sage butter. "A local delicacy," he explained.

At Nell's suggestion, Mia ordered the lamb chops with sticky rhubarb jam.

"It's from a sheep farm down the way," Nelladine said. "Very fresh. I know the farmer's daughter."

"*Also* very fresh," Ville quipped.

Nell grinned. "For once you happen to be right, Ville."

The cuts of lamb were so tender Mia's knife slid through them like soft butter.

She missed the taste of butter. She missed the taste of everything.

They ate on a low balcony overlooking the White Lagoon. Back in her normal clothes, Mia felt more herself. The carved frostflower sat quietly in her lap. She would ease the conversation casually into the terrain of science, like easing a boat into the sea.

"What makes the lagoon so white?" Mia gestured toward the visitors below, who were laughing and splashing each other with chalky water. "I bet *you* can explain it to me, Ville."

"Right you are!" He puffed out his chest. "Back in the old days, freshwater and saltwater mingled together in fyre ice caves deep underground. The fyre ice sparked a paroxysm that made the water very, very hot, releasing minerals that gave it an otherworldly sheen. By the time the water bubbled all the way to the surface, it was the perfect temperature for bathing. Of course, once the fyre ice ran out, the lagoon lost its appeal. What good is a hot soak that isn't hot?"

Ville rapped his knuckles on the table. "But here we are! Fyre ice fully restocked beneath us, so we can indulge in our excesses once again. Even the floors are warm."

He toed the hard marble, then flashed Mia a grin. "Nice and toasty, isn't it? Which reminds me." Ville turned to Zai. "Did you get the shipment?"

"I meant to show you down at the dock." Zai grinned. "Everything you said is true. I took her out for a spin this morning, and she purrs."

Ville whooped. "What did I tell you? Burns clean as a whistle. And so much power!"

"I've never seen anything like it."

Nell let out an exaggerated sigh. "Boys and boats, an ongoing love affair. Even if they have a fundamental misunderstanding of what a boat truly is, what it *means*." She poked playfully at Zai. "I'd still like to know how you managed to buy yourself a heap of fyre ice. Must've cost a pretty penny."

"He owns an alehouse," Ville boomed. "He's a man of profits. Leave him in peace!"

"I'm only saying—"

"Good Græÿa, Nell. Don't you know that's exactly why the Grand Fyremaster's discoveries are so revolutionary? Clean fuel at an impossibly low cost! Thousands of new pits in the heartlands.

A natural resource that never depletes."

"But doesn't every resource deplete?" Mia asked. "If it's natural, it's finite. You said yourself Luumia has run out of fyre ice before."

She realized the table had gone quiet. Both Zai and Nell looked expectantly at Ville, like they'd been wondering the same thing.

Ville's gaze cut into Mia.

"I don't expect you to understand, Raven. Luumia is the first kingdom to harvest a self-replenishing source of power, and the system is complex. As this is my field of expertise, I could explain *how* we reap that power—but I'd have to teach you a lesson in advanced mechanics, which frankly would ruin my mood."

He leaned back, cupping his hands behind his head.

"I may play the clown, but I'm the brightest one here."

Nell snorted. "Speak for yourself, Ville."

"I *am* speaking for myself."

Mia hadn't meant to insult his intelligence. Her pulse thrummed against the ink flower on her wrist. She couldn't risk upsetting Ville, not when she needed his help.

A new strategy crystallized. She would appeal to his vanity. Play the ignorant Glasddiran girl with adorable freckles and a compass she didn't know how to use.

As she leaned forward, a blaze of scarlet in the water caught her eye.

The fork fell from Mia's hand. Below them, a red-haired woman was standing in the White Lagoon.

Her mother.

125

Wynna stood tall and fearsome, her pearly skin nearly as pale as the water around it. Wavy red tresses pinned in the Luumi style, swept up in a clasp at her nape. Wide hazel eyes. She was looking straight at Mia.

She was not smiling.

Mia's memories flooded back in a torrent. Karri, blood soaked on the forest floor. Pilar, shrinking back into the forest, bow hot in her hand. Zaga, cold and furious in the castle crypt. The dullness in Quin's eyes as he raked his hands through Angelyne's tresses, kissing her with manufactured passion, helpless against the enthrall.

And in the midst of everything: her mother's final gift. A way to save her heart by stopping it. Wynna had used this gift herself—and fled to the snow kingdom, never to return.

Mia felt grief and joy and white-hot fury. She didn't know if she could ever forgive. Yet in that moment, all she wanted was to throw her arms around her mother and never let go.

Hatred will only lead you astray. Sometimes love is the stronger choice.

"Mother!"

Mia stood with such force it sent her chair flying. She sprinted down to the lagoon and leapt in fully clothed. When she tried to run, the water slowed her limbs, so she dove under the surface, streamlining her body as she kicked.

When she emerged, gasping for breath, her mother was gone.

No. *No.* She couldn't have vanished. She was *right there.*

Mia splashed through the lagoon, her heart pounding in her eardrums. "Mother!" she shouted. "*Mother!*"

The hair should have been a beacon, crimson against creamy white water. "Have you seen a woman with red hair?" she said, over and over. The same question she'd asked for months, only now it would finally yield the right answer.

None of the visitors had seen a red-haired woman.

"Except for you," one man murmured.

A hush fell over the lagoon as Mia grew increasingly frantic. "She was standing right beside you! Right here!" The visitors regarded her with curiosity, then discomfort, then fear.

"Raven?"

She whirled around to find Zai standing in the water, his brow creased with concern. "Who are you calling to?"

"She was here, I swear it. My mother was here."

Mia no longer cared if Zai knew she was looking for her mother. She should have told him from the beginning, pushed aside her foolish pride. She saw the others standing a ways back: Nell chewing her bottom lip, Ville uncharacteristically quiet.

"Maybe we should go back to the pub," Zai suggested. "For a calming drink."

She shook her head fiercely. She was done drinking. Done hiding. Done pissing her life away in White Lagoon. She had a mother to find, a moonstone to shatter—and a prince to save.

"I have to find her, Zai."

He pressed his hands together. "A red-haired woman came to my alehouse two nights past."

Mia forced herself to breathe. Two redheads in all of White Lagoon, and he hadn't thought to mention he'd seen the other?

"I don't know for sure it was her," Zai said slowly, "but if it *was* your mother, I can take you to her."

"What do you mean, take me to her?"

"In my boat. She's headed to Valavïk to request an audience with the Snow Queen."

Mia's heartbeat ricocheted through her rib cage. "How do you know this?"

"She told me."

19 DAYS TILL THE WEEPING MOON

Sister of mine,

Let me tell you a story.

Once upon a time, there was a little ogre. He lived with his family in a cozy ice kabma at the foot of a mountain. But "cozy" is just a nicer word for small. There was never enough food to eat, never enough space to think. The ogre's mother loved him very much, but he was the littlest, and by the time she had ladled out enough lamb and potato stew to feed her five elder children, there was hardly any left for him.

But the little ogre had a gift.

He could render.

He kept a row of sharp, brightly colored pencils underneath his straw pallet. Whenever he was lonely, when his sisters and brother played with one another and not with him, he would take out his pencils and draw the most beautiful things.

Orange marmalade kittens. Strawberry cake. An ice leopard about to pounce.

It did not take him long to discover his drawings were different. When he rendered a picture on the page, he rendered it on the landscape of the mind.

He could make his family see things. Images so real they would reach out to stroke the kittens or cut themselves a slice of cake. He made one of his sisters flee in terror from the ice leopard she swore had barreled down the mountain, baring its razored yellow fangs.

He even made his family see angry villagers encircling the kabma, fiery torches clenched in their pale fists. While the little ogre spooned more lamb stew into his bowl, his sisters charged outside, only to find no villagers at all.

Legend has it that when the villagers did come, surrounding the kabma with torches dipped in oil and fire, the little ogre frantically drew portrait after portrait, trying to paint a different picture of his family in the villagers' minds. But this was where his talents failed him.

Perhaps it is only legend. After all, we do not know how the witch's children died. Only that they died.

Today the little ogre goes by a different name. He is the Renderer. And though he is the smallest of Graÿa's children, he is known as the Second Soul of Jyöl. He is, the Luumi tell their children, one of the kinder Souls. But every night of Jyöltide, you must leave a blade on your front stoop so the Renderer may sharpen his pencils. If you do not, he will draw monsters that haunt your dreams, so full of terrors you can no longer tell when you are sleeping and when you are awake.

My men have found curious artifacts in the Twisted Forest. First: an empty box with claw marks made by human fingers. Second: two of my men. One with a severed windpipe, drowned in his own blood. The other skewered through the heart . . . and no knife.

It appears you, sweet sister, did not leave a blade behind.

My men have arrived in White Lagoon, along with my army of Dujia. A charming town, they tell me, candles strung up over the streets with no strings, bewitched by some strange spell. Are you close? Floating in the lagoon, perhaps?

Come home and I will not meet you with torches and knives. On the contrary: I have something to offer you. You are a victim of your own delusions. Though Zaga tells me you are lost, I have hope that I may yet be able to save you from yourself.

I will render you a better world in bright, vibrant colors.

I will skewer the old world through its dark, rotted heart.

Tenderly yours,
Angelyne

Chapter 15

HOME

"Take me to the queen."

Pilar stood on the steps of the Snow Queen's palace. Hands bound behind her back, elbows jutted out on either side.

They'd made it to Valavïk after a miserable three days. Bumpy roads, choppy seas, more bumpy roads. Reports of the snow kingdom being a "land of progress" were sorely overrated. Despite the strange nature of the carriage Pilar and Quin had been locked in—a box that bounced along with no horses to pull it—the roads had more ruts and ridges than a washboard. Not to mention they reeked of shit.

She stared hard at Freyja, leader of the guardswomen. Freyja with her sharp silver eyes and shaved head. After three days on the road, her scalp was beginning to show signs of black stubble.

Pilar lifted her chin. "Dove said the queen would want to see us."

"I heard him," said Freyja, leader of the guardswomen. "I was there."

"Get on with it, then."

The other two guardswomen watched, stoic. They talked about as much as two large rocks. Pink-cheeked Lord Dove had scuttled off as soon as they arrived at the palace. But Freyja remained. She always seemed vaguely amused.

Pilar wanted to punch the grin right off Freyja's face.

Or you could use magic.

She'd thought about it a hundred times along the journey. She'd even *dreamed* about it, when she wasn't dreaming of Princess Karri. Freyja and her two large-rock lackeys wore no protective stones. When the lumbering guards escorted them outside to piss, it would have been easy to unblood their hands and make a run for it.

But Pilar had sworn not to use magic, especially against other women. Besides. Despite her beef with Freyja, Pilar couldn't deny the guards had brought her exactly where she wanted to be. She didn't like the *way* they'd done it, or that it wasn't on her terms. But there she stood on the steps of the Snow Queen's palace. In nineteen days, her father would stand in this very spot.

Not to mention the guards had earned her grudging respect. After a wandering thief stole a carton of apples from the carriage, they'd caught up to him easily on horseback—all three women were excellent riders. One punch from Freyja laid the thief flat in the snow.

"As head of the queen's guard," said Freyja, extending her hand, "let me be the first to welcome you to the palace."

Quin reached out a hand, until Pilar looked daggers at him.

"We don't shake hands with our captors."

"For someone so intent on seeing the queen," Freyja said, "you haven't tried very hard to be cordial."

"I never pretend to be something I'm not."

"That I can respect." She pulled back her hand. "A round of introductions. That's Frigg"—she jerked a thumb toward the bigger guardswoman—"and that's Fulla." She pointed to the smaller blonde.

"You can't be serious." Pilar blinked. "Freyja, Frigg, and Fulla? Are you a nursery rhyme?"

The other two guards stared at her, unlaughing. There was no punch line.

"The queen is a busy woman," Freyja said. "She will see you when she sees you."

Pilar glared at Quin, waiting for him to say something. He'd come to Luumia to ask the Snow Queen for help. Why wasn't he demanding to see her?

But he kept his eyes fixed on the ground.

Pilar shook her head in disgust. Coward.

"What are we supposed to do while we wait? Sit on our asses?"

"Not at all." Freyja grinned. "We'll give you the tour."

Once again, Pilar found herself at the butt end of an ax.

The guardswomen prodded them through the snow palace. Pilar's broken toes throbbed, but she wouldn't give the three Fs the satisfaction of seeing her limp.

The palace was a world apart from the black shadows of Kaer Killian. The walls, floors, and ceilings were blazingly white, so bright they hurt her eyes.

They walked past a vast indoor garden with a scummy fish pond and a grove of snow plum trees. Then giant drawing rooms with paintings and marble busts—stern-looking noblemen and plenty of proud, curvy women. A refreshing change of pace from the Kaer, where King Ronan preferred to decorate the halls with the Dujias' dismembered hands.

Maybe Luumia really was a land of progress. Or at the very least a land of pendulous breasts.

They had stopped in the middle of a corridor.

"Here we are," said Freyja.

Pilar frowned. "Here we are where?"

No sooner had she said it than a curved line appeared in the white wall. Fulla heaved her shoulder against it once. Twice. Three times. The line deepened into an arch.

A doorway.

Freyja sliced through the ropes around Pilar and Quin's wrists. As the door scraped open, she pushed them into a small dim chamber.

"We're not sheep," Pilar snapped. "I can goad myself."

"Self-goading sheep! My favorite kind." Freyja nodded toward the room. "You may be here a while. Make yourselves at home."

Quin let out a muffled laugh. "*Home.*"

The door vanished into the wall, sealing them inside.

Chapter 16

BRAGGARTS AND THIEVES

PILAR AND QUIN WERE surrounded by beasts.

Seven beasts, to be exact. Three reinsdyr, two emerald eagles, one small red bird, and—most impressive—a gigantic silver ice leopard.

All silent. All stuffed.

They were fascinating . . . for about five minutes. The longer Pilar waited, the more the dead animals lost their shine.

The walls and floor of this chamber were different than the corridors outside. Here sprawling purple lines reached across the white marble. They looked like tree branches, or lightning bolts. Pilar thought of the elder Dujia on Refúj—their wrinkled, veiny hands. That was what the purple marks looked most like. Human veins.

Pilar paced the chamber, dragging her bare knuckles over the marble, hoping to find a crack. The only light came from the walls glowing pale purple.

"You're not going to find the door," Quin said. "It disappeared the minute they did."

He lay face-up on the floor, leather pouch resting comfortably on his stomach, his hands folded over it.

"How long have we been in here?" Pilar said.

"Somewhere between three hours and three hundred. We're like everything else in this room."

"Dead?"

"*Captured.*" From the floor Quin waved a hand. "The Doomed Duet of Pil and Kill! Playing in a dungeon near you."

"This is some kind of test. Freyja's been toying with us from the start." She nodded toward his pouch. "We could try and use your dead men's stones. Make the door reappear."

His hands tightened around the pouch. "Stones won't do us any good. This room isn't magic."

"Then why do the walls have veins?"

"I don't know. Science?"

"They're warm, too." She pressed her fist against the marble. "Feel it."

"Why do you think I'm down here? The floor is nice and toasty."

"Nice to see you put up a fight."

"And you pacing in circles has been so incredibly effective." He sighed. "This is precisely where you wanted to go, remember? You made it to the palace, and—wonder of wonders—you didn't even have to arrange transportation! Relax. Unload. Take some nice, deep breaths."

Pilar hated being told to breathe. She turned away before she said something she regretted.

Quin wasn't wrong. She knew full well she'd hitched a free ride to the Snow Queen's palace. But she couldn't stand being confined against her will. It reminded her of the long months she'd spent trapped in the Kaer, enkindled by her mother or Angelyne, the nasty moonstone dangling from their hands. The desire to kill them flooded her mouth with the sweet taste of blood.

It took her a moment to realize she was biting the inside of her cheek.

Pilar paced more quickly. The minute she stopped moving, her breath would stick in her throat. The Kaer wasn't the only time she'd been a prisoner in her own body. She might see things from the cottage by the lake. Thick wooden beams. A broken bow.

"I think they want us to find our way out," she said.

"Good luck with that."

"Typical. The prince of the river kingdom sits on his ass."

Quin sat up. "Is there a bone you'd like to pick with me, Pilar? Because it certainly seems that way."

"Why didn't you pull some fancy royal card? Demand an audience with the queen?"

"I'm sure she'll see us eventually."

"For someone who's supposedly so determined to go back to Glas Ddir and save Dom, you sure aren't trying very hard. As far as I can tell, you haven't spent a single second thinking about the kingdom you left behind."

"You don't know what I spend my time thinking about," he snapped. "And why do you, of all people, want me to storm the castle and proclaim myself king? Descendant of the men who have been killing Dujia for generations, long before my father took the throne?"

Her mouth twisted. "You could choose *not* to kill Dujia, you know. It's not like that's part of the job description."

"A fair point." He shook out his curls. "I don't approach a challenge the way you do, is all. I prefer diplomacy to unfettered bouts of violence."

"Do you?" Pilar snorted. *"The Diplomacy of Lying Flat on Your Ass."*

"If you're so keen to get out of here, why didn't you use magic on the guards? At any point on this journey you could have easily escaped."

"I told you. I don't use magic anymore."

"Right. *The Obstinacy of Being Pilar."*

"You met my mother, right? Does she seem like a nice person to grow up with? All she cared about was magic."

She shook her head. "As a girl I believed everything she told me. She said magic was how we Dujia got our power back—how we made the world right again. But that was a lie. Magic is just another way to abuse power. My mother didn't care who she hurt."

Pilar bit down on her lip. Why was she telling Quin all this? She hated being vulnerable.

"I don't expect you to understand," she said.

"You're right. A parent who hated you, lied about magic, and killed innocent people?" He arched an eyebrow. "I obviously have *no* idea what that's like."

Some of the tension leaked out of Pilar's chest. Maybe he did understand.

"All I'm saying is, I don't ever want to be like my mother."

Quin cocked his head. "You could choose *not* to use magic to hurt other people, you know. It's not like that's part of the job description."

A smile tugged at the corners of her mouth.

"You do have a way of throwing my own words back at me, don't you?"

He shrugged. "They're good words."

She plopped down beside him on the warm floor.

"The thing is, I *did* escape. First from Refúj, then the Kaer. I don't have to be who I was on the island. That girl is gone."

Pilar stopped to consider what she'd just said. She had never put it into words before, but it was true. During her months as a scullery maid she'd dreamed of returning to Refúj and asking her Dujia sisters for forgiveness. But she didn't *have* to go back. After she killed her mother, what was keeping her from finding a better sisterhood somewhere else? Sisters who both listened and believed?

"For the first time in my life," she said slowly, "I get to see who I am without magic. Who I *really* am, not the person my mother wanted me to be."

Quin was quiet a moment. Then he said, "Maybe this is what it means to grow up. We see our parents for who they truly are, then get to choose whether or not to follow in their footsteps." He traced a purple vein in the marble floor. "Gods know I never want to be like my father."

Some of the tension crept back into her shoulders. She *was* trying to be like her father. A man who killed Dujia, no magic required.

She reached into her pocket and touched the silver coin, then the bone carving. Freyja and her guards had poached Pilar's dagger, but she'd managed to keep the coin and flower hidden. They gave her comfort.

Restless, she forced herself back onto her feet and stepped onto the raised platform where the beasts stood. If she were right about this being a test, maybe they held the clue.

Of the seven dead animals, the ice leopard was most striking. Curved yellow fangs. Cold blue eyes. Six silver blades on each paw, more like sickles than claws. Pilar had never seen a real leopard, only heard about them. Vicious, bloodthirsty carnivores with paws big enough to crush a child's skull—or hers, since she wasn't much bigger. True to their name, an ice leopard's pelt wasn't fur at all, but barbed silver ice.

She reached out a finger and poked the leopard in the eye.

"Why doesn't he melt?"

"I'm sure they replace the ice with glass," Quin answered.

"Is that how they keep the eyes from rotting?"

"Precisely. The flesh mounters scrape out all the blood and fat and tissue so they can stuff glass orbs into the eye sockets. It's quite mesmerizing. I used to watch the mounters work on my father's stags in the Kaer."

"Your father kept an army of flesh mounters in the castle?" She grimaced. "You royals are a strange breed. If you kill an animal, you should eat it, not parade its skin around. You're all braggarts and thieves."

"I won't argue with that."

They fell silent once again.

How long would the queen keep them imprisoned? Freyja had said "a while," which for all Pilar knew could mean forever. What if she were still a prisoner on the last night of Jyöl—a stone's throw from her father, yet unable to reach him? The thought made her throat burn.

To calm herself, Pilar drew the coin from her pocket. She dragged it over the ice leopard's pelt, silver clinking against the glass like the tines of a fork. She poked the reinsdyr with her finger. The emerald eagles were green. No surprise there. The small red bird had no feathers. Unlike the other animals, he was made of hard stone.

Pilar unclamped the bird from his marble platform. He was heavier than she expected. When she touched him, her pulse hummed, the way it always did when she sharpened her fojuen arrows on Refúj. The bird was made of fojuen, too.

"Maybe Freyja wants us to lose our minds," she said, more to herself than to Quin.

"Maybe it's working," said a voice that wasn't his.

Chapter 11

GUTTURAL

Freyja stood tall in the chamber, the door a shadowy outline behind her.

"How long have you been standing there?" Pilar said.

"Long enough."

Freyja cracked her neck, then her knuckles. Grinned.

Anger churned in Pilar's chest. She hated being trapped. Hated being under someone else's control, unable to get away.

"How long do you intend to keep us here with your dead beasts?"

Freyja nodded toward the red bird. "I see you've been making friends."

Pilar slammed the bird down on the marble platform, wishing

he would shatter. For Freyja this was all a game. A game Pilar had no interest in playing. She was done poking stuffed animals and waiting to be summoned by the Snow Queen.

New plan. Escape this chamber. Hide out in Valavïk and circle back the last night of Jyöl. Find Snow Wolf, kill mother, be free.

As for Quin? His fate was his own. She didn't owe him anything.

Pilar sized up the door, still visible in the wall. Freyja had come far enough into the room that there was space for a person to slip behind her and out into the corridor. Not *much* space, but Pilar was smaller, faster. Plus, she was coming at an angle. If she ran, she could make it.

She charged. Feet moving before her mind could say no.

Inches from the door, she made an instinctual decision. Why not punch Freyja? She'd been dreaming about it for days. One solid bone strike on her way out. A parting gift.

Pilar pivoted. Swung her arm back and aimed for the soft spot behind Freyja's ear.

But she miscalculated. The guardswoman stepped back, swatting Pilar's fist away like a moth—and shoving her off balance. Freyja crooked her elbow. In one swift move she'd snaked her arm around Pilar's neck.

"I admire your spirit," Freyja said, as Pilar's vision began to cloud. Orry, her fight teacher, would hold her in chokes just like this. She'd wake up dazed on the hard dirt floor, unsure how much time had passed.

Pilar dug her nails into the guardswoman's arm, but Freyja's grip was iron.

"Let her go!" Quin cried. "You're hurting her."

"You're making this harder than it has to be," Freyja said. Her words held no malice—they were almost kind, which was worse.

She let go. Pilar staggered forward, coughing.

Freyja cracked her knuckles. "Your instincts are good. But you trust them too much. You should have run while the door was clear."

Pilar hated how weak she looked. To the head of the queen's guard. To Quin.

"I don't—need fight—lessons from—you," she gasped.

"I think you might," said Freyja.

"I'm lighter—on my feet. I should be—quicker."

"You *are* quicker. But when you abandon your own strategy, the only opponent you're fighting is yourself."

Freyja brushed her hands on her trousers. "Save your strength. You'll need it."

In one move, Freyja swiped the red bird off the marble platform and hurled it against the far wall. The air glittered and hissed. Where the fojuen struck, the wall's purple veins ignited, spilling in every direction like rivers of indigo ink.

Quin glanced over his shoulder. Gave a start.

"Pilar. Look."

She wheeled around. Both Freyja and the door had vanished.

So had the wall.

Pilar and Quin stood at the threshold. Or what *had* been the threshold a few moments ago. Now there was nothing but pitch-black space.

Pilar stretched out her arm. Wiggled her fingers. Couldn't see them for shit. The shadows gobbled everything after the wrist.

"Where's the hallway we walked down?" Quin asked.

"Poof. Gone." She yanked back her arm, more disturbed than she wanted to admit. "I *told* you Freyja's been toying with us."

"I'm starting to come around to your point of view on that."

Pilar walked forward into the dark. Every step was a leap of faith—and one step farther from the room of dead beasts. The floor was slick, then coarse. Her boots bit into gravel.

Rough dirt.

"Pilar, wait. Could you slow down for one second?"

She quickened her pace. "I was right. This is some kind of test."

The air grew colder. Pilar could see her own breath in white puffs. She had a feeling they weren't inside anymore, but in a forest. The smell of pine needles confirmed it.

Something cold and wet plopped onto her cheek.

Quin let out a mangled laugh. "Is it actually . . .?"

"Snowing," she finished.

Pilar peered up. A fat white moon dripped over the tree branches like spilled milk.

It wasn't snowflakes on her cheek. It was melted moon bits.

"Maybe we shouldn't go any farther," Quin said, uneasy.

Pilar heard a sound like footsteps. Fast and light.

"What was that?"

He tensed. "What was what?"

She was sure they were being followed. But then she looked over her shoulder, she saw only the room of dead beasts. A glowing white box floating in the black. It seemed farther away than it should have, like she and Quin had been walking for hours.

"Nothing," she said, even as a chill knocked down her spine.

The ground shifted underfoot. She staggered forward, catching herself with her hands. The floor was no longer made of snow or dirt. Her fingers snagged on splinters.

Wood beams.

The room flipped upside down. Or at least *she* did. She was kneeling on the ceiling, the rafters casting shadows like a cell.

Quin stared up at her from below. "What in four hells is going on?"

The ground shifted again. Pilar clung to the beams as the room righted itself. She and Quin were back on equal footing. In the darkness she saw ribs. Bellies. A sea of corpses.

She was kneeling on a lake of broken violins.

"Quin," she said slowly. "I think we're inside our own heads."

"What in four hells?" He pointed at a cloud of black smoke in the distance. "Is that the ice kabma?"

She tried to stand, then stumbled. Her palms smacked against cold skin.

The dead Addi boy.

He started sinking into the violins. She tried to catch him. To hold onto his shoulders, his hands. But the icy water sucked him down.

Out of the corner of her eye, Pilar saw movement. She whipped around.

"Leopard," she said.

Quin spun. The white box was still suspended in the black, the stuffed ice leopard at the center.

But he was no longer stuffed.

The leopard sat on his haunches, licking one gigantic paw. Long yellow fangs. Eyes narrowed into cold blue slits. He watched them.

"You're seeing this, too?" Quin whispered.

"I saw it first."

The leopard dropped his paw to the ground. Pilar heard the click of his silver claws against the marble as he stepped over the threshold. His body one giant muscle. Coiled. Ready.

"Run," Pilar said.

They pitched themselves into the darkness. But it was too late. The leopard was faster. In seconds she heard him at their backs. He let out a guttural roar—and pounced.

Something warm and red spattered Pilar's face, but she felt no pain.

He hadn't attacked her.

He'd attacked Quin.

Chapter 18

TWISTED

QUIN LANDED WITH A thud on his back, pinned against the marble. Somehow they were back inside the room. His feet twitched and convulsed, the rest of him crushed beneath the ice leopard.

Pilar couldn't see Quin's face. But she saw the dark red stains on the beast's muzzle. Heard the wet sounds of teeth tearing flesh from bone. Smelled fresh blood.

The prince was being mauled. He screamed so loudly it echoed in Pilar's mouth.

No. He wasn't screaming. *She* was.

Pilar charged forward with a feral roar. She hurled herself onto the leopard's back. The barbed ice cut into her chest and belly, but she couldn't feel it. It was always like that when she fought.

She tried to hook her arm around the leopard's neck, throttle him in a blood choke. Freyja had given her the idea.

The beast reared and knocked her on her ass. She skidded across the marble.

If Quin was torn limb from limb, she would never forgive herself.

She got up and tried again.

This time the leopard swatted at her face, his claws slicing open the old scar on her cheek. She reeled back. Howled in pain.

She wouldn't give up. Pilar bent her knees, shifted her weight to her lower half. She would save Quin. She had to. The prince was spoiled, ornery, infuriating . . . and he was all she had.

"Pilar?"

She spun around.

Quin was standing behind her. Unbloody. Scared.

She blinked. She had smelled his blood, heard his skin rip.

"How did you . . .?"

She wheeled back around to where she'd seen him being shredded. In place of Quin, a reinsdyr lay on the marble. She was panting heavily, eyes two white orbs rolled back in their sockets as the leopard tore into her, jowls wet with blood.

"Look," Quin murmured.

Pilar turned to where the other animals had been. The remaining two reinsdyr chuffed and pawed at the wall, trying to escape.

"The birds, too," he whispered.

The emerald eagles were perched on the antlers of the reinsdyr, cawing.

Had every dead beast in this room come to life?

The room tipped like an hourglass. The leopard roared and split into a thousand shards of ice. The eagles screeched as they fractured into green teardrops and shattered on the floor.

"Quin?"

Pilar lurched forward, grabbing hold of him. Their eyes met. He was just as lost as she was.

They held onto each other as the walls fell away.

Pilar was standing barefoot in an icy stream. A dagger strapped to each thigh, bow slung over her shoulder. Red sand squelched beneath her toes.

Orry stood on the far bank.

You're not trying, he said. *Come at me again. Come at me like your life depended on it.*

Pilar crouched, wrapping her hands around her naked ankles. She was ashamed of her bare skin.

You're better than this.

Orry's voice was distant, but when she looked up, he was standing above her, his breath sticky warm.

The second he's on top of you, he's already won.

She reached for the third dagger—the one hidden in her boot. But when she pulled it out, she found herself clutching the horse-hair bow of her violin.

When she slashed at Orry's throat, the bow snapped in two. Like a twig. Like nothing at all.

The broken pieces sank into the stream.

She sank with them.

Pilar was falling. She pitched through space, icy air slicing open the cut on her cheek.

Her body struck hard ground. She rolled onto one side, eyes adjusting to the candlelight.

She was in the library on Refúj.

A pregnant girl walked between the shelves, trailing her hand along the books. Long black hair twisted up at the nape of her neck, olive skin, thin brown eyes.

Her mother.

Zaga stared straight at her, eyes piercing.

He did not want you. When I told him you were his, he left.

Her mother's hair fell out in chunks. Her skin shriveled and fell off the bone, stomach deflating. One by one, the fingers of her left hand curled into her palm. Pilar saw the moonstone pendant noosed around her throat, glowing more brightly as the rest of her grew dark. Mold spilled out of Zaga's mouth and down her neck.

Something soft spread across Pilar's collarbone.

She tried to speak, but her mouth was full of petals. She stumbled toward her mother, arms outstretched. Her fingers grazed shiny glass.

Pilar wasn't looking at her mother. She was looking into a mirror. The moonstone seared a circle in the space between her breasts.

She screamed, and black moths flew from her mouth.

Pilar peered into the mouth of a dark cave. She'd been here before.

But this time there was no Princess Karri bleeding out onto

the snow. Instead she saw six small figures in a perfect circle, each staring into a black sheet of ice.

Children.

When her eyes settled on the sixth child—a boy with amber skin and dark freckles—she felt a jolt of hope. The violinist was alive.

Or was he? The boy stood stock-still, eyes vacant as he watched dark images flicker over the shimmering ice.

Then Pilar saw a seventh girl.

She was older than the others. Short in stature. Sharp eyes, strong jaw, dark hair chopped at the chin. And on the ice in front of her: a series of images Pilar knew well.

Thick wood beams. Rough dirt floor. Broken horsehair bow.

The girl lifted her fist and drove it into the ice. Over and over. The scene fractured beneath her knuckles, splintered and broke. But instead of falling, the black shards floated. A hundred bladed icicles suspended in the air.

It's over, said a voice.

Pilar looked up.

Orry was crouched above her. Feet planted on the cave ceiling. Dark red cloak hanging down like a curtain, blocking his face.

She found a jagged blade of ice in each hand.

Pilar let out an inhuman howl. She ran up the wall effortlessly, her body lifting off the ground until she too was upside down. She plunged both blades into the back of Orry's neck. Skin tore. Tendons stuck. His neck a kind of instrument, her blades a kind of bow.

Her intonation was perfect. Not a single wrong note.

As he crashed to the ground, face slamming into the rough cave floor, his cloak crumpled and fell away. She saw the back of his head, gray hair thinning at the crown. He was too old to be Orry. Too frail.

Pilar, the stranger burbled, strangling on blood.

The daggers fell from her hands.

My little girl. My angry little girl.

Her father struggled to his knees, blood pouring from the wounds in his neck. He reached toward her, tilted his head back.

He had no face.

Pilar awoke facedown, her nose smashed against cold white marble. Breath jammed in her throat. Her head hurt worse than if she'd polished off a bottle of rai rouj. If only.

She felt something move in her mouth. *Black moths.*

It moved again.

Not moths. Just her tongue.

Pilar lifted herself onto her elbows, woozy. Had she been dreaming? She'd visited multiple places—multiple lives, it felt like. All the pieces jumbled together, some strange, some familiar.

"It's time," said a woman's gravelly voice. "The Snow Queen will see you now."

Pilar peered up, eyes blurry. One of the blond guardswomen was holding out her hand. Frigg, she thought. Or maybe Fulla. Did it matter? She settled on Frigg.

"Up you go."

She stared at Frigg's hand, unmoving.

"Quin," she said. The only four letters she could mash together.

"There." Frigg jerked her head across the room, where Fulla was pulling Quin to his feet.

Pilar felt a wallop of relief. He was in one piece. Unmauled. Alive.

She tried to speak, but the words got stuck somewhere between her head and her mouth.

"You'll talk soon enough," said Frigg, hoisting Pilar off the floor. "For now, you walk."

As the guards herded them out the door, Pilar snuck one final glance at the room. Her jaw dropped halfway to the floor. The beasts were back in place: three reinsdyr, two emerald eagles, one ice leopard. All silent. All stuffed.

All but one.

The red stone bird was gone.

The guardswomen prodded them through the corridors. More gently than before, Pilar thought, though she wasn't sure. It didn't matter—she was too dizzy to fight them off. She kept staring at her hands, expecting to find them sticky with blood. Hadn't she stabbed someone in the neck?

"Here," said Frigg.

She'd brought them to a wide wooden door, one that didn't appear magically out of the marble.

"Throne room?" Quin croaked. He was doing a better job speaking than Pilar was. She kept gluing letters together in her mind, only to have them fall apart before they landed on her tongue.

Fulla seized a metal loop in the wood and pushed the door open.

It *was* a throne room. Of sorts. High vaulted ceilings, and, at the far end of the hall, something vaguely thronelike. Dozens of flowers were—floating? The same purple color as the room where the dead animals weren't actually dead. The floor was a carpet with white and silver stars. It flattened under Pilar's feet.

"Go," Frigg said, nudging them forward.

As Pilar stumbled toward the throne, the Snow Queen came slowly into focus. She wore a snow-fox cloak that shone bright white against her tawny amber skin, a heavy strip of metal twisted around her neck with a purple stone at the center.

Broad shoulders. Silver eyes. Head freshly shaved.

Freyja sat tall on the throne.

Chapter 19

A VIOLATION

"*You're the Snow Queen?*" Quin said.

He looked about as shocked as Pilar felt. She could only spit out one word: "You?"

Freyja's silver eyes sparkled with amusement.

"Me."

Pilar thought of several choice words to shout at Freyja, but her mouth wasn't working right.

"Your Grace," Quin mumbled, attempting a half bow.

Freyja waved a hand. "Don't bother with all that. We're not so fond of the *Your Grace* business here in Luumia. We try to keep things simple. Take this hall, for instance."

The chamber looked nothing like the ridiculous throne room

Pilar had seen at Kaer Killian. There were no flags or drapes hanging from the ceiling, no gold. Other than the floating flowers, the room was simple. Same white walls with purple veins and a carved wooden chair for a throne. It sat on the floor so the queen's eyes were level with theirs.

"My ass," said Freyja, "needs no gilded chair."

No gilded crown, either. Other than the twisted-metal necklace with its glowing purple jewel, Queen Freyja looked no different from Head Guard Freyja. Confident, easygoing, maddeningly good-natured. She looked like she belonged.

"Another game you play." Pilar was crawling back into the land of complete sentences. "Costumed as a guard?"

"I prefer to get to know my guests *without* the throne obstructing my view."

"Trick. All a trick."

"More of a test." Freyja tilted her head, thoughtful. "What would you have me do? Two strangers arrive at my borders. Both children of powerful people, born in kingdoms that have not historically been our allies. You, Quin of Clan Killian, had a murderous father, and you are now bound to a murderous wife. You, Pilar Zorastín d'Aqila, have a murderous mother who sits at the new queen's side, moving people like chess pieces from one bloody square to the next."

Pilar's eyebrows shot up. "You knew who I was?"

"What kind of queen would I be if I didn't?"

Until Pilar's time as a spy in Kaer Killian, no one knew she existed, because no one knew *Refúj* existed. But somehow the

Snow Queen had known.

Pilar was pleased. Even if she'd never show it.

"Is that why we're your prisoners?" Quin said.

"You're not prisoners. You're just not quite guests." Freyja leaned back in the throne. "When I stumbled across you, you were concealing the corpse of a young boy."

"We weren't concealing him!" Pilar said. "We were trying to revive him."

The queen drummed her fingers on her thigh. "The snow kingdom is not always kind to the people in it. Over the last twenty years our long winters have claimed many lives. Yet we are a peaceful people. When Luumi die, it is usually the fault of the elements, not other Luumi. Foreigners from other kingdoms, however—they play by different rules."

She nodded toward the corridors. "I know the Watching Chamber can be brutal. You did very well. Now let's see what you brought me."

Freyja motioned to Fulla, who unballed her fist. At the center of her palm sat the red bird.

The fojuen stone cracked. The bird lifted one wing, then let out a sad warble as it stepped onto the queen's finger.

Dead, not dead. Dead, not dead. Pilar wished the animals in Luumia would make up their minds.

"You stole that." Quin's eyes bored into Freyja. His voice was hard. "The red wren belongs to Mia Rose."

"You're wrong," said the queen. "It belongs to her mother."

When she turned to Pilar, she was no longer smiling.

"Ready to see who you are?"

Before Pilar could respond, the Snow Queen pitched the wren violently against the wall. It sparked and crackled, erupting into flames. Purple fire shrieked through the wall's veins.

A gust of wind snuffed out all the floating candles.

The world went dark.

What happened next was hard to explain.

Gray and black shapes moved across the wall like torch shadows. But there was no torch.

As Pilar watched, the shadows stretched into scenes. Dread knotted in her stomach. These were *her* dreams. *Her* nightmares. She saw everything she'd seen in the Watching Chamber—and more. Only difference was, now she had an audience.

Just as the shadows began to shape themselves into the inside of the cottage by the lake, Freyja raised a hand.

"I've seen enough," she said.

Instantly the shadows evaporated. The candles sputtered back to life. The wall was white again, with quiet purple veins.

It didn't matter. Whether or not she saw it on the marble, Pilar saw it in her mind. The shame was so rich she could taste it.

"What you've just seen," said the queen, "is a peek into your truest mind. A blending of past and imagined future. Your darkest fears, darkest truths, and—perhaps most interesting—darkest desires. The Watching Chamber exhibits your Reflections. It holds up a mirror to who you truly are."

"We came here for your help," Quin said, his decorum cracking. "And you locked us up in that miserable room and marched us through a parody of our own memories. Now you mount a public show of Pilar's private thoughts for your own sordid amusement?"

Pilar's heart lifted. Quin had come to her aid. He was right: what the Snow Queen had done was unforgivable. Even if Freyja was merciful to not show the whole story, she had peeled back the skin of Pilar's most painful secrets.

How much had Quin seen? How much had he understood?

Maybe it was better if he saw. At least then he'd know what Pilar had done.

"No," Freyja said, answering Quin's question. "It doesn't amuse me."

"And the characters in these delusions?" he spat. "Are they real or imagined?"

"Nothing in the Reflections is pure invention. They are simply the mind bending its own truths, twisting them into something strange but familiar. Our brains have a way of stitching people together from composite parts."

"That doesn't explain how *you* were able to see into Pil's thoughts."

"That's where the bird comes into play," said Freyja. "Your mind holds the Reflections already. The Watching Chamber makes them visible. The ruby wren simply watches."

She gestured toward the red bird on the marble, which had hardened to stone once again.

"The wren bears witness, then shows me what she's seen. Her body is made of fojuen, but her eyes are made of fyre ice. Sometimes our objects know the truth, even when we don't."

"Was the leopard made of fyre ice, too?" Quin scoffed. "He

could have killed us!"

Freyja shook her head. "Nothing can harm you during the Reflections. Even *I* can't reach you. What happens there happens in a space between."

She walked to the wall and rapped it with her knuckles. "How much do you know about fyre ice?"

"I know you Luumi used it for heat and light before you mined it all."

"Fyre ice has long been one of our great natural wonders. It is an embodiment of the physical world, the purest form of elemental magic: a perfect balance of fire and water. A single sliver can create a miniature paroxysm powerful enough to light a whole room."

The queen stooped to pick up the fallen wren. "But fyre ice gives us far more than heat and light. My uncle has discovered new mines that yield a much more powerful fyre ice than Luumia has ever seen. He has cured sickness and invented new ways of growing and preserving food. In so doing he has saved thousands of lives, and will save thousands more."

Freyja rubbed the stone wren between her fingers. "The Grand Fyremaster has been able to harness this new power in ways our ancestors never could have imagined."

"Fojuen is inanimate." Quin jerked his head toward the bird. "So is fyre ice. Gemstones are just that: gemstones. They can store up a magician's magic, not create it. You expect me to believe you brought a stone bird to life?"

"Stones are rocks shaped by humans with an ax to grind.

Rocks were forged at the mouths of volqanoes, carved by oceans over thousands of years. To say the physical world is not alive is to impose a very narrow view of life on the world you inhabit. But then, I doubt they teach the Elemental Hex in your Glasddiran schools."

The prince jutted his jaw, defiant. "I wouldn't know. I had a tutor."

The queen tossed the bird from one hand to the other. "With a curriculum carefully selected by your father, I'm sure."

Quin was quiet.

"Magic has always been about an imbalance of power," Freyja said. "We humans are merely the newest landscape on which that imbalance is reflected. The six elements of the natural world—Fire, Water, Wind, Wood, Earth, and Stone—are reflected in the body: eyes, blood, breath, bone, flesh, and aether. Of course humans are also made of fear and pride, jealousy and hate. We have honed a new set of tools to oppress and subjugate the bodies of other people. Violence. Pain. A lust for power. And so, our magic has grown."

Quin frowned. "What is aether?"

"The most dangerous—and perhaps the hardest to describe. The place where mind meets spirit." Freyja kissed the red bird, then tucked it into her snow-fox cloak. "Aether is the part of us that can be most easily manipulated by what our hearts long for, and what our eyes see."

"Magic was a gift from the Duj." Pilar's voice came out steely. "But it's been twisted by people like my mother. People like *you*."

"Is this why you've chosen not to practice magic?"

Pilar opened her mouth, then clamped it shut. She didn't owe the queen an explanation.

"You could have easily beaten the ice leopard," Freyja said. "But you did not."

Guilt seeped through Pilar. The queen was right. When she'd attacked the leopard, why *hadn't* she used her magic? She could have unblooded him. Shattered his bones. Instead she'd come at him with her puny fists.

"Don't change the subject," she hissed at Freyja, shoving her guilt aside. "I didn't give you permission to gut my memories and play them for everyone to see. How is what you did any better than my mother and Angelyne enkindling us in the Kaer?"

The queen's expression was grave. "I won't argue. To use magic in such a way is a violation. I am never proud of using magic to subvert the power of another human being."

"And yet that's exactly what you did."

Freyja shifted her weight.

"As queen I am asked to make decisions every day. Some are difficult. Some cause pain. I try to choose the path that causes the least pain for the fewest of my people. I do not always succeed. But I always try."

Freyja straightened. "I have seen your Reflections, and I am satisfied. You came to Luumia of your own volition, not your mother's. You do not use magic to hurt innocent people—and you didn't kill the boy."

Pilar laughed, incredulous. "*That's* your most reliable means of interrogating your prisoners? I didn't kill the boy, and I'm here to find my father, the Snow Wolf. There! You could have just asked."

She pointed at Quin. "He didn't kill the boy, either. You've seen my memories. At least spare him the humiliation."

The queen fixed her attention on Quin. She started to say something, then stopped.

She heaved a deep, long sigh.

"I invite you both to join me in the Feasting Hall. We'll have something to eat. But first." Freyja took a step toward Pilar, her face softening. "Your feet."

"My feet?"

"Aren't you sporting a broken toe or two, on account of my guards? Fulla can be a bit overzealous."

With all the adrenaline pulsing through her, Pilar had forgotten all about her toes.

"And the scar on your cheek?" the queen pressed. "There's a story there, no doubt."

If Freyja thought the two of them were going to kick back with a bottle of vaalkä and compare battle scars, she was mistaken.

The queen reached out her hand. Pilar recoiled.

"I don't mean to hurt you. I mean to help."

"Doubtful. And I don't like being touched."

"Then I won't touch you."

The queen slipped the purple jewel out of her necklace and clenched it tightly in her fist. She closed her eyes. Exhaled.

Pilar felt a strange jarring in her bones. A vibration. It coated her in an easy, melted sort of bliss.

"There." Freyja opened her eyes. "Better?"

Pilar wiggled her toes in her boot. Unbroken. She opened and closed her mouth. She hadn't been able to move her jaw without pain in months. The fractured cheekbone and the scar that marked it were both gone.

The queen had healed her without touching her skin.

"Despite my Addi heritage," said Freyja, "I am the only one in my family who does not have magic. I must rely on my stones."

"Then I suppose I was wrong that stones can only store a Dujia's magic," Quin said darkly. "They appear to be able to yield power to people who do not have any power themselves."

Pilar was angry. She hadn't asked to be healed. But she was also struck by Freyja's expression. The queen was beaming. Healing those wounds had made her happy.

Pilar was reminded of something she'd nearly forgotten: magic wasn't always dark.

"Come," said the queen, cracking her neck. She slid the purple gemstone back into the twisted metal band around her neck. "Our supper awaits."

Chapter 20

ONLY ONE

THE FEASTING HALL WAS ugly. At least Pilar thought so. Long table. Low bench. Wooden rafters.

She didn't like rafters.

"We are a people of many stews," Freyja explained, nodding toward the steaming bowls being carried out from the kitchen. "Reinsdyr, lamb, fish—they say a hearty stew is the best way to stave off the cold winters. Sometimes we add lobsters for good measure."

Pilar glanced at Quin, who looked away. They were both starving.

"No poison." The Snow Queen picked up a lobster tail, drenched it in melted butter, and popped it in her mouth. "Just lobster."

Pilar took a sip of vaalkä. Her first ever.

It was even better than she'd imagined. Like drinking a spiced cinnamon apple. She took a bigger sip. More of a swig, really. The slab of butter at the bottom of the glass greased her lips.

If the queen were trying to kill them, she'd have done it already. Pilar stabbed a filet of arctic char and dunked it in sweet dill sauce. Her tongue exploded with flavor.

Quin was more cautious. She watched him spear a boiled egg on the tip of his fork.

"We have Addi mooncake for Jyöltide." Freyja motioned toward a tray of sweets. "Peanuts and taro—very rich. Be sure and try the snowdrops, too. Black licorice cake balls dipped in ivory chocolate. They're a Luumi delicacy."

She offered them the platter, then swiped one herself.

"If it makes you feel any better," she said between chews, "I walk the Watching Chamber myself on occasion. Afterward I invite my uncle to observe my Reflections."

"Why in four hells," Pilar said, "would you willingly subject yourself to that?"

"It keeps me honest. If I'm hiding from some unpleasant truth in my own life, the Reflections ensure that I don't hide from it for long. What right do I have to interrogate others if I don't first interrogate my own mind?"

Pilar considered it. Though the effects of the Watching Chamber had faded, she still felt exposed. How was what Freyja had done any different than Angelyne with her moonstone, that foul white orb always swinging from her neck?

Still, the Snow Queen seemed different than Angelyne. Her methods were unorthodox, blurring the line between right and wrong. Her chamber of nightmares was brutal. But when Freyja said she tried to cause the least pain for the fewest of her people, Pilar believed her.

She felt another lick of guilt. After watching her mother use magic to cause people pain, Pilar had sworn it off entirely. But what if *not* using magic caused a person pain? She'd watched Quin getting gored right in front of her, when she could have saved his life.

Pilar had a disturbing thought. Most of her life she'd practiced magic because it was what her mother wanted. Now she was *not* practicing magic, because it was the opposite of what her mother wanted. Didn't that mean, at the heart of it, her mother was still controlling what she did?

"I'd hoped to introduce you to my lady"—Freyja nodded to the empty place beside her—"but she isn't feeling well tonight. Lord Dove, however, should be along shortly. Of course you've met already."

"Do I hear you gossiping about me, Niece?"

A lean older man with a full white beard hurried into the Hall.

"Lord Kristoffin Dove," the queen announced, smiling. "My most trusted advisor. The Grand Fyremaster of Luumia. And perhaps most important: my jolly uncle."

Pilar recognized him immediately. During their journey from Glas Ddir he'd stayed on the outside of the carriage, bundled up in heavy cloaks and scarves with just his blue eyes peeking out. But she remembered the twinkle. He *looked* jolly. At the time she'd found it insulting.

"At last!" Dove cried. "Forgive me my tardiness. Now we can

meet on proper terms, without a carriage wall between us. My niece has some funny ideas about making new friends."

Pilar wholeheartedly agreed.

"Pilar d'Aqila!" Lord Dove pumped her hand with vigor. "Daughter of the fire kingdom, with a spirit to match. And you, young Killian prince!"

Dove extended a hand, which Quin stared at. After a moment the older man clapped him warmly on the back. "Very well, very well. It's a pleasure to be reacquainted with you both."

He settled himself on the bench next to Pilar. When she started to dip a forkful of lobster in a mysteriously lumpy cream sauce, he leaned in and whispered, "It's full of clams."

"Who puts clams on lobsters?"

"It's ludicrous." He tucked a napkin into his collar. "An affront to good sense."

She couldn't help it. She liked Lord Dove.

"So, my dear niece." He turned to the queen, one eyebrow raised. "I assume you've thanked the Seven Souls for this Jyöltide feast?"

"You assume wrong."

"*Ever ensnared by assumptions, this is a man's lot.* Do you know who said that?"

"Let me guess. You're about to tell me."

"Takk, the great Addi poet three centuries ago. A fine purveyor of moral truisms!"

The queen sighed. "You'll pardon my uncle. He's always pilfering old proverbs. He speaks of dead men as if they sit among us."

"Do they not? Their words have the power to carry them into this room, hundreds of years after their bodies have moldered in a crypt."

"We're eating, Uncle!"

"Who are the Seven Souls?" Pilar asked, genuinely curious.

Freyja waved a hand. "My uncle is referring to Græÿa and her six children. We pay homage to them every year at Jyöltide. It's an old Addi myth, one that's become very popular with the new visitors. Some believe Græÿa and her children did in fact exist, only to meet brutal ends."

"Your dear old uncle, for one." Dove turned to Pilar. "A culture is only as strong as its mythology. I believe our myths teach us about our own inclinations, both good and bad. What are we without our origin stories?"

"What do you care about those stories? You're not even Addi!" Freyja waved a dismissive hand. "My uncle is a man of science, yet curiously also a man of faith. I myself have never been super-stitious. I believe we each have the power to be goddesses of our own choosing. There is magic and majesty inside us all."

"But you don't have magic," Quin said icily. The first words he'd spoken since sitting down. "It would appear there is *not* magic and majesty inside us all."

The queen's grin remained as good-natured as ever.

"As I said, magic does not belong to us, though we often act as if it does. The natural world has its own system of balances and imbalances. This is the power of the Elemental Hex. It is why the discovery of new fyre ice is so valuable, and why my uncle toils night and day in his laboratory to harness its power. He has merged magic with science in a way that no longer requires human pain."

Pilar leaned forward, rapt. "You're saying you've found a kind of magic that doesn't come from an abuse of power?"

Lord Dove nodded. "I have divorced magic from suffering. The extraction process hearkens back to a much older time."

He sat up straighter. "The history of Luumia is colored by the dark stain of the past. But we all bleed crimson. Oppression is a uniquely human legacy, one we can—*must*—change. Fyre ice has given us a way to exploit the world's natural counterbalances for good instead of evil. It is both catalyst and container, a tool and a gift."

"How does it work?" Pilar asked. "How do you extract the magic?"

Dove chuckled. "Forgive me, but the process is a bit technical. I'm sure you'd find it all rather boring."

"Thanks to my uncle," the Snow Queen said proudly, "we have emerged from a land of darkness into a land of light."

Pilar was staring at Quin's place, which no longer held Quin in it.

She pushed back her chair.

"Leave him be," said Freyja. "He can't have gone far."

"Try the music room," Lord Dove said. "I have a sixth sense about these things."

The queen cast a sideways glance at her uncle, then picked up another lobster tail. Her fingers were slick with butter.

"East wing. But you should know—"

Pilar didn't hear her. She was already gone.

It wasn't hard to find the music room. Pilar followed the sounds of the piano.

The doors were propped open, but she lingered in the shadows behind them.

Quin had his back to her on the piano bench. The piano was solid white, just like everything else in the room, including two violoncelloes and a hideous clavichord.

Pilar noticed a pale birchwood violin mounted on the far wall. She wanted to touch it but didn't want Quin to see. He might stop playing, and she loved hearing him play.

Quietly she leaned against the purple-veined wall. The strain of guilt she'd heard at supper was getting louder, mingling with the notes. *I should have used magic to save him.*

Pilar hated that she had one more thing to feel guilty about. One more apology she owed him. Like Karri and Mia Rose weren't enough.

She closed her eyes. Instantly she was back in Kaer Killian. Lurking in the library with Quin at the shiny black piano. The song he'd played that night had power. The song he played now had even more.

His fingers stopped moving.

"I hear you," he said.

"Liar," she shot back. "I haven't made a sound."

"I feel you, then. Come in."

She hugged the perimeter of the room as she entered. Made a playful attempt at punching the walls, which were warm.

"Fyre ice walls here, too."

"It would appear the whole palace is one giant fyre ice cube." Quin patted the piano bench beside him. "I'll teach you a simple duet."

"No." She stayed upright, feeling suddenly shy. "Play me something."

He didn't need much convincing. The melody began in the lower octaves, the sounds as round and deep as thunder claps. Pilar felt the notes in her belly, and when his hands moved up an octave, in her chest.

When Quin closed his eyes, she could watch him unnoticed. She liked his expression when he played. It wasn't that he looked calm or peaceful—the opposite. Sometimes he scrunched his nose until creases appeared on his forehead, curled his lip like a note had caused him physical pain. The prince didn't look pretty. He looked real.

The melody was winding down. Quin's fingers stilled.

"I wrote that for you," he said.

"Don't lie."

"I'm not lying. Only I suppose I shouldn't say I wrote it—I haven't composed music in some time. At least not on paper."

He dragged his hand from the highest key to the lowest, the notes clanging together. Pilar winced.

Quin smiled. "I did make it up with you in mind, though. It used to be my favorite thing: sitting down at the piano in the library with no idea what I was going to play, then plunking my way toward something beautiful. It felt like I wasn't in control, like there was some greater force flowing through me. Almost as if my fingers had a mind of their own."

"You really made that up just now?" She sat on the bench, an inch of space between them. "I could never do that with violin."

"Different instrument. Different musician."

"You play music like it hurts you," she said.

"Doesn't music hurt everyone?"

Pilar wanted to hug him. Instead she folded her arms over her chest.

"When I play violin, it hurts," she said. "But when I don't play, it hurts more."

"Music is meant to be a gift. For me it's become an instrument of grief." He splayed his fingers over the keys, struck a sweet-sounding chord. "You sure you don't want to learn a duet?"

"You mean the Doomed Duet of Pil and Kill?"

"*Gods* no." He leaned in, nudging her shoulder. "I was thinking something more cheerful."

Pilar's cheeks felt hot. Fiery.

"I didn't know cheerful was your style, Killian."

"I have been irredeemably glum, haven't I?"

"I bet you could still redeem yourself."

She pressed one knuckle into a skinny key. The sound hummed through her bones. For a moment she felt happy.

A truth settled into Pilar's heart. She was scared. And not of the ice leopard.

Scared of losing Quin.

"I'll play a duet with you," she said. "But you're on piano." She nodded toward the violin hanging from the wall. "I'm on violin."

"All the better. Then I can feast my ears *and* my eyes. You really are beautiful when you play."

Pilar stood abruptly, hoping Quin wouldn't see her pink cheeks. Her eye caught something small and brown on the music rack.

"Your dead men's stones!" She reached for the leather pouch. "I'm dying to know what treasures you've been hiding in here."

"I'll take that back now."

"Don't be so sentimental."

"Give it back, Pilar." Quin's voice had an edge.

She squeezed the contents between her fingers. To her surprise, she felt only one stone: a perfect round orb.

A knot formed in her belly's pit.

"What's in the pouch, Quin?"

He wouldn't look at her.

"What have you been hiding?"

Pilar willed her hands steady as she shook out the leather pouch. Even before it thudded into her palm, she knew.

Angelyne's moonstone.

Chapter 27

KISSED BY FYRE, STEELED BY ICE

"IT ISN'T WHAT YOU think," Quin stammered. "I can explain."

Pilar stood and backed away from the piano bench. She ripped the moonstone off the chain, clutched it so tight her fingers turned white. She wanted to crush it to dust.

"Angelyne sent you. You're her spy."

"It isn't like that. Please, I'm begging you—"

"And the protective stones you stole from the dead men in the Kaer? Was that a lie, too?"

"I . . ." He stared hard at the piano. "I started to steal them. That was the plan. You know what it was like, being in that place, under her control."

Quin's face was so pink and flushed it made her sick.

"I did go to the Hall of Hands." He looked up at her. "That's not a lie. But Angelyne found me. I tried to use the stones against her, but she was too strong."

"Why should I believe you? You've told me nothing but lies."

"He's lied to us both," said a voice behind her.

Pilar whirled around. It was Freyja, of course. The Snow Queen had a habit of creeping into rooms undetected. For once she wasn't flanked by Frigg and Fulla.

"Why didn't you watch his Reflections?" Pilar hissed. "Why did you only watch mine?"

"The wren only shows the Reflections you ask it to. And you asked me to leave him be."

Pilar thrust out a hand. "Give it to me."

The queen didn't argue. She reached into her snow-fox cloak and pulled out the ruby wren. When she whispered into the cage of her hands, the bird flew across the music room.

Pilar snatched it from the air. She turned on Quin.

"Let's see who you are, Killian. Who you *really* are."

She coiled her arm, then chucked the bird as hard as she could against the marble wall.

At first, nothing. Maybe all nightmares had to be watched in the throne room.

Then on the wall, the purple veins ignited—and the darkness split into shadows.

It was a strange thing, watching someone else's nightmares. A dark-haired boy hunched over a piano. The scene shifted: the boy was on his knees, screaming in a crypt. A man stood over him with a sticky knife.

The walls of the crypt melted, churned into a black river. Pilar saw a girl and boy pressed together. The boy was Quin, his curls glued to his skull like wet blood. He looked happy. At least happier than she'd ever seen him.

The girl was Mia Rose.

Of course it was. Quin loved Mia. The fact that he'd lost her changed nothing. In fact it probably made the love feel even more real.

But that wasn't what Pilar was looking for. As the shadows shifted, she saw a pile of bodies in the Hall of Hands, faces crumbling and limbs black with rot. Quin crouched over them, his hands rifling through their pockets. His back to the door as Angelyne glided into the room.

The river queen looked frailer than Pilar remembered. She imagined how easy it would be to fell Angelyne with one blow. A well-aimed bone strike to the temple. Maybe to the throat.

But Quin didn't fight. He froze when Angelyne bent beside him, whispered something in his ear. She unsnapped the pendant at her nape and folded it into his hand. Quin's eyes blackened, then cleared. He nodded. Smiled.

Pilar's heart closed like a fist.

"End it," she said to Freyja. "I've seen enough."

The Snow Queen waved her hand, and the shadows ceased.

Quin was very still, his head hung low. He wouldn't look Pilar in the eye. She hated him for it. Hated that he'd been lying from the start.

Pilar turned to the queen. "Leave us."

Freyja's mouth twisted. "You realize what we've just seen

changes everything. The river prince is not to be trusted."

"Don't worry," said Pilar, "I don't."

The Snow Queen gave a sharp nod. "I'll give you five minutes. Use it well."

She pulled the music room doors shut behind her.

"Pilar." Quin stepped away from the piano, eyes pleading. "There was nothing I could do. No way to resist."

"And yet I resisted." Scorn welled up in her throat. "She's enthralling you right now, isn't she?"

"Angelyne never asked me to harm anyone. She only sent me into the forest to find out who was loyal to her and who wasn't. Instead I found you."

"I can't trust a single thing you say." Pilar flung her hand toward where Freyja stood outside the doors. "I trust *her* more than I trust you!"

"Angelyne's magic is different now. Subtler. My mind is still my own. My speech, my actions: all mine. It's more like . . . a suggestion."

"If you're so in control, you could have told me the truth." Pilar stiffened. "Is she in your head right now? Is that why you're defending her?"

"No. I—" He tugged a hand through his hair. "It's Zaga who stacks people's bodies in the Hall. I get the feeling Angelyne wants to find another way. Not that what she's doing is good, either. That hasn't changed. I'm babbling, I know I'm not making any sense . . ." He straightened. "I just need you to understand that it hasn't *all* been a lie."

Pilar's fist tightened around the moonstone. "You were never going to give the guards gold, were you? You were going to show them this stone so they'd know you were the queen's little errand boy. Here I thought you were helpless, that you needed my help. But you were lying even then."

"Pilar, please. I'm not—"

"Destroy it."

"I . . ." He deflated. "I can't."

"You're weak. If you were brave, you would have fought."

"I tried, honestly I did. But she was too powerful. I'm not like you."

"An understatement." She held the stone high. "Since you're too much of a coward, let me help you."

"No! Wait!"

She hurled the orb onto the floor with all her might. When it didn't shatter, she crouched. Grabbed the stone. Slammed it into the marble. Again and again.

"Please, Pilar!" Quin shouted, trying to grab hold of her arms. "Please stop."

Each time she smashed the moonstone into the ground, the impact shot up her arm, jarred her whole body. She knew she'd find bruises on her fingers later. But she'd rather have a million bruises than the kind of pain that lived beneath the skin.

Just a few minutes earlier, she had leaned into Quin on the piano bench, wanting to stay there forever. How quickly things could change.

Pilar was out of breath. The orb still perfect and unbroken. She paused for half a second—and Quin swooped in, snatching the stone off the ground. He cradled it in his hands.

"Are you trying to kill me?"

"I'm trying to free you."

"You don't understand. You can't imagine what it's like to be in my head every second of every day, reliving the deaths of all the people I cared about. It's not like I want to be enthralled. But at least, when Angie's in my head . . . at least there's someone."

Pilar's pity burned down to rage.

"Of course Angelyne got in your head. You don't even know who you are."

He glared at her. "You want the truth? I'm jealous of you. Even when you hate yourself, you *know* yourself. I've never been able to be that honest. Growing up in the Kaer, I lied to everyone. I knew how cruelly my father would punish me for my desires. And I was right. Dom wasn't the first boy I cared about. The boy who taught me to play music . . ."

Quin cast a painful glance at the piano. His face hardened.

"I have always been ashamed of who I was."

Pilar was no stranger to shame. It had lived inside her for years. A bitter, breathing thing.

She stomped out the spark of sympathy before it grew into a flame.

"Do you really want to kill? Your own mother?" Quin said softly.

"My mother and Angelyne lied. They hurt and betrayed us, killed innocent people. They said they were acting for the good of the Dujia."

"I'm certain they still think they are. You know what they say: every villain is the hero in her own story."

"A villain is a villain. And you're still lying to protect one." She jerked her head toward the moonstone. "Keep your jewel. Take it back to your queen like the sniveling little prince you are. I don't give a sheep's shit."

Quin's eyes blazed a violent green. "Let me come with you. I'll help you find the Snow Wolf. We'll go back to Glas Ddir, kill your mother and Angelyne, then save Dom and all the other innocent people suffering under the new regime. I'll destroy the moonstone. I'll do whatever you want. Just don't leave me."

A window creaked open in Pilar's chest. She slammed it shut.

"I don't keep company with liars."

Her own words smacked her in the face. Wasn't she lying, too? She hadn't told Quin what happened in the cottage by the lake, why she *really* came to the Kaer as a spy. He didn't know her truth, either. At least not all of it.

Why did her mind keep trying to forgive him? What he'd done was inexcusable.

She struck the door three times with her palm. It swung open to reveal Freyja on the other side, this time joined by Frigg and Fulla, three new guardswomen, and Lord Kristoffin Dove.

"Good Græÿa," Dove said softly, taking in the scene.

Pilar set her jaw. "We're done here. Do what you want with him."

The guards pushed past her. She turned away. She didn't want to see them seize Quin, even if he deserved it.

The queen's silver eyes flashed. "You, Pilar d'Aqila, are free to go where you please. But I may be able to help you. You say you have come to find your father. The Snow Wolf will be here at the palace the night of the Weeping Moon. However, if you are impatient—and you do strike me as impatient—you'll find him in the heartlands, outside Kom'Addi. I will furnish you with a ship."

The offer was generous. *Too* generous.

"Why would you help me?"

"Because I didn't trust you, and I should have." She motioned toward the lump in Pilar's pocket. "Your rune may come in handy. The one you've been hiding on your person since you arrived."

"How did you—?"

"Our objects often reveal us, even when we don't reveal them."

Pilar fished the frostflower out of her pocket. Placed it on her palm.

"That chalk mark you drew on the door of the ice kabma," she said. "It's the same as this flower, isn't it? Six spokes, six petals."

Freyja nodded. "The rune is meant to represent the Elemental Hex. We use it to mark the houses where someone has died. A way of calling the elements back into balance. It's an old Addi ritual, one my father taught me." Her voice softened. "The carvings are believed to lead children back to the family they seek. A way of calling lost souls home."

"But this flower isn't mine. Won't it lead me to the wrong home?"

"In the right hands, it adjusts." Freyja paused. "Are you sure you want to find the Snow Wolf? To answer violence with more violence? In my experience, violence is best used in service of some nobler purpose. Justice. Love."

"*Love?*" Pilar scoffed. "What place does love have in all of this?"

"Often the greatest place." Freyja glanced at Quin, now bound by the guards, then back at Pilar. "Sometimes the greatest violence we inflict is upon ourselves."

Pilar didn't feel like being lectured. "Sounds like bad poetry."

For once Freyja didn't smile. "I speak from experience. I have seen your Reflections, and I know the guilt you carry."

Pilar's face flushed. She could feel Quin watching her.

"I have one request," said the Snow Queen. "Come to the festival of Jyöl. We haven't enjoyed the Illuminations in many years, and my uncle has outdone himself. When your father comes to the palace, you should accompany him."

"This is a request, not a command?"

"Yes."

"Enjoy your lights in the sky. I have work to do."

"What did I tell you, Niece? *Kissed by fyre, steeled by ice.*" Lord Dove's eyes sparkled. "A scrap of wisdom from an old Addi mystic. The greatest warriors burn with passion but act with cold resolve."

Freyja nodded. "Very well. You'll sail south across the Lilla Sea to the port of Suvi West. From there you'll chart a path into the heartlands. Two days by boat, another three by foot to Kom'Addi."

"How do you know where the Snow Wolf is?"

"I know where everyone is. At least everyone who matters. It's my job to keep an eye on all those in Luumia who might cause harm."

"And the river prince? What will you do with him?"

Freyja grunted. "Ship him back to Glas Ddir where he belongs."

On cue, the guardswomen marched Quin past, his hands bound behind his back. So close Pilar could reach out and touch him.

What if she never saw him again? Was she really damning him to a lifetime of being enthralled?

But he lied, she reminded herself. He lied to you.

If a person wasn't in control of their lies, did it still count as lying?

No. Quin could have told her. He could have found a way. He had betrayed her, just like everyone else.

Pilar could still see the rafters in the cottage. Wood beams casting shadows like a cell. Tiny rocks on the rough dirt floor, biting holes into the soft skin of her back. So many moments she couldn't remember. But the ones she did remember, she would never forget.

She watched the guards march Quin down the too-white corridor. Freyja was wrong. Love wasn't some nobler purpose.

Love was a fist with broken knuckles. A knife with a blunt blade.

Good, then. When someone came at you with broken

knuckles—when they brandished their dull little knife—they were easier to beat.

Where love bloomed, Pilar would cut it out. And in the space it left behind, she'd set the world aflame.

17 DAYS TILL THE WEEPING MOON

My bewitching, elusive sister,

They tell me you are not in White Lagoon.
I should have known you'd journey to the queen's
palace to find whom you seek. I fear you will be
gravely disappointed. But then, what is a Dujia
if not a constellation of failures with the occasional
glimmer of success?

While we wait: another story.

The youngest of Graja's daughters had a dark
secret. She tried to eat the hearty stews her mother
prepared: tender hunks of lamb meat swirling in
brown broth, savory mushroom caps and sweet onions,
pearl barley from the village and dandelion dust from
the fields. But with every spoonful, she fought the
urge to retch. She had no appetite for stew.

Unlike her mother, the girl had an appetite for
human flesh.

When her mother journeyed to the village, the girl followed. She started with the little things, pieces no one would miss: a thimble of fingernails, a discarded tooth. But the teeth were sour and the nails scraped her throat. They never satisfied her hunger.

Before long, she found the barber.

The barber was not known for his gentle touch. He was ever ready with his cleaver, keen to hack off appendages at the villagers' request: fingers blackened from infection, toes frozen in the bitter cold. The girl could smell the fragrant flesh, ripe for the taking. She crept into the barbershop at night, unwrapped the parcels of red-soaked cloth, and feasted.

But as is often the case, the more she fed her appetite, the more it grew. Dead flesh was no longer enough. She thirsted for the warm, sweet drizzle of fresh blood.

The girl made rules for herself. She would never eat the flesh of those smaller or weaker. Not the old. Not the destitute. And never a single child.

But still the weight of her hunger burned a hole in her belly, made her sick with shame.

So she devised a better system. For every piece of flesh she stole, she would lay her hands on someone else's broken flesh to heal it. She traveled to the ice kabmas, sought out the Addi children who wept and suffered. She healed flesh and mended bone.

None of that mattered, of course, when the villagers came for her.

They say the Flesh Thief still haunts the villages of Luumia. Today she is the Third Soul of Jyöl. Be good and she will patch your scrapes and bruises. Be bad and she will eat you in your sleep.

The Jyöltide celebration is nigh, sister. The Weeping Moon rises. Soon you will see the Illuminations in the night sky. I urge you to remember that even the most resplendent light is invisible if not pitched against the darkness.

We are each of us evil, and each of us good.

Inside ourselves we hold both light and shadow.
The question is: How big a fire must you kindle to
illuminate the dark?

Fervidly yours,
Angelyne

Chapter 22

WRENCHED

Mɪᴀ ʟᴏᴀᴛʜᴇᴅ ᴛʜᴇ ᴡᴀᴛᴇʀ. It was unpredictable and vindictive, ready to drown you at whim. The ocean couldn't be trusted. No matter how diligently you charted the tides, the sea would not hesitate to kill you.

Now, on Zai's boat bobbing on the Lilla Sea, Mia had a peculiar thought: maybe *most* things would kill you, if given the chance. Take her mother's moonstone. What had once been an instrument of healing turned out to be an even more powerful instrument of death.

"Seasick?" Zai called out from the deck. He was tinkering with the rigging as the sunlight waned. "You'll feel better if you come outside. Breathe the fresh air and fix your eyes on the horizon."

"I don't get seasick," she called back. The truth.

Instead Mia stayed in the galley, lost in her own thoughts.

The memories had come back.

Seeing her mother in the White Lagoon—or the apparition of her mother—had loosed a tide of recollection unlike any she'd ever known. Zaga's cruelty. Angelyne's betrayal. The moonstone dangling at Angie's throat as she enkindled Domeniq, Pilar, the Hunters, Mia's father. All sitting in the Grand Gallery, pinned in place like bugs to a cork board.

And Quin. Always Quin.

Every time Mia closed her eyes, she saw the agony on Quin's face as he crouched over his dead sister. And she saw the blank terror in his eyes as he kissed Angelyne under the enthrall.

Somehow, in the midst of falling for the prince, Mia had destroyed him.

She hated herself for the months she'd squandered in White Lagoon. She'd let herself get distracted. All the drinking and fyre ink and night companions—they were a failed attempt to feel something. She'd been so desperate to live inside her own body again, she'd conveniently forgotten that Quin was a prisoner in his.

And now she was sailing in the *opposite* direction of Kaer Killian, with a boy she found undeniably appealing.

What was wrong with her? How could she be so selfish?

Because you're broken, said a voice inside her. *And you broke Quin, too.*

Zai strolled back into the galley. "The water will smooth out soon."

They'd left White Lagoon that morning for the palace in Valavïk. If Zai was right—if her mother had indeed surfaced at his alehouse two days prior—Mia was closer than she'd ever been. Maybe she still had time to make things right.

"Tell me again," she said to Zai. "Every single detail."

He sat beside her on the bench. "She was a big woman. Hazel eyes, I think. She ordered two thumbs of rai rouj and drank it in a single swallow."

"What else?"

"She asked if I knew the fastest way to get to the palace. Said she was seeking an audience with the Snow Queen."

"That's all?"

"I'm sorry, Raven. I've told you everything I remember."

Mia folded her arms over her chest. "You have a boat. You could have made a pretty penny ferrying her to Valavïk."

"I don't like leaving the alehouse unless I have to."

She flourished a hand around the boat. "And now?"

"Now is different."

"Why?"

He leaned back. "If you'd seen yourself at the Lagoon, you'd understand."

Mia frowned. She knew how it must have looked as she splashed around the lagoon, shouting: like she'd lost her mind.

Maybe she *had* lost her mind. One minute she knew in her bones the woman who'd come to Zai's alehouse was her mother; moments later, doubt dug its hooks. If Wynna really had left the port town two days ago, how in four hells did Mia see her in the lagoon? Grief was a potent paint, but its colors were muted pastels, its brush strokes blurry. The redhead in the lagoon was not some grief-soaked phantom. What Mia saw was real.

Yet no other visitor had spotted a red-haired woman standing in the water. That troubled her most of all. She could no longer trust her mother, her father, and certainly not her sister. But after the numb haze of the last few months, Mia was beginning to wonder if she could trust herself.

Trust your heart, even if kills you.

She rolled her eyes. It had, in fact, killed her.

"Rest easy, Raven." Zai rapped his knuckles gently on the table. "If this woman was your mother, then she's safe and well, only two days ahead of us on the voyage to Valavïk. She seemed like the kind of woman who gets what she wants."

Mia smiled a little. That *did* sound like her mother.

"I'm curious about your family," said Zai.

"I'm curious about yours," said Mia, deflecting. "You haven't said a word about them, though you seem to have put as much distance between you and them as possible."

He shifted. "There isn't much to say. My family herds reinsdyr in the heartlands and lives off the land. Yours?"

"Oh, they're into this and that." Magic. Murder. "What brought you to White Lagoon?"

"My ambition. I wasn't going to stay in Kom'Addi for the rest of my life. I wanted to see more of the world."

"Me too," she said. "As a child I wanted to be an explorer."

"And here you are." He tipped his head toward the ocean around them. "Exploring."

"Something like that."

Zai's black hair had freed itself from the leather band again. She watched him sweep back the loose strands. The fact that she found him handsome—that she could even be *thinking* about another boy when Quin remained in the Kaer, waiting to be rescued—was an equation she didn't know how to solve.

"You know," she said, forcing a yawn, "I'm quite tired. Perhaps we could discuss sleeping arrangements?"

"Of course." He stood and cribbed the last green apple from the hanging basket, then leaned against the wall, slicing it into quarters with a pocketknife. "You've seen the cot in the corner?"

She had absolutely seen it. It was tiny and—most important—had no twin.

"Oh. Are we going to—"

"The cot is yours, of course."

"But where will you sleep?"

"I don't sleep much. When I do, I can sleep standing up."

"You don't mean that."

He slid his blade under the surface of the apple, loosing the skin from the flesh. "That might be an exaggeration. But I sleep as soundly sitting as I do lying down."

The thought of sleeping on the cot while Zai sat on the bench—staring at her, since the bench directly faced the cot—was mortifying.

He handed her a tart apple wedge speared on the blade of his knife. When she took it, she caught him studying the indigo frostflower on her wrist.

"I'm sorry I offended you with my fyre ink," she said.

"I know you didn't mean any harm. It's just that visitors come here with no understanding of what the marks mean. They take Addi symbols of great significance and treat them like pretty ornaments to wear on their skin."

Mia cringed. That was precisely what she'd done.

"What does the frostflower mean? If you don't mind me asking." Her eyebrows shot up. "Is my mark actually a compass?"

"Yes and no." He gestured toward her wrist. "May I touch you?"

Her heart climbed up her collarbone and nestled in the back of her throat.

"Yes."

Zai traced a finger over the ink, petal by petal. If Mia closed her eyes, she could pretend his touch fired a cavalcade of chills up her humerus and across her clavicle.

"In nature frostflowers grow above the fyre ice pits—the *old* pits—in the heartlands. Even long after the pits were emptied, the flowers continued to grow. They're not as fragile as they look."

His finger lingered on her mark.

"The bloom represents the Elemental Hex."

"Hex as in a hexagon with six sides? Or a kind of spell?"

"Both. Do you remember my mark?"

"Not really," she lied. "Can I see it again?" Even if she couldn't *feel* sensations of pleasure, she could still *look*.

Zai's mouth lifted in an almost smile. "I'll show you the original sketch tomorrow. I gave it to the ink painter so he could blade the fyre ink. But I rendered the mark myself."

Mia was surprised. Zai struck her as more of a craftsman than an artist. All day she'd watched the way he double- and triple-checked every rope knot, how thoroughly he ran his fingers over the railing. Whenever he found a splinter, he dug out a scrap of coarse paper and patiently sanded the offending wood down to a fine gleam.

"I didn't take you for an artist," she said.

"I didn't take you for an explorer. You seem to hate the sea."

She cocked her head. "I suppose you're right. I always wanted to sail the four kingdoms, but somehow I neglected the fact that to do so would involve actual sailing."

Zai walked to the cot and brushed it off with his hand. He tried to plump the tragically flat pillow. It didn't plump, but Mia was touched by the effort. There was a lumbering gentleness to him that made her want to rest her head on his shoulder.

"Sleep well, Raven. Når päivö aukoja, fura liekki." He handed her the thin pillow. "*When day breaks, frost becomes a flame.*"

She dreamed of the wooden box.

Mia was choking on her own tongue. She balled her fists and smashed her knuckles into the lid, over and over. Wood slivers stuck to her skin as she fought her way out of the coffin.

Only after she'd tumbled onto the forest floor did Mia realize she was not alone.

Pilar d'Aqila stood between the trees, watching. She reached for the quiver on her back. Nocked one fojuen arrow. Drew the bow.

Mia tried to speak, but the words turned to dust in her mouth.

The arrowhead glimmered red, still wet with blood. Was it Karri's? Quin's? Or someone else's?

It's over, said Pilar.

She loosed the string.

Mia awoke clenching both fists. Her breathing was erratic, panicked; she willed herself calm. It took a moment to remember she was on a boat, not in a box. Also, she wasn't dead.

A mouse scratched at the walls. A boat mouse? Did those exist? She lifted herself on her elbows.

A candle flickered on the round table. Zai hunched over a stack of loose papers, drawing feverishly. The scratching wasn't a mouse, but a piece of charcoal being raked across the page.

He was so focused on what he was doing he didn't notice her approach. When she reached for one of his sketches, he flinched.

But Zai didn't stop her as she picked up the papers and began leafing through them. She saw a drawing of the port, the boats rendered with perfect precision, all crisp lines and billowing sails. She saw the alehouse, patrons nursing their spirits in various states of inebriation. She saw a family gathered around a fire wearing striped wool scarves in what she imagined would be festive Jyöltide colors if not rendered in charcoal grays.

"Zai," she murmured. "These are lovely."

"Running an alehouse can be tedious work. You find things to do to pass the time—whittling, playing dice, sketching. It's always a welcome change of pace when a pretty girl stumbles through the front door."

Was he talking about her?

"Probably not when she's literally stumbling," Mia blurted. She brushed the loose curls out of her eyes, attempting to regain her composure. "Would you render me?"

Zai set his piece of charcoal down on the table. It rolled sideways, tilting with the boat before nesting in a deep groove.

"I don't render people."

"I just saw a sketchbook full of people."

"They're strangers. I don't draw people I know."

"But you don't really know me, do you?"

"I can't render you, Raven." His voice was gruff. The sea waves churned and slapped against the boat, reminding Mia of a sound she couldn't quite place.

He took the sketches from her hands. As he did, they splayed apart like a silk fan. Mia caught a glimpse of red amidst the charcoal. A shock of scarlet in a sea of black and gray.

Her fist closed around the page. She felt Zai stiffen, but before he could stop her, she wrenched the paper free.

And there she was, clear as day.

Mia's mother.

Chapter 23

BITE-SIZED

Zai had rendered Wynna Rose flawlessly. She sat tall on an alehouse stool, two thumbs of rai rouj in her hand. Long wavy hair pinned at her nape in the Luumi style. Most of the sketch was in charcoal, but he'd made her eyes a greenish-gold hazel and stained both her hair and the drink with some kind of rosy pigment. She was not smiling.

Mia sank onto the cot, still clutching the sketch of her mother. On one hand, she was thrilled. Zai *had* met her mother. That meant they were definitely headed in the right direction.

On the other hand, she was livid.

"Why didn't you show me this?"

Zai lowered his head. "I didn't want to upset you."

"If you'd shown me I would have known immediately it was her!"

"When you thought you saw your mother at the lagoon . . . I don't know how to explain it. It's like you went wild with grief. When you described her to me, I knew immediately she was the woman who had come to my alehouse. And I knew I could take you to her. But I thought, if I showed you this sketch and you saw her image . . ." He shook his head. "I wanted to spare you any additional pain."

"And additional delusions, you mean."

"Raven, whatever you saw—"

"You think I'm unstable. A danger to others."

"Not to others," Zai said carefully. "But maybe to yourself."

The walls were closing in. "I'm not crazy."

"I never said you were." He walked to the cot and sat beside her. The frame sagged under his weight.

"Your mother made an impression on me." He gestured toward the sketch clenched in Mia's fist. "That's why I drew her. She had a ferocity in her, a wildness. I think you have it, too."

"Wild isn't the same as crazy."

"I know."

"I saw her, Zai. I know I did. She was *right there*."

The paper was crimped on one edge from Mia's fingers. She sat the sketch on the pillow, as gently as she might have tucked a child into bed.

"I don't know what's happening to me."

She dropped her head in her hands. A moment later, she

sensed a dull thud across her back.

Mia looked up to find Zai's arm around her shoulders. She let him pull her close, her body snug against his broad chest. She knew his skin was warm, but she couldn't feel it. Such a kind, simple gesture only made her feel more broken, more alone.

If this was her life now—if this was a permanent side effect of dying—why live at all?

A sound sliced through the quiet. Outside Mia heard the low murmur of voices, then the splash of oars.

"All hands on deck!" came a muffled shout. "You're about to be boarded by pirates!"

The voice was swallowed by raucous laughter, followed by a hearty, "Good Jyöl!"

Mia and Zai hurried onto the deck.

A wooden canoe bobbed on the waves. Nelladinellakin sat tall at the stern, wearing a sparkly purple gown that seemed entirely inappropriate for sailing. Nell looked gorgeous, her long legs folded into the small canoe, an oar balanced on her knees.

At the other end, Ville struggled to heft an oversized cask of ale onto his shoulders—and nearly toppled over the side.

"This ale might actually kill me. Permission to board, Captain?"

Mia glanced at Zai to see if he'd expected this, but he looked as shocked as she was.

"Ville?" he said. "What are you doing here?"

"You didn't really think we were going to let you two have

an adventure all by yourselves, did you? Where's the fun in that?"

Nell beamed and waved. "Hello, Raven, Zai! I hope this is a pleasant surprise, at least maybe halfway pleasant?"

"I'd settle for a quarter pleasant," Ville said. "Good Græÿa, this thing is heavy."

Mia's heart lifted. Nelladine and Ville provided a terrific distraction. Perhaps this was why people had friends: to distract them from their own bottomless despair.

But being with people was also exhausting. She could handle Zai; spending time with him felt easy. Nell and Ville, on the other hand, were more vivacious. Between all the laughs and jokes and banter, Mia had to work extra hard to pretend to be normal.

"This will be fun, like our very own Jyöltide celebration!" Nelladine gathered the velvet folds of her plum gown as she stood. "One big happy family piling into a snug little boat!"

"Family?" Zai cocked an eyebrow as he helped Nell into the boat.

"Oh, shove off, Zai." Ville slapped him on the back. "You know as well as I do we're the best family you've got."

It took Nelladine all of three minutes to excoriate Zai for how poorly he'd stocked the kitchen.

"You were going to sail to Valavïk on *this*?" She held up a paltry pouch of carrots and strips of cured meat.

"We have potatoes," Zai countered.

"Three days of boiled potatoes?" Nell lifted one from the

hanging basket. The eyes were sprouting green buds.

Ville plopped a crate of baked bread and milk jars onto the stone slab in the galley. "Leave the poor boy alone! We've brought libations and sustenance, so the great potato crisis is averted. Though I must say, Zai: she does have a point. Your hospitality could use some work."

Mia had yet to see Zai blush, but as he turned toward the deck, his cheeks were flushed. Ville stepped in front of him, blocking his escape.

"Why don't you and I make supper for the ladies?"

Zai lifted a brow. "You cook, Ville?"

"I second that," Nell joined in. "When have you ever cooked a day in your life?"

"Never too late to start," Ville quipped. He picked up a linen towel and looped it around his waist like an apron. "I hear women like a sensitive man."

Nell appraised him, hands on hips. She sighed.

"Do you think you can manage to cut the cabbage?"

"I was born to cut cabbage."

"Highly debatable." Nell dug into the crate and pulled out a purple head of cabbage. She handed Ville a sharp knife. "Slice on a diagonal. Bite-sized pieces, please."

Nell turned back to the crate, then stopped, her attention arrested by a mustard-yellow mug. She lifted it off the stone slab, inspecting the work from top to bottom. Then she set it back down with a hard clank.

"I don't know why you buy this garbage, Zai." She sighed.

"The craftsmanship is insulting. Look at the bleed on that glaze!"

Zai started to respond, but he was drowned out by the sound of screaming.

Ville had sliced open his hand.

Chapter 24

A LITTLE MORE MAGIC

THE KNIFE HAD CUT clean through the webbing between Ville's thumb and forefinger. Thin streams of blood spilled over his wrist, his palm.

Mia couldn't tear her eyes away. All she could think about was Princess Karri, the arrow buried deep in her belly. Mia had tried so hard to save her. She had failed.

"Ville," Nell shouted. "Stop waving your hand around. Don't be such an infant! Give it here." She snatched him by the wrist and pulled his face level with hers. "Do you want me to help you?"

He whimpered a response.

"I need to hear you say it. 'Help me, Nell.'"

"Help me, Nell!"

She took his hand between hers. Nelladine's skin was deep brown, but her palms were lighter, creased like pink satin. She placed them on either side of Ville's injured hand and squeezed.

Instantly he stopped howling. Swallowed. Stared.

Mia watched, mesmerized, as the webbing regenerated. Tiny filaments of tissue stitched themselves back together. In under five seconds the gash was gone completely.

Safe to say, Nelladine had magic.

She smiled and patted Ville's arm. "There. Better?"

Gingerly he touched his fingertips to the webbed folds.

"Thanks, Nell. I owe you one."

Zai's face relaxed. "You sure you're all right, Vi?"

"Dandy and fine. Nice to have someone who can always put me back together the way the sweet goddesses intended." He winked at Mia. "In other words: as charming as ever."

Nell groaned. "I should have put you back another way."

Mia couldn't believe how normal they were all acting, like this happened every day.

She gestured toward Ville's hand. "Can I see it?"

"For you, Angel of Ashes? Anything."

She wasn't trying to be coy. She wanted to examine the wound.

But there was no wound. When Mia had mended Quin's arrow wound all those months ago, it wasn't as if the tissue didn't hold the memory of the damage: it sutured a fishbone scar around the gash. Ville's skin gave no indication it had ever been anything but whole.

What baffled her most, though, was how, when Mia healed someone, she was decimated for hours, wrenched and depleted, like a cloth wrung from both ends. Nelladine strode over to the galley slab, humming to herself as she parceled a bud of garlic into cloves. She popped a clove into her mouth and swallowed it whole.

Nell appeared to have paid no energetic cost whatsoever.

"How did you do that?" Mia asked.

"What? Eat a garlic?"

"No." She nodded toward Ville. "*Him.*"

"Oh, that? That's nothing, I'm sure you've done it yourself."

Mia swallowed. "You knew I had magic?"

"You think I haven't heard about the Angel of Ashes?" Nell smirked. "For all its lofty aspirations, White Lagoon is still a small town. Everyone knows everything."

"Then you know I'm an utter disaster when it comes to calibration. Even when I heal my own superficial burns, it exhausts me so deeply I can barely stand."

"Calibration?" Nelladine raised a brow. "It's magic. Not ingineering. I bet you're just not balancing the elements, which is a common enough mistake." She flipped the long dark braids off her shoulders. "I can teach you, if you want. On one condition."

Mia tensed, but Nell's smile was impish.

"I get to do your pigment first."

They ate a modest supper of roasted potatoes, flame-toasted bread, and non-bloody cabbage stew, topped off with ale from

Ville's cask. As Zai cleared the plates off the stone slab, Nelladine instructed Mia to sit on the bench.

"Hair first," she said. "Pigment after."

She pulled a wide-tooth comb out of her satchel, then stuck three hairpins between her lips.

"Will you help me with the jib, Ville?" Zai said. "The luff keeps coming loose."

Ville stood and stretched. "I do love a loose luff."

"Reroute the halyard back to the mast," Nell said, pins still in her mouth.

Zai scratched his head. "Tried that already. Puts too much pressure on the furler."

"Then untie the halyard from the shackle, pull it down hard, and have Ville push the jib up the furler slot." Off Mia's look of surprise, Nell added, "Oh, did I forget to mention? I'm a better sailor than either of them."

"It's true," Zai confirmed. "Ask Nell how old she was when she sailed all the way from Pembuk. Just a girl and her boat."

"How old?" Mia asked, genuinely curious.

A shadow passed over Nelladine's face. Mia had seen that shadow once before, in the disrobing chamber.

"Not old enough," Nell said.

"To hells with the furler," Ville said, rubbing his hands together. "Show me the new fyre ice, Zai. We'll leave the girls to their women whimsy."

"Excuse me?" Nell said, affronted. "*Women whimsy*?"

"You misunderstood me! I said *whim and whimsy*."

211

He gave a droll wink as he strolled out of the galley, Zai on his heels.

"That boy." Nell clucked her tongue. "He studies fyre ice day and night, but that doesn't seem to matter, he's still a kid in a candy store every time he sees it."

Mia waited to see if she'd bring up the boat from Pembuk. But Nell said nothing as she began working her comb through Mia's curls, carefully pinning up one plait at a time.

"Your hair is almost as curly as mine, though mine has more texture, obviously. You've got all these little red silk ringlets, have you ever thought of braiding it? I think a headful of red braids would look stunning on you."

Mia assessed her dented reflection. There was no mirror on the boat—Zai the consummate bachelor did not sit preening in front of a looking glass. Nell had fashioned one out of a shiny pewter plate. The reflections were slightly distorted, but frankly that felt more indicative of Mia's mental state.

"My mother used to comb my hair," she said. "She was the only one who ever had the patience for it."

"Was it awful? My mother used to comb mine, it took *hours*. One of us was always screaming by the end, though it was a coin toss as to which."

Mia's smile was genuine. "For us it was the opposite. We never stopped laughing."

If she closed her eyes, she could pretend she was still a little girl with wild, unruly tresses. Sitting in front of the looking glass for hours on end, talking and giggling. *Tell me something I don't know about you*, her mother would say.

"You don't have to talk about why you're looking for her," Nell said. "Unless you want to."

Mia thought of the many *somethings* she'd told her mother over the years, things that seemed gigantic at the time. She'd snuck scraps to a pig in a market stall. She'd peeked through a window in Ilwysion and seen so-and-so take off her glove. She'd had a dream about kissing Domeniq du Zol.

Then she thought of the much larger *somethings* her mother had never told her.

"She's not who I thought she was," Mia confessed. "She lied to me my whole life. But I still need her. I have to go back to Glas Ddir to help someone, and I can't do it without her."

Nell looked contemplative. "Did she actually lie? Or did she just keep secrets?"

"She liked to say secrets are just another way people lie to one another."

Nelladine laughed. "I think I like your mother. I always say that secrets are what make us real. Which is really the same thing, isn't it? People lying to one another is part of what makes us human, we wouldn't be very interesting if we only told the truth. *There.*"

She pinned the last of Mia's plaits, then squeezed onto the bench, scooting the candle closer.

"Pivot, please."

Mia pivoted toward her. Nell cupped her chin in her palm.

"How do you make your skin so soft?" Mia asked.

"What do you think all the lotions are for? I don't use them for moral reasons!" Nell angled Mia's head to catch more of the candlelight. "Good, stay just like that. And don't blink."

"Didn't you say you'd teach me magic?"

"Yes, yes, I'm getting to that."

Mia watched her stride to the stone slab and heat two small silver tins over a flame. Nell unrolled a strip of black linen and laid out all manner of pots, vials, sponges, and long brushes with white bristles, as meticulous as a surgeon lining up her tools. After she'd arranged everything, she sauntered back to the slab, where she poked at the substance bubbling inside the first tin.

"Nice creamy consistency, good. Should be ready now." Nell spooned rosy-beige cream into an egg-shaped bowl. Then she brought the bowl back to the table, dipped a sponge wedge into the clay pot, and began brushing the cream up Mia's cheeks.

"Let me know if it's too hot."

"It isn't."

"See how I'm applying pigment in the hollows? We want a touch of shadow, then we tint it lighter to make your cheekbones pop. Always rub it smoothly into your skin so it looks natural; if you don't do it evenly it'll cake."

Nell turned Mia's face toward the dented mirror. "Look! Marvel at yourself! Doesn't that look pretty? I'd kill for your bone structure."

Mia had to admit: her cheekbones had never been so strikingly defined.

"What's it called, the thing you just did?"

"Bleeding the pigment."

"That sounds awful."

"Why do people always think bleeding sounds awful?" She shook her head. "I think it's strange to be so frightened when someone mentions blood. Blood is the most natural thing there is! In Pembuk, we have moon circles every month, where women come together and celebrate their moon cycles."

Mia's mouth dropped open. "You bleed . . . together?"

Nell laughed. "Not simultaneously. We don't all bleed onto the same blanket, Raven! But we sit and eat and talk together, honoring the elements in the physical world, and the elements in our bodies. It's a time of communion, of being proud to be a woman. Proud to be a witch."

Mia couldn't imagine it. Like everything else women did in Glas Ddir, bleeding was something to be ashamed of.

"Are all Pembuka women like you?" she asked. "Proud of who they are?"

The same shadow flitted over Nelladine's face.

"The glass kingdom is a good place for women to live. But that doesn't mean it's a good place for *all* women."

When Nell laid down her brush, Mia could feel her steering the conversation into safer waters.

"Here's the thing, Raven." She lifted Mia's chin. "Practicing magic is not so different from applying pigment. It's a way of bleeding and blending, of seeing things as more than the sum of their parts. Magic means taking what already exists and highlighting some parts, shadowing others. It's that in-between place, the balance between opposites, where true beauty resides."

She stood, stretching her long arms overhead. Mia watched her reach into the ample space between her breasts and pull out a small flask, which she placed on the table.

"Speaking of secrets: your bosom is a treasure trove of them."

Nelladine laughed her husky laugh. "Look that over while I mix the paste."

Mia tipped the flask upside down and gently tapped the bottom. A tiny scroll of parchment popped out. Then another.

"Careful," Nell called over her shoulder, scooping the contents of the second tin into a small scalloped pot. "They roll."

Mia shook out more scrolls, at least a dozen, maybe more. The parchment was worn thin, well loved—or at least well read—the words inside smudged from years of finger oils. She unfurled one scroll.

There were no words. Only symbols.

Runes.

She was struck by one rune in particular: a circle bisected by three bold lines, each with three fletchings at the end. As the lines sliced through the circle, they carved it into six identical wedges, like a stoneberry pie.

Mia felt certain she had seen the symbol before.

Nell sat down with her pot of warm paste. She began sorting through the scrolls, muttering to herself. "I think I lost one of the Fires—doesn't matter, the only one you really need is the Hex. Oh! Right. I don't know where my head is half the time, I truly don't." She dipped her fingers into the pot. "May I touch your eyes?"

"Haven't you already been doing that?"

"This time is different. A little less pigment, a little more magic. I need to hear you say it."

"Yes, Nell. You can touch my eyes."

"Good. Close them."

She began slathering paste onto Mia's eyelids, asking "Too hot?" But of course, it wasn't.

"Gorgeous, perfect," Nell said. "Now open."

Mia sucked in her breath.

The scrolls were no longer covered with symbols. The runes had become words.

Chapter 25

EXPERIMENT

THE SCROLLS TEEMED WITH words, all scribbled in large, bold handwriting.

Mia touched her eyelids. "How did you . . .?"

"Magic, obviously. Sometimes our eyes need a little help to see what's right in front of them."

Nelladine unrolled a larger version of the six-spoked symbol, setting two pots of paste on either end.

"Why don't we start here? Read those to me, the six points on the Elemental Hex."

Mia cleared her throat and began.

WIND
–Breath–

FIRE
–Eyes–

WATER
–Blood–

EARTH
–Flesh–

STONE
–Aether–

WOOD
–Bone–

She stopped halfway through. "I don't understand."

"Already?" Nell teased. "And here I thought you were bookish."

"I was taught there were four elements: Air, Water, Earth, and Fire. And why are these linked to human anatomy?"

"All books are limited in what they can teach, the books in Glas Ddir most of all. There have always been six elements, and they are all connected, a system of balances that is constantly shifting. You know magic is about the imbalance of power, yes?"

"Of course."

"But people misinterpret what that imbalance means. Magic has been around long before humans were abusing power." She flourished a hand toward the black ocean. "Wind and Water. Two of the original tyrants. You think human beings created tyranny? The elements have long warred with one another. But there *is* a system. What that means for us—the people who practice magic—is that the elements are split into three pairs. Three counterbalances. Earth and Water, Wood and Wind, Fire and Stone."

"And what is a counterbalance, exactly?"

"Magic is a response to an imbalance of power, that's true—an *external* imbalance. What people don't always talk about is how, if you want to be a good magician, you have to balance the elements *inside yourself*."

Mia pointed to the other words around the Hex. "But I don't have Wood inside myself. Or Stone. Or—"

"It's not literal, more of a resonance. Sorry, give me a second, it's been a while since I've tried to explain this." Nell wrinkled her forehead. Then she brightened. "You said you've healed someone?"

Mia nodded. "Most recently, myself."

"Gorgeous. And what do you think about when you heal yourself?"

"I . . . I'm never entirely sure what to think about. My old teacher taught me that a gifted Dujia should empty her mind."

Nell snorted. "You can't use magic without thinking! Magic is where your head and heart meet."

Mia winced. *Empty your mind*, Zaga had said as Princess Karri bled out on the snow.

"Let me put it another way," Nell said. "What images do you conjure when you heal someone?"

"When I'm healing a burn, I conjure up cold things. Snow and ice."

"Perfect, yes, that's exactly it! Your flesh is the element of Earth"—Nell tapped the easternmost point of the Hex, then drew her finger to the left, landing on the westernmost point—"and when it burns, when it blisters, you counteract it with images of frozen Water."

"Shouldn't Water and Fire be on opposing ends?"

"I didn't make the Hex, Raven. I can only tell you the way I've come to interpret it. It's not an exact science. Each element is in relationship with the other four elements on the Hex, too, not just its counterbalance."

Mia scrutinized the Hex. "Who invented it?"

"No one. It just *is*. Of course magicians tweak the Hex in their own ways. Mine was passed down to me by my grandmother. When I was younger, I had trouble controlling my magic, but it got better when I learned to balance the elements.

Take what I did to Ville. The knife cut into his flesh, Earth. The wound jolted that element out of the body's natural balance. "So I conjured up the counter element. I called up a memory of myself crouching beside a mountain stream in Pembuk, reaching down to cup sweet, cold water in my hand."

"That's such a beautiful image," Mia murmured.

"I've found the more beautiful the image, the more pleasurable the magic. The trick is to have a rich inner life. Sensual memories are best, and they're always more powerful if there's a strong feeling. Love. Loss."

Mia frowned. She wasn't exactly earning high marks in the "sensual feelings" department.

An image sprang to mind: Nanu, Dom's grandmother in Refúj. Mia had touched Nanu's chest to clear her lungs.

"Once I healed a woman who was having trouble breathing," she said. "I guess the element of Wind was out of balance? But I didn't counteract it—I thought of the same element. I remembered the wind in Ilwysion where I grew up."

"Is Ilwysion a forest, by any chance?"

Mia blinked. "How did you know?"

Nelladine tapped the Hex, triumphant. "Wood. You were thinking of Wood, you just didn't know it. Wood balances Wind."

"You're right," Mia said, astonished. "I remembered the sound of the trees whispering. I saw myself hiking with my mother to the top of a mountain, where I could see the forest so clearly."

"And if her lungs were full of fluid," Nell added, "her Water was out of balance, too. You intuitively knew to think of hiking through the forest. Of Earth. Of course, you don't always invoke the counter element, sometimes you want to make more of the same element. Once my brother had hiccoughs for a full day. Relentless! He needed more Wind element, so I conjured a glass terror, a nasty kind of windstorm we have in Pembuk. The Wind whips the sand into a cyclone and the sun gets so scorching hot, it melts the sand into glass. You never want to be caught in a glass terror."

"I had no idea any of this even existed! How have I been able to do magic at all?"

"You don't need to understand magic to practice it. But the Hex helps you practice it *well*. My hunch is you're inherently good at healing, probably a gift you inherited from someone, maybe your mother. You're just lucky it hasn't gone disastrously wrong."

Mia saw Princess Karri lying in the forest, her skin rapidly losing its color.

"Dear gods," Nell said, reading her expression. "It *has* gone disastrously wrong."

"It's all right," Mia said, even though it wasn't. "It feels like half a lifetime ago."

Nell regarded her for a moment, then tapped the center of the Hex.

"I haven't gotten to the part you asked about. You conjure up the counter element when you heal someone, but you *must bring yourself back into balance* afterward so you're not depleted. After I healed Ville, I thought of Earth. I imagined plunging my fingers into soft clay, shaping it on my wheel. I thought of a silly little doll my brother gave me made of dried mud. Such a small thing, but I carried it all the way from Pembuk, only to lose it in the Lilla Sea."

Her voice softened. "I miss that doll. It reminds me of home."

If Nell sounded sadder than usual, Mia barely noticed. Her mind was clicking and whirring. She loved that feeling more than anything, the feeling of the world snapping perfectly into place.

"So *that's* how you recovered so quickly. You called the elements back into accord! That's what I've been missing—the thing I've been doing wrong." She gestured to the other scrolls. "What are these?"

"Just my little notes on magic: things that worked before, things that didn't, and all the memories that are dear to me. You can reuse the memories, sometimes, though they tend to lose their luster after a while. I guess most things do."

"And the paste you put over my eyes?"

"We call it Jouma's Brew, after my grandmother. She cooked it up. When you slather the paste onto someone else's eyes, they see what you see. Very helpful when your grandmother wants to show you how naughty you've been from her point of view."

She nodded toward the silver tin. "The recipe is simple. Grind magical gemstones into powder, then heat them until they turn to paste. A little Stone, a little Fire." Nell tapped the mysterious sixth branch of the Hex, the only one they hadn't discussed. "It opens the eyes with the help of the aether."

"I was going to ask about aether. That's not something I've seen on any anatomical plate."

"It's the trickiest of the bunch. I'll be honest, I don't fully understand it. Some say aether is soul or spirit, the fiery life force that binds us all together. Others say it's the mind. Magicians who work in the aether often work with Stone. They use the stones to manipulate memories, dreams, and desires."

That explained how Angelyne was able to enthrall people with the moonstone. She could shift what their eyes saw—and what their hearts believed.

"Can you counterbalance the magic in a stone?"

"Of course. You can counterbalance almost anything."

Mia bristled with excitement. This was the answer, the way to neutralize the lloira's dark magic. Her mother was a gifted Dujia; she would counter the elements to sap the moonstone of its power.

And if for some reason her mother couldn't do it, Mia would learn herself.

Hope soared inside her chest.

She could save Quin.

"Can you teach me how to balance the elements?"

"I can teach you some things, but really it just requires practice. The relationship between counter elements is complicated. I guess it's more of an art? I'm sorry, I can tell that disappoints you."

"It's true. I'm always trying to quantify magic. I want there to be a system, a methodology. If something can be systematized, it can be controlled."

A smile played at the corners of Nell's mouth. "That isn't how magic works, sad to say. It's about thoughts and fears and longings and subtle shifts in a person's mind and body. Really it's about the messiest and most indecipherable parts of a human heart."

She waved a hand at the scattered papers. "These memories are precious to me, but they wouldn't work for anyone else. You have to draw on your own memories, your own internal truths. You have to be aware of your own body, your own heart, at all times. But you also must be *attuned to other people*. That's the most important thing, Raven, if I can teach you anything it's this: you cannot privilege the sensations or desires of your own body, your own heart, over that of others. You must only touch them if that is what they truly want."

"Which is why you made Ville give you permission. Then me."

"Yes. I do not use magic on anyone without their knowledge and consent, no matter how good my intentions." She threw back her shoulders. "Magic is not yours to control. But it is always, *always* your choice how you use it."

Nell tugged on one of her braids, thoughtful. "You should also know there are certain things you cannot counterbalance. You can't bring a person back once they're gone."

Mia shifted in the chair. She wasn't sure that was true. She caught Nelladine's eyes, and for a moment, she felt certain Nell was inviting her to disagree.

Could she summon the courage to tell Nell the truth?

"You also can't create life out of nothing." Nell poked one of the runes, and the paper curled around her fingertip. "No magician has ever put a baby in someone's belly."

"Are we talking about babies?" Ville strode into the galley, Zai trailing a few steps behind. "Love babies."

Nell groaned. "Don't even start, Vi."

He held up his hands in mock surrender. "I know better than to discuss such a delicate matter with two women. Though, Nelladine, as I've said on many occasions: you do have the most magnificent childbearing hips."

It was sometimes hard to tell if Ville was paying a compliment or lobbing an insult. Mia waited to see if Nell would object, but she looked quietly resigned. Every time Nelladine began to show vulnerability, she sealed it off once Ville came around.

"Anyone thirsty? I could do with a pint right about now." He sat beside Mia on the bench and kicked his feet up on the table. "What have you two been up to, anyway? Working your feminine wiles?"

"Nell's been teaching me things about magic I never knew I never knew."

"Sounds fun. Why don't you try some out on me? I do love a good experiment."

Mia looked hopefully at Nell. She had an insatiable urge to test out what she'd learned, to move her understanding from theory into practice.

Nell shrugged. "Fine with me."

Zai frowned. "I don't think we—"

"No buts!" Ville cried. He tipped an imaginary hat and winked at Mia. "A gentleman never says no to magic."

He really should have said no.

Chapter 26

BREAK YOU

IN THE BEGINNING, EVERYTHING was fine.

"I'm going to give you hiccoughs," Mia said.

Ville turned to Nell, pretending to be aghast. "Good Græÿa, you wicked demoness! You've taught your pupil the darkest of all dark magic."

Nelladine rolled her eyes. "Pay no attention to him, Raven, hiccoughs are an excellent choice for a first lesson."

"I don't approve of this." Zai leaned against a reinsdyr pelt in the corner, arms folded across his broad chest. "Not that anyone asked."

"Live a little!" Ville rubbed his hands together and winked at Mia. "Do your worst."

She put one hand on the top of his abdomen and the other gingerly on his throat.

Nell coughed, then looked pointedly at Mia.

"Oh, I thought he already . . ." She looked into Ville's eyes. "May I touch you?"

He grinned. "By all means."

"Wind," Nelladine instructed. "That's the element you want to counter, Raven. To bring it out of balance, you're conjuring Wood. Imagine chopping the breath into smaller segments, like breaking a stick into pieces, or hacking firewood with an ax. You want to fragment the Wind as it flows from his belly to his mouth. Does that make sense?"

"Yes, thank you," said Mia. She didn't want to correct her new teacher, but Nell had the anatomy wrong: hiccoughs were involuntary contractions of the diaphragm, the dome of tendon and muscle attaching the thorax and abdomen, not the belly itself. When the diaphragm contracted, so, too, did the larynx. The air didn't flow into the mouth; rather, it rushed into the lungs. That's what caused the *hic* sound.

Mia felt a flush of pride. Even if she hadn't mastered the Elemental Hex, she knew a thing or two about human anatomy. She could whip up a batch of hiccoughs in no time.

She pressed a palm to Ville's lower ribs, visualizing the diaphragm drawing air into the lungs. Then she imagined the trees of Ilwysion where she grew up. She saw herself as a girl, peeling long strips of bark from the brown oaks and white birches, snapping them into smaller and smaller pieces, then planting them in the ground like seeds.

Even as a child, she had longed to escape Glas Ddir. She'd pretended the bark would grow into trees that would be made into ships that would carry her far, far away. An illogical fantasy, yes, but a powerful one.

Ville's chest seized. They all looked at him, expectant.

"You're a wit*chic*!" he crowed, pumping his fist into the air. "Angel of the Ash*hic*es strikes again!"

As the others laughed, Mia shimmered in silent triumph. When Nelladine leaned in to say, "Beautifully done, Raven, you're a natural," her chest swelled with pride. She'd missed being praised by a teacher.

Was that really all it took? A childhood memory or two? Her heart thrummed with hope. So what if she couldn't feel anything in her body? Her mind was perfectly capable of evoking the *memory* of sensations, even if she could no longer feel them.

She closed her eyes and kept her hands on Ville's chest, dredging more from the memory. She saw the tallest trees of Ilwysion being felled by large burly men. She summoned shipbuilders hacking the timber into logs, logs into planks. It was all so vivid, so real, as if the men were right beside her, laying the planks side by side, building ships, every knot and splinter tossed by the waves until the ship finally landed in a bustling port town in a distant kingdom, ale slung from the hips of strong women, mud soft under the mariners' boots as they stumbled onto—

"Raven?" Nell's voice was sharp, urgent. "*Raven!*"

The ship vanished as the world snapped back into focus.

Mia's hands were still on Ville's stomach, his shirt blooming red beneath her fingers.

He was coughing up blood.

"Get back," Nell said, shoving her aside. Mia couldn't believe what she was seeing. Ville's ribs had ruptured his skin. The bones were expanding as she watched, ripping through tissue and stomach fat. They were cracking, splintering from their own untempered growth, like a birdcage lifting from his chest.

Mia staggered back, trembling.

"It's all right, Vi," Nell said, even as her voice shook. The composure she'd shown healing his earlier wound was gone. *"A gale, a tempest. A tempest, a gale."*

But Ville's ribs continued to expand. He was drifting out of consciousness, blood sleeping through his shirt.

"The wind caresses the trees," Nell whispered. An incantation. *"The breath caresses the bones. Wind kisses, breath heals."*

In a panic, Mia began shuffling through the scrolls. If she could just find the right one, some powerful Wind memory to counterbalance Wood, she could hand it to Nell.

But as she touched the papers, they curled and smoldered.

"No, no, no," Mia cried, trying to save the scrolls. Every time her fingers grazed a piece of parchment, it ignited.

"Please," Nell begged, her voice breaking. "Please stop." She couldn't save her papers, because she couldn't leave Ville. She cradled him in her arms, blowing cool air onto his broken chest.

It was working. Mia watched as Ville's solar plexus began to deflate. Nelladine mended his ribs, shrinking them back beneath his skin, then patching up the puncture wounds. Sweat beaded on her forehead, her shoulders bowed from exhaustion. She was clearly so focused on saving Ville she wasn't balancing the elements inside herself.

Mia couldn't look at them. If she did, her guilt would devour her. Instead she looked at the table where Nell had lovingly unfurled her scrolls.

Every note, every paper, every memory had burned to ash.

Minutes later, Ville stood on deck in his bloodstained shirt, inches away from Zai. All his playfulness had evaporated the minute he saw the red holes where his ribs had pierced the linen.

"She has to leave," he said. "Immediately."

"She didn't mean to hurt you," Zai said quietly. "She doesn't know the extent of her own magic."

Nell's eyes were bright with tears. "It doesn't matter whether she means to or not, Zai, don't you see?"

"She won't do it again." Zai turned to her. "Will you, Raven?"

Mia was speechless. She couldn't find the words.

Ville grunted. "Very reassuring. Maybe we should push you overboard so you can murder the fish instead?"

"You are a guest on my boat," Zai said tersely, "as is Raven. My guests will respect each other."

"Are you that dense, Zai? Did you not see what she just did?" Ville flourished his arm toward the galley. "She didn't just make the ribs pop out of my chest. She set fire to paper! Paper is wood, my friend. She's a 'guest' on your very wooden, very flammable boat. Are you trying to get yourself killed?"

"It was an accident," Mia said, her voice a whisper.

"I'd rather cut off my own hand," Ville growled, "than stay within spitting distance of you."

Zai's face hardened. "Then leave. Get off my boat."

How had everything changed so quickly? Half an hour ago, they were all enjoying each other's company. Now the tension in the air was so thick Mia could slice it into wedges and serve them on a plate.

"I'm not the problem here," Ville said. "I'm only trying to help. But you never accept help, do you? The Great Zai needs help from no man."

"I said get out."

Hurt shone in Ville's eyes. "I was already leaving." He beckoned to Nell. "Come on, Nelladine. I can tell when we're not wanted."

He stomped off down the deck, pitching himself over the side and landing with a hard smack in the canoe.

Nell hesitated. She stared into Mia's eyes, searching, perhaps for some kind of explanation. Mia wanted to tell her, to apologize for everything. But where would she even begin?

"I don't understand why you couldn't feel it," Nell said softly. "Why couldn't you feel that you were hurting him?"

The truth singed Mia's tongue. The problem with feeling nothing was that you didn't feel anything. She couldn't feel Ville's pain because she couldn't feel her own.

"What is it you're not telling me?" Nell pleaded. "I am trying to help you, Raven. I want so much to help you. But you almost killed my friend."

Mia should have felt something. But she only felt exhaustion. She was too tired to lie.

"I can't feel anything," she said.

"What do you mean, you . . ." Nell stopped. "Is that what happened in the disrobing chamber? Why you couldn't feel your hands in the ice tub? Or do you mean *here*?" Nell thumped her own heart. "You can't feel anything inside?"

The numbness enveloped Mia like a shroud. She struggled to pluck a single word out of the haze.

"Everywhere," she said.

Nelladine's face was a patchwork of shock and compassion, sympathy and fear. For a moment Mia thought Nell might pull her close, stroke her hair, and tell her things would be all right. Mia had just confessed her biggest secret, and if it was true that secrets made a person real, then she was more real than ever.

"People say I feel too much," Nell said slowly. "But I can't imagine living any other way. Who's to tell me my lows are too low or my highs are too high? Isn't that what it is to be alive?" She took a breath. "The one thing that truly scares me is being numb to it all. I think I'd rather be dead than feel nothing."

Nelladine's face was changing. A new emotion burned in her deep brown eyes, so fierce and pure it blotted out all the rest.

Horror.

In an instant, Mia's worst fears were confirmed. She was broken. Defective. Dangerous. When she crawled out of the wooden box in the forest, she'd left some vital part of herself behind. Not just her magic or her senses. The part that made her human.

"That's why you're looking for your mother, isn't it?" Nell took a step back. "You're not trying to help someone back in Glas Ddir. You're trying to help yourself."

"No." Mia shook her head vehemently. "This has nothing to do with me. You told me stones can manipulate the aether, and you're right. I've seen it. There's one stone that's being used to kill and hurt thousands of Glasddirans. But in the past the same stone was used to heal people, and I think if my mother can bring the magic back into balance—"

"I don't buy it, Raven." Nell's voice was deadly sharp. "I don't think you do, either. It's time you start being honest with yourself. You think your mother can unbreak you, and you've dragged us along for the ride."

Nelladinellakin stood tall.

"I know I said secrets make us real. But you should have told us the truth. This whole trip has been one grand experiment, a way for you to feel something again, and you don't care who gets hurt along the way."

The words landed like an arrow in Mia's chest. She was too stunned to argue. She watched, helpless, as Nelladine turned to Zai. Gently Nell pressed a hand to his cheek.

"Zai K'aliloa. Come home with us. It's not too late."

A part of Mia felt terrified Zai would turn the boat around.

But another part of her hoped he would listen. She was murderous, unpredictable. She'd become the worst kind of scientific variable: uncontained.

Zai peeled Nell's hand off his face.

"No more magic, Nelladine. Not tonight."

It took Mia a moment to understand what had just happened. Nell wanted Zai to come back home—for his own protection, no doubt. But she'd used magic . . . and she hadn't asked permission.

"Wait," Mia stammered, "I thought you said—"

"What I said," Nell snapped, "was that you have to adapt. We break our own rules all the time, especially when we're trying to survive, trying to protect the people we love. *That's* what makes us human."

She tossed her long braids over her shoulder, the moonlight drenching her ebony skin in a soft, silvery glow.

"But if you can't control your own gifts, you'll only hurt other people. You have to learn the rules before you can break them. Because I promise you, Raven: if you don't learn how to break the rules of magic the good way, the *right* way, it's only a matter of time before they break you."

Chapter 27

NOT A NORMAL GIRL

MIA COULDN'T SLEEP. SHE tossed on the thin cot, heavy with regret. Every time she shut her eyes, she saw bones growing where they shouldn't, ribs ripping through flesh.

Ville's face blurred into Karri's, then Karri's into Quin's. Mia wanted so desperately to earn high marks in magic, but she was failing every test. At least when she'd first bloomed, she'd had the power to heal. Now she only knew how to wound and destroy.

As the boat carved a path through the waves, it was not lost on her that she was traveling farther and farther from the boy she'd sworn to save.

It's time you start being honest with yourself. You think your mother can unbreak you.

The words echoed in Mia's mind. Was it such a crime to want to feel something? Nell herself had said she'd rather be dead than numb. Mia hated that she'd opened herself up completely, only to be rejected.

Who needed friends, anyway?

Nell was wrong. Mia had charted a course for Valavïk so she could go back and save Quin. But along the way . . . if her mother could show her how to coax the sensations back . . . what was the harm in asking?

Mia kicked the sheets off the cot. To hells with sleeping. Even if she did manage to nod off, nothing awaited her but the wooden box.

She could see Zai out on deck, leaning into the railing and staring up at the sky. Should she go talk to him? The idea flooded her with shame, but the alternative was to be alone with her thoughts, which flooded her with despair. A delightful duet.

Her eyes swept the galley, snagging on a small silver tin. *Jouma's Brew*. In Nelladine's hurry to get off the boat, she had left it behind.

Mia swept her hand along the stone slab and palmed the tin. Half empty. Or half full, depending.

She dropped the brew into her pocket. You just never knew when you might need someone to come around to your point of view.

By the time she joined Zai, he had his eyes on the curling black sea. Mia felt a pang. He'd stood up for her, argued that she should stay on the boat—and perhaps lost his two closest friends because of it. Considering her inability to mitigate her own magic, he could lose a lot more than that.

Mia kept her distance. Her voice was quiet against the low hum and rumble of the waves.

"Nell was right. It isn't safe for you to take me to Valavïk."

Zai turned, studying her for a moment. He nodded to the empty ocean.

"See anyone else you'd like to hire for the job?"

He made a decent point. Mia couldn't exactly paddle water while she waited for another ship to pass.

She took a breath. "I will confine myself to the galley for the rest of the journey. Once we arrive at the palace, I ask that you depart immediately. You'll have done your duty, and I will no longer be your burden to carry."

Zai was quiet a moment. Then he tipped his head toward the sky.

"Have you ever seen the Ribbons? I doubt you have. Glas Ddir is too far north. Here in Luum'Addi on very clear nights, the Ribbons light up the sky."

All she saw was a sheath of dark purple—a calm, starless night.

"I don't see anything."

"You will. The conditions are perfect tonight." He smiled. "We just have to wait."

Mia tried to smile back, but she couldn't quite get it right. Sometimes she wondered how no one else could see the cloak around her shoulders. The numbness had begun to feel like a part of her, as if the guilt and sadness had seeped into her flesh, bled into the marrow of her bones.

"You can come a little closer," said Zai. "I know you're being careful. But it's all right."

She took the tiniest step forward so as not to offend him.

"Are the Ribbons the same as the Illuminations?"

"No. The Ribbons have been lighting the sky for thousands of years. The Illuminations are a human invention, fueled by fyre ice."

"They were all anyone talked about in White Lagoon."

"That's because we haven't had them in so long. Of course the new fyre ice will be used to do much more than entertain people—the festival display is just a small sample of their potential. But for people my age, this is the first time we'll get to see the Illuminations."

He folded his arms, then unfolded them. "Can I tell you a secret?"

"According to Nell, secrets are what make us real."

"Yes, that's one of her favorites. She's always saying things that get me thinking. Even if half the time she goes and contradicts herself." Zai smiled. "I guess we all do that."

"I like her. And I'm sorry she left. I seem to drive people away."

"Not me. I'm still here."

She came an inch closer, still leaving plenty of space between them. "Are you going to tell me your secret?"

He shifted his weight. "Sometimes I'm not sure fyre ice is the magic elixir everyone says it is."

"Really?" Mia said, surprised. "You seem like a pure devotee."

"You asked Ville how fyre ice could be a self-replenishing resource. I've asked him the same thing. He always avoids the question or tells me I wouldn't understand. But I hear whispers. Not everyone thinks the new pits are such a good thing. Especially among the Addi."

"And you?"

"Me? I have a foot in both worlds, I guess."

"But didn't you tell me the Grand Fyremaster is using fyre ice to right a lot of prior wrongs? I thought he was trying to make reparations for all the ways the Luumi have hurt the Addi."

"I'm sure he intends to. But with every advancement, there is always a cost. The colonizers thought they were 'helping' the Addi, too. Bringing civilization to an uncivilized land." Zai shook his head. "It's remarkable how often the word *civilize* has been used in place of *oppress*."

He sighed. "I don't want to talk about it anymore. Not tonight."

Mia nodded. When he looked skyward, she did too.

"There's something special about the Ribbons," he said. "In Kom'Addi my family would hike several hours into the heartlands to get away from all the noise and lights. We'd lay out blankets and lie on our backs. Sometimes we waited for hours in the freezing cold. But it was worth it. When I see the Ribbons, I feel like the sky has picked up a paintbrush."

Zai's face took on a warm, ruddy glow.

"My Addi ancestors told each other stories to explain the celestial bodies they saw above. They believed the sun was a vengeful god and the stars were his children. He scattered them through the sky once he grew tired of them."

"You never hear stories of jolly gods, do you?" said Mia. "It's all rage and revenge. If these beings created the world, you'd think they might slug back an ethereal ale every once in a while. Pat themselves on the back and celebrate."

"It's easier to dwell on the mistakes you've made than the good things you've created."

He shot her a sideways glance. Was he talking about her?

"I'm sorry, Zai. About Ville. I really am."

Zai shook his head. "Ville asked you to do magic. He's always tempting fate."

"Do you believe in fate?"

His eyes met hers. Soft, inscrutable.

"I do."

When he beckoned, she took a full step in his direction, then stopped. She could see hints of lines around his eyes, perhaps from all his hours in the sun. They lent his face an air of wisdom, as if he knew things Mia hadn't yet discovered.

Zai was beautiful. She couldn't deny it. His hair had come loose from its leather band, a few black wisps framing his face. She had a fierce urge to smooth them.

Instead, she stayed rooted in place. Nell's words haunted her. *You don't care who gets hurt.*

Zai peered up into the darkness. "They say the sun god's children were lonely all spread out across the sky."

Mia nodded. She knew what that was like.

"So they called out, seeking comfort. The Ribbons are how they speak to one another."

Silence. Then Zai touched the railing by his side.

"It's all right, Raven. You won't hurt me. I'm not afraid of your magic, even if you are."

The cloak tightened its grip around Mia's shoulders. She was desperate to feel something—*anything*—besides the endless numb.

Slowly, carefully, Mia walked to the space he'd made for her.

They stood side by side. Mia checked the sky for Ribbons. It was still dark. Still purple.

"I don't know what I'm—"

"Look," he said.

The sky rippled with light.

In an instant, the Ribbons unfurled. They appeared out of nowhere, long jagged strips of lime green and blushing pink. They snaked into lines, curving one way, then the other, some bursting into wider swaths of color. The Ribbons moved like liquid, flowing and flickering, gleaming streams of brightness poured out onto the night.

Mia's eyes filled with unexpected tears. She had felt alone for such a long time. Shipwrecked and broken on an empty shore, no one to comfort her, no one to whisper she would be all right. How strange that green light ribboning through a night sky could make her feel less alone.

The guilt and sadness roiling inside her were replaced by something else: wonder. Mia had never believed in myths. She found no comfort in the idea of all-seeing, all-knowing creatures rolling the dice of destiny. But as she stood beneath the moving, breathing sky, she wondered if there *were* a divine being, a wry old woman in a rocking chair, throwing the Ribbons with a flick of her wrist, like a ball of celestial yarn.

The sky was whispering, speaking. Speaking to *her*.

Deep in her chest, something frozen began to thaw.

For the first time in months, she was grateful to be alive.

"Beautiful, isn't it?" Zai's voice was a quiet hush as he slid his hand closer to hers on the railing.

"Yes," she said, terrified by his closeness—and wanting so much to feel his skin against hers.

"Zai," she whispered. "May I touch you?"

"Yes."

She reached out and laid her fingers over his, lacing them between the cracks.

Then his arms were around her, one hand on the scoop of her lower back, the other cradling the nape of her neck as he pressed her against the railing. His lips found hers, his mouth on her mouth, a kiss that was both question and exclamation mark.

"Raven," he whispered into her hair. He kissed the corner of her mouth.

She wanted to inhale him, breathe him in. She imagined the scent of wood dust on his skin, the tang of tart apple on his lips.

But he was scentless, tasteless.

We shouldn't do this.

The words echoed through her mind. Unsayable.

Something was wrong. Or rather, something wasn't right. Her

breath locked up, lodged in her throat. His mouth moved against hers like wet sand.

His caresses, his touch—she wanted desperately to want them. Hadn't she been admiring him quietly ever since they'd met? The soft swell of his biceps; the smooth, easy rhythm of his hands. He was here, and he wanted her, and he was beautiful.

But her body was numb. Rigid.

She didn't know what she wanted. But she didn't want this.

He brushed the hair off her neck.

"Zai," she whispered. "This isn't the right time."

Immediately she felt him slacken. He pulled back, his eyes seeking hers.

"Oh no," he said. "I'm sorry. I thought . . . I didn't realize . . ." He fumbled for the words. "I'm sorry, Raven. I misunderstood, I misread everything."

He stepped back. She was relieved she could breathe again, but then the air clotted in the space he'd left behind. An acrid shame coiled down her throat. She heard Ville's words: *If you write messages on your body, you should know boys are going to read them.*

What about the messages she'd written *with* her body? Holding Zai's hand? Wanting to be near him? And perhaps most of all: kissing him back?

Had he misread, or had she miswritten?

What did she even want?

Mia saw the stricken look on Zai's face. She hadn't told him about the cloak, her broken body, the emptiness yawning inside her. How was he supposed to know she was not a normal girl?

245

"It isn't you," she said, the words tumbling out. "You didn't do anything wrong. It's just I'm . . . I can't . . ." She choked back tears. "There's something wrong with me."

She wanted to make herself disappear. For a moment she thought of pitching herself overboard. The wall of salt water pressing at her eyes might drown her anyway.

"I'm sorry," she said, backing away. "I'm so sorry."

She fled into the galley, where she stayed until Valavïk Bay.

Chapter 28

PLUNGED

THE PORT WAS LIKE any other. Filthy. Swarming. Alive.

As Mia stepped onto the dock, her patellae trembled, her knees unaccustomed to the solidity of land.

To Zai's credit, he had respected her need for solitude. They'd spent the last few days in silence, moving around each other the way the wind parted around the boat. She sensed him being careful with her, delicate.

"Have you ever seen a glacier?"

Zai's voice was hoarse after days of silence. As he secured the boat to the quay, he nodded toward the snowy mass in the distance. The glacier reminded Mia of a giant iced cake nestled between mountains. Deep fissures snaked down the front side, splitting the ice into long jagged fingers.

"No," she said. "I haven't."

"It melts a little more each year. That's what glaciers do. But they say one of these days it'll melt entirely, and then all hells will break loose."

Zai hoisted a coil of rope onto his shoulders. Once again she found herself admiring the breadth of his shoulders, the corded muscles in his neck.

Mia was embarrassed and confused. But mostly angry.

Not at Zai. Angry at herself.

If there was one thing magic had given her, it was the ability to trust her own instincts. But this, too, had been stripped away. She could no longer trust her eyes: she had seen her mother when her mother wasn't there. She could no longer trust her hands: her magic had hurt innocent people. She could no longer trust her heart: she'd thought she wanted Zai, but the moment she had him, her desire warped into something she didn't recognize.

She couldn't feel her body. She couldn't know her mind. And without these things, without the ability to trust the most basic aspects of herself, what was left?

"I have to do one thing," Zai said. "Will you wait here?"

She nodded, careful to step aside as he brushed past. He disappeared down the pier.

The memory of Zai's kiss stung. Mia tried to banish it to the far corners of her mind, but it kept oozing back. She closed her eyes. The second she did, she was back in the wooden box. Her eyes flew open.

For the first time she understood something. The cloak was just the box in another form. It was always there, siphoning off every modicum of life and joy and happiness, pulling her back into the darkness. She carried the box with her, *around* her, always.

After what happened on the boat, first with Nell and Ville, then with Zai, Mia felt emptier than ever. At least, once she found her mother, she would no longer be alone. Wynna had stopped her own heart and awoken from the dead. If she had managed to resurrect herself—to find a path back to a life worth living—then maybe she could help her eldest daughter do the same.

Nell was right. Beneath all her clamoring efforts to destroy the moonstone and save Quin, she had come to the queen's palace for a selfish reason.

She wanted to feel again.

Mia stared out at the smooth silver waters of Valavïk Bay. One of the queen's ships had just left the wharf, its sail draped in Jyöltide mauve and silver. If Mia squinted, she could make out a short dark-haired boy on deck, leaning over the railing. The weak sunlight kissed his head and turned his hair a bluish gold. Even from a distance, she could tell he was the sort of boy who wore his confidence like a second skin.

When the seaman lifted his chin, Mia recognized something in the gesture. It wasn't a boy at all. She was staring at a girl—proud shoulders, black hair cropped short at the chin. Addi, or maybe Fojuen. Not much older than Mia and out to sail the seas. Why not? Anything was possible in a queendom, where a woman sat on the throne.

Jealousy flamed in Mia's chest. There was the life she'd wanted, an explorer charting a course between the four kingdoms. Tasting new foods and inhaling new scents, meeting people from different cultures, reveling in the beauty of a rich and vibrant world.

As the boat slipped out of the harbor, she felt her dream slip away with it. Every taste, every scent, every moment of that wild and wondrous freedom had vanished.

"Good news," Zai called, hurrying down the dock. "I asked around to see if anyone remembers your mother. Turns out, *everyone* does."

Mia willed her bones quiet, even as the blood glittered in her veins.

"Where is she?"

"The palace. They say she's with the queen." Zai straightened. "I'd like to take you there, Raven. If you'll let me. After that you can be rid of me for good."

She hadn't looked him in the eye since the night of the Ribbons. The memory was too painful. She harbored no anger toward him—he'd done nothing wrong, and he'd stopped when she asked him to. It was her own shame that festered inside her, like a wound she did not know how to treat.

"Very well," she said. "To the queen."

They didn't wait long to be admitted. Mia couldn't believe how easily she and Zai were ushered in to the palace. They could have been spies, poisoners, foes—though she supposed it helped that they carried no weapons. When the blond guardswomen asked them to shake out their boots, all that clattered onto the ground were nubs of gravel.

Mia hardly noticed her surroundings as the two guards accompanied them through the spacious corridors, other than a fleeting observation that the dazzling marble was whiter than a bone scrubbed clean. Her excitement mingled with her disbelief. After all this time, she was finally about to see her mother. Her mother, who for unknown reasons had travelled to Valavïk to visit the Snow Queen.

"You're sure my mother is *here*?" she murmured to Zai.

"She's here," answered the bigger guardswoman. "You'll wait on the balcony at her request."

Mia felt a flash of irritation and a flush of hope—irritation at the guard for eavesdropping, hope that her mother was just a few winding corridors away.

Her mother, who had been dead for three years.

Her mother, who was alive.

Her mother, who had lied, enthralled, betrayed, and abandoned—and who had loved Mia with her whole heart, protected both her daughters, and tried to teach them compassion and gentleness in a world carved of bigotry and hate.

"This way," said the guard, ushering them up a spiral staircase and through two glass doors onto a balcony. In the sky overhead, the sun cowered beneath a dark blue veil.

"Stay," the other guard commanded, turning on her heel.

Seconds later, Mia and Zai were alone.

"I can't do it," she said suddenly, the words rushing out. "This was a mistake."

"You've made it this far—you can't turn back now."

"She never came home. She clearly doesn't want to see me. If she did, she wouldn't have spent the last three years pretending to be dead."

Mia hadn't said any of these things aloud; she'd barely dared to think them. Now the words clung to the air, taking on more weight.

"People don't always do the things we think they should," Zai said. "But they often have good reasons. Even if those reasons are ones we'll never understand."

His gaze was steady. "She loves you, Mia. We always hurt the ones we love the most."

Her eyes locked onto his.

"What did you just say?"

"I said she loves you. We always—"

"You said Mia." The blood echoed in her ears. "I never gave you that name."

Zai watched her, his expression blank. The silence clogged the air like smoke, until Mia was choking on everything his mouth didn't say, and everything his eyes did.

Then it no longer mattered, because her mother swept onto the balcony.

Her mother.

Luminous red hair pinned in the Luumi style, woven into interlocking plaits. A heavy snow fox cloak draped over her shoulders. Older, but somehow younger, too. Wide hazel eyes.

Alive, alive, alive.

Mia's thoughts splintered into pieces.

Mother.

The whisper never left her throat. Her heart was tangled up inside the word, a bloody, broken sob.

Mother.

But it wasn't right; something was off. She was looking straight at Mia, but her eyes were cold, distant, the life sapped out of them.

"Mother?"

Mia took a tentative step forward, frightened by the deadness in her mother's face.

"My red raven. You've come at last."

Mia wanted to receive her mother's words, to be bathed in their gentleness. But the vowels were hollow, the consonants stripped of warmth. They didn't close the space between them. If anything, they emphasized it.

"I've missed you," Mia said, hating how small she sounded, how young.

Her mother exhaled, so long and deep Mia wondered if she'd been holding her breath for three years. Surely this would break the spell. Her face would ease into the smile Mia knew so well, her hazel eyes dewed with happy tears. Wynna had always possessed a natural warmth that drew people to her, an effervescence of spirit and an ease in body that had embarrassed Mia as a girl— and that she now longed to emulate.

Mia needed that warmth. But when she looked into her mother's eyes, they were dark. Wooden.

"Thank you, Zai." Her mother clasped her hands together. "You have done exactly as I asked."

The world slipped through Mia's fingertips.

Zai knew her mother.

He'd done exactly as she asked.

Awareness landed with a dull thud. She was not charting her destiny, plotting her own course as she'd imagined. She had not brought Zai here.

He'd brought her.

Mia staggered toward the balcony—to fling herself off the ledge or to vomit, she wasn't sure.

"Take her to my chambers," Wynna said. "I'll tend to her there."

They were too late. Mia's knees buckled beneath her. Her body stayed on the balcony, but her mind plunged into the dark.

11 DAYS TILL THE WEEPING MOON

My silent sister,

Do my stories bore you? Perhaps you are not listening as closely as you should. Any storyteller who does not tell another, deeper story beneath the words has failed.

I assure you, I have not failed.

The quiet boy was the middle child. As is often the case with middle children, he sank into the unseen space between.

They were a gifted family; magic was the air they breathed. But the boy possessed none himself. He was more human than witch. For many years he resented it. Then, as his siblings twisted into strange, unnatural shapes, he began to feel proud of his humanness. He wanted to know his father, the man who had made him.

Over and over, the quiet boy pleaded with

his mother to tell him about his father. "Was he handsome? Was he strong? Is he still alive?"

Her answer was always the same: "Your father was not a good man." And that was that.

So the quiet boy resolved to find out on his own.

When his older sister crept into the village at night to sate her hunger, he followed her. He peeked into the houses while the men slept, trying to find a face he recognized, a face like his own.

And finally, after months of searching, he found him. The quiet boy sat beside the bed in silent reverence until his father stirred. One look at the quiet boy and the man knew exactly who he was.

"Do you have magic?" his father said.

"No," said the boy proudly. "I'm not like the others."

"I have three human children already. You are of no use to me unless you can do things they cannot."

The quiet boy's heart was broken. But he did not abandon hope. He returned to the ice kabma and watched his siblings—the way they plied their magic, bent the elements to their will. Bit by bit, he learned to pilfer the remnants they left behind.

When he returned to his father's house, he could commandeer magic that did not belong to him. He had the power to melt sand to glass, turn certain kinds of stones into a weapon or a gift.

His father's eyes gleamed. "You will make me a fortune," he said, pulling a pair of shackles from behind his back.

But as the shackles snapped around the quiet boy's wrists, something strange happened. He felt his arms soften into wings. His fingers were now gray feathers, velvety and thick, the tips alight with silver flames. As he rose above his father, the plumes licked the wooden walls, and the boy watched while both the house and the man inside it smoldered down to cinder.

The quiet boy flew home and bragged to his siblings that he was now the most powerful of all.

But because he had stolen magic from the others, his hands were stolen from him.

The Silver Sorcerer is the Fourth Soul of Jyöl. He follows on the heels of the other Souls, spooning up the scraps of magic they leave behind. In the olden days, he would leave every child a gift on the last night of Jyöltide. The good child wakes to a small glass bird on her pillow. The bad child wakes to a thin glass feather in her heart.

Perhaps a story is both a weapon and a gift.

Perhaps, as you will see, the two are not so different.

Ever yours,
Angelyne

Chapter 29

MORE DEATH

THE SNOW WOLF WAS the best kind of assassin. Silent. Invisible. Lurking in the shadows, waiting to slit his victim's throat.

Pilar could respect a man like that. She just couldn't *find* him.

"Drink?" said the woman behind the bar, as Pilar plunked herself down on a wooden stool. The barmaid was thick hipped and quick fingered, with weathered brown skin and lines of icy blue ink flowing up both arms. More of a bar matron, really. She wore the Addi red cloak.

"No drink," Pilar said. "I'm looking for someone."

"This isn't generally a place people come to. It's a place people leave."

Pilar stifled a groan. She'd heard this, or some version of it, everywhere.

Kom'Addi wasn't a village—at least not in the way she'd originally thought. It was a cluster of connected villages filled with Addi reinsdyr herders. For the past three days, Pilar had dragged herself from one community to the next, always clutching her carved frostflower. But the rune hadn't revealed a path to her father, and when she showed it to people in Kom'Addi, they looked at her like a common thief.

So she'd tried more traditional methods. She sat in taverns and alehouses. Talked. Listened. Plied patrons with spirits to loosen their tongues.

No one knew anything about the Snow Wolf. Most people had never heard of him, and those who knew the name had no idea where he was. Pilar had come to understand that the Illuminations, the Jyöltide festival, the Wolf standing on the steps of the queen's palace—none of it held any interest to the Addi. "Those are just Luumi tricks," one boy had told her. "If you want to see magic, go outside and look up at the Ribbons."

Instead of helpful information about the Snow Wolf, Pilar was learning an awful lot about reinsdyr. She learned herders were moving their herds inside fences to protect them from predators (silver lynxes and ice leopards in winter, scarlet bears in summer). She learned how angry people were that a Land Council in faraway Valavïk had accused one Addi herder of overgrazing, demanding that she slaughter forty-one of her one hundred beasts.

"You can't survive with a herd of fifty-nine," a man with a kind face had confided at the last tavern. "She has children to feed."

When Pilar asked if the family would starve, he'd shaken his head. "We won't let them. Kom'Addi is a community, and we act like one. This isn't the first time some fool from Valavïk has tried to interfere with our livelihood. The Council is the newest chord in an old song."

"Did Queen Freyja create the Council?"

"No, her uncle. Isn't that lucky? When he isn't busy 'saving' all of Luum'Addi with his magic ice, he still has time to meddle in Addi affairs."

The Addi never said Luumia. When they spoke of the snow kingdom, it was always Luum'Addi.

Pilar had noticed something else over her three days in Kom'Addi: there was no fyre ice in sight.

"Who is it you're looking for?" said the bar matron, polishing a glass. "I know all the thirsty souls who come around, so I might be of use. Though I'll also say we've had quite a few foreign visitors lately. Very unusual for us."

Pilar slid her frostflower across the bar. "Does that mean anything to you?"

The woman cocked a brow. "What are you doing with a rune like this? You're not Addi. None of my business, but your coloring is Fojuen, if I had to guess. Maybe half Glasddiran."

"I am *not* a river rat. I'm half Luumi."

"You sure?" The bar matron tapped the bone carving. "If you were, this rune would have led you home."

Pilar swiped the frostflower off the bar. She didn't feel like defending her parentage to a stranger.

"I didn't steal it, if that's what you're asking. The Snow Queen gave it to me."

"I see." The bar matron swapped out the clean glass for a dirty one, kept right on polishing. "Would you like me to be impressed?"

"I'd like you to help me find the Snow Wolf."

The woman shrugged. "The Wolf doesn't hunt here. Never has. I've heard he doesn't hunt in the other kingdoms, either. Killing magicians has gone out of style."

A dormant assassin was impossible to find. Why couldn't the Wolf wait to hang up his hat till *after* he'd helped her kill Zaga and Angelyne? Then he'd be more than welcome to retire to Kom'Addi, plant a nice garden, and herd reinsdyr till his hair went white.

Pilar tried to imagine a future as the mild-mannered daughter of a reinsdyr herder, living in an ice kabma with a rose garden out back. She couldn't fathom it.

That was the problem. These days she had a harder and harder time imagining her future at all. She'd spent the better part of the last year dreaming about her triumphant return to Refúj, being embraced by her Dujia sisters, and finally earning her redemption. But the longer she spent off the island, the less she wanted to go back. She never thought about any of those women. The one person she *did* think about was Quin.

Cowardly, backstabbing Quin.

"There is one odd thing, though." The bar matron dunked her towel in soapy water. "You've heard of the three sisters?"

"I have not."

"None of my business, but a curious thing happened here in Kom'Addi a few months back. The sisters had just lost both parents to the pox. They were living with their grandparents in a kabma down the road from mine. One night they tucked the girls into bed, and the next morning, they were gone."

"All three of them?" Pilar leaned forward on her stool. "They just vanished?"

"Without a trace. Some say they wandered out into the snow and got lost. But the frostflowers weren't in the sisters' room, which means they had them. And those runes should have led them home." She wrung out her towel from end to end. "I think someone took those poor girls. They had a good bit of magic between the three."

"Three Dujia go missing," Pilar said slowly, "and you still don't think the Snow Wolf had something to do with it?"

"I told you: he doesn't hunt here. We've had peace in Luum'Addi for decades." The bar matron slapped the towel onto the bar and began scrubbing out old rings. "The queen herself came to Kom'Addi to meet with the grieving grandparents. Drew the Hex on their front door. A nice gesture, though I suspect mostly for appearances."

Pilar leaned back, pondering this new scrap of information. Freyja herself had said all agreements could be broken. If three Dujia girls had gone missing, why weren't people at least *talking* about the Snow Wolf? Was there something—or someone—the Addi were more afraid of?

Frustrated, Pilar tucked the carving into her pocket. If she really had dead-ended, she didn't know what to do next. Without her assassin father, she couldn't kill her mother—which meant she couldn't save Quin.

She hated that she'd trusted him.

She hated that she missed him.

Pilar slouched lower on the stool. At least Freyja had given her a fat pouch of coins. Small comfort, but something.

She pointed to the bottle of silver death.

"I'll have a dram."

The bar matron nodded. "Thought you'd come around. Hoarfrost?"

Pilar shook her head. "Just give me two thumbs."

"Have three." The woman reached for the bottle. "You need it."

It didn't take long for the licorice spirits to make Pilar's blood thrum.

She scanned the tavern. It was cozy, all dark wood and candles. Mellow orange instead of fyre ice purple. At a nearby table, three black-haired men played cards with a hulking boy around Pilar's age, a pasty blond with a tuft of ugly yellow hair above his lip.

Blond hair on face: not appealing. Blond curls on head: appealing.

She was thinking about Quin again.

For the last week Pilar had warred with herself over whether she should have left him. He was a pawn, a puppet, a liar. She couldn't forgive him.

But she'd been too hotheaded in the music room to think things through. He wasn't in control of his own actions. Pilar knew how it felt to be enkindled, a prisoner in your own body. Surely enthrallment was even worse.

Was he already back at Kaer Killian? Recaptured by her mother? Enthralled by Angelyne? Had she blamed the victim when she should have been focusing on the people who had hurt him?

Pilar ordered another dram of silver death. She had never believed in regret. But you didn't have to believe in something for it to exist.

A warm voice slid through the air.

In the far corner, a young girl stepped onto a makeshift stage. She wore a silky silver dress and reindeer-skin slippers curling up at the tip. Dark red hair and dewy brown skin—a combination Pilar had never seen.

But it was the girl's voice that rooted her to the spot. Low. Haunting. The guttural sounds formed deep in the girl's belly, then flooded her mouth, rich and full. No words, but the song didn't need them. The same few notes over and over told a story. The girl had lost someone.

Pilar was struck by the simple beauty of the song, how much it revealed with so little. But no one else in the tavern even noticed. The bar matron kept scrubbing out rings. The card players didn't look up from their game.

Heathens. They couldn't even appreciate music.

Quin appreciated music.

There he was again. Four hells.

265

The last note of the song clung to the air. The girl sat on a stool, stage creaking beneath her. She fixed the silver folds of her dress. Pulled a small table toward her and began laying out objects.

Pilar turned to the bar matron. "Is she the entertainment?"

"We don't pay her. But she still comes. Sings the same Yöluk every night. The Luumi outlawed our native songs years ago—thought only witches sung them. Today Yöluks aren't forbidden, but you don't hear many outside of Kom'Addi."

She shooed Pilar off the stool. "Go, go. You'll want to see what she does next."

Pilar settled in a chair close to the stage.

The girl was younger than she'd thought. Underneath the thick layer of skin greases, she couldn't be more than thirteen. There was something in her movements that Pilar understood. She was quick, watchful. Half her attention fixed on her hands, the other half elsewhere. Ready to strike.

The girl laid out a row of trinkets carved from silver rock: an hourglass, a crow's wing, a rose. She licked her fingertips, then picked up the rose in her left hand and closed her fingers around it. She fixed her gaze on Pilar. Her eyes were deep brown.

"Which hand?" she said, presenting both fists.

"I don't do magic tricks."

"Which hand?"

Pilar nodded toward the girl's left hand. "That one."

But of course, when the girl opened her fist, there was nothing there.

"Let me guess," Pilar said dryly. "There's a rose in the other."

"Wrong."

The girl unclenched her right fist. Silver liquid pooled in her palm.

It was thick and syrupy. As the girl tipped her hand, the puddle slid from side to side.

"Fine," Pilar said. "You have my attention. How'd you do it?"

"Magic."

"Obviously. I meant what kind of magic?"

The girl closed and opened her fist again. This time the silver had shaped itself into a miniature ice leopard. The beast opened its mouth and roared.

Pilar leaned forward, intrigued. "Again."

The girl obliged. Over and over, the silver in her palm shifted.

A cloud raining silver hail.

A boat bobbing on the sea.

A flock of silver birds.

Pilar was fascinated, then wary. A magic of objects could be used for evil, just like all the rest. How were the silver birds any different from Freyja's red wren? The queen had said nothing could harm you during the Reflections, but surely the act of being dragged through your darkest memories was harm enough.

Sometimes our objects tell the truth, even when we don't.

As long as Quin had the lloira, Pilar couldn't trust him. But over the last few days she'd started to wonder. What if he destroyed the moonstone? Would she forgive him then?

And another thing. How was Angelyne controlling everyone else in the river kingdom if she'd sent her moonstone off with Quin?

Pilar kept thinking about something he'd said in the forest. Angelyne was storing her magic in new objects now, ones they wouldn't even recognize.

She massaged her temples. Her whole head hurt.

A whoop of laughter sounded from across the tavern. The blond boy was dragging a heap of silver coins toward him. He gloated while the other men grumbled and chugged their pints.

"I could make them pay attention," the girl said. "If I wanted."

She closed her fist again. This time when it opened, a dozen tiny silver spheres rose above her palm.

She flicked her wrist. The spheres flew so quickly they were invisible.

The card players swore. Pilar spun around, expecting to see blood. But the men were unharmed.

Their drinks, on the other hand, were destroyed, punctured with tiny holes. Every glass on their table had shattered, oozing ale and spirits all over their cards.

"Witch!" sniped one of the men. "Keep your sorcering to yourself!"

The girl said nothing. She turned to Pilar.

"You're very gifted," she said.

"*I'm* gifted?"

"But you don't use your gifts. Why?"

Pilar frowned. "I don't know what you—"

"My show is only as good as the magicians who come to it. And usually"—she sniffed at the men mopping up their spilled drinks—"no one good comes."

"You're not making sense."

The girl sighed like she'd explained this a hundred times.

"I'm a sorceress. I tap into other people's magic. I'm at my best when a magician is refusing to use her own gifts, because then there's more magic left over for me to play with." She pursed her lips. "It builds up in your body, you know. You should be careful. Someday you're going to explode."

An idea was forming in Pilar's head.

"You're saying there's a way to siphon off a Dujia's magic . . . and use it for yourself?"

"Yes." The girl stiffened. "But I don't hurt people. Ever. That isn't how this works."

In one move, she swept all the talismans into her skirt.

"Wait," Pilar said. "That wasn't what I—"

"Good night."

The girl hurried up the tavern stairs. One of the card players cursed her loudly as she left, shaking his soaked cards.

Whatever idea had been forming vanished along with the girl.

Pilar went back to the bar and flopped down on her stool.

"More death."

The bar matron poured a generous thumb. "The sorceress is strange, isn't she? No family. No friends. Arrived here in Kom'Addi after the river queen opened the borders."

Pilar sat up. "Angelyne opened the borders?"

"Why else would all you Glasddirans be coming around?"

"I told you, I am *not* Glasddiran."

"No? Well *he* is."

The bar matron waved toward the far end of the bar, where a blond patron hunched over his spirits. Pilar nearly dropped her silver death.

She was staring at Prince Quin.

Chapter 30

FIERCE AND LOVELY

"You're drunk."

Pilar's first words to Quin as she stood behind him.

He spun around on the stool. His face was smudged with dirt. He looked tired but otherwise safe.

Quin's green eyes warmed for a moment. Then cooled.

Pilar felt happy. Then furious. Then confused. What in four hells was he doing in Kom'Addi? The queen had shipped him back to Kaer Killian a week ago.

"I'm not drunk," he said flatly. "For a sniveling little prince, you'd be surprised how well I hold my spirits."

He turned his back.

So he wasn't happy to see her. Fair enough. They hadn't parted on the best of terms. Still, the sight of his cold back stung.

Pilar had a fierce and sudden urge to apologize. She shook the idea out of her head. *He* should be the one apologizing to *her*.

"This stool taken?" She sat on it before he could answer. "You don't seem surprised to see me."

"I'm not."

"Really? Because last time I saw you, you were being carted off to Glas Ddir."

"Mmm. Thanks for that, by the way."

She noticed the backs of his hands were caked with dirt and grime. When he saw her staring, he moved them off the bar.

"Turns out mining is dirty work."

His voice sounded thick—with bitterness or exhaustion, she couldn't tell.

"Mining?"

"Yes, Pilar. The Snow Queen gave me a choice. Either she would ship me back to the river kingdom on her fastest ship—back to Angelyne, back to your mother—or I could go to Kom'Addi to work in the fyre ice mines."

Pilar shifted on her stool, uncomfortable. "And you chose the mines."

"They say a man isn't a man until he's done manual labor."

"Who says that?"

"Me. Just now."

Quin held up his palms. His hands weren't just caked with grime: they were red and blistered, so raw it made her wince.

"I don't imagine I'll be playing much piano."

272

Pilar kept noticing new things, like how much his shoulders sagged. Or the fresh purple bruises on the inside of his arms. The air was stuffed with words he wasn't saying.

"When did you—"

"Get here? Same time you did. I was in the brig belowdecks."

She was astonished. "You were on my ship?"

"I'm sure Queen Freyja assumed you'd stay above deck, where the *non-prisoners* reside." He flagged down the bar matron. "Three thumbs of death, please."

"Hoarfrost?"

"The more the merrier."

The bar matron licked her thumb, swirled it once around the rim, and stamped the glass into a plate of ice crystals.

Pilar stared at the crusted saliva. She was glad she'd said no to the hoarfrost.

"They give us three coins a week," Quin said. "That way they can call us workers, not slaves."

When the bar matron slid his death across the bar, he tossed her a silver coin.

"As you might imagine," he said sourly, "a week's wages don't go very far."

Maybe Quin was lying. Maybe this was all a ploy to get sympathy.

"Why aren't they here? Don't they worry you'll run?"

He snorted. "Run to where? It's three days to Suvi West by foot. Even if I made it that far, the only way out of the port is on one of the queen's ships. I'm stuck in Kom'Addi forever. Or at least until I'm too old to be of any use in the mines."

Pilar shifted from one ass cheek to the other. She didn't like the idea of people being forced to work in the mines. It didn't match up with the bright picture of progress Freyja and Lord Dove had painted.

"Oh, but I destroyed Angelyne's moonstone," Quin said. "That's what you wanted, right?"

He thrust a hand into his pocket and pulled out the mangled pendant. The metal had been pounded with an anvil or some other blunt instrument until the gem dislodged. Quin handed her the empty scoop.

Pilar held it on her palm, a tide of conflicted emotions rising. Why wasn't she pleased? She could still hear herself in the music room, furiously demanding he destroy it.

But she could also hear Quin begging her *not* to destroy it. Pleading with her. *You have no idea what I've lost.*

She tried to give back the warped piece of metal, but he waved her off.

"Keep it. Something to remember me by."

"For all I know you're keeping the lloira somewhere else."

He shoved his hands into his trouser pockets, tugged them inside out. "Come see for yourself."

She hesitated, then set the pendant on the bar. She leaned over and felt his pockets. Pinched the thin fabric between her fingers. Ran her hands down his legs. Up his hips, his stomach, his chest. No stone.

His body was warm.

Her face was scalding.

Pilar retracted her hands, suddenly unsure what to do with them. She tried her lap. Her sides. She felt furious for having hands at all. Finally she balled them into fists.

"You should know I did it of my own volition," Quin said. "Before Freyja could force my hand."

"And how has it been? Without Angelyne in your head?"

"Lonely."

He lifted his dram of silver death and licked the hoarfrost from the rim. Tipped it back. Swallowed in one gulp.

"Cold frost for a dead heart," he said darkly.

She'd seen Quin morose before. But even in the forest, there were still flickers of feeling—when they'd fought, or when she kneaded his shoulders, or when he talked about the violin. The boy sitting beside her now reminded her of the pendant: the bright heart had been pounded out.

This was her fault. He had begged her to show mercy and she'd showed none. All she'd wanted was to punish him for hurting her.

But hadn't she hurt him first?

You have no idea what I've lost. All the people I cared about.

She'd killed his sister. Killed Mia Rose.

Quin believed the world needed gentleness. But Pilar hadn't been gentle. She'd cared only about herself. *Her* pain. *Her* suffering.

The epiphany landed like a punch to the gut.

She was just like her mother.

Pilar stared hard at Quin's empty glass. The pleasant heat she'd felt from her own dose of death had faded. She wasn't sure she deserved to have it back.

She cleared her throat. Took a breath.

"Listen. I . . ." She unclenched her fists. Stared at the lines in her palms. "I want to . . ."

Why was apologizing so hard? She could never find the right words.

"No need to say you're sorry. I'm just a liar, right? Weak. A coward." He angled his body toward her. "You want to know the truth?"

"Always."

"It was cruel, what you did."

Her stomach twisted. "I know. That's what I'm—"

"Let me finish. It was cruel, but I understand why you did it. You were right. I'd been lying to you since the moment you charged into that copse of swyn trees to save my skin. Every time I didn't tell you about the moonstone, I knew it was wrong. But I couldn't stop. I didn't have the *power* to stop. So I'm not angry at you."

Quin stared at his hands. "I'm angry at everyone else. Angry at the way this world works, how it holds us hostage. I cared about a boy and was punished for it. I cared about a girl, and I lost her, too. First my father was the villain, then Angelyne. Now I'm at the whim of some Luumi bastard barking orders in a giant pit. Someone else always decides who I get to be. I'm angry I haven't had a choice—a *real* choice—my entire life."

He looked up at her. "I *did* want to save Domeniq. I still do. Of course I want to go back and protect all the innocent Glasddirans from the horrors they're facing. It's what my sister would have done. But even when I told you why I was going to Luumia, I knew I'd been stripped of all my power to actually do it."

Quin's smile was bitter.

"You know what kills me most? I'm angry that I can't feel angry. Because every time I try to feel that rage, to let it live inside me, all I feel is shame."

Shame was the air Pilar breathed. She'd tried to fight it with her fists, to choke it out. But the shame was always just beneath the surface. Like sweat. Like blood.

For the first time, she understood something. The world had held them both hostage in different ways. Pilar had spent her life stuck on an island full of women who were supposed to be her sisters. But when she needed them most, they had betrayed her.

And yet there she was, still trying to win them over. She so desperately wanted them to forgive her. Which meant she still believed she had every reason to be ashamed.

Maybe they were right. Maybe what happened in the cottage was her fault. Maybe she deserved it.

Pilar felt suddenly desperate.

"We could leave," she said. "Break you out of the mines. Go somewhere together. Anywhere. Pick a kingdom."

He shot her a dubious look. "What happened to finding your father and claiming your bloody revenge?"

"Maybe that doesn't matter."

"That's all you wanted, Pilar. It's what you've been living for."

"It isn't *all* I want. I want other things, too."

She realized that was true. What if her mother didn't have to die for Pilar to choose a different ending? What if she could make a choice *now*?

"The Snow Wolf isn't here." She set her jaw. "And I don't care. I should never have left you behind."

She reached out. Lifted his chin until his eyes met hers.

"I'm sorry, Quin. Sorry for all of it. I'm sorry I left you. And I'm sorry I killed your sister. I could never be sorry enough for that."

"I don't blame you for the people I lost. It wasn't your fault."

Tears pounded at her eyes. "I'm sorry for Mia, too."

Pilar could never be Mia Rose. Nor did she want to. But she refused to punish Quin for feelings he had every right to feel. It was time to put her own complicated emotions aside.

"I know you loved her. And I want you to know it's all right."

She placed her hand over his. "You were right, too. I don't want to be alone. I've been lying to myself about what I wanted. I thought, if I found my father . . . if I could make him believe me . . ."

"Believe you about what?"

The warmth of Quin's skin warmed her own. "The world has tried to break us both. But we won't let it. You get to make a choice."

He shook his head. "I don't know if I even know how."

"Of course you do. You can *always* make a choice. No one can take that away from you. What is it you want?"

He stood from the stool, leaned down—and kissed her.

278

His lips tasted like licorice. She expected to feel fear, her body freezing, retreating into itself. Instead she felt a softening.

She pulled back. "Quin? Is this really what you want?"

"Yes." He kissed her jawbone, then the soft place where it met her neck. "You, Pilar Zorastín d'Aqila, are fierce and lovely and impossible."

Heat pulsed through her as he murmured in her ear: "Is this what *you* want?"

She raked her hands through his curls. Drew him toward her. "Yes."

This time when he kissed her, she kissed back.

Chapter 31

THICK WITH PLEASURE

In the small room above the tavern, their clothes didn't come off easily. Quin's shirt got stuck around his neck. Pilar's socks snagged around her ankles. She laughed at how clumsy they were.

"I'm sorry," Quin said, fumbling with her trousers. "I'm not very—"

She put her hands over his and guided the button through the hole. He eased the fabric down over her hips until the trousers fell in a clump to the floor. She sat on the bed as he knelt between her legs, planting kisses on her stomach, her hipbone.

"You have beautiful breasts."

"They're small."

"Small and beautiful."

Quin peeled off her undergarments, inching them down her thighs and knees. He was being so gentle. She wanted to put her arms around him and never let go.

"I want you," she said.

"You have me."

He tugged a sheepskin sheath out of his pocket. Pilar watched him put it on, her desire growing. When she leaned back onto the bed, she banged her head on the wooden headboard and swore.

"Are you all right?" he said.

Pilar laughed.

She wrapped her arms around him, his long lean body pressed into hers. He looked just as good unclothed as she'd imagined. And she had imagined it many times, ever since the prince arrived in Refúj all those months ago, handsome and terrified. His stomach was lean and taut. His arms hard without being over muscled. His skin smooth and warm.

But as they tried to get the angle right, something wasn't quite connecting. Skin slapped against skin.

"Not comfortable," she said.

"Sorry! I'm sorry. I think . . ." He buried his face in her hair. "I think I'm exhausted. And a little nervous."

"But this isn't your first time! I've seen your Reflections, remember? I saw you in the river with Mia Rose."

He blushed fiercely. "Do we have to talk about Mia?"

"Fair. I don't really want to be thinking of you and another girl while you're in bed with me."

"Though since you brought it up . . ." His cheeks were still bright pink. "You know when you had your bow and arrow in the Royal Chapel, but then your arrow didn't quite go where you wanted it to?"

She raised an eyebrow. "Is that supposed to be a metaphor?"

"It's a good one!"

"You must not want me very much."

"My gods." He looked stricken. "Are you joking? You are driving me wild."

She kissed his nose and nudged him off her. He plopped onto his back. Groaned.

"How mortifying," he said.

"It's all right."

Pilar hooked her leg around his leg. Laced their fingers together and brought his hand to her mouth.

"Go to sleep." She kissed his thumb. "When you wake up, we'll try again."

Pilar knew how to touch herself. She'd figured that out when she was nine years old. In the beginning, she'd used her magic to whip herself into a frenzy—what Dujia hadn't? But before long she discovered she preferred just her fingers. They were magic enough.

Once she began training, she learned to do other things with her fingers. Curl them into a fist. Test the sharp point of an arrow. At seventeen, she stopped touching herself completely. After what happened in the cottage, her own fingers felt dirty, poisoned. The shame was much bigger than the pleasure ever was.

But there, in the room above the tavern, something shifted.

Pilar awoke in the middle of the night, Quin pressed beside her on the too-small bed. Her body alive with desire.

She kissed his bare shoulder. "Are you awake?"

He stirred. Still dreaming, maybe.

For a moment she doubted herself. What if he was pretending to be asleep? What if he didn't want her?

Her flesh was singing. She wanted to touch herself, but she wanted Quin to touch her more.

Then he leaned his head into hers, nuzzling the side of her face.

"Not awake," he murmured. "But I bet you could wake me."

She climbed on top of him. Leaned down to kiss the scar on his chest. The scar she had given.

When she sat back up, he was looking at her, a strange smile on his face.

"Why are you looking at me like that?"

"Nothing. It's just." He traced the shape of her mouth. "You're so tender. I didn't expect that."

She bent and kissed his brow, his nose, the curve of his jaw. Grazed her teeth along his perfect lower lip.

This time, everything fit.

Her lips lingered on his as she began to move her hips in a slow, easy rhythm. A warm wave of sensation curled inside her. Pilar wanted to cry from relief. Her body felt like hers again. She didn't think she would ever feel this softness again.

The wave rose from her hips and flooded her belly, blooming in her chest. Her body thick with pleasure.

This was not the first time she had been with someone.

It was the first time she'd enjoyed it.

Chapter 32

COTTAGE BY THE LAKE

PILAR AWOKE TO QUIN kissing her shoulder. His warm mouth
sent shivers tumbling down her spine.

"You make little noises when you sleep," he whispered.

"What kind of noises?"

"Charming ones." He tucked a strand of black hair behind her
ear. It slid out again. She could have told him that would happen—her hair didn't like being restrained.

"You're beautiful," he said. "And I'm not saying your worth is
in any way contingent upon—"

"Oh please." She nipped playfully at his nose. "Don't ruin the
moment."

"You're so beautiful I want to kiss you again." He kissed her forehead. "And again." Her eyelids. "And again." Neck. "And again." A little lower.

"We're going to need another sheepskin," she murmured, her skin tingling with desire.

She wanted to stay in bed with him forever. In the past she'd never felt that way. To be fair, she'd never been in a bed, only on a hard dirt floor. Staring up at the thick wooden beams, counting the seconds until it was over. Sometimes her mind left her body, floated up to the rafters and watched the scene unfold from above. In those moments she would have sold her soul to be anywhere else—another cottage, another kingdom, another skin.

Pilar closed her eyes. Those days felt very far away. Now, as Quin planted kisses down her stomach inch by inch, her body hummed with pleasure. She couldn't remember the last time being in her own skin felt so delicious.

I never have to go back.

The same thought welled up from the night before, filling her with wild, giddy hope. She never had to go back to Glas Ddir *or* Refúj. With Quin at her side, she could go anywhere she chose.

Assuming he wanted to go with her.

"What do you like about me?" Her voice was soft. Vulnerable.

"Other than you're beautiful?" He trailed a lazy finger around her navel. "You're brave. Obviously. You know how to give *and* take a good punch. Since you don't practice magic, I never have to worry you're enthralling me. So that's nice. Oh and you're an uncommonly fine violinist. I want to make music with

286

you someday. Promise me we'll play a duet—and I mean a *real* duet, on violin and piano, not the lovely song our bodies made together."

Pilar groaned. "Did you really just say that?"

Quin smiled. "That might be the very best thing about you. You don't lie. To anyone, ever. You're brutally, unabashedly, brilliantly honest. And you never apologize for who you are."

The words looped a knot in Pilar's belly.

She didn't want to dredge up the memory, to ruin this perfect moment of being kissed, being held. But she was sick of keeping secrets. If she wanted him to understand who she was, he needed to know what she'd done.

"Quin?" she began. "There's something I want to tell you. Something that happened."

He grew serious. "Is it about one of your Reflections?"

When she nodded, he sat up. "I haven't wanted to ask about it. But it's not because I don't care. I *do* care. I knew you'd tell me if and when you chose."

"I do want to tell you." Pilar hugged the sheet tighter around her bare chest so she didn't feel so exposed. "No. I don't want to. I *need* to."

He wrapped his arms around her. She could hear the thump of his heart.

"Whatever it is," he said, "it's not going to change how I feel about you. I promise."

A heavy thud sounded from the room next door. Followed by a deep, throaty moan.

Quin raised an eyebrow. "Thin walls."

A girl cried out, quick and sharp. Then a man laughed.

Pilar felt the hairs on her neck rise. There was something not right about that laugh.

"Should we do something?" Quin asked, reaching for his clothes.

Pilar already had her feet halfway through her trouser legs. On instinct she snatched her frostflower. Yanked her shirt over her head and stumbled forward. She unhooked the latch and the door swung open, spewing them both into the corridor.

The sounds from inside the room were louder now. Inside the room, the girl was crying.

"Should we get the innkeeper?" Quin said, his voice tight.

"No time."

Pilar slammed her hip into the door. Again. Three times, until she heard something snap. She shoved the door open.

The red-haired girl huddled in the corner. *The sorceress.* A large blond man loomed over her.

"Please," the sorceress begged. "*Please.*"

Pilar knew exactly what to do. Left hook to the back of his skull. Punch the mirror above the washstand, seize a shard of glass, split his throat into two equal parts.

But she did nothing. Just stood on the threshold, paralyzed.

"Get off her!" Quin shouted, and the man whirled around. But he wasn't a man at all. He was the blond boy from the card game—the one with the yellow tuft of hair above his lip. For the first time she saw the white carvings on his belt. *Frostflowers.*

Pilar tried to move forward, to make her feet work. But she was no longer in the room. She wasn't in the tavern, wasn't even in Luumia. She'd traveled all the way back to Refúj.

She was in Orry's cottage by the lake.

Chapter 33

LIAR

IN THE BEGINNING, SHE'D wanted him.

That was the worst part. The part that made it impossible to forgive.

Pilar was fifteen when Morígna and Orry arrived on the island. Many of the Refúji—especially the older, crabbier Dujia—weren't in favor of husbands accompanying their wives. But everyone adored Orry. The young couple was a bright spot in a dark, ugly world. Orry with his underground fight school, teaching girls to keep themselves safe. Morígna with her music.

Soon Pilar began finding excuses to drop by their cottage. They weren't old enough to be her parents, but she liked to imagine it. They were funny, playful, beautiful, kind. Best of all, they cared about her. They knew she was lonely, and they gave her ways to make the loneliness bearable. Morígna taught her to play violin. Orry taught her to fight.

Over and over, they told her she was special. "You have an ear for music," Morígna said.

"You're a natural fighter," Orry said. "You have a gift."

Pilar loved them both. But it didn't take long for that love to blossom into something more specific. She thought about Orry when she went to sleep at night. His wavy brown hair and clear blue eyes. The curve of his forearms. The scruff on his face that wasn't there in the morning but always started to grow back by the afternoon.

For three long years she wanted his attention. Craved it. Every time he corrected her right hook or demonstrated how to land a dropkick, she welled up with longing. And whenever he complimented another girl during a sparring match, her jealousy flared. Orry was *her* teacher, *her* friend. He'd told her she was special—and she believed him.

And so, the first time his hand lingered on the small of her back after adjusting her stance, she let him. When he pulled her close and pinned her arms to her sides, testing her reflexes, she let him. When he peeled off his shirt, claiming to be too warm, she let him.

When he peeled off *her* shirt, she let him. Even as dread knotted in her stomach. Even as the nervous flutter in her chest turned to hot bile in her throat.

She didn't want it. Not anymore. But she never said no.

Orry only touched her when his wife wasn't in the cottage. Morígna left often, to shop at the merqad or visit her pupils for their music lessons. "Save enough energy for the violin once I'm back, love," she'd say to Pilar, giving her a peck on the cheek. "And don't let Orry wear you out. You know he's only hard on you because you're his favorite."

The word sank like a brick in Pilar's belly every time. *Favorite*.

Wooden rafters. Hard dirt floor. Gravel too small for anyone to see, big enough to bite holes into her back.

"You know we can't tell people about this," Orry would say afterward, buttoning his trousers. "They wouldn't understand what we have."

Pilar figured that was true, if only because *she* couldn't understand it. She'd spent three years dreaming about Orry. Now she had him. Wasn't this exactly what she wanted?

So she smiled. Moaned. Pretended to enjoy it. She never used magic to defend herself—and she never said no. Every time scared her worse than the time before.

And she lied. Lied. Lied. She couldn't tell anyone, couldn't find the words. And she couldn't make it stop. Orry had taught her to protect herself, but in the end, the only person she needed protection from was him.

Even that would've been survivable, if not for what happened next.

Morígna came home early from the merqad. She walked in to find Orry, his hairy back slick with sweat. Grunting and panting with Pilar trapped beneath him.

Morígna didn't fly into a rage: she *became* rage. She seized Pilar's horsehair bow and struck Orry's neck, over and over, until the bow snapped in two. She wrapped her hands around his throat. Used magic to draw the blood to the surface until every vessel popped. His neck folded in on itself. Bones crumbled. Flesh tore.

Then Morígna turned on Pilar.

"Get out," she snarled. "Never set foot in this house again."

So Pilar ran home. She went to the cave and called her mother's name. All she heard were echoes. She spent a sleepless night pacing the shore of the lake, too numb to feel the cold.

The next morning, Morígna called a meeting in the Biqhotz. All the elders—and any Refúji looking for a good scandal—crowded into the sanctuary. Pilar lurked on the outskirts of the circle, confused and heartsick, but grateful someone else would tell the truth. She knew the other girls would judge her for what had happened, but at least Orry wouldn't be able to hurt her anymore.

Morígna stood tall in the center of the circle. Pilar held her breath. The shame would strike first, she knew. Then surely the relief would follow.

"You may soon hear rumors," Morígna said to the gathered Dujia, "that my husband has acted in an unnatural way toward one of his students. I assure you, these rumors are lies. My husband wants only to protect these girls, and it is the great desire of his heart to teach them to protect themselves. He has given so much to this community, and the fact that he has been targeted with false accusations makes me angry."

Morígna turned her head and looked directly at Pilar. She stared long enough that everyone in the circle turned their heads, too. Hundreds of eyes scraped over Pilar's face, her body. Like being flayed with a hundred knives.

"But I am a Dujia," Morígna continued, raising her chin. "I hold myself to a higher standard. There will always be girls who are so starved for attention they must lie to get it. Girls who pretend to be victims when they are anything but. So I beg you, my sisters. Do not punish girls like this. They deserve our compassion, not our wrath."

It was a neat trick. By calling for compassion, Morígna ensured Pilar got none.

The woman who had once been her friend and teacher made a choice: preserve her husband's reputation—her *own* reputation—at all costs.

Later that day, Pilar saw Orry buying a stalk of broccoli at the merqad. Morígna had healed him. His neck was back to normal. Everything was back to normal. Fight lessons at the cottage recommenced the next day. Not for Pilar, of course. She would never set foot in the cottage again.

Defend yourself, but do not hesitate to hurt him.

Pilar had failed on both counts. She had not defended herself, and she hadn't hurt him. Three years of training and she was still cowardly. Still weak.

Nothing made sense anymore. Every Dujia on Refúj looked at her like she was dirty, broken, *wrong*. And that was when they looked at her at all. When Pilar drummed up the courage to tell one of her sparring partners the truth, the girl called her a liar. Another girl slammed a door in her face.

Desperate, Pilar tried to tell her mother what had happened.

"Orry is a gift to the Dujia," Zaga said. "Do not poison that gift."

Pilar had started at her in disbelief. "You're my mother. Why don't you believe me?"

"Did you fight? Did you kick and scream and push him away?"

When she didn't answer, Zaga shook her head.

"Even if what you say is true, you have no one to blame but yourself."

Maybe her mother had it right. Maybe it *was* her fault. Pilar knew all the horrible things a man could do to a woman. She'd been trained to protect herself from these exact things. But her memories were chopped into jagged pieces. The wood beams. The broken bow. The way she'd felt lying on that floor, her mind floating out of her body and up into the rafters. She could no longer remember exactly what happened—the images were tangled and unclear.

Pilar started to believe Morígna's version. Maybe she *had* been lying. Pretending to be a victim when she was anything but.

So when her mother gave her the chance to be a spy in Kaer Killian, Pilar took it. Refúj had become unbearable. She was downing half a dozen nips of rai rouj every night just to drown out the silence.

"You must kill Mia Rose," her mother said. "Perform this task and you may win your redemption."

Pilar wanted desperately to prove herself. Show the women of Refúj she wasn't the liar they thought. But it gnawed at her, the mission she'd been given. To reclaim her place in the sister-hood, she would be forced to kill a girl who—under different circumstances—might have been her friend.

But then she heard Mia Rose speak in the Grand Gallery the night before the wedding. The way the word *Gwyrach* was a curse in her mouth. Instead of standing beside her fellow women, Mia wanted to strike them down. This spoiled and cocky river rat would never be a true sister to the Dujia.

Honestly, none of the "true sisters" on Refúj had turned out to be so true.

Pilar knew weak men had always been afraid of powerful women. What she'd never expected was that powerful women would turn their power against one of their own. Orry hurt her, but her Dujia sisters hurt her worse. They had remade her into something she had never been. *Two* things.

A liar.

Ashamed.

"Her."

The word wrenched Pilar back to the present. She was in the room above the tavern. Frozen in the doorway. The sorceress on the floor, pinned down by the blond boy. But something had changed.

The girl was pointing at Pilar.

"Her," the sorceress gasped, tears streaming down her cheeks. "She has magic. She's the one you want!"

The boy lurched toward Pilar, reaching for her throat. A solid *thwack* pulled him up short. He groaned and sank to his knees, collapsing face-first onto the floor.

Behind him was Quin, holding a plank of wood. His face white as bone.

"Pilar," he said, but she didn't wait to hear the rest.

She turned and ran.

Chapter 34

AS GOOD AS DEAD

PILAR SHOT OUT OF the tavern, feet pounding the hard-packed snow. She didn't know where she was going. Didn't care.

The boy in the tavern had brought everything back. Orry's touch. Morígna's betrayal. Her mother's cold indifference.

And everything that happened after. Karri. Mia. Buckets of blood on her hands.

When forced to choose between shame and rage, Pilar preferred rage. At least anger was a kind of fuel.

But as she ran, she thought of something Quin had said. *Every time I try to feel that rage, all I feel is shame.*

She wondered if, when you cracked rage open, you'd always find shame at the core.

What good was Quin's forgiveness if she couldn't forgive herself?

Her pace slowed. The ice kabmas had thinned into barren white nothingness. A light snow began to fall.

The boy from the tavern wasn't coming after her. No one was.

Pilar didn't want to run anymore. She'd run from Refúj, run from the forest where Karri lay dead, run from Kaer Killian. She'd even run from Quin, the one person she actually wanted to be with. She was running from the past—but also from the future.

Pilar Zorastín d'Aqila, the girl who'd thought herself a warrior, was a coward.

She doubled over, hands on her knees. Tears rammed up her throat. She choked them back down.

A sheet of whirling snow swept over the tundra. When it cleared, Pilar saw a herd of reinsdyr not far from where she stood. She walked forward slowly, in case they bolted.

But they weren't afraid. The beasts were easy in their bodies, lean and muscular. Short fur mottled white, gray, and brown. They rooted through the snow. Pawing. Chewing. A gray cow nudged her calf toward a fresh eating patch. They were just animals, she knew, but somehow they seemed noble. Kind.

Pilar thought of the reinsdyr come to life in the Watching Chamber, the way the ice leopard tore smoothly into the soft flesh. She thought of the reinsdyr stew she and Quin had eaten in the palace.

She reached out her hand, let it rest on the reinsdyr's nose.

So mighty, so strong. And still so easily devoured.

Orry

Orry

Orry

No matter where she went, no matter how far or fast she ran, he found her everywhere.

The cold sliced into her skin as she struggled to hold herself up. She touched her shoulder, trying to remember the warmth of Quin's kiss. The memory of his gentleness made her crumble. She didn't deserve love. How had she ever thought she did?

Regret eroded you from the inside out, like a poison. Shame was a curved blade. It eviscerated you, scooped out all the parts you thought were worthy. Shame carved an empty space nothing could ever fill.

Pilar's chest shuddered and cracked open. She sank to her knees on the tundra. Wrapped her arms around herself, with only the reinsdyr there to see.

She was alone. But then she'd always been alone.

In the middle of the wilderness, she sobbed.

It took Pilar some time to pull herself together. She couldn't remember the last time she had sobbed like that. Probably never. Her eyes stung from crying. Her skin was cold and raw, tears frozen to her cheeks.

Her heart felt heavy—and also somehow lighter. Maybe hearts got smaller and smaller every time they broke until you were left with nothing but a bloody stump in your chest.

By the time she stood and brushed the snow off her trousers, her fingers had gone numb. The sun wouldn't rise for hours. She knew she should go back to the tavern. Back to Quin.

Pilar scanned the horizon. She thought of the three missing girls. It was easy to vanish in a place like this, especially with no one looking.

She took a breath and walked deeper into nowhere.

The snow under her boots crunched, then softened abruptly. She looked down and found herself trudging through a field of frostflowers. Blooms so thick they made a silvery white blanket.

She stooped and plucked one. The flower was velvety soft. So different from her bone carving. When she stroked a petal, it ripped in two. Beautiful and fragile.

Fierce and lovely.

She pushed all thoughts of Quin from her head. Rolled the white blossom into a tiny scroll and chucked it as hard as she could. The frostflower fell sharply, as if it had been sucked down into a pit.

That was how she found the quarry.

Pilar stood on the ledge of a massive canyon. Below she saw cranks and pulleys, coils of cables, rusted iron tubs. Quin's fyre ice mine, she assumed, or one like it. There were probably hundreds of pits like this around Kom'Addi.

The moon sagged in the night sky. All the workers were out at the taverns, greasing their misery with silver coins. The pit was dark, empty.

Only it wasn't. Not completely. At the far end of the quarry, she spotted a soft blue light. Someone mining midnight fyre ice, maybe. Pocketing a few slivers for themselves.

The road down into the pit was easy to find. Brown dirt stamped by wagon wheels and some footprints, too. The path snaked down the rock, spitting Pilar out at the bottom of the canyon. She headed toward the blue.

It didn't take long to realize the light wasn't coming from a human, but a cave.

The opening was only as high as her hip. She ducked, crouching low as she made her way inside. When she looked up, she gasped.

The walls were carved of clear blue ice. But "carved" wasn't quite right. She had the feeling no human hands had ever touched this cavern. The ice had formed naturally into plates. Like armor, she thought. Or a dragon's scales.

Not that she'd ever seen a dragon. On Refúj she'd never even seen a snake.

She dropped to her knees and crawled farther into the cave. Dizzying rows of scales stretched across the walls and ceiling. What made the ice glow? She couldn't find a source of light. Maybe a hole dumped moonlight from overhead? Or maybe all fyre ice glowed of its own accord, like the violet walls of Freyja's palace.

But something didn't add up. Fyre ice was purple. And wasn't it always warm? That was the whole point: the Grand Fyremaster had brought heat and light back to Luumia.

Pilar reached out to touch one blue scale. Cold and silky smooth.

Intrigued, she crept a few feet deeper. The ground, too, was icy, the cold seeping through the knees of her trousers. She was in a tunnel now, surrounded by bright blue on every side. Some scales had tiny objects trapped beneath the surface. Bubbles. Petals. A brown bug frozen forever on its back.

Her hand struck a barrel of carved trinkets. She dug out a bird and scraped it against the wall. When that didn't work, she hurled it with all her might. Freyja had said a single sliver of fyre ice could create a paroxysm.

Nothing happened.

A chill spread over Pilar's skin. If this wasn't fyre ice, they'd been lied to. And if it *was* fyre ice, then the rest of Luumia was mixing theirs with something else.

A low thud echoed through the canyon. Rhythmic.

Pilar tensed. Horse's hooves.

She cursed herself. Why had she crawled wide-eyed into the cave? Now she had nowhere to run.

The hooves echoed louder. Sweat licked the back of her neck. *The blond boy from the tavern.* It had to be. He'd awoken from Quin's plank to the skull with a lump on his head and rage in his heart.

Pilar dug her hand into the barrel and seized the sharpest piece of blue ice she could find. Not ideal, but something. She backed out of the cave on her hands and knees. Stood. Braced herself.

The boy was in the quarry now, coming quick. Horse and rider masked by a cloud of brown dust. All she saw was a shock of fair hair.

Pilar swallowed. She was alone. Trapped. As good as dead.

Would she use magic to defend herself? She didn't know. But this time, she wouldn't turn and run like a coward. She would fight.

The horse reared inches from her face. She clutched the makeshift knife so tightly she felt it break skin.

"Pilar?" shouted the rider.

Her heart leapt out of her chest. "Quin?"

"Thank the gods!"

He dismounted and rushed toward her. Wrapped his arms around her shoulders. Pulled her close. Could he tell she'd been crying? She didn't care. She sank farther into his arms. He was the only thing holding her up.

"The most amazing thing happened, Pil." He stepped back, his face flushed. She held onto his arms, not wanting to let go. "After that lout tried to attack you, I ran downstairs to get help. I couldn't find the tavern keeper, but you'll never guess who I found instead."

Pilar tried to smile.

"If I'll never guess, you're not going to make me guess, are you?"

"Griffin Rose."

She blinked, not understanding. "Mia and Angelyne's father?"

"Yes."

"Wasn't he rotting in the dungeons back in Kaer Killian?"

"Not anymore, I guess. When I told him what happened, he drew his dagger and charged up the stairs. But the boy was gone."

"That's not good news."

"We made a full report. The boy won't be able to show his face in that tavern or anywhere in Kom'Addi again. But you're missing the point. Griffin Rose has come to Suvi West with a ship."

Quin looked at her, expectant.

"So what you're saying," she said slowly, "is that the leader of the Circle of the Hunt, the man who killed too many Dujia to count, is here in Kom'Addi. And this is good because . . ."

"Because he's here for you and me. He's come to rescue us."

Chapter 35

SOMEHOW FAMILIAR

PILAR REJECTED THE IDEA of rescue. She'd come to Kom'Addi of her own free will, and she had zero reason to go back to Valavïk. She certainly didn't need a man to save her—let alone Griffin Rose, leader of the Circle of the Hunt. Everyone knew what the Hunters could do. What they *had* done.

Of course, Pilar had never heard his full story. Not till the night Angelyne enkindled them in the castle. That's when Zaga had revealed her love affair with Wynna, the woman who would enthrall Griffin Rose—and give birth to Mia and Angelyne.

Angelyne, who threatened to reveal her own mother for being a Dujia.

Wynna, who cut her life short before Angelyne could reveal her.

Mia, who wanted to kill Dujia before discovering she was one.

Griffin, husband of Dujia, father of Dujia, killer of Dujia.

And Pilar thought *her* family had problems.

"Orange?" Quin said.

They were in the ship's galley eating breakfast. Nothing spectacular: thin flat cakes made of flour and butter, cold tea, and slightly moldy oranges. A pauper's feast.

Pilar had yet to see the infamous Griffin Rose. When she and Quin returned to the tavern, they'd found an Addi guide waiting with two fast horses. The ship was waiting in the harbor once they arrived in Suvi West. The sailors welcomed them aboard, told them to eat and drink whatever they found in the galley.

Now Rose was off in his private quarters, doing whatever people did in their quarters on a ship.

It had all been suspiciously easy.

"Come on now," Quin prodded, holding out the orange. "You don't want to get scurvy."

Pilar snatched the fruit and smashed it into the table. He raised a brow.

"What did that orange ever do to you?"

"Nothing." She rolled it in circles with the heel of her palm. "It loosens the peel."

When she dug her fingernails into the skin and stripped it off, the orange meat plopped out in a perfect orb.

"Why does Rose think I want to go to Valavïk? I came here to find the Snow Wolf."

"I thought that wasn't what you wanted anymore."

"I said it wasn't *all* I wanted."

"Well you haven't found him, have you? In just a few days your father will be at the queen's palace. You'd be a fool not to be there, waiting."

Pilar ripped off a wedge of the orange and swallowed it without chewing. Even if Quin was right, she didn't have to like it.

"Since when has Griffin Rose owned a ship in Luumia?"

"I think it's one of the queen's fleet."

"Another reason to distrust Freyja, if you ask me."

She squeezed the orange too hard, and sticky juice squirted everywhere. She swore.

"Why do *you* want to go back to Valavïk, Killian?"

"Must you really ask?"

She felt a clutch of fear. "Answer the question."

"No, no. I'm not trying to be evasive. I'm just . . ." He sighed. "I'm going to Valavïk because *you* are, Pilar. And I want to be with you."

The fear released its grip. She smiled. Then felt shy. Then felt the need to hide the fact that she felt shy.

"Want some orange juice?" She held up her sticky hand. "Better lick it off. You don't want to get scurvy."

Before he could answer, a burly sailor appeared in the galley.

"Pilar d'Aqila? Lord Griffin would like a word."

Griffin Rose's quarters were stately. Dark, shiny oak desk, thick red curtains, chairs with pieces of gold stuck in the wood. It was all a bit rich.

Rose gestured toward a chair. Pilar didn't sit.

"You don't look well," she said.

It was true—his hair had gone straight gray since she'd last seen him. He looked impossibly tired.

"It's been a long few months for us all," he said.

Pilar almost laughed. He didn't know the half of it.

"Last I heard you were rotting in the dungeons. You seem to have made it out of Kaer Killian just fine." She looked around the room. "And stole a ship, apparently."

"It's on loan."

"Nice loan." She folded her arms. "Why am I here?"

"Could you sit, at least?"

"Why?"

"So we can have a proper conversation."

"I don't do proper."

"Very well." He stood, hesitated, then leaned against the wall. "We'll stand."

"You don't get to decide what I do." She slammed herself down in the chair to prove a point. "I'll stay in your boat, and I'll go to Luumia. But I have nothing to say to you."

Rose lowered himself back into the chair. He met her gaze. His eyes were a sad, muted gray.

"I have committed atrocities too numerous to count," he began. "Until my wife was taken, I never thought to question the narrative I inherited. But for the past three years I have tried to fight *for* the Dujia, not against them. I have dedicated my life to atonement. I know it will never be enough. I deserve neither your sympathy nor your forgiveness."

"Good. Because you're not getting them." She folded her arms over her chest. "What do you mean, the past three years?"

"After I learned the truth, I stayed in the king's employ. But I did not continue his campaign of slaughter. I was a Hunter who did not hunt. I used my position to help as many Dujia as I could."

Pilar hadn't expected that. Was it even true?

"And now your daughter carries out her own campaign of slaughter. You birthed a monster as bent and twisted as you."

Rose's eyes softened. He looked down at the desk.

"I have had a good deal of time to reflect the past few months. More and more I think the bond between parent and child is not as I understood it."

"Fair," Pilar said. "Since a monster birthed me."

"I don't hold you responsible for any act your mother has committed."

"Thanks. I *do* hold you responsible for the acts your daughter has committed. You taught her how to hate. Clearly she's learned the lesson well."

"What you're saying is true. I don't dispute it. But my daughter is not what she was. Some say she is horrified by the dark turn her reign has taken, that she grows weak from the weight of her guilt. The view from the castle dungeons is limited, and a rumor is precisely that: rumor, not fact. But I know she opened the borders in an attempt to reestablish trade routes, to show the other kingdoms that Glas Ddir is not the intolerant, hateful dominion it once was. She did this without Zaga's approval, and I fear she has paid the price."

Rose's eyes narrowed. "Your mother has always been drawn to magic's darker currents. With all of Glas Ddir crumbling by her hand, she has been given the opportunity to indulge her appetites."

"I've known her my whole life, and I assure you, she's never had any trouble indulging those."

"Do you remember the night in the Grand Gallery? When we all sat at the feasting table, enkindled? The night my . . ."

He didn't finish. They were both thinking it: *The night Mia died.*

"Of course I remember."

"You will recall your mother speaking of Wynna Merth, the woman she loved. The same woman who would enthrall me for two decades as a way of paying penance. My wife."

He looked away. "I was fodder for their experiments. But before Wynna and I started our life together—before the grand experiment began—it was your mother I loved."

Pilar frowned. "My mother loved no one."

"I never said she loved me back." His smile was tight. "I was wrong about many things back then. So many things I did not know, no matter how much I might have wished to."

He laid his hands on the desk. "The list of wrongs I have committed is long. I have dedicated the rest of my life, however short it may be, to atonement."

"You said that already. It doesn't make me like you."

"Nor should it. But if there are any lies I can turn to truths— any people I have wounded to whom I might still be of service—I will do everything in my power to help them."

He reached into his jacket and drew out a stack of yellow parchments tied with brown twine.

"It was Angelyne who freed me from Kaer Killian," he said. "She gave me these."

"Angelyne let you go?"

He didn't answer. Just held out the stack of papers.

"What's this?"

"Six letters. They were meant to come one at a time, but life intervened."

"What could Angelyne possibly have to say to me?"

He set the parchments on the desk between them. Pilar's curiosity won out. She plucked the top letter off the pile, unfolded it, scanned the first few lines.

She shook her head. "These letters aren't for me. They're for Mia." She tried to hand back the parchment. "Looks like sweet demented Angie is writing to the grave."

Rose pushed the stack of letters gently toward her.

"No, Pilar. They're for you."

"It says right here, 'My dearest sister.'" Pilar grabbed the next letter. Shook it open. "'Beloved sister.'"

She looked up at Rose, who held her gaze. His gray eyes were somehow familiar. Almost like she'd been staring into them for years.

The room spun.

Rose stood slowly. "I loved your mother, Pilar. There was a time when I thought we would have a life together. A family."

"No." Pilar couldn't breathe. "That isn't possible. You can't be . . ."

The Snow Wolf. The greatest Dujia killer in all four kingdoms.

Griffin Rose bowed his head. His voice cracked like a cup, spilling words.

"Mia and Angelyne are my daughters," he said. "But you were my daughter first."

1 DAY TILL THE WEEPING MOON

My undeserving sister,

The moon weeps, and still you have not answered me.

Very well. I will tell you the one story I have not yet told: the story of the sisters.

When the witch crept into the village under the canopy of night; when the Renderer sharpened his colored pencils; when the Flesh Thief purloined her bits of flesh; when the Silver Sorcerer poached their magic and used it for himself . . . the three sisters stayed behind. There, tucked safely into the kabma, they did what all sisters do.

They told each other stories.

The eldest sister told tales of battle. Dreams of fierce mares galloping over white fields, their hooves flattening the flowers. Sometimes she was a demon with a breastplate of silver. Sometimes a sea monster, sometimes just a girl. But no matter the shape of her body or the length of her teeth, she was always a warrior.

The middle sister told tales of wonder: mystical fog-cloaked lagoons and lights rippling through the sky. Her curiosity was insatiable. Her stories became ways to simmer mystery down to truth.

The littlest sister didn't care for truth. She was a liar.

The best storytellers always are.

In her stories she was not reviled by the villagers. She was a lovely human girl with dazzling wit and devastating grace. She turned heads as she swept through opalescent ballrooms, silken gown rustling like a velvet summer breeze. The ladies admired her, the men loved her. She was not the daughter of a monster. She was a queen.

When the villagers came for Græja's children, carrying torches dipped in oil and fire, the eldest sister relied on her fists. She tried to hurt them, even as red flames licked the thatch roof. The middle sister relied on her intellect. She appealed to their reason, trying desperately to prove her family's innocence.

It was the littlest sister who saved them. She knew these men would not be defeated by blood or logic. So she dipped her quill in ink, pulled out a fresh piece of parchment, and wrote a different ending.

Once upon a time, the monsters survived.

As with most endings, it is really a beginning.

The myth of Græja goes like so: we do not know how the witch's children died, only that they died. But there is more than one kind of death—and more than one means of survival. New life can come from the deadest of places, if you only know where to look.

You have now met all the Souls of Jyöl. The Warrior and Wonderer number five and six. But I am far more interested in the Liaress, the Seventh Soul. She is the most powerful. The Liaress made the other Souls immortal, all with a few strokes of her pen.

A reckoning is at hand, sister. Tomorrow, when the moon weeps light into the palace, you must choose how to align yourself.

Remember the things I have told you.

Sometimes the men are the monsters.

Sometimes the monsters are the light.

Truthfully yours,
Angelyne

Chapter 36

PERFECT LIKENESS

WYNNA'S CHAMBERS IN THE snow palace glimmered. White marble floors swirled with gold and copper; a deep porcelain tub ringed by milky candles; gilded sconces reaching for the ceiling like claws. The Luumi crest was emblazoned over the fireplace: a frostflower crushed beneath an ice leopard's paws.

The bed curved into a sumptuous canopy, dark cherry wood carved as birds and blooms. The bed itself boasted snow fox blankets half a foot deep. Heavy velvet drapes dripped vermillion from the bay windows, reminding Mia of frosted blood.

Outside, the balcony offered a view of the seaside: boats kissing the horizon with sails of pale blue, gleaming copper hulls bobbing on the bay. In the distance the glacier loomed large, its ivory fingers reaching down into the ocean. Dollops of smoke rose above the bustling port as cream-capped waves frothed at the shore, snow frilling the water's edge like a fringe of lace.

In a word: horrific.

Mia pulled the drapes shut.

Before she'd fainted, she had a vague memory of her mother saying she would "tend" to her in her chambers. But Mia had awoken on the canopy bed, alone. No sound save for the crackle of logs in the hearth, a wolfskin rug laid before it.

Why did her mother have her own chambers in the queen's palace? Did she *live* there? As if it weren't betrayal enough that her mother had hired Zai to ferry her from White Lagoon to Valavïk.

Of course the irony was that Mia had *wanted* Zai to ferry her to Valavïk. But she could have done without all the subterfuge.

Secrets are just another way people lie to one another.

Her mother had forged an endless rope of lies, one woven into the next.

Mia kept replaying the moment on the balcony. When she'd imagined their reunion, she always saw her mother rushing toward her, bundling her in a tender hug. Wynna would beg for her daughter's forgiveness, and even though Mia had sworn she'd never give it, she would feel months of icy numbness thawing in her chest.

In reality, their reunion hadn't resembled that fantasy in the slightest. Her mother's face was cold and distant. If she had instructed Zai to bring Mia to the palace out of love or longing—aching to see her daughter, missing her terribly—that was one thing. Even regret would have sufficed: a bone-deep remorse over all the pain and suffering she'd caused.

But Wynna's words were transactional. Emotionless. Mia felt no joy rolling off her mother, only a sense of resignation. *You've come at last.* Not a celebration: a verdict.

Mia straightened. It didn't matter that her mother hadn't released a thousand golden butterflies for her return. What mattered was that Wynna would be able to counter the magic in the moonstone so they could beat Angelyne and save Quin.

Mia could be transactional, too.

A knock echoed through the room.

Her heart leapt. She hurried to the door and pressed her ear against the wood. Was she still holding out hope that her mother would ask for forgiveness? She loathed herself for even thinking it.

"Mia," came the muffled voice. "It's Zai."

Her stomach clenched.

"Can I please come in? I want to apologize."

"I don't care what you want," she called through the door.

"I have food."

"I'm not hungry."

"She made you a potato cake with sweet brown mustard. Just the way you like."

Mia's resolve wavered. Her mother knew better than anyone that potato cakes were her favorite. A simple meal from simpler times.

She adjusted her jacket and opened the chamber doors.

It struck Mia how different Zai looked. His black hair was no longer confined to the leather band; it hung free, kissing his chiseled jawline. He leaned into the doorway with a new swagger.

"Good morning, Mia Rose."

She extended her hand, palm facing up. "Potato cake."

Zai started to give her the copper plate, then hesitated.

"I'd like to sit with you."

"I don't have anything to say."

"We don't have to talk. You can eat, and I'll just . . . watch you eat."

"Why would that appeal to me?"

He shrugged.

Mia snatched the copper plate and started to close the door. But she paused halfway. She couldn't resist.

"Was *any* of it real? The alehouse? The boat? Your stories about your family?"

She started to close the door again, but Zai caught it with the toe of his boot.

"It was *all* real. I own the alehouse. The boat is mine. My family lives in Kom'Addi—all but one cousin, who chose a very different direction." He paused. "I came to White Lagoon to make my own way."

"I see. And at what point did you become my mother's lackey? Or since you brought me here to the palace, should I say the queen's?"

He frowned. "I don't work for Freyja. I work for myself. From time to time I make shipments when the price is right."

Mia almost laughed. "I'm a shipment, then."

"No. That isn't . . ." He rapped the door with his knuckles. "I mean, yes. You were a shipment. But only at first."

She rolled her eyes. She had zero interest in hearing the rest of this monologue, about how she'd gone from being a shipment to someone he cared about, his feelings blossomed into something more, et cetera.

"So you're a man of coins. Tell me: what do you spend it on? Fyre ice for your boat, perhaps? Casks for your alehouse? And do you carry whatever cargo they tell you to? Even when it means luring girls onto your boat under false pretenses?"

He regarded her closely, with that same piercing gaze. She hated that she found him handsome.

"I won't lie to you, Mia. I was waiting for you. A few months ago your mother told me you'd be coming to Luumia, and she offered me a handsome sum to bring you to Valavïk. But then you came, and it wasn't at all like I expected."

Zai pressed one palm into the doorframe, leaning toward her.

"I'll tell you anything you want to know. No more secrets."

"I sense a contingency."

"All I want is to sit down. My foot is tired of being a doorstop."

"All you want is a chair, and you'll tell me anything?"

He flashed a roguish smile. "Make it a good chair."

Mia had never seen his expression anywhere close to roguish. It unnerved her—and intrigued her, too. Who was the Zai she had spent the last week with? And how close was that Zai to the real one?

"Why should I trust you?"

322

"I never outright lied to you, Mia."

"That itself is a lie."

She started to close the door with his toes still underneath it. Zai yelped.

"You're right. I did lie to you. But only once."

He stared into the empty room behind her. Ran a hand through his black hair.

"I said I couldn't render you. That I don't draw people I know. The truth is, I *do* draw people I know. That's what I'm best at. But the other part . . . that was true."

She raised an inquisitive eyebrow.

"I couldn't render you because by then . . ." He shook the hair out of his eyes. "You weren't just a shipment I was carting between ports. I didn't want to hurt you. Sometimes, when I render people, they get hurt."

"You're saying when you draw someone in charcoal, they get hurt in real life?"

"You really don't know, do you?" His round brown eyes were soft, almost playful. "Honestly, you ask more questions than anyone I've ever met. But during all those months in White Lagoon, you never once thought to ask this one."

She looked at him, baffled. He held her gaze.

"Do you remember what I drew, Mia?"

She thought of Zai sketching feverishly on the boat, the way he bristled when she came too close. No wonder he'd captured her mother in flawless detail: he'd seen her in real life.

And then Mia remembered seeing her mother in the White

Lagoon, fierce and silent. The same way he'd drawn her.

The *exact* same way, come to think of it. Same voluptuous red tresses pinned in the Luumi style. Same wide hazel eyes. Same unsmiling expression. Every curve and wrinkle—even the tilt of her head—identical.

One minute Wynna was there in the lagoon, flesh and blood. The next minute, she'd vanished.

The wheels were turning in Mia's brain. All this time she'd feared her sanity was fraying. But her mother had never been in the lagoon at all. Mia had seen her perfect likeness because Zai had sketched her on paper . . . and etched the image into Mia's mind.

He opened his mouth to speak, but she spoke first.

"You have magic," she said. "You're a Dujia, too."

Chapter 37

FAMILY OF GHOSTS

"This doesn't make sense."

Mia paced her mother's chambers, trying to organize her thoughts. Zai had thrown open the drapes so that bluish sunlight spilled into the room. After all the fuss about a chair, he hadn't taken one. He sat barefoot on the rug in front of the roaring orange fire, his arm slung over a low chair. His toes were angular, all roughly the same length.

"You're trying to fit magic into the box you were given," he said. "But your box is too small."

"In the river kingdom I was taught only Gwyrach could have magic. We looked like women, but really we were demons. In the fire kingdom I learned we had another name. We were Dujia, daughter of the Four Great Goddesses. We were angels. Either way, there was one constant in the equation: we were always women."

"I'd argue you were women most of all."

"But that's exactly why magic was born inside us. For centuries men have treated our bodies as vessels to bring them pleasure, or bear their children, or whatever they chose. We wear the scars of that heavy history. Magic was created the first time a woman's body rose up against oppression."

"Do you think only women have been oppressed?"

Mia stopped pacing. She stared at him, unblinking. For once in her life, words eluded her.

"You are correct," Zai said, "that women have suffered from violence. Magic was the body's answer to these abuses. But you are not the only ones who fought to survive."

He dragged his fingers down the wolfskin rug until he reached the muzzle.

"Remember what I told you about the physical world? Fires, oceans, wild beasts—all become bloodthirsty when their survival is at stake. This violence is echoed in the human heart. We're the ones who cut our bloodlust into a blade, sharpened it like a set of teeth."

He tapped the wolf's yellow canines.

"The violence of animals is pure. Eat or be eaten. It isn't personal. But we muddied ours with hatred."

He met Mia's eyes. "Growing up in Glas Ddir, did you know any Addi?"

"Not a one."

"Why do you think that is?"

"Because our king was a bigot. He hated anyone he perceived to be different."

She thought of Quin and the boy who'd taught him piano, and what Ronan had done when he discovered them together in the crypt.

"That's right," Zai said. "When Ronan sealed the borders, it wasn't just to keep you in. It was to keep us out."

He pushed himself to his feet and walked to the window, where he gazed out onto the port.

"I won't bore you. You already know the Addi bear a long history of oppression. When the colonizers came to Luum'Addi, they were threatened by our music, our dress, our language. They forbade us from singing the Yöluk or worshiping our gods. Addi who looked like me"—he gestured toward his rounded eyes and dark hair—"had it hardest, because to them we looked the most like monsters. But we all suffered."

"I'm sorry," Mia said, and meant it. Once again she'd been ignorant, confined by her own assumptions. Had she really thought only women faced imbalances of power? It seemed hopelessly naive. But why had she never heard anything about men practicing magic? Her mother didn't mention it in her journal, and there certainly weren't any male Dujia on Refúj.

She thought of something Pilar d'Aqila had said. *That's what you don't understand about magic. It isn't evil—it's a way of combating evil. A way to topple the power structures that have held women captive for thousands of years.*

Mia felt vaguely smug. At least Pil had been wrong about *some*thing.

"The Grand Fyremaster is trying to make amends to all Addi," Zai said. "Women and men alike."

A detail snapped into place. "You know Kristoffin Dove. Of course you do! He was drinking at your tavern the night we met." Mia frowned. "Did he know you were dragging me off to the palace?"

"We may have discussed it. He was headed in the same direction." He sighed. "I would never cause you harm, Mia. That night on the boat—"

"No need to talk about that again."

"We never did talk about it. I want you to know that my putting you in that position . . . feeling forced to do something you didn't want to do . . ." He turned from the window to look at her. "I read everything wrong. I can't forgive myself for it."

"There's nothing to forgive," she said stiffly. "I thought I wanted something, but I was wrong. When I told you to stop, you stopped."

She leaned hard into the mantel above the fireplace. "But not all kinds of harm are physical. My mother spent the last three years lying to me. You picked up the lie and carried it farther."

"I'm sorry. I should have told you the truth from the start."

The tension in her shoulders began to ease. She knew her anger at Zai was misdirected. Yes, he'd lied to her. But only at her mother's behest.

Where *was* her mother? After three years of not seeing Mia's face, it hurt that Wynna had evidently decided her time was better spent elsewhere.

"You said you'd tell me anything I want to know," she said to Zai.

"And I meant it."

Mia didn't want to fight anymore. She wanted to understand. She joined him at the window. "Do all Addi have magic?"

"I think many of us have magic in our blood," he said, thoughtful. "But this knowledge has been crushed to powder, like so many other truths inside us. So small we can no longer see them."

Mia didn't have to feel the fire-warmed room to know it was a good deal hotter than the snow outside; the contrast in temperature had coated the glass in a thick film of condensation. She watched Zai etch a perfect circle into the fog, then section it into six parts.

"Some of us embrace the full potential of the Elemental Hex," he said. "We've learned to bend the natural balances. Others are afraid of the Hex's power."

Mia wanted to be delicate and respectful; at the same time she was dying to ask him about his magic. This ability—to render an image on the page, then in someone's mind—was new to her, both terrifying and exhilarating.

"Do you know where the Hex first came from?" Zai asked.

"The elements, I thought."

"There are different origin stories. Six has always been an important number in Luum'Addi."

"I imagine it's why the frostflower has six petals."

"It's the other way around. Because the frostflower has six petals, the number six became important. The bloom has special meaning to the Addi. It's why I first questioned your ink."

"But the bloom is all over Luumia." Mia nodded toward the crest over the fireplace. "It's even on the flag."

"Yes. The Luumi thought the flowers looked especially nice when crushed underfoot by an ice leopard."

"Colonialism in a nutshell," she muttered, feeling pleased when she earned a wry smile from Zai.

"The number six isn't only about the elements. It goes back to Græÿa." He gestured toward her wrist. "May I?"

When she nodded, he carefully peeled back her sleeve, his fingers grazing the frostflower inked onto her skin.

"This symbol has been passed down from the earliest Addi. It's the mark of the witch. One petal for each of her six children."

"Is that why the runes are supposed to guide children back home?"

"Not just home—back to each other. The Six Souls are most powerful when they're together. That's how they survived."

"I thought they *didn't* survive."

"Everyone has their own theories. I believe not only did they survive, they grew up to have children of their own, who had children, who had children. The lineage continues." He broadened his shoulders. "I'm a proud descendant of the original Renderer."

Zai began tracing shapes into the condensation on the windowpane, etching a family of ghosts.

"The Renderer," he said. "The Flesh Thief. The Silver Sorcerer. The Warrior. The Wonderer. And the Liaress."

He wiped his misty finger on his trousers.

"There you have it. The Six Souls of Jyöl. Take a look."

She stepped forward to examine the drawing more closely.

"No, no. Not there." He pivoted her gently. "*There.*"

Mia inhaled sharply.

Six figures stood in a circle across the room.

The family of ghosts had come to life.

Chapter 38

A MOTHER'S TOUCH

THE GHOSTS WERE ALIVE.

At the very least, they weren't dead.

Mia stood in awe. "You rendered them."

"Hard to make a masterpiece on a wet window," Zai said. "But good enough."

Their outlines were wispy and indistinct, like their smudged shapes on the glass. When Mia inched closer, she saw lopsided mouths, eyes gouged out of foreheads; their bodies lumpy and irregular, as if molded out of clay. Or rather, fog.

Their shoulders rose and fell. Almost imperceptibly, but she caught it.

"Are they . . ."

"Breathing? Yes. I can make them breathe."

"But do they . . . I mean, are they . . . *real*?"

"Depends on how you define real. If your eye sees something—and your mind believes it—does it exist?"

Mia reached out to touch the closest Soul. Her hand slid through empty air.

"I can't make them material," Zai said. "They live and breathe only in your mind's eye."

"Phantoms," Mia whispered.

"They're pictures. Nothing more. A trick of the aether."

The figures were beginning to fade, first from the glass, then the room.

"What a remarkable gift," she said. "Thank you for showing me."

"There's something else I need to tell you, Mia."

She wasn't sure she could take any more surprises.

"I mentioned my cousin doesn't live in Kom'Addi with the rest of my family," he said. "That's because she lives here."

"In Valavïk?"

"Here in the palace."

Mia raised a brow. "One of the queen's guards?"

"Not exactly."

The realization struck.

"Four gods. Your cousin is the queen."

"I wanted to tell you," Zai said. "It's just . . . I didn't want to overwhelm you. You've had to digest a good deal of new information since coming here, and—"

"Does that mean Lord Kristoffin Dove is your *father*?"

"No, no. Other side of the family. Dove is her uncle on her mother's side. Freyja's father was Addi. Remember how I told you the late queen fell in love with a boy from Kom'Addi? That boy was my uncle. My mother's brother."

He let out a long sigh. "My mother wasn't happy when her baby brother took up with a Luumi woman, particularly a royal. She felt like he turned his back on who he was. Thought he was ashamed of being Addi. Some families might be happy to have an open invitation to the Snow Queen's palace, but not mine. My uncle stepped into a very different world, and once he got a taste of it, he never looked back."

Mia was reeling. "No wonder you could afford a shiny new batch of fyre ice for your boat."

"I've never asked my cousin for a single coin," he said sharply.

"And yet you run her errands. Retrieving girls in White Lagoon and tricking them aboard your boat."

"I told you: I help Freyja from time to time. She's a paying customer, and she pays well. But I've worked for everything I have. I bought my alehouse and my boat. The fyre ice came from Dove, yes, but I paid for it. I wouldn't—"

"Any more secrets you've been keeping from me? Just when I thought you might finally be trustworthy."

"Like I said: I've always had a foot in both worlds."

"That's truer than you know. You speak ill of the Luumi royals who used fyre ice to fuel their excess—yet you seem perfectly happy to reap the benefit of those excesses."

Zai bristled. "I swore I would make a good life for myself somewhere else. A *better* life. But I also swore I wouldn't be like Freyja's father—or Freyja herself. I have never turned my back on who I was. I am proud to be Addi. Proud to call Luum'Addi my home."

He tapped his chest. "You've seen my fyre ink. The frostflower serves as a reminder of where I came from. But I'll never let myself be poor and hungry again. I will never go back."

"If your frostflower is meant to bring you back to your family," Mia said, "then it has failed."

The silence stretched taut between them like a rope waiting to be snapped.

A hard knock echoed through the chambers.

"Mia?"

Her mother.

He was already moving toward the door.

"You finally got what you asked for," he said. "Don't waste it."

Wynna stood in her opulent chambers, staring out the window at the wind-whipped sea. She hadn't looked at Mia once. Who was this cold and quiet stranger? Her ivory skin was paler than it had ever been in Glas Ddir. Less sunlight in the snow kingdom. Or perhaps her mother spent more time lounging in the palace while the queen's servants fed her candied grapes.

"So you live here now." Mia's voice was cold. "In your palatial chambers."

"I live here now," her mother said simply. Something in her

tone made Mia think the last three years had not been a merry cavalcade of parties and idle pleasures. The lines around Wynna's eyes had deepened. She seemed thinner, her figure swathed in thick snow fox cloaks.

"Are you cold?" Mia asked.

"I haven't felt cold in some time." Without turning from the window, her mother asked, "Have you?"

"No," she answered honestly. "I haven't felt much of anything."

"It was the same for me. And the fyre ink?" Wynna tapped her own wrist. "Did you feel it?"

Mia realized her frostflower mark was still exposed. Self-conscious, she rolled her sleeve back down.

"No."

"I fear this is the legacy I've left you." Her mother pressed her palm into the glass pane, as if she were trying to absorb the cold. "The numbness. The endless gray fog."

Mia's heart plummeted. *You think your mother can unbreak you.*

Nell was right. Mia had traveled from Glas Ddir, stumbled through White Lagoon, hitched a ride with a strange boy—who turned out to be a lying smuggler—all on the desperate hope her mother could fill up the empty space inside her.

Even as Mia's heart sank, a piece of it lifted.

At least someone else knew how it felt to be broken.

Her mother's hand dropped to her side. *"A body without sensation is like a broken violin. Still beautiful, but empty without the music that made it sing."* She smiled a little. "Kristoffin taught me that. It's an ancient Luumi saying."

"So you're trading colloquialisms with the queen's uncle?" The words spewed out with more vitriol than Mia intended. A moment ago she'd felt herself opening; now the drawbridge was hinging shut.

"I think you'll like Kristoffin."

"You seem quite at home here in the Snow Queen's palace."

"They have been kind to me."

"Mm."

A minute in and they'd already exhausted all conversation. Hurt and hope warred inside Mia's head.

"All this time," she said.

"All this time," her mother echoed.

Slowly, painstakingly, Wynna turned away from the window. When her hazel eyes settled on her daughter, they were full of emotions Mia couldn't read.

"None of this is easy, my raven girl. For either of us. I don't want to lie to you. There's been far too much of that already." She fidgeted with the pearl clasps on her cloak. "So much can happen in three years. I don't even know where to begin."

"How about at the beginning?"

Her mother gave a small nod.

"Won't you sit?" she said, motioning toward the snow plum vanity.

"Why?"

She gestured toward her daughter's unruly curls. "For old time's sake."

Mia didn't want to sit at a vanity. She wanted her mother to tell her how to balance the elements and neutralize Angelyne's moonstone so she could go get Quin. And of course, more truthfully, she wanted to know if she would ever feel alive again.

But Mia was so tired. She pulled back the chair and sank into it numbly.

"My little red raven." Wynna placed a gentle hand on her shoulder. "Your hair has never been in greater need of a mother's touch."

Nor have I, Mia thought. Nor have I.

Chapter 39

FAIRY TALE

Mia perched warily on the chair's edge, her eyes fixed on the oval looking glass. She didn't want to look at her mother. Didn't want to feel the pang of knowing her mother was not looking back.

"I don't know how I lose these things," Wynna muttered to herself, rummaging through a messy drawer stuffed with combs, pins, and brushes. "Here we are." She pulled out a pearly tortoiseshell comb.

Memories poured through Mia's head of the nights she'd spent in the cottage, her mother patiently worked a tortoiseshell comb through her curls. It was all achingly familiar.

"Do you remember the tangles you would get when you were

a girl? You'd run free in the forest all day and come home with a headful of knots."

Wynna began to draw the comb through Mia's ringlets, first delicately, then with more confidence. They were both slipping back into old motions.

"I'd never dealt with curls before, not like yours. Neither of us knew what we were doing. You'd sit before the looking glass, clenching your little fists, while I combed out one tangle at a time. It took us hours sometimes. But we always managed. We'd work through every knot, untangle every snarl, together."

Mia sensed this was not only about her hair.

"You've grown up," her mother murmured. "As clever as always, and lovely, too. You have your father's eyes. But you look like my mother, at least how I remember her. You were always more Wren than Rose."

Her mother tipped the comb onto one edge and dragged a straight line from crown to nape. Mia tried to conjure up the tingling sensations on her scalp; the warmth that had once sat in her chest, tight and cozy, while they swapped stories and spilled secrets.

It was all gone. The easy conversation, the delectable tingles. There was only the cloak.

"*Tell me something I don't know about you,*" Mia said, her voice low and pointed.

The comb stopped moving. "Oh, Mia."

In the looking glass, her mother looked so much like Ange-lyne. The hours leading up to the royal wedding bled back: Angie painting Mia's face with skin greases, whipping her into a giant white soufflé of a bride, all the while knowing Pilar was poised in the chapel with an arrow ready for her heart.

"I'll go first." Mia's eyes bore into her mother's reflection as the words bubbled to the surface. "Angelyne wanted me dead. Did you know that? My own sister tried to murder me—and your Dujia sisters helped her do it. Zaga sent her daughter to do the deed."

Her mother's face clouded. "You've met Pilar?"

"Who cares about Pilar? I'm talking about my sister. Angie wears your moonstone around her neck, but it's no longer a healing stone. She uses it to control people, to kill and destroy. And if we don't stop her . . . if we don't go back to the river kingdom . . ."

She didn't finish. Her mother set the comb on the vanity, the uneasy clack of tortoiseshell against wood exposing the tremble in her hands.

"I don't expect your forgiveness, Mia. But I am asking for your compassion."

"I'm not sure you deserve it."

Wynna let out a long breath. "I knew you had magic. When we had our fight, I could feel it, even if you didn't yet know. I was terrified the Hunters would discover you. I never expected your sister would find out first."

"Angie threatened to reveal you. You must have known she would reveal me, too—that if you stopped your own heart, there wouldn't be anyone to protect me. But you did it anyway. You saved yourself and left me behind."

The words stung. Wasn't that exactly what Mia had done to Quin?

"I was afraid." Her mother's eyes glistened. "I panicked. There wasn't time to make prudent choices. No Dujia wants to break the Second Law. But I knew your father would protect you. I had already entrusted him with my journal—he knew that, if something happened to me, he was to give it to you when you were ready."

"Ah, yes. Father, Hunter of Dujia. And a journal that led me to the fire kingdom, far from where you were."

"I thought I would be there! I was supposed to be there."

Wynna's shoulders sagged. "We knew the river kingdom was more dangerous than ever, especially once the king began to suspect Griffin was no longer loyal to the Circle of the Hunt. Your father and I were making plans to flee—all four of us. But life rarely follows the plans we make for it."

"Father was going to leave the Circle?"

"He was consumed by remorse. Even before the night Angelyne discovered my magic and threatened to reveal me, Griffin was beginning to understand the Gwyrach were not the demons he'd believed. We had long, honest conversations. I told him that if my life were ever threatened, I would stop my own heart."

She bowed her head. "It was your father who arranged for my body to be quietly removed from the castle crypt. He knew people in the snow kingdom. He knew the late Snow Queen herself. Here in Luumia, he goes by a different name: the Snow Wolf. The legendary assassin, traveling between kingdoms to hunt. But your father no longer kills women like us. He has helped dozens of Dujia escape the river kingdom and find safe haven."

"He knew about Refúj?"

"Of course. He helped you find it, didn't he?"

Mia thought of the journal her father had hidden in the train of her wedding gown. "So Father was secretly helping the very women he was supposed to kill."

"As leader of the Circle, he found himself in a unique position. No one was a better Hunter. So he kept hunting. Only, instead of killing Dujia, he ferried them to safety."

Wynna picked up the comb, running her finger over the teeth. "Your father is deeply grieved by his own deeds. For years he has done everything in his power to make reparations." She smiled a little. "Sometimes people can surprise you."

Mia arched an eyebrow. "An understatement."

"It's been a gift to watch your father become a good man. He comes to the snow kingdom once a year on the last night of Jyöl. He sails a ship into the harbor, full of Dujia who are seeking refuge."

Mia was floored—and it had nothing to do with the shipful of Dujia.

"So Father's grief was a fabrication. He's been taking regular jaunts to the snow kingdom, sipping tea with his wife this whole time."

"*Former* wife. And it wasn't a fabrication. Your father did lose me, just not in the way you thought." She placed a tentative hand on Mia's shoulder.

343

Mia wished she could feel it—the softness, the warmth.

"Was there anything either of you ever did," she said quietly, "anything you ever told me, that *wasn't* a lie?"

Wynna removed her hand.

"I know you're angry. You have every right to be. We fed you a steady diet of lies. Your king, your father. I lied to you as well. It wasn't your fault. Children are hungry; they eat what they are given."

She steadied herself on the vanity. "I didn't want to stop my own heart, Mia. No one does. You of all people should know that."

"I don't blame you for stopping your heart. You did what you had to do to survive. I blame you for everything after. For what you *didn't* do. You left us alone in our grief. What happened to Angelyne . . . what happened to *me* . . ."

Mia stared up at the ceiling, furious at the tears pooling in her eyes.

"I don't know how to use my magic," she said, "because you weren't there when I bloomed. I listened to the wrong people. I killed Princess Karri. I will always have her blood on my hands, all because I trusted Zaga when I shouldn't have. How am I supposed to forgive you if I can't even forgive myself?"

Her mother laid a palm over her own heart, as if the words caused her physical pain.

"I know I failed you and your sister. I failed *all* my Dujia sisters."

"I don't give a shit about them! I needed my mother. You told me to trust my heart, even if it killed me. It *did* kill me.

Even now, sitting here with you, feeling nothing, I'm not sure I'm entirely alive."

Mia clenched her jaw. "But I've come to set things right. Angelyne was hungrier than I was. She swallowed more fear, more hatred. We have to stop her. The only way to do that is to balance the elements in your moonstone so she can't use magic to hurt any more people. We have to save Quin. We have to save them all."

She turned from the looking glass to look into her mother's eyes. "We'll work through every knot. Untangle every snarl, together."

Her mother's gaze was steady. "I admire you, my raven girl. You ask questions, and you demand the truth." Slowly she exhaled. "For a long time, I fought. But I am tired of fighting. Tired of the fear and the lying. I have other things calling for my attention. Quieter places to put my heart."

She took a step back. "I'm not going back to the river kingdom, Mia. My life is here now."

If her mother had speared her through the heart with a dagger, it would have hurt less.

"Since your life is here now," Mia spat, her voice like poison in her throat, "I take it you're quite cozy with the Snow Queen?"

"Her name is Freyja."

The way her mother said the word—the gentleness buried in the letters—told Mia everything.

"You're in love with her. That's why you chose to stay."

Wynna knit her hands together. "There was something

between us from the moment we met. A spark I hadn't felt in many years."

The knowledge shook Mia to the core. Three years of grief withering her own heart while new love bloomed in her mother's.

"How wonderful for you. You flee a wicked land, leave your husband and sad little daughters, and find love in the land of frost. No wonder you don't want to come with me to the river kingdom. You're living in your very own fairy tale."

Her mother inhaled deeply. "Not a fairy tale. Just a new beginning."

She tugged open a smaller drawer at the top of the vanity.

"I do have something for you. Newly arrived from the glass kingdom." She pulled out a small vial of sand-colored liquid. "A brilliant Pembuka innovation. It doesn't make all the sensations come back—I still can't feel hot or cold—but last week I tasted the licorice in a chocolate snowdrop. Yesterday I caught the scent of wood burning in the hearth. And I can feel joy, too, in tiny, precious slivers."

Mia stared at the vial. Despair slashed at her throat, puncturing the words.

"Did you feel a sliver of joy when you saw me?"

Wynna's eyes fell. "I was relieved to see you, yes. And I felt happy. But I'm not sure happiness will ever be what it was. Not for me. I hope it will be different for you."

She held out the vial.

"One drop before anything you want to savor and enjoy, like a pleasant conversation or a fine meal. You may be able to taste food again, if only for a moment."

Mia stared at the vial. Wasn't this what she'd wanted? Relief from the cloak—and a way out of the box.

Only it didn't bring back joy. Not really. The "magical elixir" teased an occasional taste of licorice and left you dead inside.

What pitiful recompense for everything she'd lost.

Mia didn't take the bottle. She stood.

"Children eat what they are given, Mother. And I am not a child."

Chapter 40

TINKERING AND TOILING

MIA MARCHED DOWN THE palace corridors, determined to erase the memory of her mother's blank face. She passed spacious drawing rooms, vaulted galleries with books and paintings, even a garden with a grove of snow plum trees.

Her mother wasn't going to help her save Quin. She wasn't going to do anything but sit in her pretty chambers, mooning over the queen. She couldn't fix Mia. She couldn't even fix herself.

Mia ground to a halt, the soles of her boots squeaking on the polished marble floors. A giant birdcage hung suspended by four iron cables at the corridor's end. It was boxy at the bottom and domed up top, wrought iron plated in bronze. At the top of the dome a hinged door functioned as a hatch; at the bottom, the gridded iron base housed a complex system of cranks and shafts.

"Care for a ride?"

Mia spun around to find a white-bearded gentleman in a long plum cloak, his hands clasped behind his back.

"Lord Dove," she said, remembering. Before she'd known him as the queen's uncle, he was simply her drinking chum at Zai's alehouse: jovial, pink-cheeked, impish.

"I thought I told you to call me Kristoffin," he said, the same paternal twinkle in his silvery-blue eyes.

"And *I* thought I was coming here to the queen's palace of my own accord," she countered. "It would seem our midnight dram of silver death was not quite so coincidental."

He smiled. "Sharp as an arrow, and just as quick." He gestured toward the cage. "I see you've found my prized invention. I call it 'The Descending Room.'"

Kristoffin stooped to fiddle with one of the cranks, then stood, grimaced, and muttered something about his creaky back. He flourished a hand.

"Care to join me?"

She hadn't yet decided how she felt about Kristoffin Dove. The droll lord before her seemed at odds with the legend of the Grand Fyremaster, hallowed savior of Luumia.

But he was a welcome distraction.

Mia cast a skeptical eye at the birdcage.

"Where does it go, exactly?"

"Ah. Well." He leaned in conspiratorially. "The Descending Room goes only one way."

"Let me guess," Mia said. "Down."

As Kristoffin scuppered them beneath the palace, the cage emitted a series of shrieks and moans. With every twist of the crank, the carriage descended another five or six feet, swaying gently on its strings.

Cables, Mia reminded herself. Not strings. That made her feel slightly safer about the whole arrangement.

"A polly's farthing renders sin!" Kristoffin shouted. "Would you lie to sea?"

She strained to hear him. "What?"

"Apologies for the horrendous din! Would you like to see?"

He lifted the hatch overhead, and Mia peered through it. One large crank grated against a series of smaller cranks, teeth grinding together as a large tube puffed violet steam.

"Fyre ice!" Kristoffin shouted, though she'd guessed that already.

Seconds later, the box came to a jolting stop. He heaved the iron doors open with an echoing screech, then offered a hand to help her descend.

"This way," he said, ushering her down a long corridor. Buried in the silver walls were thousands of tiny lights, lustrous specks of ivory and lilac no bigger than pinpricks. Despite being dozens of feet underground, the hall was as bright as a moonlit night in Ilwysion, the skies lanced with opalescent stars.

"You'll excuse an old man his dabblings," Kristoffin said, gesturing toward the walls. "But I do so enjoy decorating for Jyöl."

"What are they?" Mia asked.

"I call them shimmers."

Up close they were shaped like tears. But they couldn't be prisms: the light they reflected wasn't from torches or candles. They glimmered from an unseen source.

"You can touch them," Kristoffin said. "I assure you they are perfectly safe."

Mia touched one lightly. It came loose, a daub of violet shimmer on her fingertip.

"I'm sorry, I didn't mean to—"

"Take as many as you like. I can always make more. Ah, here we are."

Kristoffin pulled a white velvet rope and a pair of metal doors clanged open. "Welcome to my little shop of tinkering and toiling."

Mia sucked in her breath.

She was staring at a monster.

Chapter 41

KINDRED SPIRITS

THE *bowels* OF A monster, to be more accurate.

Kristoffin's shop was a gaping maw, snaked with pipes of brass and copper. They reached across the walls and floors, looping and coiling like the intestines of a giant.

And that wasn't all. Half a dozen laboratory assistants—five men, one woman—bent over tabletops alive with movement: boiling liquids in thin glass tubes; elements mingling together on silver observation plates. This place was a scientist's dream.

"Forgive me," Dove said. "We've been working such long hours to prepare for the Illuminations. It's a bit of a mess."

"It's incredible," Mia murmured.

He took a dramatic bow. "Aboveground, I am Kristoffin Dove,

the Snow Queen's senile uncle. Down here, I am the Grand Fyre-master."

A boom sounded from across the room, so loud Mia jumped.

"Good Græÿa!" Kristoffin swore. "It appears we haven't quite—"

Another deafening boom. He threw his hands into the air.

"My apologies. We still have some wrinkles to iron out, apparently! Can't have the Illuminations scaring the little ones."

He pointed toward the culprit: a giant glass box. Mia moved closer for a better look.

Two copper pipes leaked colored vapor into the cube: one blue, one red. Where the vapors collided, they formed a sphere of purple fire. The ball hovered a few inches in the air, hissing, crackling, spewing indigo sparks.

Mia traced the copper pipes, trying to source the origin of the vapor. But they diverged sharply once they reached the floor; she lost track of them in the nest of twining cables.

The flaming orb expanded in a sudden paroxysm—and this time, Mia covered her ears. She watched as long lavender tendrils broke off from the sphere, fluttering like hair ribbons against the glass.

"These are the Illuminations?" she called over her shoulder.

"Yes," Kristoffin said, a few inches behind her. He was closer than she'd thought. "A small-scale version, anyway. I've been testing them elsewhere in Luumia, but it's nice to have a controlled indoor space. Stunning, isn't she?" He beamed at the orb. "I've always thought of fire as a woman. Elegant and all-powerful, beautiful but deadly. As the old mystics once said: *When you strike a woman, you strike a match.*"

"You like these sayings."

"I collect them. We Luumi have a rich tradition of proverbs from men far wiser than I. Wisdom itself becomes a kind of fuel. It grows stronger the more you use it."

"Not many fuels do that."

He winked. The wink looked wrong on the Grand Fyremaster's face, yet somehow eerily familiar.

"This is precisely what makes fyre ice so unique," he said. "A natural resource, it can never be depleted."

Mia wanted to ask Dove the same question she'd asked Ville at the White Lagoon. Didn't all natural resources deplete?

"I know you think me a doddering fool," he said. "But I speak the truth. The fyre ice of twenty years ago is no more. We have found a new strand that's far more powerful—one that burns clean."

"I thought the new fyre ice was purple?" Mia scrutinized the blue and red vapors feeding separately into the box.

"Different varieties, of course. You wouldn't believe what we've been able to accomplish in such a short span of time! We've found ways to grow food even in the dead of winter. To *cook* food to kill off the animalcules that make people sick. We've discovered not only cures for the pox, but inoculations to prevent it. And look at this."

He waved her over to a different tableau, shooing two assistants away. A giant map of Luumia unfurled across the wall.

Mia inhaled sharply.

The map was alive.

In Kom'Addi, miniature brown reinsdyr grazed on the tundra, munching mushrooms with tiny caps. To the east, Fojuen volqa-noes loomed, bubbling quietly at the mouth. To the west, orange sands whipped over the glimmering glass cities of Pembuk. To the north Mia saw her own kingdom: majestic forests and jagged cliffs, the black Natha River winding through the trees.

And stretching between all four kingdoms: a network of roads.

"Imagine the potential," Kristoffin said excitedly, "of expanded transportation. A way to bolster trade and cultural exchange. To connect instead of isolate. Our discoveries will no longer be ours alone. They will belong to all four kingdoms."

He pointed to a tiny wheeled carriage chugging along with no horses or reinsdyr, its rear pipe expelling clouds of empurpled steam. A shrunken version of the one Mia had seen in White Lagoon.

Kristoffin gestured around the laboratory. "This is only the beginning. We are on the cusp of transformation—and I am in dire need of assistance to usher it forth. From what I've seen, you possess a thirsty and inquisitive mind. I could put it to good use."

Mia frowned. "You speak as if I'll be staying indefinitely."

"You could stay with your mother. Make the palace your home. In fact I have something that might help ease your transition."

He pulled a small vial of sandy liquid from a nearby drawer. "There are some wonderful new elixirs coming out of Pembuk."

Mia stiffened. "My mother already tried to give me this. She didn't exactly give it a ringing endorsement."

Kristoffin held the vial between his thumb and forefinger. "Forgive me, but I believe we are kindred spirits, you and I. But a scientist stripped of sensory perceptions is like a hollow wooden box. How can one investigate life when she can't feel it herself?"

Mia froze. Had her mother told him?

Nell's words circled through her mind once again. *This whole trip has been one grand experiment, a way for you to feel something again, and you don't care who gets hurt along the way.*

She stared at the vial, gripped by shame.

Mia had been lying to herself since the moment she woke from the box. She hadn't really come to Luumia to save Quin. The truth was far simpler.

She wanted to be alive. To *feel* alive.

She took the vial and dropped it in her pocket.

"Wonderful!" Kristoffin said, clearly pleased. "I hope this means you'll consider being my assistant. Of course we'll need to train you first. We can't have you breaking any bones, not in my lab!"

Mia gaped at him. How did he know she'd broken someone's bones?

She was being paranoid. Kristoffin was Zai's uncle, or uncle once removed—whatever that relationship was called. Zai probably gave him a full report.

By the laboratory doors, a brass bell swung to and fro at the end of a long rope, the chime clanging through the room.

"A ship has arrived in the harbor." Kristoffin smiled. "Just in time for Jyöl! Remember when we met in White Lagoon, I told you I was carting foreign goods for the queen? One of those goods is a Glasddiran you know quite well."

Mia's heart seized in her chest. *Angelyne.*

"My sister is *here*?"

"No, no, no." His laugh was jolly. "I mean your sister's husband. Quin has returned."

Chapter 42

DUET

QUIN WAS BEAUTIFUL.

Mia had always thought so. Even in the beginning, when he played the part of the ice prince so well, she'd feasted her eyes on the sharp cut of his cheekbones, his tousled golden curls. He was beautiful when he lay dying in the underground tunnels, an arrow lodged in his chest. Beautiful in the snow-smothered mountains, the steamy hot spring, and in the Natha River the night they pressed their bodies close. Beautiful the day she left him in the castle, helpless against her sister's enthrall.

Now, as he walked from the port to the palace, it had never been more true. The other passengers piled off the ship, but Mia hardly noticed. All she saw was Quin. In a land of limited sunlight, his hair caught every ray.

Quin was beautiful. He was safe.

And he was not alone.

From her hiding nook on a window seat, perched high in the palace, Mia watched Quin climb the stairs with a dark-haired girl by his side. *Not* her sister, which came as a relief. The girl was short, lithe on her feet, slick black hair chopped close to the chin. There was something proud in her carriage, familiar. Try as she might, Mia couldn't distinguish her facial features. But then she couldn't distinguish Quin's, either.

She didn't need to. She remembered everything. Seeing him stirred something deep inside her. Feelings she thought she wouldn't feel again.

When he reached for the girl's hand, she wove her fingers effortlessly into his. The gesture stung. For a moment Mia almost wished he were being enthralled—an awful thing to wish on anyone, let alone someone she cared about.

But somehow she knew this wasn't enthrallment. Quin's posture was easy, natural. More comfortable in his own skin than she had ever seen him.

She stopped watching after that.

Mia sank into the ivory cushions of the window seat, arms wrapped around her knees. The Grand Fyremaster—or the queen's uncle, she supposed, now that they were back aboveground—had scurried off to prepare for their visitors. She was glad Kristoffin had left her alone.

Quin was safe. That was the important thing. Angelyne hadn't hurt him—at least not visibly. Of course Mia knew all too well that some wounds cut deep into the heart. She could only imagine the torments he had been subjected to in the castle. All those months.

All those months she hadn't gone back.

Quin was happy. That was the important thing. He'd found a way out of Kaer Killian, met someone else along the journey. A Luumi girl, perhaps. Could Mia blame him? For all he knew, she had died that night in the crypt. Dead was a permanent state of being—for most people, anyway.

She wasn't sure how long she spent hunched on the window seat. Enough time to replay every moment she'd ever shared with Quin, every smile, every maddening fight. They'd spent two weeks in each other's company. Hardly that, even. Half the time they'd been running for their lives. The other half they were careening toward their own doom, though they didn't know it.

Two weeks. A laughably tiny sliver in the grand scheme. Not enough time to even *know* another person, let alone love them.

"Are you all right?"

She gave a start. Zai stood quietly in the corridor.

"How long have you been there?"

"A little while."

Seeing him standing there so still and respectful made her want to cry.

"What are you doing here, Zai? Shouldn't you be headed back to your alehouse?"

"Freyja said I could stay for the Illuminations. We'll be up on the northern balcony. You can join us, if you like."

Mia forced herself up off the window seat. She couldn't feel the soreness in her muscles; only when she stumbled forward did she realize how stiff they were.

Zai reached out to catch her, but she straightened.

"The queen has visitors," she said. "I'm going to see them."

"You mean Quin?"

An inscrutable expression flickered over Zai's face. Sadness? Disappointment? She didn't ask. Now that Quin was here, any dalliance she'd had with Zai—or with any of the boys she'd met in White Lagoon—suddenly seemed empty.

"Yes," she said. "I mean Quin."

He nodded, as if he'd expected it. "I saw him in the music room."

Zai led Mia down one winding white palace corridor after another until piano music wafted down the halls, haunting and deep.

It had to be Quin. The song reminded her of the one he'd played in the castle the night before their ill-fated wedding. This melody was different—sadder—but boasted the same elegance.

Zai stopped in front of a pair of frosted glass doors.

"The music room," he said.

Mia stood to the side of the glass, suddenly nervous. What would she say to Quin? How to explain that, yes, she'd been alive all this time . . . but she hadn't come back for him?

"Anything else I can do for you?" Zai said curtly.

She searched his face, trying to tell if he was angry or simply hurt. But his eyes were hard. Inscrutable.

"No. I . . ." The words wilted before they reached her mouth. "Thank you for everything."

Without a word, he turned on his heel and hurried down the hall.

Mia couldn't waste time worrying about Zai. She edged closer to the doors, peering through the frosted glass. She saw two people in a white room. One standing, one sitting. Mia waited, pulse pounding in her ears. When the song came to an end, she put her hands on the glass handles and pushed.

The doors swung open too softly for anyone to notice. No sooner had Mia stepped into the room than the melody started up again. This time, there were two instruments instead of one.

In the quiet torchlight, she found herself staring at a cream-colored piano with Quin at the bench. He was angled away from her, facing the large window, but she'd know him anywhere. At his side was the dark-haired girl, horsehair bow clasped lightly in her fingers. She had a white violin tucked beneath her chin.

They were playing a duet.

Mia couldn't see Quin's hands, but she could see the girl's. The torchlight made the violin look almost wet, the bow sailing over the strings like ripples on the sea.

Mia stood in the doorway, transfixed by the music. The notes laced themselves together, one instrument blending exquisitely into the other, like two voices in perfect harmony. Even Quin's song in the library at Kaer Killian couldn't compete. He was far better with this girl than he was alone.

He said something Mia couldn't hear. The girl tipped back her head and laughed. Mia saw her face.

Pilar d'Aqila.

Mia's failed assassin. Daughter of Zaga, the woman who had loved Mia's mother, corrupted her sister, and betrayed the Dujia—including Pilar herself.

Pilar saw Mia, too.

The violin dropped from her hands, clattering to the marble floor.

"Shit."

The music ceased abruptly as Quin pivoted on the bench.

"Mia?" A question.

"Quin."

All the shock Mia expected to see on his face materialized on Pilar's instead. Her olive skin had drained of color, now more gray than gold. Pilar stepped toward her, then stopped, as if she didn't know whether to move forward or back.

"How in four hells are you here, Rose? You're supposed to be dead."

Mia didn't answer. She was watching Quin. His eyes didn't leave hers, even as he reached into his jacket and extracted a piece of yellow parchment folded crisply into thirds. He shook out the creases with one sharp flick.

"Now that I have you both together," he began.

Pilar wheeled around, hands balled into fists. "What did you just say?"

Mia didn't understand what was happening.

363

"Quin?" she said again, hating how plaintive her voice sounded. She took an uneasy step forward. "Aren't you surprised to see me?"

"I'm happy to see you, Mia." He stood from the piano bench. "But no. I'm not surprised."

Pilar looked like she was ready to shove his face through the window. "What the fuck is going on?"

"I promise, this will explain everything." Quin flourished the letter. "But it's rather long. Why don't you two take a seat? Get comfortable?"

Neither of them sat.

"Very well." He cleared his throat. "Let me tell you a story."

Quin began to read.

THE NIGHT OF THE WEEPING MOON

Pilar, my fearless warrior. Mia, my tireless wonderer.

My lovelies, my darlings, my elder sisters. Reunited at last.

Did you know you were bound by blood? When you first met in Refúj, could you feel it? When I first summoned you to the river kingdom, Pilar d'Aqila, and commanded you to lodge an arrow in my sister's heart, I never imagined that you, too, were my sister. Zaga failed to share this little detail, as she failed to share so many others.

A love affair before a love affair: our father enthralled by your mother, Pil, before he was enthralled by ours. Who would have taken Griffin Rose for such a lady-killer? But then I suppose he's been killing ladies all along.

I knew you weren't dead, Mi. As much as you claimed you'd do anything to protect me, you always chose yourself in the end. Even now, haven't you chosen your own welfare? You pretend to make noble sacrifices for others—to save your darling prince. But these are fictions you tell yourself. Though you went to Luumia under the pretense of saving Quin's life, from the moment you woke in that box, what you truly wanted was to save your own.

I have always been more generous than you. I am not opposed to second chances. I saw, in those final moments, something in your eyes I'd never seen before: an admission of defeat. You knew you'd been wrong: about me, about magic, about everything. And so I resolved to help you.

It was I who ensured your body be safely carried out of the crypt of Kaer Killian. I who sent you into the forest with two stones: fojuen to stop your heart, and lloira to restore it. I who sent the prince to revive you.

Quin brought you back to life in that wooden box, Mia. But I made sure he was long gone before you emerged. I left the frostflower rune in your possession, knowing you'd take it as a sign from our mother. I knew you'd stop at nothing to find her, because this is how you are: like a dog with a bone.

Relentless, even when all the meat is gone.

And I knew I'd be able to find you, when the time was right. That's the thing about sending someone on a mission they think they've devised themselves: they go right to where you want them.

But you, Pilar. You were always more unpredictable. One night I got your mother drunk on blackthorn wine and made her tell me everything about the circumstances of your conception. I knew then I'd found the sister I always wanted. The sister I deserved. My sister the warrior, who would gallop into battle alongside me and her fellow Dujia, righting the wrongs of this broken land.

I awoke the next morning to a rotten headache and even more rotten news: Pilar d'Aqila had run away. You'd left me alone in the castle with your mother, who in a way became mine.

I must be honest: Zaga was unperturbed by your escape. But I was heartbroken. My whole life, I'd dreamed of a sister like you, only to have you ripped from my arms the very moment I found you.

And then an idea occurred to me. I knew you'd be looking for your father, based on the lies your mother had told you, lies mingled with truths. If you journeyed to the snow kingdom, I realized I might be able to gather both my sisters in one place. I didn't have to lift a finger or send any of my men: I could let you ferry yourself to our rendezvous point. But I needed someone to accompany you, someone who could ensure you were headed in the right direction.

Someone like my husband.

Quin was to stay by your side every step of the way. If he was successful—if he is speaking these words to you both right now—then he fulfilled his duty. Do not be angry with him. He has cared for you both, has he not? In a way only he can do. And finally, after all this time, you are together in the Snow Queen's palace. All that's missing from this equation, my sisters, is me.

Pilar, I know you hate lying. From this day forth I swear to always tell you the truth. And so I must impart some heavy news: Zaga is dead. I killed her without ever touching her skin.

If I thought her loss would wound you gravely, I would wrap my arms around you and wipe the tears from your cheeks. But you know as well as I do she never loved either of us as a mother should. Zaga only loved herself. She wasn't there when you needed her the most.

I will not abandon you. I believe you. I will fight beside you in every battle, now and always.

Mia, you are either for us or against us. I hope you will fight beside your sisters. You have made many mistakes: now is your time to correct them. The Dujia of the river kingdom are hungry for the reign of their new queens. The Dujia of every kingdom cry out for a better tomorrow. And they deserve one.

You both failed to see me as I am. One of you wanted to save me; the other, to destroy me. Make no mistake: I could enkindle each of you with a snap of my fingers. It would be easy to make you want what I want. But I want you to choose it. As you once told me, Mi: if I were strong, I wouldn't need to enkindle people to make them follow me. I assure you, I am stronger than you think.

The veil has been lifted from my eyes. You've both been clinging to the old world. Old rules, old grievances, old revenge. Mia, you've been searching for Mother. Pilar, you've been searching for Father. You both thought you could find your family—that this would be the magic elixir to fix your broken hearts.

But the old world is dead. Our parents have failed us; they betrayed and abandoned us, fed us lies and hate. They tried to break us, but we will not be so easily broken. We are all that's left.

You are together at last. You have found one another. And soon I will find you, too. But first there is something I must do.

Good Jyöl, my sweet sisters. The Illuminations are starting soon. Meet me where the darkest night sparks the brightest dawn.

Your littlest,
Angelyne

Chapter 43

ONE LAST MISTAKE

PILAR BARELY WAITED FOR Quin to finish before she ripped the letter from his hands. Shredded it. Shoved the scraps into one of the torches, singeing her fingertips. Not that it mattered. She would have ignited the whole palace if she could have. Quin included.

Her mother, dead. A few lines in a letter and that was it: scraped off the earth like a scab off a knee.

Pilar thought she'd feel happy, or at least satisfied. But mostly she felt angry. Not that Angelyne had killed her mother—that she hadn't gotten to do it herself.

Zaga was dead, and Mia Rose wasn't.

Dead didn't amount to much these days.

Pilar was still reeling from the *other* letters. She didn't want to accept that Griffin Rose was her father, or that she'd inherited two half sisters: one dead, one deranged. In the midst of her whole world caving in, Quin was the one good and steady thing. But he'd been lying to her. Even after he'd sworn he wasn't. Even after *she'd* sworn never to trust him again. With or without the moonstone, he was still Angie's little errand boy.

"So this—everything, you and me—was all a lie."

He shifted his weight. If she had to hear him clear his throat one more time, she would clear it for him. With her fist.

"Pil," he said. "You know that isn't true."

"Answer the question."

Silence.

"To be fair," said Mia Rose quietly, "you didn't technically ask a question."

Pilar glared at her. None of this was Mia's fault—she knew that. But if the girl was going to go around rising from the grave, she could at least keep her mouth shut.

"Sisters," Mia whispered, more to herself than anyone.

"Oh that? Your father and my mother?" Pilar shrugged. "That's old news."

She was posturing. The news wasn't *that* old. She'd spent the last two days on the ship from Kom'Addi, ranting endlessly to Quin. No shortage of things to rant about. Pilar had raged, cursed, even gotten a little teary one night after too many nips of vaalkä. She'd cried on Quin's shoulder about how much she used to want a sister. Someone to play with. As she got older, someone to talk with. And after everything with Orry: someone to stand beside her. To believe.

But Pilar wanted nothing to do with Angelyne Rose. She hated that they shared even a drop of the same blood. Same with Griffin. All those wasted years dreaming about meeting her father. Now that she finally had, she couldn't stand to look at him.

Quin had been a good sport as her moods slingshot wildly. That was the thing about Quin: he was always a good sport.

A good, lying, backstabbing sport.

"I did destroy the moonstone," he said quietly. "But Angelyne is stronger now. Her magic goes deeper. Once she buries an idea in my head, I can never be free of it—not until I do what she asks. But then, sometimes . . ." He groped for the words. "Sometimes what she wants is what I want, too."

He turned to Mia. "I woke you up because I didn't have a choice. But I was also glad to do it. I thought you died in the crypt. When your sister told me we could bring you back, I didn't hesitate for a second."

He turned back to Pilar. "And I really was trying to escape. I thought, if you were strong enough to fight the enkindling, maybe I could fight the enthrall. But she caught me and told me to follow you. At first I only did it because it's what she wanted. And then, the more time we spent together, the more I got to know you—"

"How many times are we going to have this conversation?" Pilar spat. "What we did in the tavern? On the ship? Was that fake, too?"

Whenever she wasn't ranting, she and Quin had spent the last two days exploring each other's bodies. They fit well together: their hands, their lips. Other parts, too. She told him how and where to touch her, and he was happy to oblige.

Knowing that he'd betrayed her—that even with their bodies tangled up together, he was steering her somewhere without her knowledge or consent—knocked her right back to Orry's cottage. Hard dirt floor. Wooden rafters. Her fight teacher crushing her with his weight.

Quin let out his breath.

"Just because I want what she wants doesn't mean I don't also want things for myself." He tugged his hand through his curls. "It's hard to explain. But she never told me how to feel about you. That was real."

He grew quieter. "This is the first time I'm reading the letter, too. I had no idea about your mother. I know your relationship was fraught, but even so: I'm sorry."

Pilar shoved the sentiment away. Forced a laugh. "Who cares about my mother? I have two sisters and a father now! What a celebration."

She turned on Mia. "How about you? Angelyne enkindling you, too? Anyone left in all four kingdoms who's *not* being controlled by your twisted little sister?"

Mia hesitated. "I suppose she's *our* twisted little sister."

Our sister. Like it was that easy. A stack of melodramatic letters and suddenly they were all one big happy murderous family.

"We still might be able to stop her, Pilar," Mia said. "If we use our magic to bring the elements back into bal—"

"I don't do magic anymore," Pilar said, cutting her off. "I'm done hurting innocent people."

She spun back around on Quin. "Anything else you'd like to tell me, Killian? Before I walk out of this room and never speak to you again?"

"I'm sorry, Pilar. You have to believe me—at least about that."

She could see it in his eyes, the sorry. But it didn't soothe. It burned.

"And I never would have hurt you," he added.

"What makes you think you haven't?" she volleyed back. "You think all wounds show on the skin? I'm sure you wouldn't have hesitated to slice my head off my neck, either, if that's what Angie wanted."

He shook his head. "She wanted you both here, together, for Jyöl. She swore on the Duj she wouldn't let any harm come to you."

"How comforting," Pilar sneered, "from the girl who's a raving lunatic."

"All I know is that this was the last task Angelyne gave me. My job was to ensure you both made it to the snow palace, safe in body and in spirit. Now I'm free."

Pilar snorted. "I've spent the last month of my life with you, and you've lied to me for the last time."

She wheeled around, then wheeled back, remembering.

"Take these. I don't want them." Pilar dug the letters out of her pocket and thrust them into Mia's hands. "Welcome to the sisterhood of the warped and broken."

She stomped out of the music room, the doors banging shut behind her.

Pilar wanted to break something.

She charged down the corridors of Freyja's palace. Her eyes snagged on a drawing room filled with clay busts of noblewomen. Good enough.

She skidded to a stop. Clenched her right fist. Hugged her elbow close to her body.

Then froze.

She needed her knuckles to fight—and she needed her hands to play violin. Not that she'd ever touch one again. She'd never played as well as she had during her duet with Quin.

The Doomed Duet of Pil and Kill.

With a roar, she shifted her weight onto her back leg, landing a drop kick on the side of the bust. Pain shot up her calf as the woman's torso soared off the platform.

The clay didn't shatter. Only cracked into three large pieces.

Maybe love was like that, too. You only soared for a second before breaking.

Quin was a liar. Pilar had known that ever since she found the moonstone in his pouch. She'd still given him her heart. He'd still broken it.

She burned with shame.

Now Mia Rose and Quin had found each other once again. A love that survived even death. Insert epic ballad on mandolin.

The thought of Mia and Quin together made her sick, but it also felt inevitable. Even if Quin *had* felt something genuine for Pilar beneath the haze of enthrallment, he could cast it off now like a soiled sock. Boys like that didn't choose girls like her—not when they had a Mia Rose.

Pilar Zorastín d'Aqila was damaged goods. No one would ever want her.

"Why, hello," said a jolly voice.

Her head jerked up. Lord Kristoffin Dove stood in the drawing room, surveying the clay bust.

"I broke it." She met his eyes, defiant. "I'm not sorry."

"Fine with me. Honestly, we're a bit overstocked in the bust department."

Pilar's shoulders relaxed, just a bit.

Lord Dove folded his hands. "I thought you were with Quin? When I passed the music room a moment ago, I heard you working your magic on violin."

"I'm with no one," she said firmly. "And I don't practice magic."

"Really? May I ask why not?"

"Because magic is just another way to make people suffer."

Dove's eyes lit up. "Then perhaps you can help me. The Illuminations are about to begin, but there is one display I can't quite get right. Would you come and take a look? I am in dire need of a woman to help me mend my one last mistake."

Pilar had no reason to say yes, but no real reason to say no. The realization hardened in her belly. She had nowhere to be—and no one to be with.

"Why not?" Pilar said darkly. "I'm all yours."

Chapter 44

SPLINTERS

Mia clutched the stack of letters. She had a sister. A *second* sister. She and Pilar d'Aqila were bound by blood.

Not to mention her first sister had been puppeteering their every move and was now careening toward them with rage in her heart.

Not to mention Quin hadn't only known Mia was alive: He had brought her back from the dead himself.

"I need a drink," she said.

"First you need to sit down," Quin said, and she realized she was swaying on her feet. Gently he took her arm and guided her toward a frothy settee with trumpets embroidered in the lace. He sat uneasily on the cushion beside her, craning his neck to stare out the door Pilar had just barreled through.

"If you want to go after her," Mia said, "go."

"It's not that simple."

Mia didn't know the whole story, but she didn't need to. The energy crackling between Quin and Pilar had made things abundantly clear. They'd been yoked—in more ways than one. And they cared for each other. That much was obvious.

She couldn't deny it stung. She knew she'd been gallivanting about with Zai for weeks, admiring the hard, rutted lines of his torso; and before that she'd brought plenty of boys—and one girl—home to her cot in White Lagoon. So it wasn't as if she'd been pining away like a lovestruck widow in one of Angie's novels.

And yet. She'd wanted Quin to pine for her anyway. Which wasn't fair. She knew that. But then, what about love was fair?

Not that she loved Quin.

"I should . . ." Quin said, but didn't finish. He scoured the room, as if he would rather look at anything but her. That hurt too.

His gaze fell on the birchwood violin. Quin scrambled across the floor to retrieve it. This time he chose the farthest chair to sit in.

"Is it broken?" Mia asked.

"One of the strings unraveled. Catgut snaps more easily in the cold." He began to untwist the peg on the instrument's neck. "Dropping it didn't help."

Mia didn't know how to talk to him. Had she really forgotten this simple act? She played out possible conversation topics:

M: How have you been?

Q: Enkindled by your sister.

M: How's your family?

Q: Dead, thanks to you.

M: Are you and Pilar . . .

Q: Of course we are.

Needless to say, they all ended badly.

"So," she began. A wildly courageous start.

"So," Quin volleyed back.

She watched him feed the string through the peg's tiny hole, looping the other end. He twisted the peg gently, the coil of string thickening as it turned. It reminded her of the night he'd prepared their supper in the Twisted Forest, how nimbly his fingers had eviscerated the dead hare for rabbit stew. He'd been quite chatty that night.

Now the silence was excruciating.

After a moment, he gestured toward the parchments without looking up. "You can read the letters. In fact you probably should."

Mia was grateful to have a task. She skimmed the parchments. But her mind was spinning too fast; it was impossible to focus. After a few minutes she'd gotten the gist: Angelyne was obsessed with the Jyöltide myths, wanted to lure Pilar back to the river kingdom, and had a penchant for purple prose.

Oh, and she was probably insane.

Mia folded the letters softly and set them on the settee. Every second she wasted, Quin slipped farther out of reach.

An idea materialized in her head.

"If you could eat anything right now," she said, hoping he'd remember, "what would it be?"

Quin didn't answer. Had he forgotten? *She* certainly hadn't. Mia conjured up the image of the two of them wandering cold and hungry through the Twisted Forest in the days leading up to the stew, Quin taunting her with his outrageous imagined meals.

"I would take some nice smoked lamb," she prodded. "Add a little sage butter on the roll, and a dram of silver death to chase it down. A delicious Luumi supper fit for a king."

"I'm not hungry," Quin said.

The violin string popped out, destroying the tension he'd been so careful to maintain. He squinted at the notches, frowning as he ran his finger over the grooves. What was it Mia's mother had said? *A body without sensation is like a broken violin. Still beautiful, but empty without the music that made it sing.*

Quin's fingers ceased to move. He looked up at her, the muscles twitching at the hinge of his jaw.

"I dreamed about you, Mia. I knew you weren't dead, but I still felt like I had lost you. I suppose, in all the ways that mattered, I had."

He almost smiled. "I'll admit it: in the moments my mind was my own, I thought you might come back. That instead of going to the snow kingdom, you would decide to turn around and help me. To free me from the tyranny of your sister's control."

She exhaled a long breath. "I was going to, Quin. I swear it.

381

Every day I searched for my mother, I was thinking about you."

Mia plucked at the lace trumpets on the settee. There was so much she wanted to say, and no possible way to say it.

"I'm sorry, Quin."

He set his jaw. "Life is too short for regret."

"Life is too long to never say you're sorry. And I am."

Once again Quin drew the violin string taut, and once again it unraveled.

She waited, blood thrumming in her wrists. No matter how much she wanted to interject, she would let him speak.

"Did you know the piano is also a string instrument?" he said. "Most people don't know that. The piano and violin look like different species—a giant and an ant. But in the end they're not so dissimilar. That's why they blend so beautifully together. Two different instruments playing the same song."

"Do you love her?" She couldn't believe she'd had the nerve to ask it, but there it was, suspended in the air. "Are you in love with Pilar?"

Quin stood. With the violin cradled in his arms, he walked over to the piano.

"Music is an instrument of grief," he said. "An instrument is useless if there's no one there to play it."

He lifted his arm, swung the violin in a wide arc—and brought it down hard on the black-and-white keys.

A dark, jarring chord clanged as a sickening crack echoed through the room.

Mia jumped off the settee.

"Quin!"

He lifted the violin and smashed it into the piano. Again. And again. The keys stuck and jammed; the discordant notes clung heavy to the air, until they didn't. Mia staggered back, away from the carnage, a safe distance from the piano's chipped ivory teeth. It hurt to look at. Like staring into a crushed, broken mouth.

The violin bent and contorted, the wood fracturing more with each strike, until its graceful curves were nothing more than splinters.

Tears pressed at Mia's eyes. Even if she couldn't play either instrument to save her life, it frightened her to see Quin destroy them. She knew how much music meant to him.

And then it was over. He dropped the decimated violin to the floor. His shoulders shook; she thought he might sob. But when his eyes met hers, they were fierce.

"What's happening?" She shrank away from him. "I've never seen you like this."

"You've never seen me at all. I'm always someone's puppet. Following you, following Pilar. Doing Angelyne's bidding. When do I get what *I* want? When am I free to choose?"

"You said you *were* free."

Quin walked to the window and peered out onto the port town below. Whatever he saw made his whole body tense.

"Look," he said.

Cautiously she edged forward.

Her gaze fixed on the ever-present glacier in the distance, reaching down toward Valavïk like the knuckles of a giant hand.

When Mia first saw the glacier, she hadn't found it ominous. Now she wasn't sure. A thin stream of water trickled off one white ledge.

But when Quin tapped the windowpane, she followed his finger to a much closer scene. Amidst the horde of Jyöltide revelers hustling to nab a prime spot for the Illuminations, she saw a ship freshly docked in the harbor. If Mia squinted, she could just make out a tiny figure stepping off the gangplank, the glint of sun on strawberry hair.

"It would appear," Quin said, "that your sister has arrived."

Chapter 45

SAPPHIRE SILVER

THE ACT OF ILLUMINATION required two ingredients: light and movement.

Take a book with pages limned in gold foil. In quiet darkness, the book was little more than ordinary. But if you thumbed through it under candlelight, the paper's edges scintillated like liquid gold.

Illumination was by nature unstable. For an object to shine, it first had to shift.

Angelyne sauntered down the gangplank, out into the bustling port of Valavïk. She craned her neck to gaze up at the starless night. The Illuminations had not yet begun. She'd assumed the Weeping Moon would resemble a teardrop, but it was thin and sharp, a silver scythe in the sky.

She waved off the mariner who tried to assist her. Beneath her skirt she'd sewn a small pocket into the hem; other than the contents of that pocket, she had no luggage. She had come to Luumia to get, not give.

The air reeked of fish and rot. She leaned into a salt-crusted wood beam to regain her equilibrium. Before this voyage, she had never set foot on a ship. After she returned to Glas Ddir, she hoped never to again.

What bittersweet irony. The girl who could make whole rooms of men drop dead with a snap of her finger couldn't heal her own seasickness. Magic was funny that way. Fearsome Angelyne, Queen of Glas Ddir, Savior of the Dujia. A waif clinging to a wharf.

"You all right, miss?" A dirt-smudged boy materialized at her side. "Need any help?"

"I'm fine."

He took a step closer. "Looks to me like you're about to heave up chunks."

"I don't need your help."

He cocked his head, silver hair masking half his face. "You're from the river kingdom."

The boy reached toward her wavy ginger tresses. She recoiled. "Are you evil too, miss?"

Angelyne had a fervent desire to crack his head open like a winter squash. What more did people want? She had reopened the borders. After dispensing with Zaga, she had rescinded her teacher's more brutal policies—they were no longer stacking bodies in the castle halls. And she had repealed *all* of King Ronan's hateful decrees, which meant Glasddiran women were now free to discard their gloves and practice magic with reckless abandon.

There had been casualties along the way, of course. Subjects who refused to kneel, proving themselves more valuable as corpses. An inevitable side effect of progress. For a kingdom to shine, it first had to shift.

"If I can't help you, miss," said the boy, "you can help me."

She felt a fumbling at her hip, then a quick tug, followed by lightness. The urchin scampered off down the pier, his dirty fist clutched tight. She didn't have to check the secret pocket in her skirt to know it was empty.

"Little thief," she muttered.

She tapped her throat. Instantly the boy fell onto the dock, face slamming into the uneven wood planks. He let out a sharp cry.

Angelyne strolled leisurely toward him. He flailed and writhed on his stomach, clawing at his throat, gasping for breath. She bent over his body.

His fist unclenched. Empty. What he'd stolen was no longer in his hand.

By now a small crowd had gathered. She heard whispers of "witch" and "monster," fear rolling off them in sweet, icy gales. Sometimes Angelyne gazed into a looking glass when she practiced the kind of magic only she could do, manipulating another person's body without ever touching their skin. She knew exactly how she looked. Savagely calm.

The boy's coughs rasped and deepened. He lurched onto hands and knees, chest seizing, as if he were struggling to hack something up. In fact he was. An object lodged in his throat, spit and breath mangling around the lump, until finally he spewed it out on a stream of bloody black.

No one said a word as the boy rolled onto his side, still choking, but breathing nonetheless. A shiver of disappointment ran through the crowd. They had missed their chance to witness a gruesome death. In Angelyne's experience, people's hunger for catastrophe almost always outweighed their concern.

The other urchins edged forward to see the object their friend had heaved up. When it quivered and extended seven black legs, they gasped.

"What *is* that?" one of them whispered, shrinking back.

Angelyne swooped down and snatched it up. She crouched on the edge of the pier, dipped it into the ocean, and shook off the remaining blood and phlegm.

"Is it a spider?" squeaked the smallest girl, who looked like she might burst into tears.

"This?" Angelyne held it up with an insouciant shrug. "This is merely a stone. He stole it from my pocket."

In her palm, the creature had hardened into a wheel with seven spokes, no bigger than a plum. Pale white particles shimmered in the lustrous black stone like snowflakes.

Angelyne crouched beside the thief, who had managed to lift himself onto wobbly elbows. She brought her face level with his, dangling the dark gemstone inches from his terrified eyes.

"You ought never to steal something," she said coldly, "when you don't know its worth."

Hordes of people thronged the streets of Valavïk as Angelyne made her way to the palace. She passed families huddled together, children bundled in festive Jyöltide scarves and striped wool hats, parents clasping mugs of cinnamon-swirled cocoa. The Luumi chatted and laughed and sometimes stared up at the sky, waiting for their history to be writ in lights.

She felt sorry for them. They were so awestruck that the Illuminations had returned after twenty years, it hadn't occurred to them to ask where the lights had come from, or what they even were.

As a girl Angelyne had been afflicted with the same wide-eyed wonderment. She'd read everything she could about the Luumi festival of Jyöl, smitten by the magic and majesty. She loved the Addi myths most of all. The story of Græÿa and her six children—the Seven Souls of Jyöl—were infinitely more compelling than the lackluster Glasddiran tales of four squabbling brother-gods creating the four kingdoms.

Of course, the more she dug into the old myths, the more she understood the darkness at their hearts. Græÿa and her children had suffered in ways too horrible to imagine.

Now, as she drew closer to the palace, she cared not one whit about the twisted scribbles that would soon paint the sky.

What she *did* care about was their source.

Angelyne hugged the eastern side of the palace and, with no guards to stop her, circled round the back. She followed a winding garden path through an atrium, then down a flower-scented corridor to an iron gate where a stout boy about her age was waiting.

"Your Grace," he said, bowing. "You're even lovelier in person."

"You're not the man I was expecting."

"When day breaks, frost becomes a flame. When dusk falls, beasts become the prey."

"And when the moon is weeping . . ."

"The witches do their reaping," they finished together.

She nodded. "Very well. And the Snow Queen?"

"Preparing to meet the Snow Wolf," he assured her.

"Good."

He pressed his palm to the frostflower on the iron gate, and it swung open.

"This way."

The boy led her down the dazzling white corridors of the palace. She passed stately drawing rooms and a well-lit music room with a large window, where a white piano looked out over the wharf. Angelyne felt a flicker of heat and the attendant memory: she and Mia twirling through the cottage in their mother's finest gowns, singing that dreadful snow plum song.

She turned away. What a child she'd been.

"Where is everyone?" she asked the boy. "I haven't seen a single guard."

"They're all outside for the Illuminations. Like pigeons with bread crumbs: so easily entertained." The boy ushered her into a large box embellished with bronze beasts. "The Descending Room, I call it."

The room was well named. It did, in fact, descend.

As they dropped beneath the palace floors, she took note of her companion. His face was a study in contrasts: dark, heavy-lidded eyes set in a round face with skin so fair it was almost translucent. He boasted a shock of ghostly white hair, with spurts of the same fine hair on his knuckles, which he cracked with obvious pleasure.

The boy was a stranger—and not the stranger she'd expected. Yet, in spite of all this: she felt no fear.

The realization coaxed a smile to her lips. There was nothing this boy could do to her, no harm he could inflict. Angelyne was untouchable. This was why she loved magic so dearly: it granted her a power she had never known.

Moments later, the box came to a bumpy stop. The boy offered his arm.

"Your Grace."

He led her down a long silvery tunnel freckled with purple dots.

"Why is Lord Dove underground?" she asked. "He's been slaving over the Illuminations for months. Doesn't he want to revel in the fruits of his creation?"

"Lord Dove tries to be everywhere at once. Sometimes he is successful."

He pulled a velvety white rope, and a pair of silver doors clanked open.

In the months since Angelyne had struck up a correspondence with the queen's Grand Fyremaster, she had spent plenty of time imagining his underground laboratory. She envisioned it wreathed in pungent smoke, an army of workers scuttling between experiments so magnificent they took her breath away.

Now, standing in the thick of it, her breath was decidedly untaken. In the middle of the room, a large mirror with an ornate gilded frame stood six or seven feet high. Lackluster tables encircled it, littered with parchments and writing implements.

"Where is Lord Dove?"

"He said to tell you we are happy to commence a new era of peace with our northern neighbor."

The boy hefted a barrel onto the closest table, heaped high with carvings in various shades of blue: azure, cobalt, luminous cerulean. Flowers and beasts, mostly.

She frowned. "This isn't fyre ice."

"No," the boy agreed. "Not yet."

She was far less interested in the blue gems than in the red stone bird perched on a nearby table.

"That's fojuen," she said.

"With eyes of fyre ice. Lord Dove finds the combination particularly effective when summoning a person's Reflections."

Angelyne knew the bird well, of course. She'd recognize the ruby wren anywhere.

Her mother was close by. Probably tucked into a cozy balcony upstairs, awaiting the Illuminations. As far as Angelyne was concerned, her mother had betrayed their family the moment she stopped her own heart, twisting the knife of that betrayal when she'd chosen never to return.

Angelyne meant what she'd said in her letter to Mia and Pilar. This wasn't a time for parents and children, old families and old alliances. It was a time for sisters. The sisterhood would rise up and save them all.

She dug her hand into the mound of blue carvings, sieving out a few choice pieces. They were cold to the touch. She dropped the carvings back into the barrel with a pitiful *clink*.

Trinkets. A pathetic, trifling magic. Fury bloomed in her chest. Did Dove really think these would appease her?

The wren, on the other hand, might prove useful.

Angelyne angled her body away from the boy, and—with a clever sleight of hand—poached the bird from the table. She dropped it discreetly down the front of her gown.

When she wheeled back around, her voice was icy.

"I didn't come all this way for baubles."

"Of course not, Your Grace," the boy said. "But these are only one ingredient."

He threw back his shoulders, round belly lifting an inch or two, and strolled in front of the gilded mirror in the center of the room.

Angelyne gasped.

In the mirror's reflection, she no longer saw a boy, but a wiry white-haired man. A gentleman, by the looks of it. Pink cheeks, pink nose, and a white beard both thick and impeccably trimmed.

His eyes sparkled a pale sapphire silver.

A thrum of excitement thrilled through Angelyne's chest.

"Lord Dove?"

"A pleasure to be reacquainted," he said with a wink.

Chapter 46

RESERVOIR

MIA CLAPPED A HAND over her mouth, willing herself silent. From her hiding place, she could see Lord Kristoffin Dove perfectly framed in the mirror's reflection. But from her unique angle, she could also see him from the side, *not* in the glass, and the flesh-and-blood figure was not Lord Dove at all.

It was Ville.

The instant she had seen Angelyne brush past the music room, a flash of strawberry hair against white walls, Mia knew she would follow. Quin had urged her not to go. When he realized she couldn't be swayed, he announced he was going, too.

"The last thing I need is my sister's lackey accompanying me," she'd said.

"I think that's exactly who you need. When it comes to the inner workings of Angelyne's mind, I have the clearest view."

She had no choice. He was coming whether she liked it or not. Together they'd stolen down the palace halls, careful to stay one corridor behind, until Angelyne and her companion—one of the queen's guards, Mia imagined—stepped into the Descending Room and were lowered inch by inch on its cables.

"What is that strange box?" Quin whispered as it dropped out of sight. "Can we ride it, too?"

Mia shook her head. "It's too loud. I have another idea."

Once the screeches and creaks subsided when Angelyne arrived below, Mia leaned over the edge and gripped hold of an iron cable, signaling Quin to do the same. Far below, she could just make out the eerie lavender glow of the box, the cranks and pipes puffing violet steam. She hoped the hazy light would be enough to guide them.

And thus began the horrifying endeavor of using two swaying cables to climb down a lightless shaft. She couldn't help but be reminded of the night she and Prince Quin had slung themselves off the cliff outside the Kaer in a dusty bronze carriage. They seemed to have a knack for free-falling down tremulous cables.

Once again, they'd survived. Mia and Quin landed on top of the Descending Room, sweaty but unscathed. "How far does this thing go?" he'd asked, as they peered into the darkness beneath them, catching their breath. She'd thought the chute would dead end where the box stopped, but, judging by the cold current blowing up from below, it kept going. Did the Descending Room plunge even deeper than Kristoffin's laboratory?

"I don't know," she'd said. "But we don't have time to go exploring."

Mia had found the hatch door in the roof of the box, precisely where she remembered. She and Quin dropped soundlessly through it and hurried down the corridor lit with shimmers. Then they crawled into Lord Dove's shop, where they crouched behind a table just as the guard stepped in front of the mirror.

The guard who wasn't a guard at all.

When Mirror Lord Dove spoke, Flesh-and-Blood Ville's mouth moved in synchronicity. Same wink. Same wry grin. Though their two voices came in different timbres, their bodies in different shapes, every gesture and inflection found its perfect twin.

Mia dragged her eyes away from Ville—or Kristoffin—and fixed them on her sister. Her heart rose in her throat. Angie had always been slender, but in a few short months she'd gone from slim to emaciated. It took Mia a moment to recall the person her sister resembled, until it struck with sickening clarity: Zaga.

Angelyne studied Kristoffin, then Ville, a smile flirting at her lips.

"Which of you is real?" she asked.

"Both, Your Grace. What your eye perceives is what the mind believes."

"What kind of magic is this?"

Mia caught the excitement in her sister's voice. There was a hunger beneath the words. Ambition.

"Are you familiar with the Renderer, Your Grace?" Kristoffin asked.

"Of course. The Second Soul of Jyöl?"

"Good, good."

Lord Dove stepped out from behind the mirror, and the moment he did, Ville disappeared. One second he stood beside Angelyne; the next, he'd vanished into air, with only the Grand Fyremaster remaining.

"Remarkable," Angie murmured.

Kristoffin looked pleased. He waved her over to the table, where he sifted through a stack of parchments and extracted a large charcoal drawing. Ville had been rendered flawlessly: round belly, dark eyes, silvery blond hair. His face was frozen mid-wink.

"This is Ville," said Kristoffin, clearly delighted. "He has served me admirably well."

"I presume you have others?"

"Of course." Kristoffin rifled through sheaves of parchment until he found another sketch. This fellow has become one of my favorites. I get to be a bit naughty, if you will. The sort of chap I never had a chance to be."

A tall blond boy slouched on the paper, with watery blue eyes and a belt of frostflower trinkets.

Mia nearly choked. Here was the lout she'd met at the alehouse a few weeks back. The same night she'd met Kristoffin Dove, come to think of it. Which means he'd been in two different alehouses, watching her.

"So this," Angelyne said, "is how you manage to be everywhere at once."

"I can only exist in one place at a time. There is only one Kristoffin Dove. But I can take on different guises. Some people respond best to a doddering old fool. Others to a virile youth in his prime."

"You're a Renderer."

He shook his head. "What I do is far more powerful. I am fully present inside each illusion, made manifest outside the palace walls. Not only can I warp what the eye perceives: I can make those illusions material."

Kristoffin licked his finger, dabbing at the charcoal sketch in his hand. "Perhaps I should explain how magic works."

Angie's jaw tightened. "I *know* how magic works."

"Forgive me," said Kristoffin, "but I thought I did, too. The work I've done, the successes I've been able to achieve . . . they have shown me things I never could have imagined."

Mia waited for her sister's temper to flare. Either Dove didn't know the extent of Angelyne's powers, or he was intentionally playing with fire.

When you strike a woman, you strike a match.

What an awful expression. Why hadn't she realized that when Kristoffin said it?

"Magic is born of a power imbalance," Kristoffin said. "In the natural world, it is physical. But when that imbalance of power is found inside a human heart . . . when one person oppresses another . . . something shifts. A shift that goes deeper than the visible world."

Mia leaned forward on her heels. Her sister leaned, too.

"In each of us there is a reservoir," Kristoffin explained, "carved from this imbalance. The deeper the reservoir, the stronger the potential for magic. Thus any living creature that bears the capacity for great suffering bears the capacity for great magic."

He gave a sad little chuckle. "Of course there are others for whom the reservoir runs dry. Fortunate devil that I am, my lake is more of a thimble, really. Left to my own devices, I could never practice magic."

"But you do practice magic. You've rendered yourself a whole army of guises."

"Once you find the right method to extract this magic, the potential is limitless. And *that,* Your Grace, is why fyre ice is so powerful."

Lord Dove broadened his shoulders, winding up for his grand crescendo.

"We have found a way to divorce magic from its legacy of pain and suffering. *Divorce* in the truest sense of the word: to separate one from the other. Fyre ice is both catalyst and container, a tool and a gift."

Mia studied her sister's face. Angelyne was inscrutable.

"Surely by now, Lord Dove, you know I am far more interested in process than results." She seized a blue bird and held it up. "I want to know how they're made."

Kristoffin rubbed his hands together. "*Sharp as an arrow, and just as quick.* Good Græÿa, how you remind me of your sister!"

A shadow stole over Angie's face. Mia could see the question in her eyes. *Which sister?*

"If suffering is a reservoir," Kristoffin said, "then the substance that most effectively fills it—the most potent ingredient—is pain."

Every hair on Mia's neck stood up. Instinctually she knew something was about to be revealed. Something unconscionable.

Come with me, she mouthed to Quin. She planted her hands on the ground, then her knees, crawling silently toward the metal doors.

"You have concealed the truth from me since I arrived, Lord Dove," Angelyne said coldly. "You've masked your true form and obfuscated the work you do here—the work I've come all this way to see. You will answer my next question truthfully, or there will be consequences."

Mia and Quin slipped through the doors, just as Angie asked her final question.

"This isn't the real laboratory, is it?"

Kristoffin let out his breath.

"No," he said. "It isn't."

Chapter 47

THE FORGOTTEN

ANGELYNE WAS GOOD AT playing coy. The trick was in the wavering voice, the tear-brightened eyes, the lowered lashes. Deferential and pliant, the kind of girl who always needed saving.

She hated that role.

As Lord Dove escorted her out of the laboratory—the *false* laboratory—rage swelled in her chest. It would be so easy to turn his breath to shards of glass, slit his throat from the inside out.

"Right this way, Your Grace," said Dove, ushering her down the corridor and into the iron box.

Angelyne swallowed her fury. She needed to get into that laboratory. After that, she made no promises.

As Dove reached for the crank, she found herself staring up

at the ceiling, the hatch door slightly askew. Just a touch, but enough for a wedge of violet light to peek through.

She pointed overhead. "Is that normal?"

Dove looked up, then frowned. "Forgive me. Sometimes it comes loose on the descent."

He jiggled the hatch door until it snapped back into place, sealing out the light.

For a moment Angelyne thought she heard a slight twang underfoot. But then Lord Dove twisted the crank and the box descended, drowning out all other sounds in a cacophony of groans.

As they plummeted deeper beneath the earth, Angelyne's thoughts grew darker. Did the Grand Fyremaster really think he could deceive her? Or was he toying with her the same way she'd toyed with him? If, after months of correspondence, Lord Dove truly thought she'd come for a pocketful of trinkets, then he hadn't been paying attention.

The truth was, Lord Kristoffin Dove troubled her. If a man who claimed to have no magic himself could somehow transform illusions into bone and flesh . . .

For the first time since arriving in the snow kingdom, she allowed herself a trickle of fear. She was powerful; no one would dispute it. And yet.

Angelyne shook her head. It didn't matter what the Grand Fyremaster conjured. She wasn't here for the end product.

She was here for its derivation.

The tunnels beneath the tunnels boasted none of the same gloss. No glowing lilac flecks adorning the walls. Lord Dove led Angelyne through caverns and passageways roughly hewn from dark rock and damp earth.

"You have assistants, I presume?" she said, hearing hoarse whispers up ahead.

Lord Dove shook his head. "Not down here. I can't risk prying eyes."

She heard the noise again: two hushed voices intertwining. The air in the corridor chilled, the same cold she sensed when subjects cowered at her feet.

"Someone is down here, Lord Dove. We are not alone."

"Of course not. But I assure you, you needn't be afraid."

In her letters she had played the part of the weak, fearful river queen, under the control of someone much stronger. Frankly, that didn't require much exaggeration: Zaga committed most of the truly egregious acts. Heap the bodies of all disloyal subjects in the Hall of Hands? The stench was heinous, not to mention the flies.

"Does Queen Freyja know about this place?" Angelyne asked.

"Not an inkling. Nor does her cousin—and I intend to keep it that way. As Ville I've grown quite chummy with Zai. As for my niece . . ."

He sighed. "Freyja rules our people with justice and compassion, but she does not understand that some sacrifices are required. There is always a cost, and always a reward."

Angelyne nodded. This was precisely why the snow queen had never interested her. Freyja struck her as the kind of ruler who believed in essential goodness. As if that were enough to rule a kingdom. Being good.

"You do her dirty work, then."

"I do what is necessary," Dove said, "for the queendom to thrive."

They had come to the mouth of a large cave, light shifting and flickering from within.

Lord Dove straightened.

"I want to prepare you, Your Grace. It's a bit of a shock at first. I ask only that you suspend your initial judgment. As they say, *Progress is two horses gained, one horse lost.*"

"More wisdom from an old Luumi mystic?"

"An old Luumi horse trader, I imagine."

"You don't need to lecture me, Lord Dove. I know as well as anyone the ends justify the means."

He nodded. "Then you're ready to meet the conduits."

Six figures stood in a circle, staring into plates of glittering black ice.

Each individual plate was cut into a hexagon snaking into larger hexagons. From above they might resemble a giant serpent—not that anyone would ever garner such a view. The cave ceiling was opaque. The rocks glinted, as if glistening with sweat.

Not sweat, Angelyne realized. *Veins.* She looked down to see red tributaries beneath her feet like blood, thickening as they bifurcated and trifurcated, then clawed up the walls, blooming overhead in a vermillion lightning storm. The veins fed into glass pipes shunting crimson vapor through the rock ceiling, presumably to the rest of the palace and, by extension, to all of Luumia.

Angelyne's eyes fell once again to the human figures below. The ones powering the kingdom, like small flickering flames.

Three black-haired girls. One willowy redhead. A boy with dark freckles, and a small blond girl. All perfectly still. Eyes fixed on the ice before them, gray and black shapes shifting over the surface. Shadows cast with no light.

"These are children," Angelyne said.

"Yes," said Lord Dove. "They tend to be most efficient."

She faced him. "*Efficient?*"

"Children have an immense capacity for suffering. Adults do too, of course, but we have more defense mechanisms at play."

She frowned. "You said magic was a reservoir. Surely our reservoirs grow deeper over time."

"You listened well, Your Grace. And you are correct. Magic is most potent when it has had time to simmer. But a child's suffering is pure, unencumbered. It produces a special kind of fuel."

Angelyne turned back to the children. She saw clear glass pipes rising from each partition, scarlet vapor churning inside. If the vapor was the fuel, then it was being shunted through the pipes that pierced the cave ceiling, where she assumed it was funneled straight into the laboratory above.

This was even more promising than she'd hoped.

"What are they watching?"

"Their own Reflections. The moments in their life that have caused them the most pain. See that boy?"

He pointed to the boy with tawny amber skin and freckles. The boy stood so close to the ice his nose almost touched the surface.

"I found him a month ago," Lord Dove said, "in an Addi village just north of the Glasddiran border. The week before, his mother had frozen to death trying to track down a missing reinsdyr. When I found him, his father was dead in his arms, sick from the pox. This poor child has known more suffering than most."

When Dove beckoned, Angelyne peered into the boy's Reflections. She saw a man shivering and retching, then growing still in his son's arms.

"He had a twin," Dove said softly. "A gifted violinist. We tested him to be a conduit, too, but the initial process . . . suffice it to say not everyone is strong enough to revisit their deepest wounds."

"So you syphon their suffering," Angelyne said, "to mine their magic."

"We have saved hundreds of thousands of lives with a mere handful of conduits: a remarkably low cost."

"Are you aware that in the old language, *conduit* means 'safe passage'? The irony is poignant. And yet this seems to bring you joy."

"Not at all. I'm not a monster."

He reached out a hand and laid it affectionately on the boy's head. "I feed them. I make sure they are bathed and clothed and cleaned. In a way, these are my children."

Angelyne had stopped listening. Instead she began to walk the perimeter of the circle. At each plate of ice, she noted a white bone frostflower swinging from a thin cord.

"How many don't have parents?" she said quietly.

"The suffering of orphans tends to be more pronounced."

"I expected only girls. But there are boys, too."

"You can be as loud as you like. They can't hear you. The conduits see and hear only the scenes playing before them." He strode forward. "And yes. Men are not immune to suffering. Especially the Addi, who carry a long history of suffering inside them." He paused. "You said you are familiar with our Jyöltide myths?"

She reached out and touched the closest plate of ice, watching as the images curled and twisted over her fingers. "I'm familiar with the *Addi* myths, yes. The ones you stole."

"Thievery is the height of flattery! I'm sure you know the *true* ending of the story? What really happened to Græÿa's children?"

Angelyne folded her arms. "I know the littlest sister made the others immortal. She wrote the stories as we know them today."

Dove chuckled. "Good Græÿa, no. The witches weren't saved by pretty words! In the end, they were saved by man's greed. The villagers did come for the little monsters—but not to kill them. They realized that magic, like a good cask of ale, could be tapped. So they found ways to channel the children's power. Their bodies were used for magic, among other things. The magic was preserved in the bloodline. Each of Græÿa's children had children of their own."

"Yes," Angelyne said darkly. "Whether they wanted to or not."

"The entire foundation of this great kingdom was built on the sacrifice of those six little souls. Isn't that true power? To give your life to spawn thousands more?"

His chest puffed with pride. "And *this* is the gift I have given the snow kingdom. I have spent years of my life following the bloodlines. Painstaking work, tracing it back over so many generations."

"What you're saying," Angelyne said, piecing it together, "is that these children descended from Græÿa?"

"Six of them did. The seventh came from an unexpected place. The missing ingredient I didn't know I needed."

Angelyne raised a brow. "The seventh?"

Dove rubbed his hands together.

"The six children you see before you are the living descendants of the Renderer, the Flesh Thief, the Silver Sorcerer, and the Three Sisters. The extraction process I have perfected—over many years, with much trial and error—hearkens back to a much older time, when men revered the sacred power of witches."

"Seems to me the men were the monsters."

"Only in our stories can we be both monster and hero."

"So you stole their power *and* their myths."

"Their power was in their myths. Don't you see?" He brandished a hand around the cavern. "These are the orphans, the castoffs, the forgotten. These seven conduits provide an invaluable service. They have saved the snow kingdom from darkness—and will now save the river kingdom from the same fate."

Angelyne looked at him with something akin to pity. What a senile fool. Did he really think she'd come to Luumia to make a trade? To broker peace between their two kingdoms?

"You keep saying there are seven," Angelyne said. "But I only see six."

"At first I was determined to only find conduits who were direct descendants. I'll admit I was being myopic—a bit of a purist, perhaps." He nodded toward the cave's farthest corner. "Sometimes true inspiration comes from the places we never expect."

Angelyne's eyes focused on the seventh of the "forgotten," shrouded in partial shadow. Hair cut sharply at the chin, hands balled into fists as she watched her own nightmares.

Angelyne stepped closer, drawn to the images on the frosted ice. A ceiling crisscrossed with rafters. A man. A violin.

Only then did she realize who the girl was.

Pilar Zorastín d'Aqila.

Chapter 48

CELL

You will always see the rafters. Those thick wood beams. You stare up at them,
imagining a game of kurkits. Yes. This is all a game.
Tiny rocks on the rough dirt floor. On an island of volqanic sand, you never
minded gravel. Not till it bites holes in the soft skin of your back.
The bow is broken. The horsehair snaps in two. Wet, like tendons in a neck.

Wood
Rough
Broken

You have magic, but you don't use it.
You have fists, but you don't use them.

You have words, but they don't come.
Daggers. Arrows. Blades. You don't reach for them.
You've forgotten how.

Wood
beams
Rough
dirt
Broken
horsehair

Your hair is black.
Your eyes are brown.
You have a scar on your right knuckle, second from the thumb.
You tell yourself these things so you remember.
So you don't disappear.

Wood
beams
casting
shadows
like
Rough
dirt
floor
Broken
horsehair
bow

You are there, on the floor, and he is there, on top of you, and she is there, on
  top of you both.
No one sees you at all.

wood
bow
rough
beams
broken
dirt
wood
dirt
rough
bow
broken
beams
wood
cell
rough
hair
broken
shadows

You have been
here
You will always be
here
wood beams

casting shadows like a

broken cell
broken bow
broken neck

You will always be
broken.

Chapter 49

SWEETEST SISTER

MIA SAW PILAR.

She was unmistakable, even in the shadowy cave: strong jaw, clenched fists, thirsty brown eyes. In the eerie light her black hair glinted with an almost purple sheen. Her cheeks were silver, wet with tears.

And fluttering over the smooth ice, in soulless blacks and grays, Mia saw Pilar's story.

She saw the cottage by the lake.

As Mia crouched behind the coarse rock, shoulder to shoulder with Quin, his breathing quickened. In her periphery she saw the horror on his face. No matter how well he thought he knew Pilar, she hadn't told him this.

Which meant she had been completely, achingly alone.

For months Mia had held Pilar d'Aqila up as the example of what *not* to be. Prone to brash behavior. Stubborn for no good reason. Manipulated by her mother—and naive enough to never question it. Yet, when Mia did the math, wasn't she guilty of all the same things? Brash. Stubborn. Daughter to a lying mother, yet still refusing to accept the truth.

Pilar wasn't the enemy. She was Mia's counterpart. Her counterbalance. Currently *out* of balance, perhaps, but not opposed.

And now, Pilar was suffering.

Her whole body trembled, face twisted in agony as she relived her worst nightmares. Mia wanted to reach out and wipe the images from the ice, wipe them from Pilar's mind. She wanted to tell her, "This was not your fault."

But she couldn't do any of these things. Angelyne was there.

Angie stood inches away from Pilar, watching the story unfold. For a moment Mia thought she caught a softness in her sister's eyes. Sadness? Compassion? Grief?

No. The glimmer in Angie's ice-blue eyes wasn't grief.

It was *delight*.

Mia's heart broke for her sister—and not the sister she'd thought.

Angelyne turned to Kristoffin.

"I thought you said a child's suffering was most pure. Pilar is not a child."

"Ah, you know Pilar d'Aqila? I didn't expect you two would ever cross paths. Pilar is an interesting case. After all, she isn't

Addi; she did not descend from the Six Souls. But the girl is a canyon of suffering, a veritable quarry of untapped potential. Our bodies store up unused magic, and hers has languished inside her, growing to unhealthy extremes."

When he placed his hand on top of Pilar's head, Mia winced.

"She's got no family," Kristoffin said. "There's no one to miss her."

Quin flinched, the tiniest sound escaping his mouth.

"I thought the pain was only in her mind," Angelyne pressed. "Why is she sweating and shivering?"

"Sometimes the conduits break out in cold sweats. They may scream or seize or faint." He hesitated. "I do coax them back into their bodies from time to time. Though only for a little while, lest they start pining for a future that is no longer theirs."

Angelyne flicked her hand toward Pilar. "Bring her out of it."

He frowned. "Pilar is the seventh conduit. She's the most powerful. If I coax her back before the Illuminations—"

"To hells with the Illuminations. There are bigger things at stake."

Dove blinked at her. When he saw she wasn't going to waver, he muttered, "As you wish, Your Grace."

He crouched, grumbling as he fiddled with the copper pipes at the base of the ice. Mia felt Quin shift beside her, his muscles tense. He was about to charge forward.

She grabbed the back of his shirt, shaking her head fiercely. A plan was forming in her brain, but if it had even the slimmest chance of working, she couldn't do it alone.

Get Zai, she mouthed to Quin.

He looked confused. *Who?*

She thrust her hand into her trouser pocket and her fingers hit hard metal. She'd forgotten she still had Jouma's Brew, the tin of paste Nell had left behind on the boat.

That wasn't what she wanted. Mia pushed the Brew aside and extracted one of Angelyne's letters. Silently she snapped a piece of rock off the cave floor, scraping it across the parchment like black chalk.

Zai. Northern balcony. He's going to draw us a way out.

Quin took the paper. She wanted him to meet her gaze, just for a moment.

But he was gone. Mia watched him crawl quietly along the cavern wall, her heart heavy. He made it to the mouth of the cave before disappearing down the corridor.

Mia turned back to see Pilar's black sheet of ice was clear.

"Good Jyöl," Kristoffin cooed, nauseatingly gentle. "Someone's here to see you."

Mia saw Pilar stumble forward, arms shielding her eyes. She doubled over, hands on her knees, trying to catch her breath. When she looked up, her eyes locked onto Angie.

"You," she whispered.

"Sweetest sister," Angelyne said, but she choked on the last syllable as Pilar's fist connected with her throat.

Chapter 50

A SPACE BETWEEN

PILAR'S HANDS WEREN'T WORKING right. Nothing was working right. Her legs felt like water bound up in pigskin. The throat punch had failed to fully connect, though Angelyne did fall to the ground. So not a *total* failure.

When Pilar staggered back, she almost fell herself. In her mind she could still see the smudged images from her Reflections.

On the fifth, twelfth, hundredth viewing of the cottage by the lake, Pilar had left her body. Her soul lifted to the cave ceiling. She saw Mia crouched in the corner, wedged skin to skin with Quin. Of course they'd found each other. They always would.

Quin with his sweet mouth and green eyes. Watching the one story she'd never told him.

Not that he was overflowing with honesty. Stab him in the side and he'd bleed lies.

Pilar wanted to murder someone. Kristoffin Dove: top choice. But when she woke from her nightmare, Angelyne was standing there instead. Pilar could've sworn Angie licked her lips.

"Do you want me to subdue her?" said a man's voice. Only then did Pilar see Dove cowering to one side.

Pilar summoned all the strength she had left. Palm strike. Blood choke. Anything.

"Don't touch her," Angelyne commanded.

As she brought herself to her feet, her eyes settled on Pilar. "You are entitled to your anger. I won't take it from you. It's a potent fuel."

Angelyne turned to face the old bastard. "Lord Dove, I want to thank you. What you've done here is remarkable. You have found a way to leverage these children's pain. The more they suffer, the more powerful you become."

Pilar gaped at the other children. She hadn't seen them when she and Dove first stepped into the cave: he'd asked for her bone carving, and like a fool she'd given it to him. By then it was too late. Seconds later she was trapped in her own Reflections.

The children were young. Too young. Overhead, glass pipes shot red fog through the cave ceiling. No wonder fyre ice was purple. Blue ice mixed with red suffering. The children's pain was a lifeblood, powering all of Luumia.

Pilar refocused on Angelyne. She couldn't believe she'd always wanted a sister. Sibling bonds were a heap of reinsdyr shit.

"I'm impressed," Angelyne was telling Dove, "that with so few children, you have accomplished so much! Luumia is a beacon for us all."

He beamed. "The quantity is one of the selling points, of course. Sacrifices must be made, but I'm sure you would agree that the fewer, the better."

"Would I?" Angelyne frowned. "Perhaps I'd agree that quantity is, in fact, one of the selling points. But we seem to disagree on logistics. You have chosen a small number of conduits, but you have focused on the innocent. I will focus on the guilty—and I can choose as many as I like."

An object flashed in Angelyne's hand. Pilar bristled. *The moonstone.*

Only, this gem wasn't white or pearly, but shiny black.

"Before I build my army," Angelyne said, "I'm going to free yours."

She held the stone high, then hurled it against the closest plate of ice. It sparked and erupted into black flames.

A wall of crushing heat rocked the cave, so forceful Pilar stumbled back. Fire licked the frost off every piece of ice. The gas pipes overhead began to melt, bright red smoke spilling into the air.

"Stop!" Dove cried. "You'll kill them! If you don't coax them back the right way . . ."

"Either way, they'll be free."

Pilar watched in horror as one by one, the children fell. Six little bodies. Used. Discarded.

But Angelyne looked *calm.* Maybe even satisfied.

Lord Dove ran toward the flames. He tried to drag one of the children out. But then, suddenly, he let go. Walked obediently back to Angelyne. Stared at her with glazed eyes.

Pilar knew that glaze. Angelyne had enkindled him.

"There is a reason I have always loved the Addi myths, Lord Dove. Græÿa in particular. In these stories, the weakest become the strongest. The children become eternal Souls, creatures with the power to enact justice on those who hurt them."

The stench of melted glass was foul. Or maybe that was melted flesh.

"People are far more powerful in their stories than in real life. Your story is that you are a good man. That you have done what you must do for the good of your kingdom. So you sought out the descendants of the Addi who suffered most. You took the weak and made them weaker, all so you could be strong.

"But tonight you told me there is a reservoir of suffering inside us all. And if this is true, then suffering is not fixed. We have the capacity to make *anyone* suffer—and to create the imbalance that makes for powerful magic. Powerful *fuel*."

She held her head high. "As queen of the river kingdom, I would like to thank you for this generous gift. I am already able to make all those who oppose me suffer. Now I can use their suffering to become even more powerful. And that is only the beginning."

Angelyne waded into the broken glass and fallen bodies, unfazed by the smoldering flames.

"For a man who touts himself a scientist, you have not been very curious. You believe the physical world is divided neatly into six elements, three counterbalances in perfect harmony. You are not alone in this. But you have invested so much time in the pursuit of balance, you failed to investigate the potential of *im*balance."

Pilar watched her sift through the wreckage.

"I have been working with stones as well, Lord Dove. Tinkering and toiling with the Elemental Hex you hold so dear. She who can tip that fragile balance is a mighty queen."

When she uncurled her fingers, the black gem nested in her hand.

"Imagine my delight upon discovering there are not six elements, but seven. Much like you've discovered with Pilar d'Aqila, the final component—the one everyone overlooks—is the most important."

Sweat beaded on Dove's brow. He couldn't speak under the enkindlement. Pilar almost felt sorry for him. Almost.

"Death," Angelyne said.

She stroked the stone. "The world is not black and white, good and evil. You think elements exist on perfect poles? Since when has wood been the opposite of wind? How does earth counter water? The Elemental Hex is a contrivance, a meager human attempt to understand a complex world. Death is the final axis, and it tilts your tidy elements askew."

She laughed. "Balance itself is an illusion. But how you people treasure it! Can you even imagine how fervently I will be cherished? The one person in all four kingdoms who can destroy peace, harmony, and *life itself*? And the only one who can bring it back?"

Her blue eyes sparkled.

"Of course this stone alone is worthless. A trinket for scaring children. To fuel it I needed a source of power forged through corrupted means. When one human is made to suffer at the hands of another, it pulls the very fabric of the world out of alignment."

Her grin was wolfish.

"Now it's time to give *you* a gift. We all have myths about who we are. Sometimes they just need a different ending."

She stepped forward. Held out her palm.

The gemstone lifted itself on seven legs, rose off her hand— and crawled into Dove's mouth.

He screamed.

Black smoke curled from his cheeks. His eyes dripped, bubbling out of their sockets. Nose crumbled. Blood gushed down his lips.

"Goodbye, little lord." Angelyne gave a wave.

Pilar backed away. She had to run. Had to get out of there.

But it was too late. Angelyne turned away from Dove's melted carcass.

"I'm sorry, Pilar."

Pilar tried to swallow. "Sorry?"

Angelyne waved a careless hand toward the wreckage. "I'll need to take one live conduit back to the Kaer so I can learn the process. It appears you are the only conduit left standing."

Pilar couldn't move. Angelyne was enkindling her. Of course she was. She'd lied about that, too.

"I'm afraid it will hurt very much. But you always wanted to be a warrior. Now is your chance."

Angelyne stooped and kissed Pilar on the cheek. "It's only for a little while, beloved sister. Once my labs are up and running, I'll set you free."

Pilar fought hard against the fog settling into her head. She wondered if *set you free* meant the way Angelyne had just set the other children "free."

"Let her go, Angie."

Mia Rose stepped out of the shadows.

"Take me instead."

Mia stood with her fists clenched at both sides. Brazen. Cocky as ever. And—to Pilar's astonishment—willing to take her place.

"How sweet, Mi." Angelyne sounded like she was talking to a child. "You want to sacrifice yourself!"

"Pilar has suffered enough."

"You feel nothing. No pain. No anything. Not much of a sacrifice, is it?" Angelyne sighed. "I need someone with a deep well of suffering, and frankly, you are the *worst* candidate."

Mia drew the vial of sand-colored liquid from her pocket.

"Unless I had an elixir that made me feel things again."

Something sparked behind Angelyne's eyes.

"Well done, Mi. You just made things much more interesting."

She leaned forward.

"If we got the dosage right, I suppose we could make you feel all sorts of marvelously excruciating things, couldn't we?"

The fog was lifting from Pilar's brain. She moved her jaw. Then her fingers.

"You're welcome," Angelyne said to her, smug as ever. "In a moment, you'll be able to run just fine. I'll take Mia back to the

Kaer, where she will suffer indescribably. But you will be free. You can start over. Make a new life. Isn't that what you wanted?"

Pilar's heart knocked against her ribs. It would be so easy to run. Leave Mia. Even Quin.

Then she met Mia's gaze. Her eyes were light gray. Funny how she'd never noticed. Pilar expected her to look scared. Instead she saw a ferocity she recognized.

She'd always thought of Mia as the enemy. The selfish, entitled river rat who had everything. Maybe Mia *had* been that girl. But they'd both lost so much. They'd trusted their mothers, struggled with the constant guilt of Karri's death. And they were lonely, searching for a family they no longer had.

In the end, maybe they weren't so different. They were proud. Reckless. Broken. And willing to risk their lives.

In other words? Fucking heroes.

Angelyne was right about one thing. They had to make a *new* family now.

"Should I help you choose, Pilar? Perhaps you'd like a brief reminder of how it feels to be lost in your Reflections."

She drew a red stone from the neckline of her dress. Pilar's eyes widened.

The ruby wren.

What was it Freyja had said after Pilar and Quin emerged from the Watching Chamber? *Nothing can harm you during the Reflections. Even I can't reach you. What happens there happens in a space between.*

Pilar turned her head, noting the black walls with their purple veins.

Just like the Watching Chamber.

She curled and uncurled her toes. Back in her body. Back in her mind.

The wren only shows the Reflections you ask it to.

Pilar had no idea if this would work. But she didn't have time to wonder.

Angelyne cupped the wren in her hand. He let out a shrill chirp as he stepped onto her finger.

In one swift move, Pilar swiped him. Pivoted. Cranked back her arm.

She let go.

The bird soared through the air and smashed into the wall.

For a moment, nothing happened.

Then the purple veins ignited.

The cave fell away.

Chapter 51

HURT YOU

MIA STOOD IN A forest of whitewashed bones.

One minute she was in the cave; the next in the Twisted Forest. A light fog wisped through the swyn. She craned her neck
and looked skyward, past the twisting limbs, expecting to see a
canopy of blue needles. But as the elegant ivory branches swelled
and intertwined, she realized they weren't branches at all.

They were ribs.

The bones expanded. They heaved, fracturing, every rib cage
splintering like wood. Overhead the sky shivered with virides-
cent light. The Ribbons curled and fell from the sky, serpents
writhing at her feet.

Mia gasped and leapt back.

Her feet struck water. It slurped at her ankles, then her knees, sucking her down. Thick and soft, a viscous milk.

Mia was dragged into the lagoon.

When she struggled to lift her head above water, the snakes had vanished.

Mia was naked, her body wrapped in thick gray fog. She ducked lower in the water, ashamed of her bare skin, not wanting the other visitors to see. But as she shrank back, they waded toward her, dozens of shapes weaving long, ghoulish shadows through the swirling steam.

They were monsters. Beasts with clawed hooves and twisted faces. Moonlight glinted off their scales and pelts and mottled skins. Noses coiled into corkscrews, teeth forked into fangs. Ears blossomed into roses.

Mia closed her eyes.

When she opened them, the lagoon was empty. Water as white and placid as a swatch of oyster silk.

She was shivering. Her bottom half toasty, top half freezing. She sank an inch lower, letting the silken warmth curl into the hollows of her collarbone, melting off every shred of cold. She inhaled deeply, recognizing the eggy tang of sulfyr.

Silken warmth. Eggy tang.

Mia gasped.

She could feel heat. Smell scents.

No sooner had she thought it than the lagoon dissolved.

429

Mia woke from the dark into the dark.

Terror clawed at her chest. She couldn't breathe. Couldn't see. But she didn't have to see to know the shape of the wooden box.

This time, she felt everything.

The deathly chill coating her skin. The stench of mold. The taste of rot in her mouth. The sound of nothing, no one.

Mia was shaking. She pressed one hand into her belly to calm her breathing; instinctively her other hand curled into a fist. But this time she didn't punch through the lid. She was so heavy, so tired. What was the point? No matter how hard she fought, no matter how many times she lifted herself out of the darkness, she would always come back to the box.

"What is this place?" said a voice.

Mia gave a start. She wasn't alone.

"Pilar?"

"Who else?"

Pilar knelt in the dark corner, heart thumping in her ears. She'd done it. Thrown the bird and launched them into the space between. Her wild scheme had worked.

Or *mostly* worked. Pilar had intended to bring them both to the forest of twisted trees. But at the moment they appeared to be in a wood coffin.

Pilar had no clue what came next.

"You just saved us, didn't you?" Mia said.

"Maybe. Don't know yet." Pilar inhaled, then gagged. "Did something die in here?"

"I think *I* did." Mia's voice shrank to a whisper. "Sometimes it feels like I'll never get out of this box."

Pilar reached out to touch the wood. Her fingers snagged on a splinter.

"For once, Rose, I think I know exactly what you mean."

The box began to move.

It tipped to the side, both their bodies thudding against the wood as the coffin toppled, then toppled again. Like a kurkits cube rolling from one side to the next.

When it finally settled, Mia crawled to her hands and knees. The box had expanded. She stood, shaky. A candle flickered on a round table, illuminating four walls.

She peered up to see a lattice of thick beams overhead. To her surprise, Pilar was crouched on one.

"Where are we?" Mia asked.

Pilar didn't answer. She was staring at the shape of her body pressed into the dirt. She couldn't look away. One indentation, two people's weight.

Pilar should have known better than to trust that filthy red bird. She'd never wanted to come back here, of all places. She wanted to be free.

"I remember now," Mia said quietly. "The cottage."

Pilar dropped from the rafters to the floor. The impact drove spikes of pain up both legs, her palms smacking the hard dirt as she fell forward. Gravel dug into the soft parts of her palms.

The same old panic. The same searing shame.

"I'll never get out of here, either."

Panic wrapped its fingers around Mia's throat. She didn't know where they were, but they needed to get out.

"We'll find a door," she said.

But as she scanned the room, she saw there were no doors, no windows. Only the candle and a broken violin.

Pilar stood. Brushed her hands on her trousers. "You know as well as I do a door won't do us any good. These places are inside us. They're stuck in our heads."

She kicked the violin, her foot connecting with a hollow *crack*. The instrument skidded across the floor.

Mia blinked, then rubbed her eyes in disbelief. A shimmering hexagon of black ice gleamed on the cottage wall, right above the spot where the violin had hit. Was the hex there before? It looked exactly like the ones in Kristoffin's underground torture chamber.

When Mia saw dark images flickering over the surface, she rushed forward, ready to shield Pilar from the familiar scene.

But she stopped in her tracks. The images were both familiar and unfamiliar. She watched, rapt, as Pilar's story played over the ice.

This was not the story Mia had seen in the cave. Or rather, she was seeing it from a different point of view.

"Pilar," she said, her voice soft. "Come look."

"No."

"Then can I tell you what *I* see?"

Pilar looked warily at the ice from across the room. Her head ached. Her fists ached. Everything ached.

"I already know."

"I don't think you do. I wish there were some way to . . ."

Mia stopped. An idea was stitching itself together in her brain. She reached into her pocket. Would she even have it? In this strange liminal dream state, she didn't know what had come with her—and what hadn't made the leap.

Her fingers struck tin.

"If you don't want me to tell you, can I *show* you?"

Pilar looked dubious. "How?"

"You have to trust me. I'll need to touch you, but only for a moment. I promise it won't hurt."

Pilar felt a flush of anger, then shame. But she didn't say no. To her surprise, she felt a tiny, guttering hope.

She crossed her arms over her chest. "Do it quick before I change my mind."

Mia's fingers flew. Her idea would work. It had to. Nervously she pulled out the Jouma's Brew. It only took a few seconds to heat the tin over the candle.

"Close your eyes," Mia said, slathering the paste over Pilar's lids. "It's warm, but it won't hurt you. Now open."

Pilar opened her eyes.

She saw a little girl.

Chapter 52

ALIVE

THE GIRL LIVED ON an island in the middle of the sea. Her mother cruel, her father missing.

So when two strangers landed in a red balloon, of course the girl mistook them for the family she had always wanted. She loved the woman who made her feel special. She loved the man who made her feel strong.

Pilar had lived this story a thousand times. But for the first time, she understood it.

Orry had tricked her. He'd used his power to make her weak and small.

And this time, when the story kept going—when it reached the parts she knew so well—she didn't look away. Strange new feelings collided with old ones. She felt compassion mixed in with the guilt. Sorrow tangled up in shame.

"It's over," said a girl's voice. She sounded very far away.

When Pilar touched the ice, it crumbled to silver dust beneath her fingertips. She turned and saw that everything had vanished. She was in a blank, empty space, an endless wash of gray. But she wasn't alone.

Mia Rose was there.

"It's over, Pilar."

Pilar's eyes blurred with tears. Mia was wrong. It wasn't over. Nothing was ever that easy, at least not for her.

"It was my fault."

"No," Mia said vehemently. "You didn't deserve what happened. It wasn't your fault."

"But I didn't fight him. I didn't."

"Of course you didn't. You were terrified."

Mia tried to think of what to say, well-crafted words of wisdom that were both comforting and profound.

But what came into Mia's head was a science lesson.

"I've always loved the natural kingdom. As a girl I devoured every book I could find about animals. Even cut a bird open once to study the anatomy."

"Why are you telling me this?"

"Because we are taught that creatures do one of two things when faced with a predator: they run, or they fight."

"And I did neither."

Mia took a breath.

"That's just it. What most people don't know is that there's a third thing. Sometimes a bird knows she won't make it if she tries to flee. And she knows that if she tries to fight, the bigger animal will tear her to pieces. So she chooses a third option. She freezes."

Pilar had gone very still. She was thinking about the reinsdyr in the Watching Chamber being gored by the leopard. The way her eyes rolled back into her head.

"The bird stops moving entirely," Mia said. "Because if the predator thinks she's already dead, he might not want her. He might find a live kill somewhere else. And even if he doesn't—even if she can't escape—the bird's body emits a natural elixir that numbs the pain. If she dies, at least she isn't suffering."

Pilar felt like she was breaking open. She was tired of fighting back tears. Tired of fighting herself.

Mia took her hand. "I'm sorry. I've only made it worse."

"No," Pilar said. "You didn't."

New truths were seeping into the cracks.

She wasn't a coward.

She didn't deserve what happened.

It wasn't her fault.

The knot of shame and rage in Pilar's chest began to uncoil. Little by little. Bit by bit.

Pilar wiped her wet nose on her sleeve. Someday she would laugh when she told this story. *My sister,* she'd say, *once tried to comfort me by telling me about dead birds.*

But for now, she squeezed Mia's hand.

They stayed like that for a while. Side by side, hands clasped. They no longer knew if they were standing or floating, dreaming or awake.

"We haven't escaped her," Pilar said, breaking the silence. "All I did was buy us time. Your sister will be waiting the moment we get out."

"She's your sister, too."

"I keep forgetting."

Sharp pain shot up Mia's arm. She winced, letting Pilar's hand fall. The frostflower on her wrist had begun to burn, a scald that went deeper than her skin. She felt shock at the sensation, followed by a wash of gratitude for being back in her body.

Then the truth sank into her belly like a snow plum pit.

"My mark is fyre ink," she said.

Pilar shrugged. "I'd take that off your list of worries. It's not like you knew."

But with the knowledge of what her mark had cost—what suffering those children had endured—Mia felt the heaviness sink back onto her shoulders. The cloak was still there. Had she really thought she could escape it?

The pain began to ebb out of her arm. Mia and Pilar found themselves back on solid ground, standing in a forest, loam and pine needles spongy underfoot.

Up ahead, they saw Karri.

The princess lay face up on a red patch of snow. Eyes open. Exactly how they'd left her.

"You see her, too?" Mia whispered.

"I see her everywhere," said Pilar.

Mia didn't want to go any closer, but when Pilar started to walk forward, she followed. Karri's eyes were terrifyingly empty. Two blank blue holes.

Quin's face appeared unbidden in Mia's mind. The pain inscribed in his eyes. What Angelyne had done to him was unforgivable. She had robbed him of his choice.

But Mia had robbed him of his sister first.

"I tried to tell myself you were the one to blame," she confessed. "But it was my fault. I'm the one who stopped her heart."

Pilar shook her head. "No. I shot the arrow. All you did was try and save her life."

"Zaga lied to us both."

They stared at Karri's body, silence feeding on their bones.

"I don't know if I can forgive myself," Mia said finally.

"Maybe we start by forgiving each other."

Pilar crouched. She hugged her knees.

"What was it like, being dead?"

"I only remember the waking. I'd give anything to forget." Mia knelt on the snow. "There've been times over the last few months where I wished I were still dead."

Pilar looked up sharply. "You don't mean that, do you?"

"Sometimes."

"You really can't feel anything?"

"*Here* I can." Mia gestured around them. "In this place I seem to be able to feel everything. But out there it all goes away."

Pilar remembered something Angelyne had said. "What about the elixir?"

"I'm scared to try it. Scared I'll get my hopes up and it won't work."

"Then we'll find something that does."

Pilar turned back to Karri. It hurt to see the princess like this. Exposed to the elements. Alone.

"You can't die, Mia."

"And why's that?"

"Because I only just started to like you."

Mia laughed. "I'll keep that in mind."

"I mean it. You didn't fight your way out of that box just to end up inside another."

Mia's smile faded. "I'm not a fighter like you are."

"It doesn't have to be with fists. You're stubborn and infuriating and brilliant and strong."

The words bubbled up from a place Pilar hadn't known existed.

"When we first met I didn't understand why you would ever sacrifice yourself for your sister. But I never had one, until now. You're a lot less broken than you think, Mia Rose."

"I wish it were that simple." Mia faltered. "I said I'd never get out of the box, but it's more complicated. It's like you said: the box is *inside* me. I'm afraid it always will be."

"Then we fight it."

"And if I'm too tired to keep fighting?"

Pilar looked her in the eye.

"Then I'll fight for you. Until you're strong enough to fight again."

Tears sprang to Mia's eyes. She'd spent her whole life caring for her little sister. But now, for the first time, *Mia* was the little sister. And Pilar was offering to fight for her.

"Thank you," she whispered.

Pilar scooped a handful of dirt. Molded it into a little mound. Her fingers were freezing, but on the inside she felt warmer than she had in a long time.

She nodded toward Karri's body.

"Help me bury her?" Pilar said.

Mia leaned forward. Cupped soft dirt in both palms.

Their eyes met, and an understanding passed between them. They had both suffered. They each bore the scars of a history they could never unwrite.

What happened to them would never be all right. But *they* would be. They had survived the worst thing—and they were no longer alone.

Pilar Zorastín d'Aqila and Mia Morwynna Rose had found each other.

They were very much alive.

Chapter 53

TERRIBLY SUSCEPTIBLE

PILAR WOKE FACEDOWN WITH cave dust on her tongue. Head pounding. Ears ringing.

A few feet away, Mia dragged herself to her knees. Could she still feel things? She pinched her arm and felt nothing. Whatever she'd experienced in her reflections—the feeling of coming back to her own body—wasn't real!

"Welcome back." Angelyne's voice dripped with vitriol. "Your pleasant little interlude did give me time to retrieve our mutual friend."

When Pilar turned, her stomach seized.

Quin.

"He was wandering around the palace," Angelyne said, "looking for your Renderer friend, Mi, so he could come back and save *you*, Pilar." She yawned. "Let me skip to my central thesis: no one is coming to save you."

"Let them go, Angelyne."

Quin's voice was soft. His head was bowed, hands clasped behind his back like they were bound, even though they weren't. He looked tired. Older than Pilar remembered.

"You can make anyone suffer," he said. "As I know from personal experience. You've been in my head for months. You took everyone I'd ever loved away from me, or *could* have loved, if I hadn't royally screwed that up."

He looked right at Pilar, his eyes so clear and green they broke her heart. In that moment she would have forgiven him anything. Every lie, every betrayal—none of it was his fault. They were both players in a play they hadn't written. Pilar wanted to start over. To begin again.

Of course now it was too late.

Quin turned to Angelyne.

"I know you could enthrall me with a single look. And I know that won't make you happy, not really, because you know it's false. You're lonely. You want someone to choose to love you. But how can they, if you've robbed them of their choice?"

He drew himself up tall.

"That's why I am making you an offer. I will come back with you of my own volition. I'll make a choice to stay by your side. I swear on my sister's grave. But don't take Pilar." He took a breath. "And don't take Mia. Take me."

That was when Pilar saw it. His right fist clenched tight.

When Quin shifted his fingers, she glimpsed the black stone. He'd dug it out of Dove's ruined face.

Pilar's heart lifted. She wanted to laugh, dance, kiss him. Gallant Prince Quin, still pickpocketing the dead.

When she saw a flash of red in his left fist, her pulse cranked up another notch.

He had the wren, too.

Quin had a plan. He was going to get them out.

"Oh, my dear husband." Angelyne sighed. "What a noble proclamation. I really have missed you. Always so eager to please, so pliant. But don't you know the truth, my love?"

Pilar glanced at Quin, who frowned. Something was wrong.

"I don't understand," he said. "The truth?"

"The truth about the moonstone, of course! I destroyed it a long time ago. I'm far beyond that kind of thing now."

"That—that can't be," he stammered. "*I* destroyed it."

"You have a weak mind, darling. A weak heart. Pure, but ineffectual. You are terribly susceptible to the power of suggestion."

Quin's face turned chalk white.

"What are you saying?"

"Your stone was a fake." Angelyne smiled. "I was never enthralling you at all."

Chapter 54

LEFT TO BURN

QUIN WAS STRICKEN. MIA watched his face twist into a series of impossible emotions, each more painful than the last. He was trembling. For a moment she thought he was afraid.

Then the confusion smoldered down to rage. Mia saw something in his eyes that scared her. Bitterness. Hate.

He opened his fists, revealing the black stone in one hand, the ruby wren in the other.

"It's past time for the Illuminations," he said. "We don't want to keep the good people of Luumia waiting."

"Careful," Angelyne hissed. "You have no idea what you're holding, or how powerful it is."

When she stepped forward, Quin hoisted the stones high.

"And now I do," he said. "You can't enkindle me, can you? Not as long as I have these. Wonder what other havoc they can wreak?"

"Quin," Pilar said, her voice tight. "Listen to me. I know you're angry. I would be too. But you don't have to do things the way she does. Don't let her inside your head."

"Apparently she never was," he growled.

"Either way," Mia said, inching forward, "you're stronger than she is."

His laugh was bitter. "When have you ever seen me strong?"

"You're better than strong," Pilar said. The three sisters formed a triangle now, edging closer. "You're good."

"Ah, yes. *Good.*"

"You said you wanted to make a choice," Mia said. "You still can."

Quin wavered. She saw something gentle in his eyes. An opening.

"You're right," he said. "I can."

He slammed the two stones together.

After that, things happened fast.

A crack echoed through the cave, swallowed by a ravenous howl. Scarlet fire bloomed between Quin's palms. An arc of light leapt from his hands and struck the closest wall, scattering into a thousand words. They spewed into the air, forming layers of text stacked so thick they were unreadable.

The walls began to ooze like candle wax. A spear of red light spiraled toward Mia. She ducked just in time.

Angelyne cried out. The fire had struck her instead.

"Stop!" Pilar shouted, charging toward Quin. The burning sphere in his hands was growing. She had to stop him. He was hurting himself. Hurting all of them.

"Don't do this," she begged.

She reached out a hand—and he recoiled. He tucked the fire under one arm, protecting it.

The answer thudded into her head, so simple she couldn't believe it.

Use magic.

Magic was just another thing she'd run from, a piece of her past she hadn't wanted to face. Of course she was wary of a power that could be so easily abused.

Zaga had wielded magic to hurt people. But Pilar could choose differently.

She could use magic as a gift.

She had no intention of enthralling Quin. He'd survived enough of that to last a lifetime.

But she had a knack for unblooding. Always had. Always would.

Pilar stepped forward, palms outstretched. She could feel magic pouring through her fingers. She'd forgotten how good it felt. How powerful.

"I will never hurt you, Quin. I promise."

He grabbed her wrist and yanked her toward him. The boldness of the move surprised her. In the split second she was off balance, he swiped his foot behind her ankle, sent her crashing to the ground.

She felt a flash of pride. She'd taught him that.

Pilar stared up at him, searching his face for the Quin she knew. But his eyes were ruthless. Cold. She couldn't find him.

He lifted the fire over his head. Ready to burn her alive.

"Sorry," he said. "You're already dead."

"Don't!" Mia screamed.

She leapt in front of Pilar and slammed her hands down around Quin's, sealing in the fire. He jerked and bucked. She held on tight.

Mia's skin was burning. Red tongues of flame licked the gaps between her knuckles. All she felt was numb.

Which meant she had the advantage.

The back of Mia's hands blistered into wet, red boils. The wound grew whiter and whiter until she realized she was staring at naked bone. Months had passed since she'd seen an anatomy plate, but she knew the names by heart: carpals clustered at the wrist, knobby metacarpals locked into the phalanges.

She didn't let go. She had to neutralize the fire, bring it back into balance. She closed her eyes and thought of Nell—her good-natured patience, her genuine wisdom. Mia summoned Stone, Fire's counter element. She conjured uzoolion, the cool blue gem from Refúj. She imagined the moonstone as it once was: a container for her mother's healing magic, Wynna's best and gentlest gift.

The fire in Quin's hands weakened.

And then suddenly Mia wasn't holding onto anything.

Angelyne had shoved her aside.

"Go," Angie said. "Take Pilar and leave before I change my mind."

The ground began to quake. Mia staggered back, the sound of shrieking metal so loud she clapped her hands over her ears. A booming crack echoed, then another. The cave was fracturing around them. Shards of rock and ice plummeted from over-head.

A deep fissure had opened at their feet. The crack widened swiftly, splitting the cave in two: Mia and Pilar on one side, Quin and Angelyne on the other.

Mia saw Angie and Quin advancing toward one another, their faces dark with fury. The two people Mia would have given any-thing in her power to protect. She had risked her health, her life, her sanity to save first her sister, then the boy she loved.

Maybe it was time to love herself.

"Hurry!" Pilar shouted, running toward the mouth of the cave.

Mia lunged after her. She had lost one sister—she wasn't going to lose another.

Together they barreled toward the Descending Room. But there they stopped short. The cage had come loose; it lay useless on its side in the corridor, the bronze softening from the heat.

"Shit!" Pilar yelled. "Shit, shit, shit."

"We'll climb up the cables," Mia assured her. "It's how I came down."

"They'll be too hot!"

With an eerie sense of calm, Mia leaned over the ledge. She surveyed the shaft. Nodded.

"Luckily," she said, "that won't be a problem."

She extended one skinless hand and wrapped her bony fingers around the cable.

"I don't have any flesh left to burn."

Chapter 55

THE SHADOWESS

CHAOS HAD ERUPTED IN Valavïk.

When Pilar and Mia tore out of the palace—no small feat, seeing as how the walls kept caving in around them—they were nearly trampled by hordes of Jyöltide revelers running toward the port.

The Illuminations had splattered the night sky, igniting many of the peat roofs and wood buildings in the surrounding village. Thick plumes of smoke shot up on every side.

"Breathe," Pilar gasped. "I need to breathe."

They doubled over on the palace steps, chests heaving. Pilar squinted up at the moon.

Typical. All she'd wanted was to get to the Snow Queen's

palace on the last night of Jyöl. To stand on the steps beneath the Weeping Moon. And there she was.

She began to laugh hysterically. Once she'd started, she couldn't stop.

"What's funny?" Mia asked.

"Nothing," Pilar said, panting with laughter. "Everything."

All that time she'd thought she was looking for her father. But what she'd really needed was a family. A sister who would stand by her. The kind of sister who would drag you up out of a dungeon with skeleton hands.

"We made it," Mia said, cradling her charred hands to her chest. "We got out." She'd already begun regrowing her skin and tissue, balancing the elements the way Nell taught her.

Another throng of panicked people careened toward them.

"Harbor?" Pilar said.

"Harbor," Mia agreed. "I know where there's a boat."

Zai's boat was gone.

Mia stood on the quay, blinking in numb disbelief. It wasn't just Zai's boat—most of the wharf was empty.

"What was that about a boat?" Pilar said.

Mia's heart sank. They knew no one in Valavïk. They had nowhere to run.

"Good Jyöl!" A warm, husky voice wafted toward them. "Or *not* so good Jyöl, really, if we're being honest."

Mia held her breath. She turned around slowly, too afraid to hope.

Nelladine stood on the pier.

"Hello, Raven."

Mia swallowed the lump in her throat. She braved a smile.

"Actually," she said, "it's Mia."

"Hello then, Mia." Nell gave a shy wave. "You two looking for a ride? Because I happen to have a boat with space for two passengers."

She stepped aside, revealing a modest boat tied to the pier.

Pilar had no idea who this girl was, but she didn't care. A new crush of people was descending on the dock, threatening to sink what few boats were left.

"Done," she said, hurtling herself onboard. She felt Mia hesitate behind her. "Get on the boat, Rose!"

Mia didn't move. She looked at Nell, heartbeat roaring in her ears.

"What made you come back?" she said.

Nelladine took a tentative step.

"You weren't wrong to want to feel something. I should know that better than anyone. You trusted me with the truth, told me a secret from the deepest part of your soul. And I did the absolute worst thing. I left."

Nell's gaze was clear and honest.

"I won't leave you again. We women need each other now more than ever. We're fighting for the same side."

She reached out her hand.

Mia took it.

Instantly she felt heat. As Nelladine pressed her long brown fingers into the frostflower mark, warmth spilled over Mia's skin. Why did Nell's touch spark a sensation when nothing else did?

An ear-splitting boom ripped through the air.

Mia and Nell whirled around.

The glacier was collapsing. An avalanche howled down the mountain, swallowing the upper half of the village in one gigantic white gulp. In a moment it would devour the Snow Queen's palace.

"*Angie*," Mia murmured, at the same time Pilar said, "*Quin*."

"No time for nostalgia, you can reminisce later." Nell was already tugging Mia aboard. "Boats are good for that."

"She really did it," Pilar said. "Angelyne tipped the world out of balance."

"Unless," Mia said, her voice quiet, "Quin tipped it first."

"I don't care who's to blame," Nell said. "All I know is that I'm getting you both out of here."

Mia tore her eyes away from Valavïk. "Where are you taking us?"

"Where I should have gone a long time ago. To the only person who can help."

"Who's that?" Pilar cocked a brow. "On that note: who in four hells are you?"

"I'm Nelladinellakin. We're going to see the Shadowess."

She gave them each an oar.

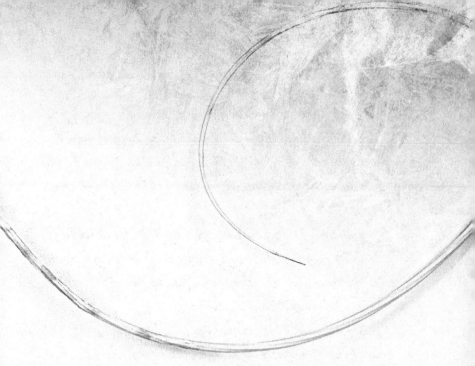

EPILOGUE

Dear sisters,

Let me tell you a story.

I once believed hurting people made you weak. I thought all heroes who hid behind their fists and arrows were cowards in disguise. That if we could simply break bread together, we might be able to come to an accord.

I don't believe that anymore.

Truthfully, I've never liked my own story. A weak boy. A scorned son. A used, manipulated lover. Whether prince or king, I have always been the pawn. I have never been the leading man.

But as a wise (albeit bent) woman once said: We all cling to myths about who we are. If you don't like them, choose a different ending.

I choose to return to the people of the river kingdom.

I choose to take my rightful place as king of Glas Ddir.

I choose to never be enthralled, enkindled, or controlled again.

And if these choices throw me into conflict with any one of you, so be it.

For the first time in my life, I feel no fear. I have always known myself to be broken. But finally, after so many years, I understand my brokenness is a gift.

Each of you has hurt me. Each of you has claimed to care about me, only to rob me of something precious. At the end of the day, your loyalties lie with one another. No matter how you carve up the bonds of sisterhood between you, you will choose each other every time.

Thanks to you, I have no sister. But credit where credit is due. They say only when a man is free of love is he free to do what he is meant to do.

Take care of yourselves, sisters. Take care of each other.

I cannot promise I will do the same.

Very truly yours,
Quin

Acknowledgments

This book was hard to write, for many reasons. I am forever grateful to the people who came to my aid.

Alex Arnold, you helped shape this story—and held my hand every time I stumbled. When Toast ate the first page, I knew I must be onto something.

Rebecca Aronson, to say you picked up the baton would be an understatement. You took my ungainly words and made them graceful and honest, like any good ballerina. #Derrida4eva.

Joel Tippie, Joel Tippie, Joel Tippie. I still regret not getting your name into the *Heart of Thorns* acknowledgments in time, so I'm thanking you in triplicate. I clearly have the best art director in the biz.

Katherine Tegen, thank you for the gift of this trilogy, and the privilege of seeing my name on it. Mabel Hsu, you are my fearless in-house champion; your kindness has meant the world. Tanu Srivastava, your emails always make me smile. Jill Amack, you have bestowed upon my inner geek all manner of grammarian delights.

Nicole Banholzer, your presence on this journey has been a blessing many times over. *Inhala, exhala.* Ante Aikio, I'm lucky to have your thoughtful insight on Sami culture and an "insider look" at the life of a reindeer herder.

Tae Keller, you saved me more than you know. You cast light into a dark room—and did so in less than sixty-five hours. This story is better because of you.

Amelinda Bérubé, you were my first reader of messy early pages, and Maura Milan, my second. When I was pretty sure there wasn't a book here, you both believed there was.

Emily Wibberley, your kind and persistent nudges restored my faith in what I was doing. Thanks to you and Austin for making me laugh uproariously in public. Wet Jams!

Emily and Mia, my favorite violinists: thanks for lending me your eyes and fingers (not literally; that'd be gross). Caden, you made my beautiful cover even more beautiful. I appreciate all your friendship and support. Lorna and Kate, you sanctioned *Tears of Frost* over bone broth. Sirpa, my translation queen: thanks for the idioms and the laughs. It's all gone to taters.

Alison, Amy, April, Aya, Bridget, Britta, Cori, Dana, Farrah, Hayley, Honora, Isabel, Kyle, Lana, Laura, Nica, Nicole, Sara,

Sarah Nicole, Sonia, Teresa, Terry, and my magical Djerassi crew—I drew so much strength from your texts and emails this year. Thank you. I needed them.

I am grateful for *all* the friends who have shared their stories with courage, honesty, and a healthy dose of female rage. I hope I've done you justice.

To my Rock 'n' Write girls—and the countless students, librarians, booksellers, and readers I've met—thank you for reminding me why I do this.

Thank you to my mom for every pep talk and word of encouragement. To my sister Cat for sharing her truth with such ferocious bravery—and inspiring me to do the same.

Christopher DeWan: you read this book more than anyone and made it better in a million little ways. You've made *me* better in a million little ways, too.

And because not all inanimate objects are truly inanimate: I'd like to thank the northern lights. When I gazed up into the sky that night in Iceland, I felt happy to be alive.

RESOURCES

The following organizations have saved many lives. Each hotline offers a live chat or text option, so even if you are not a phone person (I am definitely not a phone person), someone will be ready and available to support you.

National Sexual Assault Hotline
https://www.rainn.org
1.800.656.HOPE (4673)
Call the 24/7 hotline to be connected with a trained staff member from a sexual assault service provider in your area.

National Suicide Prevention Hotline
https://suicidepreventionlifeline.org
1.800.273.TALK (8255)
The Lifeline provides 24/7, free, and confidential support for people in distress, prevention and crisis resources for you or your loved ones.

The Crisis Text Line
https://www.crisistextline.org/texting-in
Text CONNECT, HOME, or any message to 741-741

Being "in crisis" doesn't just mean suicide: it's any painful emotion for which you need support. Crisis Text Line serves anyone, in any type of crisis, providing access to free, 24/7 support and information via text.

And if you or a loved one is in immediate danger, call 9-1-1. Tell the operator this is a psychiatric emergency and ask for an officer trained in crisis intervention.

You got this. As Pilar and Mia come to understand by book's end: you are not alone.